The Peacemaker's Code

A Novel

Deepak Malhotra

To request permissions, or to inquire about foreign and translation rights, contact the author: ProfessorDeepakMalhotra@gmail.com

Publisher: Deepak\Malhotra
Paperback: ISBN 978-1-7365485-0-9
e-Book: ISBN 978-1-7365485-1-6 / ASIN B08TLR3HCT
Audiobook: ISBN 978-1-7365485-2-3

Cover art by Adam Hall.
Formatting by Polgarus Studio.
Book Website: www.ThePeacemakersCode.com

To my parents. To my teachers. To my wife.
For making it possible.

To my friends and family.
For making it better.

To my students and my children.
For making it worthwhile.

And to all who deserve a more peaceful world.
For inspiring it all.

Code / ˈkōd /

Noun

1. a system of words, letters, figures, or symbols that are employed for the purposes of secrecy.

2. a set of rules, principles, and standards adhered to by an individual, group, or society.

Contents

Part I

the observer

They walked him down a dimly lit corridor—the kind you encounter after the employees have all left for the evening and the building has shifted to energy-conservation mode.

But this was no ordinary office building. Access to the lobby had required a retinal scan. Security cameras were everywhere. And the buttons in the elevator were unmarked. One of his guides had punched in a rather lengthy passcode to get them up to the appropriate floor.

Every door they walked past was shut, and presumably locked. Only one of them had a window—a rectangular bit of glass that you might find on a door that leads to the stairwell. *A way out.*

After almost thirty yards, they came upon a conference room on their right. Its large glass wall was frosted over, except for eighteen inches at the top and bottom. On the other side of the wall was a long table that might seat a dozen people, but the frost made it hard to say much else about the contents of the room.

He noticed that they slowed down, just a tad, as they approached the conference room. As if his guides had considered going inside, only to realize that it was not the right room. Affixed to the door was a small nameplate that told him they had just chosen not to enter *Dolos 3*. He decided that was worth keeping in mind.

After another fifteen yards, on the other side of the hallway, they arrived at their destination—a room that looked identical to *Dolos 3,* but which was assigned a different moniker: *Apate 3*.

As they approached the door to Apate 3, Agent Lane, who had been leading the way, stepped aside to allow Agent Silla to take the initiative. Agent Lane was just shy of six feet tall and probably in his mid-thirties. He had light brown hair, a clean-shaven face, and appeared to put his gym membership to good use. Silla was five-foot-seven, with an athletic build and dark shoulder-length hair that framed a captivating face. She could have passed for thirty, but Agent Lane's deference toward her suggested she might be the older of the two.

Silla put four fingers on a scanner above the door's handle. Three seconds later, he heard a click. Lane held the door open for them, and the lights in the room turned brighter the moment they stepped inside.

The long mahogany table in the center of the room was surrounded by twelve black leather chairs. On the wall to the far left of where they had entered, only a few feet past the head of the table, hung a large flatscreen TV. It was a standard conference room setup, but with some perceptible differences. The table held a keyboard, a touchscreen panel, and a speakerphone, but without the mess of wires that typically accompanied such an arrangement. There were no whiteboards, flipcharts, or recycling bins, but a large paper shredder sat adjacent to the door. Wedged into one corner of the room was a small table with a few pencils, some sheets of paper, and a metallic receptacle about the size of a shoebox. There were at least two security cameras in the room.

The secret of the metal shoebox was laid bare when Agent Lane asked him to hand over his cell phone. Lane and Silla placed their own phones—they each had two—inside the container as well.

"That really isn't necessary," he pointed out. "My phone has been dead all afternoon."

"Sorry," Agent Lane responded. "We still have to follow protocol."

Those were the first words any of them had spoken since they arrived at the building, apart from the almost inaudible "After you" that Lane had uttered when they walked into the elevator.

Agent Silla offered him the seat at the head of the table, closest to the TV screen. Lane and Silla skipped the chairs next to his before sitting down across from one another. He had been told that they would be observing an important, hour-long meeting. The meeting was taking place elsewhere, but it would be streamed for them into the conference room. For that long of a viewing, he was seated uncomfortably close to the screen. For whatever reason, Lane and Silla had ignored his convenience in favor of an arrangement that allowed them to keep an eye on him during the meeting. *What kind of reaction are they looking for? How could it possibly matter?*

Silla gave a nod and Lane grabbed the keyboard. A moment later, the bright light reflecting off the table revealed that the TV behind him had come to life.

Silla took a deep breath and then kicked things off.

"I know you have a lot of questions, Professor Kilmer. Soon enough you will understand why we couldn't answer most of them. But let me start by thanking you for joining us today."

It suddenly occurred to him that he had come to this place, if not eagerly, then at least willingly. But something in the way she thanked him—it was a slight pause before she found the word—left him wondering whether they would have let him reject the invitation. Silla and Lane had met Kilmer at his home that afternoon, shortly after he had returned from a visit to the hospital. They displayed their credentials and asked him to call the Central Intelligence Agency, using a publicly available phone number, to confirm that two agents had been sent to his house. He told them that his phone was dead, and Lane let him borrow one of his. After the call, the agents told him that his "unique expertise" was needed on a national security matter of vital importance. He needed only to accompany them to their office, where he would watch and listen in on a meeting, and then answer some questions about what he had seen and heard. That was it—he would be back by midnight.

No, he did not have time to think about it. No, they could not tell him what this was about. No, he could not call anyone else to find out whether this was legitimate.

Putting together what little information they had provided, the best that Kilmer could come up with was still a bit of a stretch—had the CIA managed to get eyes and ears on a terrorist group that was planning an imminent attack? *Not sure how my expertise helps with that.* He had asked a dozen questions, none of which were answered, before he decided that the only way to learn anything would be to go along with them. He might even be able to do some good. Two hours later, they had arrived at this building.

"Let me answer some of the questions you asked earlier, and a few others that you probably wanted to ask," Silla continued. "Agent Lane and I belong to a department of the CIA that is not officially on the org chart. It exists and functions like a standing committee comprised of select employees from three different CIA directorates: Analysis, Operations, and Science & Technology. Informally, our department is referred to as *Triad*. It's a name that most of us hate—and yes, I know it sounds like a comic-book crime syndicate.

"The meeting we are here to observe will begin soon. When it does, you will be able to see and hear the participants, but they will not be addressing you—nor will you be able to talk to them. You will see a dozen people seated around a large table, and you will recognize a few of them. Familiar faces might include Vice President Nielsen, Defense Secretary Strauss, National Security Advisor Garcia, and CIA Director Druckman. Others, whom you are less likely to know, include the energy secretary, the chief scientist at NASA, and General Allen, who is the chairman of the Joint Chiefs of Staff. You will also see two people sitting farther away from the table, against the back wall, just taking notes."

Silla paused and looked at Kilmer. It was not a look that invited questions. She was gauging his reaction. If she was even moderately well trained, she must have noticed his surprise. He had leaned back, and his eyes had widened, ever so slightly, the moment she mentioned Vice President Zack Nielsen. She might have also noticed that Kilmer had been holding his breath, and that he exhaled only after she finished listing the attendees.

This was not what he had imagined.

The Vice President. CIA. DoD. NASA. The secretary of energy. *Are we on the brink of nuclear war? Have the Russians or Chinese developed or deployed some new weapon? Is it Iran or North Korea? Nuclear terrorism?*

And then he remembered what Silla had said, almost in passing: *They will not be addressing you.* The list of attendees, combined with the setup that she had described, was extremely troubling.

Are we spying on a meeting in which the VP is participating? Are the attendees unaware that we—or I—will be watching? Kilmer decided that even this question would have to wait. He did not want to redirect the conversation, or to have Agent Silla become more guarded, just when she was starting to share information.

"Please continue," he said to her.

She nodded, slowly, and for a moment he thought she was still trying to gauge his reaction. But no, that wasn't it. She wasn't evaluating him at all. She looked... *disappointed.* As if she had wanted him to react differently. To be more impressed, or more curious, or more... something.

Silla continued. "To put it simply, Professor Kilmer, we are in a crisis. Once we give you the details, and once you overcome your initial shock, you will agree that the stakes have never been higher in the history of our country. Very few people are aware of the situation we are in, and we need to keep it that way.

"So, why are we telling *you* about it? It's because what we're about to observe is a strategy meeting, and it has a lot to do with your area of expertise. You have taught your students about President Kennedy's deliberations with the ExComm during the Cuban Missile Crisis. You've analyzed Chamberlain's cabinet meetings during the Sudeten crisis. You've studied Churchill's debates with Halifax over whether to fight or make peace with Hitler. You have reinterpreted Pope Gregory VII's humiliation of Henry IV during their meeting at Canossa. And you have offered a unique and compelling explanation for why the Spartans voted for war against Athens.

"If you ever wanted to be a fly on the wall in any of those meetings... well, then this is your lucky day. But I need you to keep in mind that you're not *just* a fly on the wall. You will shape what happens here. For reasons that will become clear to you before this night is over, your voice will not be ignored. If we survive this, and if books are written about this moment in human history, you will not be a mere footnote."

If we survive this. Kilmer did not react. He was no longer thinking of questions to ask. He was only listening.

"As to the attendees. Most of the people participating in this meeting had never heard of you. But there are also a few who believe that your advice could prove invaluable."

Her choice of words managed to ease one of his concerns. Most participants *had* never heard of him. In other words, they knew of him now. They must know he would be observing—or, at least, that he was involved.

Kilmer was not keen on spying on the US government, no matter the reason.

"All we are asking of you, Professor, is that you share your frank, unfiltered assessment of the discussion you are about to see. What stands out to you? Which arguments do you find compelling? What's missing in the analysis? In short, are we likely to make the right call here?"

There was a knock on the door. Agent Lane checked to see that his tie was in place as he rose to his feet. Agent Silla stood as well.

Lane opened the door, and in walked a distinguished-looking man with more gray hairs than you would expect given how few wrinkles he had on his face. He looked like he had ironed his suit in the hallway just before entering. He stood ramrod straight with his shoulders back, exhibiting the kind of posture that an ergonomist might insist upon, but which most people find unnatural. He shook hands with Lane and patted him on the shoulder.

"Good to see you, sir," Lane said. The older man gave a friendly nod. He walked over to Silla and repeated the same ritual with her. He then turned to Kilmer, who was also standing by now, and offered his hand. It was, as expected, a perfectly curated handshake: firm but comfortable grip, friendly eye contact, and a smile that looked so natural you had to believe it was genuine.

"It's nice to see you, Professor. Thank you for coming. You don't know me, but I've heard a lot about you."

Kilmer flashed back to his time as a graduate student. His adviser was the only other person he'd ever known who would use "nice to see you" instead of "nice to meet you" when meeting someone for the first time. After spending decades in and around campus, the adviser couldn't remember all the people he was expected to know. He gave up on "nice to meet you" after one too many awkward conversations with people who had to remind him that they'd met previously. It was *nice to see you* from that point on—for everyone.

The man with the well-ironed suit continued. "You can think of me as the director of Triad—although, technically, Triad has no director, because Triad does not exist. Less complicated is the fact that my name is Arthur Capella. Please call me Art—not Arthur or Agent Capella. My younger colleagues here insist on calling me 'sir,' and I am tired of telling them to cut it out."

Lane and Silla smiled.

Art turned toward Silla. "Have you already told him who will be in the meeting?"

"Yes, sir. That's about as far as we've gotten."

"Okay. Let's have a seat then," Art suggested.

Art took the unclaimed spot between Silla and Kilmer, but he pulled the chair back a little to get a wider lens—he could see them both without having to turn his head. Lane picked up his pencil and waited, as if he were the designated note-taker.

"You are wondering, Professor Kilmer, what exactly is going on—and why you are so relevant. You've probably made some educated guesses by now, and they're not totally off the mark, because one way to think about this is quite simple: we are trying to avert a devastating war. Beyond that, I'm afraid, you're probably way off track."

Kilmer acknowledged his limited understanding of the situation with a simple nod.

Art remained silent, but Kilmer could see it was not for dramatic effect. *He's struggling to find the right words.* Finally, Art leaned back and took a deep breath, as if he had decided to go ahead with the best he had come up with so far.

"Professor. Do you know what room we're in?"

"Yes. It was labeled *Apate 3*."

"Right. And there is another conference room on this floor. Care to guess what it's called?"

"*Dolos 3*. I read the nameplate."

"Right again. Do you know where those names come from?"

"I do. They're named after the Greek god and goddess of trickery and deception. Should I be concerned?"

"Well, in my line of work, one always has to worry about Dolos and Apate," Art conceded. "But, to your question, the answer is no. In fact, I only bring it up to clear the air. If you're like most people, you have certain assumptions about the CIA and the work we do. Most of those assumptions, and especially the less flattering ones, are incorrect—at least, those things are no *longer* true. But I'm aware of the reputational baggage the CIA carries. I want to assure you that we do a lot of very important work, and we do it properly. Am I sounding a bit defensive? Yes. All the same, it's important that I say this up front.

"As for Dolos and Apate—they're just a bit of fun. The agents on each floor get to select the names for their conference rooms. The rooms on seven are called *Possible* and *Impossible*. The rooms on four are *Chess* and *Checkers*. Some of the other names I prefer not to say in polite company. The point is, they don't mean anything."

"You said you wanted to clear the air," Kilmer reminded him. "Are you about to tell me something about your work that I'm not likely to support? Or to believe?"

Art looked at Silla and Lane. They responded with expressions that would typically accompany the shrugging of shoulders. Art turned back to Kilmer and leaned closer, resting his elbows on his legs.

"More so the latter. You won't believe much of what I'm about to tell you. But that's not really a problem, because soon enough, you will see that I'm telling you the truth."

"You seem confident of that."

"I'm *certain* of it. But I don't want to waste precious time convincing you of things you will eventually believe. I want our time spent more productively. So I'm asking for a favor. For the next hour, please keep in mind that if I'm lying, then this entire conversation is irrelevant—and you can walk away having wasted only an evening. But if I'm telling the truth, lives depend on you suspending your disbelief and taking our discussion seriously."

The request seemed reasonable enough. But there was another way to interpret it: *Don't question anything I say.*

Kilmer audited the situation. His presence here appeared voluntary, but maybe it wasn't. A few of his concerns had been addressed, but most had not. He was expected to answer their questions, but he was not allowed to ask his own. And now, they wanted him to believe whatever they told him—no matter how incredible it might seem.

Before Art could press ahead, Kilmer took to his feet. The three agents turned to each other, unsure what was happening. Was he about to walk out? Did he just need to stretch his legs? Kilmer walked slowly, as if he were still considering Art's request, until he reached the other end of the table. Then he eased himself into the chair directly opposite the one he had occupied earlier. The agents and the TV screen were now on the far side of the room from him. He waited a few seconds for everyone to get used to the new arrangement before he spoke.

"I'm ready to hear what you have to say, Art. And I'll do my best to give you the benefit of the doubt."

Art smiled. "Thank you." Then he pulled his chair closer and rested his forearms on the edge of the table, his eyes suddenly brandishing a level of seriousness that most people would find hard to muster.

Lane readied his pencil.

Silla leaned forward.

Art pulled the pin. "It's not Russia or China. And no, it's not North Korea or Iran either. I wish it were that simple."

Then he launched the grenade.

"Tell me, Professor. Do you believe in the existence of extra-terrestrial life?"

What in the actual hell?

Kilmer's mind raced to consider all the ways in which the question might have been intended. Are you open-minded about things? Are you able to discuss topics that go beyond your understanding? Are you prone to believing things for which there is no evidence?

Or was Art really asking him about the possibility of encountering *aliens?*

He waited for Art to provide additional context, or to clarify his question—but Art said nothing more.

Is this some kind of test?

"How do you mean, exactly?" Kilmer asked.

Lane jotted something down.

"I mean precisely what I asked: do you believe in the possibility of extra-terrestrial life?"

"Do I believe in *aliens?*"

"We don't use that term. But yes. That's what I'm asking."

It suddenly felt like a parlor game—a discussion you might have with friends over a few beers. *Do you think there might be life elsewhere in the universe?* Kilmer decided to give his standard answer.

"Probabilistically, yes. The universe is too large for there not to be living things somewhere else. There might even be microorganisms trapped in water somewhere in the solar system for all I know. But do I think there are aliens that are sophisticated enough to travel great distances in space, who will find Earth, and who will just *happen* to visit our planet—which is over four billion years old—during my lifetime? No, I don't think so. The odds are infinitesimally small."

That was the extent of his view on the matter, and because no one had interrupted his monologue, he had managed to recite all of *Kilmer's Thoughts on Alien Encounters* in just under thirty seconds.

"This is clearly not the first time you've thought about this question," noted Art.

"Everyone has spent at least a little bit of time thinking about it."

"Some more than others, I assure you."

Kilmer decided it was time to start asking questions. "What, precisely, does Triad do, Art? And what exactly is this about?"

"I'm getting to that. But first, let me confirm something you said. If there was an explanation for why extra-terrestrials might visit Earth during your lifetime, would you be more open to the possibility of an encounter?"

Kilmer forced himself to take the question seriously.

"Provisionally… yes. That would go a long way in making this a more interesting conversation. It's not hard to believe that there is life elsewhere in the universe. It's also plausible that there would be *intelligent* life, as we conceive of it. That they would have the technology necessary to allow interstellar space travel seems like a stretch, but they might have been leveraging the scientific method for a million years, while we've only embraced it for a few centuries. But the biggest hurdle, in my casual estimation, is that we have to multiply all of those small probabilities together, and *then* multiply by an even more remote possibility—that they just happen to show up when human beings are around and evolved enough to notice."

"Great," said Art, as if significant progress had already been made. "Now, I'm going to make this quick—and this is where I ask you to give me the benefit of the doubt. We can get into the details later, but the short of it is this: we know with *certainty* that extra-terrestrials exist. We know that they are intelligent, that they can find us, and that they have chosen to do so in our lifetime. This is not a theoretical finding, or a probabilistic assessment, or an interpretation of some aberration we've detected in the cosmos, like the bending or redshifting of light from a distant galaxy. We know all of this based on firsthand experience."

Kilmer said nothing. He was focusing on Art's words—and looking to see how the other agents were reacting. Silla and Lane showed no signs of surprise or anxiety. They sat impassively, as if they were part of a hiring panel that was interviewing him for an entry-level role at the agency, and Art had merely read out the job description.

Art, meanwhile, was speaking faster now, like a man racing through non-essentials to meet a deadline.

"Yes, they can travel great distances. Yes, they have chosen the United States as their destination. And yes, we have every reason to worry that they mean to do us harm. Now, what I need you to—"

"I'm sorry," interrupted Kilmer. "Are you saying that aliens have already *landed* on Earth—in the US?"

Agents Silla and Lane turned toward Art, as if they were unsure how he would respond to the question.

Art slowed down. "As I'm trying to explain, Professor, the extra-terrestrials *have* made their way to Earth. We have even managed to communicate with them. All of this will require more time to explain to you, but for now, I just need you to accept what I'm saying so that we can move on to the reason you're here."

Kilmer noticed that Art had not actually answered his question. *Why share so much information but still dodge the question about whether aliens had in fact landed in America?*

"Okay. So, why exactly *am* I here?"

"To help us avoid a war," said Art. "And if that proves to be impossible, then to help us win it."

"Avoid a war?"

"Correct."

"Against aliens."

"Correct."

"And if that fails, then to help you *win* the war?"

"Correct."

"Against aliens."

"Yes."

Kilmer took a deep breath as he searched for the right words.

He found them.

"Are you out of your goddamn minds?"

The agents glanced at each other.

"Why do you say that, Professor?" Art asked.

Just as Lane readied his pencil, poised to take notes, Kilmer caught his eye.

"Put the pencil down, Agent Lane, or I walk out of this room and I don't come back."

Lane looked at Silla. Silla looked at Art. Art nodded.

Lane put down his pencil.

Kilmer continued. "Here's why I say that, *Arthur*. You're telling me that you're in contact with an alien race that has traveled trillions of miles to planet Earth, and that if I can't help you avoid a war with them, you want me to help you win it. And no one here sees the problem with that?"

Silence.

"Okay. Let's do some backward induction. Why would aliens travel all this way only to *lose a war*? If they decide to fight, it's because they have good reason to believe they can win. And based on the fact that *they* found *us*—while we can barely make our way back to the Moon—well, I'm guessing they probably have the edge when it comes to technology. They just might have what it takes to beat us in a war.

"But let's imagine for a moment that we do, somehow, end up having a military advantage. If they don't already know it, they'll figure it out soon enough. At which point, why will they stick around to continue fighting a war they will lose? They can just turn around and leave. It's not like we can follow them home to finish the job."

"So, what you're saying is…"

"What I'm saying is, if our Plan B is to defeat a highly advanced alien race, one that has traveled trillions or quadrillions of miles across space, in a war that *they've* initiated, then our Plan A had better be an impeccably crafted strategy of unparalleled friggin' genius."

Silla and Lane looked at Art. For the first time, Kilmer sensed a hint of concern. But Art remained composed.

"Is it your judgment, Professor, that we only survive this crisis if the aliens have peaceful intentions?"

Kilmer shook his head. "No, Art. I'm not saying that your only hope is that they want peace—because winning isn't the only alternative to losing. History might seem like nothing but a series of wars, but most of human history is a story about wars that did *not* occur. Just because we can't win a war doesn't mean we can't avoid it."

"So you might be willing to threaten the use of force to get them to change their calculus?" Art asked.

"It's unlikely to be quite that simple, but I don't know enough about the situation to offer specifics. I only want to point out that while having a Plan B is usually a great idea, the existence of a fallback option introduces its *own* element of risk. Having a Plan B makes it easier, when the going gets tough, to abandon your Plan A. And that can be disastrous if Plan B is a beacon of false hope—an *ignis fatuus*."

Kilmer turned to Silla. "Agent Silla, you asked me earlier if I would have enjoyed being a fly on the wall when Chamberlain or Churchill were debating alternative strategies. Let me tell you what I would have *really* liked to witness. The meeting where Hitler decided to break the treaty he had negotiated with Stalin, and to invade the Soviet Union. I would like to have been in the room when the Japanese decided to bomb Pearl Harbor. These people were not stupid. They were not irrational. They debated the pros and cons. And yet, somehow, they decided to light the fuses that would ultimately burn their own empires to the ground."

"You're worried that we might end up making the same mistake," Silla said.

Kilmer shrugged. "I don't know. First of all, I have no idea what we're dealing with. For all I know, you've been feeding me a bunch of BS and there isn't any alien threat at all. But if the threat *is* real, I need a lot more information before I can make predictions or offer advice. Simple logic suggests that you can't expect to win such a war—and if your strategy can't even stand up to simple logic, you're in serious trouble. But we can't rely *exclusively* on simple logic either. Strategy has to meet the demands of simple logic, but it should never become a slave to it."

Art glanced at his watch. "The meeting is about to start."

Kilmer looked at his own watch. It was 8:04 p.m. *Interesting.* "Any chance I can get some coffee before it starts?"

"How do you like it?" Lane asked.

"Black, and as hot as possible."

"Anyone else?"

"I'll have it the same way," Silla responded.

Kilmer couldn't help but wonder whether Silla's request was some carryover from basic training, where CIA agents are taught how to build rapport. *Strategy #9: Order the same drink as the asset you're trying to cultivate.*

Lane left the room and Silla started to work the keyboard.

"Am I allowed to take notes?" Kilmer asked.

Art walked over to the small table in the corner and returned with a pencil and some sheets of paper for Kilmer.

"One more question," Kilmer said.

"Shoot."

"Do the participants in the meeting know that I'm observing them?"

Art eased himself back into his chair. "Don't worry, Professor. All the participants know you're watching."

The response was more comforting than Kilmer had expected. The issue must have been bothering him more than he realized.

Art changed the topic. "I hope the meeting will go better than you expect. But if we are on the wrong track, we need someone to help us figure that out. If we're heading toward disaster, we need someone to warn us. I hate to say this, Professor, but you might be the only one who can pull this off. That will sound very strange to you, I'm sure, but you will eventually understand why I think so."

"You're right, Art. It does sound very strange. I'm afraid you might be seriously overestimating the value I bring to the table. As for the meeting, I really don't harbor any expectations about it. I've learned, over the years, that when it comes to solving the most vexing problems, nothing ever turns out quite as you expected at the start."

Art smiled dimly. "Professor, you have no idea how right you are. But you're about to find out."

In the silence that followed, Kilmer saw the expression on Art's face change—as if he was having a hard time resisting the urge to say something more. A moment later, Art gave in to the urge.

"Before we start… I feel like I should warn you," Art confessed hesitantly. "You know that whole thing I told you about there being an alien invasion?"

Kilmer tilted his head and furrowed his brows, as if to say, *Yeah, what about it?*

"Well, Professor… that's not even the part that's *really* going to blow your mind."

~ 3 ~

~ Interlude: A different time ~

It was early morning, and Chief of Staff Salvador "Salvo" Perez was waiting in the Map Room. Located on the ground floor of the White House, the room had been used by President Roosevelt to monitor progress during World War II. The room no longer contained maps, and it was no longer heavily guarded, but it had managed to keep its name. It occurred to Perez that there wasn't a map in the world that could help them chart progress in the war that now seemed imminent. He made a mental note of that—yet another problem that someone, somewhere would have to take responsibility for addressing.

Perez had only been waiting for a few minutes when President Whitman, dressed in an expertly fitted navy-blue suit, walked in. Whitman and Perez met in the center of the room for what would be a short meeting.

Perez started things off. "I'll get right to it. As of this morning, we count approximately two hundred alien spacecraft. As you know, a few days ago, there were fewer than ten. General Allen and Secretary Strauss agree that an attack could come very soon. But we have no way to know for sure."

President Whitman took a deep breath. "Okay. I'll discuss the situation with the alliance. They've let us take the lead until now, but this could change things. We need Earth-side to remain coordinated—now more than ever."

Perez nodded. "I'll have the team in the Situation Room by 10 a.m. And I'll have those calls set up for you between now and then. Do you have any preference for the order?"

"Let's do NATO first. Beyond that, let's not be picky. Fit the others in however you can."

"Understood. I'll get that done."

"Thanks, Salvo."

Salvo Perez had known Whitman for thirty-five years, and they had been

19

close friends since they served together in the Army. But Perez still observed protocol, even if no one else was present, like waiting for the president to dismiss him. Whitman gestured toward the door, and Perez walked over to hold it open for the president.

Ten minutes later, President Whitman was sitting in the Oval Office, finishing a phone call.

"3:30 is fine. We'll see you then. Thank you, Art. And please convey my gratitude to him."

Whitman reached over to the table behind the desk and picked up one of the decorative fighting sticks that had been gifted by a delegation from the Philippines. The president stood up, gave the arnis stick a few expert swings, and then walked over to the east doors of the Oval Office.

President Marianne J. Whitman looked out at the new day that was dawning over the Rose Garden.

The first woman to be elected President of the United States.

The first woman to serve as Commander-in-Chief in the history of the Republic.

So, yeah.

Of course there would be an alien invasion.

~ **End of interlude** ~

~ 4 ~

Agent Lane announced his return to Apate 3 by knocking on the door with his foot. Silla opened the door to let him in, and Lane walked in carrying three cups, including one for himself. Silla took her coffee, and Lane delivered one to Kilmer. It was not nearly as hot as Kilmer liked it, but warmer than he expected. Lane and Silla took their seats. With the meeting about to commence, Kilmer was now sitting farthest from the TV, and he had everyone in his sights as they sat facing the screen.

The screen flickered on, showing a large, circular table in the middle of an enormous, brightly lit room. It occurred to Kilmer that he'd been expecting a darker room with a long conference table—like a scene from *The Star Chamber* with Michael Douglas. It was a helpful reminder that he had not, in fact, entirely discarded his presumptions regarding the meeting. He would have to be more careful not to allow his expectations and assumptions to filter what he saw and heard during the meeting.

There were twelve chairs around the table, and all were fully visible. Most of the participants were already seated—some looked to be conversing while others stared at their cell phones. The picture quality was excellent, and Kilmer could make out the faces clearly, except for the people who were seated with their backs to the camera. Kilmer recognized two of the attendees. The first was Secretary of Defense Robert Strauss. Before President Whitman had asked him to lead the Defense Department, Strauss had been a senator, and before that, he had spent many years in the military. The other familiar face belonged to CIA Director Noah Druckman. Kilmer had seen him on TV during more than one Congressional hearing. He was a CIA insider, and had been at the agency for over three decades.

The other people he expected to recognize were not in the room.

The camera that was streaming the meeting was situated high on one of the walls, and it showed most of the room, except for what was directly below it. For now, a least, there was no sound. The entrance to the room was through a door that was directly across from the video camera. Also against the far wall were two additional chairs, both of which were occupied. These were probably the two notetakers Kilmer had been told about. There was a table on the wall to the right, and it held a metal box that Kilmer now knew was used to collect cell phones. The wall to the left featured a row of old-fashioned file cabinets, the tops of which gave the impression of being one long countertop. Above the file cabinets hung an old analog clock that probably hadn't been used in a long time. It looked like it had died at 7:50 some years ago. There was a camera on every wall, but none of the walls that he could see had any artwork or windows.

Kilmer looked at his watch. 8:09 p.m.

On the screen, the door to the meeting room opened, and in walked four people—not three—whom he recognized. Vice President Zack Nielsen, National Security Advisor Victoria Garcia, and Chairman of the Joint Chiefs of Staff General Allen were accompanied by a young woman who was holding a stack of papers. The foursome appeared to be finishing up a conversation. VP Nielsen was the first to peel away from the group. He said a few words as he backed away, with body language that might have accompanied, *Okay, let's continue this discussion later.* Nielsen made his way around the table, shaking hands and exchanging a few words with each person. He disappeared off-screen for a few moments and then returned, finishing his stroll around the table.

The young woman who had entered with the others was Trina Morgan, and she was the next to separate from the group, leaving only NSA Garcia and General Allen to continue the conversation. Trina walked around the table, not saying hello to anyone, but looking at the name cards. At one point, she smiled and waved in the direction of someone whose back was to the camera. The person didn't appear to wave back. If he smiled or said anything in response, the camera didn't catch it. The non-waver was busy fiddling with his laptop, moving its screen up and down and side-to-side. Then he stood up and walked out of view of the camera before returning fifteen seconds later to sit back down. He checked his screen again and then started talking to the person on his left. They appeared to be laughing about something.

Trina had found her seat, but a minute later, she got up again and went to deposit her cell phone in the metal box. Some others saw this and remembered to do the same. She sat quietly now, as others at the table continued to chat with one another. Kilmer remembered how it had felt, back when he was a young professor, to be invited to events where the biggest names in the field were gathered. No one was lining up to talk to him either, back then.

Trina was a former PhD student of his, but she had left the program early to join the State Department. That was six years ago. She was a great student, but Kilmer was still surprised to see her here. After all, not many people in the world would be asked to join the first line of defense at the inception of an intergalactic war.

Then again, Kilmer had *two* former students in that meeting.

And the other one was pretty darn impressive as well.

~ 5 ~

Once everyone was seated—twelve people around the table and two notetakers against the far wall—the sound came on, as evidenced by the ambient noise now being streamed into Apate 3.

It was clear that Vice President Nielsen would be running this meeting. All eyes were focused on him, waiting for him to kick things off. Nielsen looked up at the clock on the wall, and then to his wristwatch, as if trying to reconcile the two. Kilmer looked at his own watch. 8:19 p.m.

Then Nielsen began.

"Thank you, everyone, for being on time. We will go for exactly an hour, and then I have another meeting. We will reconvene tomorrow morning. If I can, I want to save the last fifteen minutes for you to ask questions and to flag any remaining concerns. If you're unsure whether to speak up, please do it. I don't want to wake up one day and discover that I'm the last man on Earth because you didn't feel comfortable telling me what was bothering you. I know how that would end for me—losing my pistol just before I shatter my reading glasses."

There were a few chuckles of the kind you would only expect to hear from high-status attendees in such a meeting. The younger crowd probably didn't understand Nielsen's reference to the classic *Twilight Zone* episode anyway.

Nielsen continued. "I want to start with what we know. After that, I'll direct your attention to the precise question President Whitman wants us to discuss. For some of you, much of this will be new. For those who are mostly up to speed on things, there might still be a few new elements. Any questions before I start?"

There were none, so Nielsen continued, providing a brief timeline of events.

* * * * * * * * *

Two weeks ago, NASA sent an urgent message to Defense Secretary Strauss, who immediately relayed it to President Whitman. Whitman informed Chief of Staff Perez, Vice President Nielsen, CIA Director Druckman, and Chairman of the Joint Chiefs General Allen. All were sworn to secrecy, first informally, and then pursuant to a top-secret executive order issued by President Whitman. Attorney General Kim was confident it would hold up to Supreme Court scrutiny if its legality was ever questioned.

NASA scientists had detected what was first thought to be an oddly shaped asteroid almost 600 million miles from Earth. Upon further analysis, it was not only the shape of the "asteroid" but also its trajectory and movements that appeared anomalous. But the alarm bells didn't go off until a few days later, when an enormous radio telescope was trained on the space object and it was confirmed that the object was transmitting at super-high frequency (SHF)— and the signal pattern was non-random. That was when Dr. Vinay Menon, the chief scientist at NASA, made the call to the Department of Defense. That call had just ended when three additional "asteroids" were detected in the same vicinity. Menon made a second call to DoD on the heels of the first.

The first forty-eight hours after that were chaotic. It took the better part of the first day to convince everyone who was in the loop that the objects were, in all probability, evidence of an alien presence. On the second day, Whitman called UK Prime Minister Barnes, German Chancellor Koehler, and French President Cordier. Each designated one of their top scientists to work with the Americans. A select group of intelligence and defense officials from these countries set up similar channels to coordinate with their American counterparts. Everyone agreed—provisionally—to let America take the lead, but the British, Germans, and French were to be consulted and kept informed on all matters. Vice President Nielsen was designated as the chairperson for all groups that were focusing on intelligence and military matters.

On Day 3, Secretary of Energy Abigail Rao, a renowned physicist, and three scientists from Los Alamos National Laboratory, were brought into the fold. Two individuals at the CIA and two at the Department of Homeland Security were also informed. That same day, Whitman called Canadian Prime Minister Tremblay and UN Secretary-General Nkosi, both of whom urged

Whitman to reach out to China and Russia as soon as possible.

The conversations with the Chinese and Russians took place on Day 4— and were much more strained. Whitman emerged from those calls with the impression that everyone was advocating for cooperation, but there were concerns, on all sides, that others might attempt to use the crisis for some sort of advantage. It was not clear to Nielsen how that would be orchestrated, but suspicions remained barely below the surface.

Nonetheless, by Day 5, Chinese President Zhao had said that he would "agree to let the Americans speak first on these matters," a phrase that American diplomats struggled to interpret with any precision. Russian President Sokolov was clearer: "We will follow your lead, until and unless we disagree. If we dissent on any matter, we expect the Russian position to be taken seriously. If not, we will go our own way." On that same day, Whitman called Indian Prime Minister Attal, who offered to help in any way that he could and obtained Whitman's assurance that he and his National Security Advisor would be kept in the loop.

Day 6 was spent making plans for all manner of logistical and administrative challenges. Plans for dealing with the media if questions were raised. Plans for when and how to share information with Congressional leadership, and with the American people. Plans for managing mass protests and riots. Plans for evacuating cities if it became necessary. Plans for deploying the military and the National Guard. Plans for dealing with mass casualties. Plans for sustaining communication if satellite activities were disrupted. Plans for ensuring the continuity of government. Plans for ensuring that private-sector technologies capable of spotting and identifying the incoming objects were redeployed, distracted, disrupted, or locked down for as long as possible. Plans for addressing chatter among amateur astronomers who might chance upon the alien spacecraft. Plans for overseeing each of these plans and for identifying additional plans that needed to be made.

By Day 7, one of the four spacecraft had moved closer. It was now 150 million miles from Earth—about three times the distance from Earth to Mars. The other three spacecraft had not repositioned. The same day, Whitman approved a proposal that scientists from Los Alamos had made a few days earlier, but which had taken some time to advance through the various military and scientific filters.

The idea was to be proactive rather than simply wait to see what the aliens would do—and to pursue three specific goals: let "them" know that they had been spotted, signal Earth's desire to communicate, and direct the spacecraft to a specific landing spot on Earth, assuming the aliens had the ability and inclination to visit the Earth's surface. SHF radio signals would be aimed in the direction of the approaching spacecraft, with the broadcasts based on different mathematical patterns: prime numbers, squares, triangular numbers, Fibonacci sequences, et cetera. These mathematical patterns would serve as a sort of crude language, which could be used to create "information packets" that might be interpretable by the aliens.

But what information to send? The plan—which leveraged decades of prior work by scientists who had tried to imagine a day when communication with extra-terrestrials might be possible—called for implementing multiple communication strategies concurrently, in the hope that at least one might succeed. Dozens were tried. Two succeeded.

The first idea was to "personalize" the mathematical patterns for the aliens by sending parameters that they might recognize as being tied to their own spacecraft's behavior. Four pieces of information were sent in each such broadcast, corresponding to the alien spacecraft's distance at that moment from the Sun, the Earth, Mars, and Jupiter. As the spacecraft's distance from these celestial bodies changed, the parameters in the broadcast were adjusted to reflect the spacecraft's new location. If the aliens noticed the changing messages and investigated the pattern, they might deduce that the Earthlings had spotted them and were letting them know it.

The second idea was to "advise" the alien spacecraft on where it should go—if it was considering a terrestrial landing. In this case, the information packets contained "coordinates" on a two-dimensional representation of Earth-as-seen-from-the-spacecraft, using the current trajectory of the aliens to establish the point of zero degrees north-south and zero degrees east-west on Earth. As the spacecraft changed its trajectory, and as the Earth rotated in front of it, the messages—essentially, the extent to which the spacecraft would need to alter its approach to keep the "landing point" on planet Earth constant—were adjusted accordingly.

The landing point had to be chosen carefully. It had to be close enough to Washington, DC, to allow for ease of travel from the capital, in case that became necessary. It had to have adequate infrastructure, especially roadways. But it could not be a city or a town, because vacating civilians would inevitably cause delays and raise suspicion.

NSA Garcia came up with a solution that appeared to address all of these constraints: Shenandoah National Park in her home state of Virginia.

The Russians and Chinese objected. They proposed an area close to the Chinese city of Fuyuan, near their common border. If that was unacceptable to the Americans, they suggested, then a neutral location—perhaps an island in the Pacific—should be selected. For Whitman, this issue was non-negotiable. And when the British, French, Germans, Canadians, Indians, and Secretary-General Nkosi all backed her proposal, Zhao and Sokolov relented—but only after Whitman agreed that Chinese and Russian military delegations would accompany the Americans at the proposed landing spot if the alien spacecraft was headed there.

Shenandoah National Park was shut down by order of the Environmental Protection Agency, which announced the need for an evacuation due to "credible reports of a potential biological hazard." Within hours, the entire park was swept clean of stragglers, and a military and scientific presence was established.

On Day 10, NASA and Los Alamos scientists reported to Whitman that, for the first time in human history, an alien spacecraft was known to be communicating with human beings. Using the same mathematical language that humans had used, the spacecraft was relaying both its location in space and the coordinates for Shenandoah National Park. General Allen asked the scientists how they could be sure this was actual communication, and not just some sort of mirroring behavior. "How do we know that our signals aren't just bouncing back to us, or that they're not simply copying-and-pasting what we sent to them, without even understanding what it means?"

That was impossible, an excited Dr. Menon explained from NASA. "The messages from the aliens were sent at different times than the ones that we sent. If we were getting back a message that we ourselves had sent previously, it would no longer accurately represent their spacecraft's *current* location or trajectory. The aliens are not only using our mathematical language; they understand it enough to adjust the data they send to us so that it accurately accounts for where their spacecraft is located when *they* send a signal."

Put simply: *We think the aliens might be on their way to Shenandoah National Park.*

On Day 12, the alien spacecraft stopped sending signals and altered its trajectory. Instead of moving toward the Earth, it started to move toward the Moon. A few hours later, it was within 50,000 miles of the lunar surface.

On Day 13, everything changed. There were three massive explosions on the surface of the Moon. A team of scientists led by Secretary Rao concluded that each impact was of a magnitude equivalent to a 30-50 kiloton nuclear bomb—roughly twice the destructive power of the bombs that were dropped on Japan during World War II.

Every agency in charge of a contingency plan was placed on high alert. Congressional leadership was rushed to the White House and fully briefed by VP Nielsen. All were sworn to secrecy under threat of incarceration. One of the Congressmen vomited in the Roosevelt Room.

On Day 14, the alien spacecraft returned to its original trajectory and restarted its communication with Earth—as if nothing noteworthy had happened the day before.

Sorry about that. Just had to swing by the Moon for a short visit. So, where were we? Right, heading to Shenandoah National Park to meet with the Americans. See you soon.

Presidents Zhao and Sokolov voiced no more complaints about the rendezvous point that President Whitman had insisted upon.

* * * * * * * * *

Nielsen looked around the table at the attendees. Then he crossed his arms and leaned back in his chair.

"That was Day 14," he reiterated gravely. "Day 15 is today."

~ 6 ~

Holy hell.

Professor Kilmer sat staring at the TV screen, transfixed. It was the longest he had ever held a cup of coffee in his hands without taking a sip. *This is real.* He forced himself to break the trance that his mind was falling into. He wasn't invited to be a spectator. He was tasked with seeing what others might miss. He had to stay sharp. But he was already starting to feel overwhelmed.

Kilmer audited his physical state and noticed that he was slightly out of breath, as if he had just walked up five flights of stairs. He took a few deep breaths and felt more comfortable afterwards. Then he evaluated his posture—leaning forward, almost literally on the edge of his seat, shoulders hunched, his entire body straining. *No good.* He leaned back, reminding himself that every ounce of energy he redistributed from his muscles to his mind would pay dividends very soon.

Now to reboot the software. *Every problem wants to be solved*, he reminded himself. It was what his father had always said to him—and he had repeated it countless times to his own students. *If you think the problem is trying to fight you, you'll only make your job harder.* He needed to reframe the situation—to look at it differently.

That this crisis was unlike any other in history was impossible to deny. Then again, no two problems were *ever* the same. Even the threat of an alien invasion was, at its core, a problem of strategy. Higher stakes, greater complexity, more uncertainty, and less information than usual—but this was all a difference of *degree* and not of *kind*. This was terrain he had navigated before. No one ever called him for help with the easy stuff.

The physical and mental reset had taken less than ninety seconds. An investment well worth making.

Now... *think.*

Kilmer tried to synthesize what he had heard so far. Nielsen's chronology had been helpful, but...

But what? Something seemed... missing. Had something been omitted? Glossed over? Concealed?

No, that's not it. I have a million questions, of course, but lots of details are always missing at this stage.

Then what was bothering him? Did he still suspect that this was all just a test—or some charade—and that at any moment it would be revealed that there were, in fact, no aliens?

No. The people assembled for this meeting were too important, and the conversation they were having was entirely genuine. The problem wasn't the missing details. The problem wasn't the aliens.

It's something else. Something isn't quite right.

7

Vice President Nielsen scanned the room to make sure everyone was following along. The group had been fixated on him as he spoke, but they now took a moment to glance at each other. They saw in the faces of their colleagues a blend of emotions that they recognized as also being their own. *Shock. Angst.*

Nielsen continued. "As of last night, the alien spacecraft was less than 150,000 miles from Earth. For reference, the Moon is about 250,000 miles away. If you've been running the numbers, you know that the spacecraft is slowing down as it approaches Earth. It covered approximately 450 million miles in the first week after its detection. The fastest man-made objects in space would have taken one and a half *years* to travel that distance. In the last two days, the alien spacecraft has traveled only 125,000 miles. We have no intel, obviously, on why they've slowed down. We also don't know whether they really plan to rendezvous at Station Zero. We only—"

Nielsen paused.

"My apologies. Some of you are not regulars, and you might not be following the lingo I'm using. Over the last two weeks, some new words have entered our lexicon, and it will be helpful for you to know the vocabulary."

Nielsen provided a two-minute crash course on the new jargon. He explained that, apart from the CIA, where they still insisted on using the term "extra-terrestrials," everyone else was referring to the visitors as "aliens." The president's inner circle was referred to as "the team." The larger group of Americans who were in the know were referred to as "the loop." The mathematical language that was being used to communicate with the incoming aliens was christened FERMAT—named, tongue-in-cheek, for the mathematician who had popularized the method of "proof by infinite descent." Shenandoah National Park was being called "Station Zero." The foreign heads of state who were aware of the crisis were "the alliance." To distinguish between actions taken by human beings versus those taken by the aliens, the terms "Earth-side" and "Space-side" were occasionally used. Most ominously, a distinction was now being made between the possibility of an alien "attack" and an alien "invasion." None of these were official terminology. There had been no committee, no executive decree, and no official memo. The words had just taken hold.

"Now," said Nielsen, "let me get back on track. As I said, we have no idea why the aliens have slowed down. We have a wide range of hypotheses, but no way to test most of them. If we're lucky, the aliens are just being cautious. Or perhaps they're incapable of landing on Earth. Or they only wish to study us from afar. Hell, for all we know, they're sitting there wondering why we haven't come up to say hello. Those are all best-case scenarios.

"If we're *un*lucky, the spacecraft could be conducting reconnaissance in preparation for an attack. They might be waiting for reinforcements before they launch an invasion. Perhaps they're calibrating or deploying a weapon system that we can't even imagine, and they want to be a safe distance away when they blow us to smithereens.

"Of course, there are many hypotheses that lie in between the extremes— some more plausible than others. For example, it's possible that the aliens plan to cover the remaining distance in smaller crafts that we can't detect. On the less plausible end of the spectrum… well, I don't want to make too many assumptions here, but I don't think they just ran out of gas."

Nielsen again drew some chuckles, but not everyone was amused. NSA Garcia responded with a none-too-subtle shaking of the head. "Damn it, Garcia, that was funny," Nielsen complained. He allowed the smile to leave his face before continuing. "Now, let me tell you why we're here."

The vice president explained that at 5 p.m. the previous evening—on Day 14—Defense Secretary Strauss had called President Whitman to discuss the possibility of launching a "visible response" to the attack on the Moon. Strauss wanted the president to respond to the provocation "with our own show of force." Whitman subsequently called General Allen to get his views on the matter, and Allen told the president he saw merit in discussing the proposal. "It's risky, for obvious reasons, and we should avoid anything that might provoke a conflict—but it could be equally dangerous if we look like sitting ducks."

At 7:30 p.m., President Whitman met with her team. She made it clear that time was of the essence, but that she would not make a final decision until the following day. "Whatever we might think tonight, I want to be sure that it still makes sense to us tomorrow. I also want a few more voices to weigh in on this. We have a healthy range of perspectives here, but what makes sense to us might seem unreasonable to others—and I want to know if there are things we have failed to consider."

Whitman told the group that she also intended to speak to the international alliance the following day, and that close to a consensus might be required before Earth-side behaved in a way that might be provocative. At 9:30 p.m., she ended the meeting and told Nielsen to lead the following day's discussion. "I won't attend the meeting," she told him, "because I don't want my presence to influence the discussion. Nor do I want people in the room to know which way I'm leaning. Understood?"

"Yes, ma'am," Nielsen replied. "Although, to be honest, I'm not sure even *I* know which way you're leaning."

"Then I'm doing a good job," Whitman said without even a hint of a smile.

This was followed by some light-hearted banter among the team about which way Whitman might be leaning. Whitman put an end to it after CIA Director Druckman joked that Whitman was leaning toward sending the aliens a map of the Korean Peninsula and the coordinates for Pyongyang.

"Okay, that's enough. Everyone out."

As the group was leaving, Whitman asked VP Nielsen and Chief of Staff Perez to stay back so they could discuss a separate matter. Twenty minutes later, Perez returned to his office to set up phone calls with the alliance for the following afternoon. Nielsen went to his office to make a few calls of his own.

* * * * * * * * * *

"That's where things stand," Nielsen announced to everyone around the table. Then he rose from his chair.

"We have a decision to make—today. Defense Secretary Strauss is proposing a show of force that would signal to the aliens that we're not entirely defenseless. If we're going to act on that proposal—or on any variation of the idea—it must be done very soon. President Whitman wants to know where we stand before she raises the idea with the alliance—a process that is likely to introduce its own delays.

"The president understands that she's asking a lot of each of you. No one wants to cast the decisive vote in what might end up being the wrong call. But she asked me to make something very clear: *you're not here to vote.* Only one person will have to live with having made this decision. That person is the president of the United States."

Nielsen could see the gravity of the situation weighing heavily on everyone. He wanted to lighten their load, even if just a little, so that they could have a productive discussion. Then, remembering some advice he had received years ago, he smiled, and his gaze shifted slightly upward.

"A professor of mine once said something that I'd like to share with you," he told the group. "*Don't reward people for coming up with the right answer. Reward them for coming up with good arguments. Only good arguments can guide you to the right answer.*

"That is our challenge. To unearth every good argument. I don't care if you're for or against the proposal—I want to know how you're *thinking* about it. Don't censor yourself, even if the second point you want to make seems to contradict the first point you made. If you have an idea, share it. If you agree or disagree with someone, *now is the time to tell us.* The very existence of tomorrow depends on your willingness to speak up today."

The group was nodding along, and the little pep talk seemed to have calmed some nerves. Nielsen looked toward the camera on the wall and gave a friendly nod of appreciation. *Thank you, Professor, for that useful bit of wisdom.*

Then he sat down and slapped the table with both palms, making it clear that his lecture had ended. "That is all. Let's get to work."

He looked at the secretary of defense. "Strauss, please get us started. Tell us what you're proposing and why."

8

For about twenty seconds, Professor Kilmer had allowed himself to feel flattered. A former student—the vice president of the United States, no less—was quoting him at a pivotal moment in history. When Nielsen smiled at him through the camera, Kilmer almost nodded back at the screen to acknowledge it. *You're welcome.*

But apart from those twenty seconds of mild delight, what Kilmer had been feeling was nothing close to joy. *Anxiety? Fear?* Whatever it was, he had to push the emotion aside so he could focus on the task at hand.

Much harder to push aside, however, was the grating suspicion that something just wasn't right. *What is it?*

He glanced over at the three agents. Art, Silla, and Lane were observing the meeting as though nothing was wrong. They looked concerned, of course, but that was to be expected. Kilmer was concerned as well—and had been throughout the meeting—except for those twenty seconds during which he had managed to get his mind off the aliens.

Get his mind off the aliens.

The words Art had spoken returned in a flash and struck him like a lead pipe to the skull.

You know that whole thing I told you about there being an alien invasion?
Well, that's not even the part that's really going to blow your mind.

At the time, Kilmer had figured Agent Capella was simply being melodramatic. But that wasn't it. Art had meant what he said. He'd even tried to stop himself from saying it.

Suddenly, the pieces started to fit together.

The explanation. The meeting. The deadline. The alliance. The camera. The clock. The laptop.

All of it.

The incongruities began to harmonize. Not completely, but just enough.

Things were not what they seemed.

Even Vice President Nielsen, smiling at him through the camera... he had misunderstood it entirely.

Kilmer felt a chill run up his spine.

~ 9 ~

After VP Nielsen handed things over to Strauss, the defense secretary held the floor for about seven minutes, during which time he advocated methodically for a vivid display of Earth-side strength. No matter how one tried to explain the lunar attack, he argued, it was impossible not to see it as a show of force by the aliens. "Why show off your weapons unless you are trying, at a bare minimum, to establish that you are the alpha dog in the relationship? We do it too. *Speak softly and carry a big stick.* Teddy Roosevelt sent sixteen battleships around the globe for everyone to see for only one reason: to make it clear that there was a new sheriff in town. And frankly, that's the *best*-case scenario here. The other possibility is that we're being tested—the way Khrushchev tested Kennedy, by putting nukes and missiles in Cuba. There isn't a Russian general alive who will deny the fact that if Kennedy hadn't pushed back, Khrushchev would have gotten even more aggressive. The Soviets would have taken West Berlin—and it wouldn't have stopped there. That's the kind of thing we might be dealing with here."

Strauss rested his case with a passionate rendition of one of the classics: *Chamberlain at Munich.*

"Humanity has learned what happens when you fail to stand up to early acts of aggression. Hitler annexed Austria. No one pushed back. So, he demanded the Sudetenland. Chamberlain made a big show of negotiating a compromise with Hitler—but when he went to Munich, he agreed to just about everything Hitler wanted. Britain and France practically forced the Czechoslovakians to hand over a piece of their country to Hitler. And in return for what? Hitler's assurance that he wanted nothing more. Of course, Hitler then went ahead and took *all* of Czechoslovakia. *Still* no retaliation. So Hitler invaded Poland. The British and French finally woke up, but the damage was already done. The only option left was total war—the deadliest war in our planet's history!"

By the time Strauss had ended his walk down Munich Lane, he was pretty worked up. But his words had a palpable effect. No one seemed eager to follow on the heels of the secretary's fervent speech.

Energy Secretary Rao asked what, *specifically*, Strauss was proposing. What would an Earth-side "show of force" entail?

One of Strauss's DoD colleagues answered. "Secretary Rao, there is a range of options, but we believe that it would have to be the detonation of a nuclear weapon in space. Ideally, it would be on the surface of the Moon itself, to make our signal crystal clear—but that will not be easy to do on short notice. If we remove the Moon from our list of targets, then we are left with an explosion somewhere in empty space where the alien spacecraft might be able to witness or detect it. We have no intel on the types of instruments they can use to detect a nuclear blast, so there is a case to be made that it should be made visible to them, albeit at a safe distance."

National Security Advisor Garcia spoke next, and she was against the idea. "I agree with Secretary Strauss that the lunar incident might represent a Space-side show of force. However, we should consider the motivation behind it. It's true that Khrushchev would have felt emboldened if Kennedy didn't push back during the Cuban Missile Crisis, but Khrushchev was himself reacting to aggressive actions that the US had taken even earlier. Whatever else he was after, Khrushchev was driven primarily by his own sense of insecurity. Which brings us to what the aliens have done. Is it possible that their show of force is defensive in nature? Maybe they're afraid that *we* will harm *them* unless they show their strength."

The discussion broadened widely at that point, with many people weighing in. "We don't need to get into a pissing contest before we even know what's going on here," someone counseled at one point.

"With all due respect, that is not what Secretary Strauss is advocating," CIA Director Druckman countered. "We just want the extra-terrestrials to know that we're not an easy target. If they bomb the closest thing to Earth and our response is to do nothing, they might conclude that they have the license to take the next step as well. Even if they *did* drop their bombs only out of fear, they're still testing us. We don't want to instigate a war, but how does it help to hide the fact that we have some defensive capabilities? The way I see it, if they can annihilate us from space, we don't stand a chance anyway. But if they want to invade and attempt an occupation, we might be able to put up a fight. I would want them to know that before they make such a decision."

"And what makes you think we can defeat them if the fighting takes place on Earth?" NSA Garcia asked.

"I'm not saying we *can* defeat them. But we don't have to be as strong as them to deter an invasion. We've learned that lesson many times ourselves— that even a much weaker enemy can wage an effective resistance campaign. Vietnam. Somalia. Afghanistan. Iraq. I don't see why we should hide the fact that we can fight to the end if necessary. It might be enough to deter an invasion—if that's what they're planning."

General Allen asked to speak next. Until that point, the chairman of the Joint Chiefs of Staff had been leaning back, taking in the conversation. He now sat up, back straight, and placed both palms on the table.

"This has been a helpful discussion. I have heard the arguments in favor of a show of force, and I think they're quite compelling. I really do. But *practically*, I don't see how we can execute on the plan without a substantial risk that the aliens will think we're launching an attack. If we detonate a nuclear weapon in space, close enough to their spacecraft to ensure it's visible to them, they might think it was a shot across the bow—or worse, that we tried to hit them and missed. I agree that seeming weak could encourage them to be more ambitious, but the risk of unwanted escalation weighs more heavily in my analysis.

"Finally—and despite my belief that a show of force is too risky at this time—I would like to add a word of caution in the other direction as well. NSA Garcia has made a good point—that we should not assume the worst when it comes to alien intentions—but I have seen enough carnage in my life to know that giving the other side the benefit of the doubt will sometimes get you killed. We must not let our guard down, no matter which course of action we choose today."

Dr. Menon, chief scientist at NASA, steered the conversation in a different direction. "If I may, I would like to offer a science-based perspective. I'd like you to think about the amount of energy—or, if you prefer, the level of technological sophistication—that is required to travel the way these aliens have done. Consider the distances covered and the speeds at which they have moved. These beings are, *conservatively* speaking, hundreds of years ahead of us in this domain. Given what we have already seen, do you consider it at all possible that the lunar explosions we detected two days ago represent anything *close* to their maximum military capability? That is inconceivable to me.

"Which leads me to two conclusions. First, we should be very worried about escalation. We demonstrate a yield of fifty kilotons, they go to a hundred, we go to a thousand, and they decide to go to a million. That is not a game we are likely to win, and we should do what we can to avoid it. Second—and this is good news—if my thesis is correct, then it means the aliens have chosen to display a relatively *small* amount of force. If they really wanted to scare us into submission, I suspect they could have done much more than they actually did."

Strauss rose from his chair just as Dr. Menon was finishing his point. He was the only one to have left his seat during the discussion. He stood behind his chair as he spoke, resting his hands atop the backrest. "I hear you, Dr. Menon. But with all due respect, I don't think you fully understand how these things tend to play out in the *real* world."

Dr. Menon smiled, as if he was used to jokes predicated on his reputation for being among the world's top *theoretical* physicists.

Strauss noticed the reaction. "I apologize," he said half-heartedly. "I'm only referring to the real world of warfare. Of military action. Candidly, the dynamics of war do not boil down to a system of equations. The decisions that are made when it's a question of life or death are not easily explained by your laws of physics.

"Think back to the bombing of Hiroshima at the end of World War II. People wonder why we nuked a city filled with innocent people, instead of targeting an unpopulated area. Why kill tens of thousands of civilians to force a Japanese surrender, when the same could have been achieved by demonstrating the bomb's effectiveness on some remote island? Now, some will argue that the Japanese wouldn't have surrendered unless they felt the devastation firsthand. And they'll give you all sorts of reasons why it was strategically important, and how it ended up saving more lives in the long run by shortening the war. But you know what I say to all that? *Bullshit.* We could have dropped that bomb somewhere else—we just didn't want to.

"Here's what your analysis misses, Dr. Menon: even if we *had* been nice enough to drop that first atomic bomb in a distant location—on the Moon, so to speak—what do you suppose would have happened if the Japanese hadn't surrendered after that? Unless the Japanese had found some way to deter us, we sure as shit would have dropped our *second* bomb on their city. So you know where I come out on this? I say, *fine.* Let's give these aliens credit where they deserve it. Their opening move is much more civilized than our first strike was against the Japanese. But that doesn't mean they're not coming for our cities the second time around. Maybe they're just waiting to see whether we surrender or give them a reason to think twice about attacking us. I am not for surrendering. But I *am* for deterrence."

Several heads nodded—some in agreement and others in contemplation.

Trina Morgan was called on next. "Secretary Strauss—I'm sorry, but the two situations you're comparing are *very* different. For one thing, we were already at war with Japan at the time we dropped the atomic bomb. The decision to nuke was made after Pearl Harbor had been attacked, after the war in the Pacific had been raging for years, after the firebombing of Tokyo, and after a long record of Japanese atrocities in Asia. That context is simply not present in the current crisis. To our knowledge, the aliens have no reason to hate us. They have no cause for grievance. I just don't see any clear motivation for them to drop a bomb on one of our cities. On the other hand, if we launch a nuke into space, they might start to rethink their relationship with us. Our aggressive actions might trigger a war that was otherwise avoidable. It would be on us."

There were only five minutes left in the hour, and Nielsen attempted to bring the discussion to an end. He had only uttered six words before Director Druckman interrupted.

"Mr. Vice President, I apologize. I know you want to bring some closure here, but this is important. If you don't mind, I'd like to respond."

"Go ahead, Noah. It's okay."

"Thank you," Druckman said as he turned toward Trina. "Ms. Morgan, I think you're blaming the wrong party. We're not the ones who sailed across the universe. Nor were we the first to deploy weapons. You also seem to conflate aggression and warmongering. These are not the same, and it is wrong-headed to think that they are."

Druckman looked around the room as he continued.

"Two coalitions have emerged here. One is for a show of force, the other against it. I have no problem with a disagreement of this kind—if the arguments are all based on reasonable assumptions. Unfortunately, there is at least one dangerously flawed assumption that has crept into our discussion. Some of you seem to believe that those who endorse the show-of-force proposal are somehow in favor of war, or that we are more *willing* to go to war, than the rest of you. That is incorrect. We know as well as you that winning a war against the extra-terrestrials is probably next to impossible. But just because we can't win doesn't mean we can't deter certain actions they might be considering. That is the goal. Our only goal.

"Like Secretary Strauss, I believe that World War II might have been avoided, if only the British and French had shown a willingness to sacrifice earlier. Two of my grandparents died in Auschwitz. Another died at Belzec. Two uncles died at Treblinka. I know others in this room also lost family in that war—on both sides. So yes, I wish Chamberlain had been more aggressive from the start—not because I'm a warmonger, but because the whole senseless, tragic war could have been averted. I don't want our children or grandchildren to say the same thing about this moment in time. Make no mistake, friends, those of us who are proposing a more aggressive course of action are *as much* for peace as anyone in this room!"

Druckman leaned forward and slapped his hand on the table, hard, to emphasize the last point. He looked deadly serious, but not angry. He paused for almost five seconds before concluding.

"I know war. I have seen it in all its forms. And I want *peace*. But history has shown, all too often, that if you will never accept the risk of stumbling into a war, you will have war thrust upon you by others."

There was silence.

Nielsen looked at the clock. Then he rose from his chair to address the group.

"Thank you, everyone, for a robust discussion. If you held anything back, it didn't show. Still, if there is something more you want to share with me privately, you know how to reach me. Just do it soon. We didn't get a chance for the Q&A, so I'll ask Secretary Strauss, General Allen, and NSA Garcia to stick around for another fifteen minutes to answer questions—if they can.

"Ladies and gentlemen, the decision we face is not an easy one—that's why smart people are disagreeing. But we all share the same goal: to ensure that our encounter with the aliens is a peaceful one. Let's not forget that, no matter how much we argue. No matter what we decide.

"That is all for now. You'll be updated later today, and this group will reconvene at the same time tomorrow. Assuming, of course, that there *is* a tomorrow."

No laughter this time.

And then, just as the people in the room started to collect their belongings, the video stream ended. The last thing it transmitted was Vice President Nielsen looking toward the camera and saying, "And thank you, Professor."

~ 10 ~

As the screen went blank, the four observers seated in Apate 3 turned to face one another. Art looked at Kilmer from across the room. He saw in the professor's face an emotion that he could not immediately identify.

Concern? Fear? Anger?

No, none of those.

Intensity.

It looked as if concentration, hostility, equanimity, and triumph had all somehow blended together to create an expression entirely devoid of valence. Like the colors of the rainbow combining to produce only white—the constituent elements almost entirely hidden from view.

"Well, Professor, do you have any thoughts?"

"A few."

"Great. We're ready to hear them."

"I'm sure you are," said Kilmer. "After all, time is of the essence, right?"

Something in the way he said it caused Silla and Lane to turn toward Art.

"Yes, it is," said Art. "I have a call with the president later tonight. She has asked me to report on what you have to say about all of this."

"Hmmm." Kilmer considered that for a moment. "So, what would you like to hear from me?"

"Let's go straight to the bottom line, Professor. Do you think a show of force is a good idea? Do you have a strong position on that? And if not, what else should the president be considering?"

"As it turns out, I *do* have a strong point of view on Secretary Strauss's proposal. Unfortunately…"

Kilmer paused, shifting his gaze from one agent to the next until it settled, once again, on Art.

"Unfortunately," he continued, "my views are not going to matter. President Whitman won't take my advice."

Silla and Lane looked uncomfortable. If the same was true of Art, he didn't show it.

"Why do you think that?" asked Art. "If the president is undecided, your opinion should carry a lot of weight."

"It *should* carry weight, but it won't. I don't believe she's in a position to take my advice right now." Then Kilmer leaned forward. "But you already know that... don't you, Agent Capella?"

There was no response. Whether Art was starting to look frustrated or confused was hard to tell.

"I'll make this easy for you, Art. I'll tell you exactly what I think about Secretary Strauss's show-of-force proposal. Once we get that over with, we're going to talk about something else. We're going to talk about what *really* blows my mind."

Kilmer looked for a reaction—and received one that he hadn't expected.

Art smiled. "Okay, Professor. You seem convinced that President Whitman doesn't care about your opinion, but you're wrong about that. So, we have a deal—let's set that aside for now. Tell me what you think she *should* do?"

Kilmer got up from his chair and looked at his notes. He had only written two words the entire time.

Constraints. Intentions.

He reached over to pick up his coffee, still full to the brim, but estimated its likely temperature and decided against it. Instead, he picked up his pencil—something to fiddle with as he walked and talked.

"A show of force can be useful," Kilmer acknowledged, "and it can serve as a deterrent. It might even prove essential at some point. But we're not there yet. The arguments that Strauss and Druckman made were coherent, but I think they relied a bit too much on imperfect analogies. They articulated a logic that supports a show of force—but that logic was not sufficiently tested.

"None of us really know how aliens think or strategize or interpret signals from potential adversaries. We don't know what their experience with war has taught them—or if they even have any experience with war. But I find it implausible that the aliens would launch an all-out attack simply because we failed to respond to what *might* have been a provocation by them. Just think of how many assumptions they would need to make before concluding that our non-response means we are weak or vulnerable. How can they be sure that we even detected the explosions? Or that we interpreted them as a warning or a threat? How can they assume that our decision not to launch a weapon into space implies that we are scared and helpless rather than strong and unconcerned? The list goes on. And unless they can be sure they've accurately interpreted *all* of these elements, the rationale for attacking us at this stage starts to look pretty flimsy."

Kilmer walked closer to the three agents. "We heard a lot of people talk about how dangerous it would be if we misinterpreted the behavior of the aliens, but no one raised the possibility that the aliens would want to avoid misinterpreting our behavior as well. It's a common mistake—we get so fixated on what constrains *us* that we fail to see the strategic constraints that the other side faces. And as I see it, they don't have nearly enough information about us to decide—based simply on our inaction at this moment—that we are weak, and that they should attack."

Agent Silla interjected. "I see your point, Professor. But can we gamble so much on our assumption about what constrains them? Maybe they're not really constrained at all, because they just *want* to do us harm. Maybe they don't care why we choose not to retaliate, because their intention is to destroy us regardless."

"That's a good point, Agent Silla. The real danger is if they wish to annihilate us *regardless* of whether we look weak or strong. But their behavior suggests that isn't the case. If they can destroy us—and if they intend to do so—why start with an attack on the Moon? There's no benefit to warning us, and it could motivate us to attack them first or build up our defenses. The attack on the Moon suggests that they either can't or don't want to wipe us out—at least not yet. In which case, even if we look weak—as Strauss and Druckman fear—their next step will not be to destroy us. They could have done that without issuing any warning at all."

Agent Silla nodded. "In other words, we have—" She stopped herself, as though unwilling to finish the thought. When she decided to go ahead with it, it was unclear why she had hesitated. "In other words, we have time."

"I think we do, Agent Silla. They might have the ability to destroy us, and they might have the intention of doing so, but they don't appear to have *both* at this time. We want to keep it that way. As Trina Morgan pointed out, that means we should avoid taking actions that could instill fear or create grievances."

Kilmer twirled the pencil in his fingers. "Of course, we need to acknowledge the fact that we're making some basic assumptions here. For example, that logic, as we conceive of it, is at least somewhat relevant to how the aliens make decisions. Then again, if we *don't* assume that, then we probably have no basis on which to strategize at all."

Kilmer had walked over to Silla's side of the table and was now standing less than five feet away from her. He studied her face—his eyes narrowing— as though he were trying to decipher a code. Her words—the ones she had tripped over moments ago—were suddenly ringing in his ears, and he had no idea why.

"I think… I like how you put it, Agent Silla. *We—have—time*," he said, pausing ever so briefly after each word.

Kilmer took another step toward her. They were looking into each other's eyes now, but it was not a romantic scene. It was as if they were both simply searching for answers and somehow expected to find them in each other's minds rather than their own.

"We… have… time." He said the words again, but this time in a whisper, like he was trying to unlock some deeper significance.

Silla didn't respond, nor did she turn away. The room was silent. Completely still.

Almost ten seconds went by before Kilmer finally looked away—and he did it slowly, as if turning away abruptly would be to breach some silent accord they had signed.

When Silla finally looked at her colleagues, they acted as if nothing out of the ordinary had just transpired. Had they been paying closer attention they might have caught the slightest hint of... *something*... in her eyes.

But only the professor saw it—and just for a moment.

And he was sure it was only his imagination.

~ 11 ~

Agent Lane placed his pencil on the table and stretched out his fingers. But it was Art who broke the silence.

"This is extremely helpful, Professor. Thank you for your analysis. I have a few follow-up questions, and I assume Agents Silla and Lane will have some as well. So what I'd like us to do—"

"Your questions will have to wait, Art," Kilmer interrupted. "We're not going to spend any more time on me explaining to you why the show-of-force proposal is unwise."

Art seemed taken aback. "Professor, if you don't mind, we're nearly done."

"I'm afraid I do mind. And we're not nearly done, we are *completely* done. I told you what you wanted to know. And you can pass it along to whoever is interested. But you've been playing games with me, Art. Now we get to find out why that is."

"Professor, we're facing the threat of an alien attack. Do you still question that? Did you not see who was in that meeting? Did that look like a joke? How am I playing games?"

Kilmer walked back to his chair, but even as he sat down, he kept his eyes on Art. He put down his pencil and clasped his hands. "I do believe that there are aliens, Art. And I believe there is a threat. But my presence here couldn't possibly have anything to do with advising the president on what to do about Strauss's proposal."

Silla and Lane looked at Art.

Art's eyes narrowed slightly, and he appeared to be calculating something. "I'm not sure what you heard in that meeting that makes you think we're wasting your time, Professor, but what we're doing here is really—"

"That!" interrupted Kilmer. "That's the mistake you're making, Art. You're wondering what I could have possibly heard to make me doubt you, because you expected me to focus only on what was said. But I did more than that."

Art said nothing.

Kilmer continued. "This is the moment, Agent Capella, where you can win back some credibility with me. If you just admit—even this late in the game—to what I already know. It's your last chance."

For a moment, Art looked like he was about to say something, but he found the discipline to restrain himself. As if it was not his choice to make.

So be it.

"My advice can be of no use to President Whitman," Kilmer explained, "because the meeting we just observed... it didn't even take place tonight. As far as I'm concerned, we've been watching the goddamn History Channel."

Art ran his fingers through his hair. For the first time that evening, he looked exhausted.

"Now, I would like to know why that is," Kilmer said, with as much patience as he could summon.

Art sighed. "You're right, Professor. That meeting did not take place this evening. Everything you saw *was* real, but what we showed you was a recording. The meeting we observed took place on Day 15, just as Vice President Nielsen mentioned during the discussion. But... well... we're past Day 15 now."

Art paused and gave Kilmer an opportunity to react. The professor said nothing, so Art continued.

"Now, you might have a hard time believing this, but apart from implying that the meeting was a live event, everything else I've said to you today has been true. Every bit of it. There *is* an alien threat. We *do* need your help. And your advice *will* make a difference."

"I'd like to believe you, Art. But if what you're saying is true—that you've tried to be honest with me—then why include that *one* lie? Why not just tell me we were watching a meeting that took place earlier? What *possible* good could come from making me think it was happening live? It makes no sense."

Kilmer was racking his brain to make sense of it even as he argued that it was inexplicable. If Art was being truthful, why deceive him about the timing of the meeting? Why ask for advice that would already be outdated because it failed to account for everything that had transpired since Day 15?

Either Art is full of shit—or I'm totally missing something.

Or both.

"I know it makes no sense," Art said. "But I *will* be able to explain it. I'm asking you to trust me. I just can't—"

"You just can't explain it to me… *yet.*"

"That's right. Before I can tell you why we hid this information from you, I need to know how you figured out that the meeting was a recording. It's important, Professor. Will you please explain it to me?"

"How did I figure it out? Ah, well that's a great question, Art. And I'm happy to answer it." Kilmer looked at Lane. "You'll want to write this part down, Agent Lane. It might be the most important thing I tell you today."

Lane grabbed his pencil and responded with a nod. *Ready when you are.*

Kilmer leaned forward—the way one does before revealing a closely held secret.

"The answer to your question, Art—as to how I figured out the meeting didn't take place tonight—is this: *Screw you guys.*" He looked at Lane. "Agent Lane, did you get all that? Let me know if you need me to repeat any of it. I'd be happy to do so."

Art sighed. Silla looked like she might be suppressing a laugh. Lane looked slightly horrified.

"Okay. Fair enough," said Art. "You feel like you deserve to get answers before we do. I don't blame you. I'd probably feel the same way if I were in your shoes. And I'd be just as convinced as you are that there's no way to explain things—or to win back my trust."

"That's a pretty good read of the situation, Art. I don't see how you're going to pull this off."

Art rose from his chair. "Well, here goes, Professor. You know how I said earlier that something was really going to blow your mind—and that it wasn't the part about the aliens?"

"Yes. And you were right. What really blew my mind was that this meeting wasn't even taking place tonight."

"No."

"Excuse me? No, what?"

"No—as in, that's not it."

"That's not what?"

Art looked at Kilmer with a mix of confusion and sympathy. "I mean to say, Professor, that the part that's really going to blow your mind... we haven't even gotten to that yet."

Kilmer felt a shiver, as if Art's words had been carried by a winter breeze. But he said nothing. He waited for Art to continue.

"I have to ask you something," said Art.

"Go ahead."

"Professor, do you... uh... believe in... the possibility of time travel?"

Kilmer stared. He would have been shocked by the question, if not for two things. First, he had just learned that aliens not only existed, but were hovering somewhere close to Earth—so it was getting harder to surprise him. Second, he noticed that Lane and Silla seemed caught off-guard by the question as well, which was a good sign.

"Do you mean, in the way it's portrayed in sci-fi movies? Like going back in time and seeing dinosaurs or killing your great-grandparents?"

"Yes, in that sense," said Art.

"No, Art, I don't believe that's possible. Science and logic both dictate that time travel of the typical sci-fi variety is pure fiction. Are you really going to try to convince me otherwise?"

"No, not at all!" Art exclaimed. "I completely agree with you. Time travel is *not* possible."

"Then why the hell are you bringing it up?"

"Because I need for us to start distinguishing between what is *impossible* and what is merely *improbable*. May I presume you have read, at some point, the works of Sir Arthur Conan Doyle? Sherlock Holmes?"

"Yes. You're referring to *The Sign of the Four*," Kilmer answered. "*When you have eliminated the impossible, whatever remains, however improbable, must be the truth.*"

"Precisely. That's it."

"And what does this have to do with time travel? Why did you need me to confirm that I think it's impossible?"

"Because I will need you to keep that in mind. When you hear what I'm about to tell you, Professor, you're going to struggle to explain it. And you will want to believe in all sorts of stuff. When that happens, I'm going to need for you to remember that some things *cannot* explain it, because some things are truly impossible. At which point, you will have to acknowledge that the explanation I give you—while highly improbable and extremely disconcerting—is in fact true. Do you understand?"

"Yes," said Kilmer. "I understand. Now tell me whatever it is you've been hiding. I'm ready for it."

Art took the keyboard and the touchscreen. He worked the controls half-heartedly, like someone doing the part of their job that they hate most. His facial expression wasn't hard to read either. It was *pity*. Plain and simple.

"No, Professor Kilmer," Art replied. "You couldn't possibly be ready for this. You only think you are."

~ 12 ~

How had Kilmer figured out that the meeting had taken place earlier? The clues had trickled in.

It was the laptop that had bothered him at first. One of the attendees had been fiddling with his computer screen before the meeting began. *He looks like he's trying to eliminate a glare*, Kilmer had conjectured. The man left his seat and disappeared briefly in the direction of the wall behind him. When he returned, the problem with his laptop seemed to have been resolved. *He must have closed the blinds on a window.* This was speculation, of course, but it was mildly troubling. If the meeting was taking place after 8:00 p.m.—near Washington, DC—why would there be light coming in from a window? Then again, Kilmer might have misinterpreted the episode.

The second clue had been the clock on the wall. Kilmer had thought it was broken—stuck at 7:50—when his own watch read 8:09 p.m. Ten minutes later, VP Nielsen looked at that clock and compared it to his own watch, and then thanked everyone for starting "on time". *Who schedules a meeting for 8:19?* On the other hand, if the clock on the wall was *not* broken, it would now say 8:00—a perfectly logical time for a meeting to begin. An hour later, Nielsen ended the meeting by looking at the clock on the wall—not his watch—as if he had earlier found the wall clock to be functional. That had caught Kilmer's eye, and he had taken another look at the clock on the wall. It read 9:00 when the meeting ended, a much more reasonable wrap-up time than 9:19.

Nielsen had provided the third and fourth clues. The night before, according to the VP, President Whitman had asked her chief of staff to set up phone calls with the international alliance for the following *afternoon*—which meant those calls would have already taken place earlier today. But in the meeting, Nielsen told the group that Whitman wanted their input "before she raises the idea with the alliance." How could a meeting that starts after 8:00 p.m. provide input into phone calls that were scheduled for earlier in the day? The sequence of events made much more sense if this meeting was taking place first thing in the morning. Moreover, why *wouldn't* this group have met as soon as possible—early the next morning, instead of late in the evening—if matters were so urgent?

Nielsen had confirmed Kilmer's suspicions before ending the meeting. At the start, Nielsen had said that the group would meet again "tomorrow morning." But at the end, he reminded everyone that they would reconvene "at the same time tomorrow." The only way both statements could be true was if this had been a morning meeting.

The glare from the window. The clock on the wall. The phone calls scheduled for after the meeting. The plan to meet again the following morning. They could all be explained if the meeting had taken place at 8:00 a.m.

Kilmer had pieced it together, a little at a time, but he still couldn't figure out why they had tried to deceive him. How could they possibly benefit from lying about when the meeting took place?

Art said he had a good reason for it.

It's possible that he does, decided Kilmer, *but not very likely.*

~ 13 ~

Art was still working the keyboard. "What I'm about to show you, Professor, is a part of the meeting we just observed—the meeting that took place on Day 15. Don't worry, you won't have to sit through the whole thing again. Just a small portion of it."

"I observed pretty carefully the first time, Art. I don't expect I missed anything too important," Kilmer said. Then something occurred to him. "Unless… am I about to see what took place before or after the segment you showed me earlier?"

"Good guess, Professor, but not quite. This will be a portion of the meeting that you already saw. In fact, it doesn't really matter which snippet I show you."

Kilmer considered that for a moment. Why did he need to see what he had already—

Of course.

"You're going to show me a different angle. You're queueing up a recording from one of the other cameras."

"Very good, Professor. Just give me a minute and I'll have it on the screen."

What could a different camera angle show that was so important? Despite knowing that he would find out soon enough, Kilmer couldn't help but try to figure it out for himself. Turning the source of his unease into just one more puzzle to solve had the immediate effect of calming his nerves.

His mind drifted to an evening some years ago. Someone had organized a dinner party for an eclectic group of people who might enjoy meeting one another. Dinner, drinks, and potentially interesting conversation. The person with the most fascinating stories that night was a deputy chief of police who had worked for many years as a homicide detective in Chicago. What was his name? Gerard? Gerald? His last name might never have been mentioned.

Kilmer couldn't remember any of the stories he told—much less the gory details—but he remembered what Gerald-something had said when someone at the table suggested that solving crimes seemed to require a lot of guesswork.

> You can't solve mysteries through guesswork. You start with what you know, and continue adding in more of what you know, until there is nothing left of what you know. Only then do you even begin to add logic, reason, and speculation. Guessing is truly a last resort. In my line of work, it's an admission of failure.

So, Kilmer asked himself, *what do I know?*

There were at least three other cameras in the room, and the one with the best chance of capturing something he had missed would be the one mounted on the opposite wall, above the two notetakers. What would that angle reveal? Two things, at the very least. First, it would show him what was on the wall where the original camera was mounted. He had already deduced that there was a window on that wall. What else might there be? Another door? Had someone else entered the room during the meeting?

The new angle would also reveal the faces of people who had their backs to the original camera. Kilmer knew who they were—everyone had spoken at least once during the meeting—but the new angle would reveal expressions and capture some behaviors he would have missed.

No, it's none of those things. Art had said it didn't matter which segment they watched, so it had to be something that was visible the entire time. Like the window, but more important. The list of things the room might contain was endless, but the subset of things that might surprise him was much more limited.

He couldn't come up with even one.

"Here we go. All set," said Art.

With the recording about to start, Kilmer looked at the three agents. He expected them to be staring at him, with Lane ready to take notes on his reactions. They weren't. Art seemed unwilling to make eye contact. Lane was looking at the screen, his pencil on the table and his hands in his lap. Silla was watching Kilmer, but she turned away when he glanced at her.

As the screen came to life, Kilmer's anxiety began to reassert itself. He could feel the adrenaline and its impact on his breathing. Almost instinctively, he reached for the cup of coffee. Something to hold on to, as if he were on a roller coaster, slowly approaching the first big drop, grasping for the handlebars.

The recording began, and he was again observing the meeting that had taken place on Day 15. Nielsen's back was to the camera now, and he was describing the events of Day 5, when Presidents Zhao and Sokolov had agreed to let the Americans take the lead. The clock was now to the right, the cell-phone receptacle to the left. The faces he had seen before were all facing away from him now. The people with their backs toward him earlier were now looking in his direction. There was no second door to the room. The opposite wall had a camera, of course, as well as a window. Its blinds were closed, but some light was still coming through.

There were also two chairs against the far wall, directly across from the two notetakers he had seen in the previous video. There had been *four* notetakers during the meeting, not two.

That's when Kilmer saw what Art had wanted him to see.

The cup fell from his hands, exploding on the carpet below. His mouth fell open, and he stopped breathing. He could feel every beat of his heart as it pounded in his chest.

Everything around him disappeared, as if he were suddenly wrapped in a whiteness that enveloped him completely. Images from the evening started to project themselves onto that blank canvas, each new memory delivering an even harder blow than the last.

Trina Morgan waving at the man across the table.
Vice President Nielsen thanking him through the camera.
Art's greeting when they first shook hands.
All the participants know you're watching.
The look in Silla's eyes.
We... have... time.

He was trembling.

He turned away from the TV screen in a desperate effort to clear his mind—to purge from it what he had just seen. Then he forced himself to take another look at the screen, hoping it would change everything.

It changed absolutely nothing.

There hadn't been four notetakers. There had been only two. The two people sitting against the far wall were not notetakers at all. Kilmer recognized them both.

One of them was a beautiful young woman who had introduced herself, earlier today, as Agent Silla.

Sitting next to her, against the far wall, was an acclaimed historian and renowned strategist—a man whose expertise would be invaluable in such a meeting.

His name was Professor Kilmer.

This is impossible.

A cacophony of images, ideas, theories, and emotions detonated in Kilmer's mind. His prized abilities—to organize, to filter, to focus—were all failing him. He put his elbows on the table and brought the tips of his fingers to his temples.

Trina Morgan hadn't been waving at some stranger.

Vice President Nielsen hadn't been talking to the camera.

Art hadn't lied…all the participants know you're watching.

Kilmer dug his fingers harder into the sides of his skull.

Think, he demanded. *Think!*

It didn't work.

Just grab on to something. Anything. Just start somewhere.

Time travel.

Art was right. It could help explain everything. No, wait…that's not what he said. Art had said the opposite. He had warned *against* the temptation to blame it on time travel. *I'm going to need for you to remember that some things cannot explain it, because some things are truly impossible.*

No, not time travel. Something else. It had to be something highly improbable, but *not* impossible.

Kilmer closed his eyes and forced himself to take a deep breath. He filled his lungs to capacity and exhaled slowly. He was still shaking.

You can't solve mysteries through guesswork. Start with what you know.

Okay. What do I know?

Nothing. Nothing at all came to mind.

Thanks a lot, Gerald-something.

He wanted to give up.

No. Keep trying. Try again. Remember… every problem wants to be solved…

And then… one thing. He suddenly knew *one* thing.

It wasn't a fact or an idea or a theory. It wasn't something he had seen or heard. It wasn't even a memory. It was only a feeling. It made as little sense as everything else at that moment, but he knew that it was real.

You start with what you know.

That was it. It was the totality of what he knew at that moment. He would build from there. He would solve this mystery. He would do it the way Gerald-something had taught him to solve it. He would do it for everyone in that room—and for everyone else who might be counting on him. Because a war was still coming—and he had to help stop it. Because Plan B was shit.

Kilmer slowed his breathing and leaned back, focusing only on that feeling now—on the one thing he knew, but which he still did not understand.

We… have… time.

He repeated the words to himself until the trembling stopped.

And then, slowly, he opened his eyes… and looked over at Silla.

She was looking back at him, tears streaming down her face.

He hadn't shed a tear in years. But that was about to change.

Part II

the adviser

Part II

~ 14 ~

Day 14. 9:35 p.m. The White House.

It had been thirteen days since the alien spacecraft were first detected by NASA—and exactly one day since the aliens attacked the Moon.

Earlier that evening, Defense Secretary Strauss had asked President Whitman to authorize an Earth-side show of force in response to the lunar attack. After reviewing the idea with her team, Whitman called for a larger group to discuss the proposal the following morning—at 8 a.m. on Day 15. She would make her decision soon after.

Whitman asked Chief of Staff Perez and Vice President Nielsen to stay behind after she dismissed the others.

She now turned to Nielsen. "Zack, you need to remember the kind of pressure we're putting on everyone. At some point they'll realize that their voice could be decisive—and the fate of humanity rests in the balance. No one should have to bear that burden. That weight can only be carried by the Office of the President—and that is where it will rest. I'm not tallying votes on this. You have to make that clear to everyone."

"I understand, Madam President."

"Now, let's talk about Professor Kilmer. Is he as good as you make him out to be? Good enough for us to be calling him this late in the game?"

"I believe he is. His academic credentials are obviously impressive, but it's more than that. I've seen how his mind works. I shared with you the advice he gave us during the Gulf of Aden crisis. And I've told you about his views on Kharkiv. He just sees things that others miss. And I know we can trust him to keep this quiet. He never asks for anything when he takes these types of calls—not even credit for the role he plays."

Whitman nodded. "I remember his views on Aden. He changed your

65

mind on that, and then you changed mine. And it saved us, there's no doubt about that. As for Kharkiv… well, that's still a damn mess."

"It is, and it played out almost exactly like he predicted," Nielsen pointed out. "He told me we had to be more aggressive. And he warned me not to agree to the ceasefire proposal that the UN was pushing at the time—said it would blow up in our faces. We just didn't listen."

"Fair enough. But then again, I'm not sure anything could have helped that situation." Whitman paused, wondering whether she really believed that. Could they have done something more? Something different? "Okay, Zack, I hear you. Professor Kilmer brings a different perspective, and that could be helpful. By the way, that book of his you gave me for Christmas—*Heirs of Herodotus*—I thought it was excellent." She smiled. "Although I'm surprised Laura allowed you to make that my Christmas gift."

Nielsen grinned guiltily. His wife Laura had been horrified to learn that he had decided to give his boss, the president of the United States, a history book for Christmas. "But it's a really good book. And it's signed by the author," Nielsen had protested. "Well, unless it's signed by Herodotus himself," Laura warned, "I don't think Marianne is going to be too impressed."

Nielsen prepared himself for the *I told you so* that now awaited him at home.

But Whitman laughed. "I'm sorry, Zack—Laura told me she gave you a hard time about it, so I had to pile on. In all honesty, Professor Kilmer's book did more for me than those theater tickets I sent to Laura are likely to do for you. He makes an interesting observation about historians—how even the best of them are driven by a need for closure. They work too hard to tie things together with a thematic bow, making sure that every event and character from history fits neatly into their narrative. As a result, we end up with 'lessons of history' that are a little too clean, and a bit too overgeneralized to provide us proper guidance in the real world. It made me think about how we make decisions around here, in fact. And how we might do a better job."

Kilmer's book had caused a bit of a stir in academic circles, receiving praise from fellow historians just as often as it was reviled. *Publishers Weekly* quoted Kilmer at length in its starred review:

"Historians should not be in the business of explaining as much as possible with as little as possible. We are not here to create trend lines on the graph of human events. We owe the world much more than that. Whatever mistakes Herodotus, the "first historian," made in this regard should have been corrected by those who came after—not amplified. Our job as historians is to extract principles, not punch lines."

Whitman returned to the issue at hand. "So, Zack, how do you want to proceed?"

"If I can track him down in time, my plan is for Professor Kilmer to attend the 8 a.m. meeting tomorrow—just as an observer. He and I can debrief afterwards. The team's on board, but with varying degrees of enthusiasm. For Allen and Druckman, he's an unknown entity—they're not sure he'll add much, but they don't see how it can hurt. Garcia is a fan; she knows his work and is aware that he helped us out during the Aden crisis. Strauss said he's okay with it, but he added that sending a professor to bore the aliens to death might be a proposal worth considering as well."

Whitman and Perez laughed.

"Let's bring him in," said Whitman. "If he tells you something I need to hear, I'll make time for it. And Zack, when you invite him, please let him know that I loved the book… and that I'd be extremely grateful if he could join us."

Zack smiled. *And people wonder how she won by a landslide.*

"Yes, Madam President."

~ 15 ~

VP Nielsen and Chief of Staff Perez left the Oval Office and walked down the hall. They were almost at the door to the chief of staff's office when Perez stopped short.

"Zack... can I have a minute please?" Perez sounded uncharacteristically hesitant.

"Sure. Is everything okay?"

"Yeah, it's just... well... you never brought it up, Zack. Not once—not even as a joke. And I give you a lot of credit for that. But I should have been the one to bring it up and clear the air." Perez paused. "It's no secret that you weren't my first pick to join the ticket when Marianne was looking for a running mate. I want you to know I regret that. And I should have had the courage to say that to you when you came on board. I'm sorry I didn't."

This was the last thing Nielsen had expected Perez to bring up at a time like this. "Salvo, there's no reason to apologize. You did what you thought was right—and a lot of people agreed with you. I didn't take it personally."

Nielsen genuinely believed that Whitman had had a lot of good VP options, but it still hurt a little to know that some of the people he now worked with had been rooting for the other guy. Regardless, Nielsen couldn't think of any reason to make someone feel bad about it right when the world was about to end. Perez was a good man who cared deeply about two things— the United States of America and Marianne J. Whitman. No one doubted that Perez would be the first in line, even before the Secret Service, to take a bullet for the president. Nielsen could respect that.

"It probably sounds like I just need to get this off my chest in case we don't get another chance to talk about it—with the alien invasion and all. Maybe that's part of it. But there's something else as well." Perez inched closer to Nielsen. "Zack, you're among the few people the president trusts to always speak their mind *and* to fully support her decisions. If we survive the next few days, things are going to get complicated. Stress levels are high, and I can see the cracks forming already. Strauss. Druckman. When the calls don't go their way, they don't take it too well. And if the president rejects their advice when the stakes are this high… I'm not sure how cooperative or forthcoming they'll be after that. I'm not sure they won't decide to, you know, *go their own way*—to use Sokolov's phrase."

"You think they have their own agendas?"

"No. I think their agenda is mostly the same as ours. To protect the American people. But if they think millions or billions of lives are on the line and the president is making the wrong call, I'm not sure how they'll react."

"I see. What do you propose?"

"I just want you to be aware. I think the people we've chosen are the right people for the job—even when the going gets tough. But when all hell breaks loose? I just don't know."

Nielsen reflected on Perez's words. If anyone was looking to undermine the president, he would certainly have no part of it. But how do you distinguish between undermining the president and following your conscience? He was suddenly reminded of what Whitman had said to him the day she offered him the VP spot. *"Zack, I didn't do you a favor today. I did what I thought was right. And I don't want you feeling indebted to me. Whenever things get rough, I need you to say and do what's right—no matter the consequences."*

Nielsen had always shared his views, candidly and respectfully, and then supported whatever decision Whitman made. Even in the worst of situations, and even when they disagreed, supporting the president had never felt like a moral dilemma. Not even remotely. But then, all hell had never broken loose before. What if his conscience told him Whitman was wrong at a time when millions of American lives were on the line? Would he still support her, like Perez was sure to do? Or would he decide to go his own way, like a Strauss or a Druckman might?

Nielsen admired President Whitman. He respected her. He trusted her. He had no doubt about any of that. But she hadn't done him a favor. That was what he needed to remember. It was what she had *asked* him to remember.

"Thanks, Salvo, for bringing this to my attention. A lot to think about."

Perez nodded in agreement, and then they parted ways.

Nielsen walked a few more steps to his office and gave his assistant some instructions, along with an address. Then he sat down at his desk and pulled out his cell phone. He had a call to make.

~ 16 ~

Professor Kilmer was at home, sitting in his library, when the call came. The developer had planned for the space to be used as a formal dining area, but that dream ended the day Kilmer moved in. Kilmer wasn't interested in having two dining rooms, and he was even less keen on having zero libraries. The makeover solved both problems. The library was Kilmer's favorite room in the three-bedroom condo where he lived alone—save for the countless spirits of scholars, strategists, philosophers, historians, and generals who drifted about his bookshelves.

The room itself was cozy, but otherwise unremarkable. The couch was more comfortable than trendy, and the pinewood coffee table was unworthy of further description. There was a desk in one corner, on top of which sat Kilmer's laptop, some more books, and a few stacks of paper; he wouldn't have been able to remember what documents comprised the bottom inch of any stack.

To be sure, there were some personal items as well. A Rembrandt print decorated one of the walls—*The Storm on the Sea of Galilee.* It was the only painting Kilmer had ever loved, or, for that matter, looked at for longer than thirty seconds. Tucked into another corner of the room was a fancy-looking globe—a gift from a woman Kilmer had once expected to marry. Five years ago, when they parted ways, she told Kilmer that it was because he would always be more concerned with what was happening around that globe than what was happening in their relationship. He had disagreed with that characterization of his priorities… but not with enough conviction to change her mind. He'd dated other women since, but as time went on, he started to think that she had been right about him—that he really was, in her words, *wired for peace, and not for love.*

And then there was the armchair, which had once belonged to his father.

It was ancient—and managed to look even older than it was—but it remained Kilmer's most prized possession.

Someone walking into the library, knowing nothing about who owned the home, would probably have imagined that it belonged to a slightly frail, gray-haired retiree who went for a walk every morning on doctor's orders.

Kilmer was forty-two years old. He stood five-foot-ten, had a healthy tan complexion, and sported only a single strand of gray in his dark brown hair. He wasn't much of a walker, either. When he needed to clear his mind, he chose to meditate; when he felt the need to exercise, he preferred to hit the gym.

Kilmer saw the name *Zack Nielsen* appear on his phone and answered on the first ring. The three seconds between reading the name and saying "hello" were spent wondering why the vice president would be calling so late on a Friday night.

"Professor Kilmer?"

"Hi, Zack. How are you?"

"Fine, Professor. Am I catching you in Boston or somewhere else?"

"Boston."

"Got it. I'm sorry to be calling at this time, but do you have a few minutes?"

"Sure. I was just reading."

"Oh, what are you reading?"

"Well, at the moment, I happen to be re-reading a few chapters from *The Causes of War*—by Geoffrey Blainey. I want to revisit some of his arguments for an assignment I'm going to inflict on my students next semester."

"Wait—didn't we read Blainey in our course? Is he the guy who says unintentional wars don't really exist?"

"Good memory, Zack. That's the guy. He says wars are never unintentional in the way we might think. That people don't just stumble into wars where there was no willingness to fight. He makes some very good points."

For each of the last seven years, Kilmer had taught an eight-week course in DC, entitled *War & Peace: The Lessons of History*. For four hours each week, a few dozen lawmakers, government officials, and military leaders would attend the class, ready to listen, analyze, debate, and distill insights from over 2,500 years of human history. Most of the students were American, but not all. Over the years, high-ranking officials from around the world had enrolled.

Zack Nielsen had attended the course six years ago. At the time, he was a senator from Michigan who sat on the Committee on Foreign Relations and the Select Committee on Intelligence. As a student, Nielsen was always respectful and well-prepared—although others in the class probably thought he raised his hand a little too often. Nielsen stayed in touch with Kilmer after the course, and they spoke at least once every couple of months.

On two occasions, Nielsen had invited Kilmer to Washington to advise on some highly sensitive matters. In one case—the Gulf of Aden crisis—they had worked together closely for weeks to resolve the problem. In the other—the Kharkiv fiasco—Kilmer's perspective was pretty much ignored from the start. It was during those meetings that Kilmer discovered Nielsen had a pretty good sense of humor, reserved mostly for the darkest of moments. Maybe that was when it was needed most.

"So, Zack. Did you just call me for a book recommendation?"

"I wish, Professor. Listen, the reason I'm calling is that we need your help. I can't give you any details, but it's important. Just… assume the worst. Can you get to Washington ASAP?"

"Do you mean ASAP in the next few days? Or ASAP tomorrow morning?"

"None of the above. I mean tonight. I mean now."

Kilmer put down the book. "I'll try to come as soon as you need, Zack, but I won't be able to catch a flight before tomorrow morning. If I get on the first one, I can probably meet you around 7 a.m. at your office. Does that work?"

"I'm afraid it doesn't. We need you right away. We have a plane in Boston that can get you here at a moment's notice, and since I figured you were probably in Boston, I already have a car on the way to your house. You still live in Brookline, right? Same address as before?"

"Yes."

"Great. If you can be out the door in the next ten minutes, you can land here by midnight and I can meet you in my office around 12:30. And don't worry, I already know… coffee, black and extra hot. I've got that covered. But can you do it?"

Kilmer was already in his bedroom and looking for clothes to change into. "Am I flying back in a few hours, or should I bring a change of clothes?"

"I don't know. Bring some clothes just in case. For two days or so."

"Okay."

"Just one more thing. This invitation isn't coming from me. It comes from President Whitman. She asked me to tell you that she hopes you can make it—and that she would be very grateful if you would agree to come. This is different from the last few times, Professor. You'll see what I mean when you get here."

This *was* different. Although Kilmer knew that his advice to Nielsen had always made it to the president in one form or another, he had never interacted with her directly—Nielsen was always the intermediary. For all Kilmer knew, Whitman had no idea who he was or that he had advised the vice president in the past.

"Okay. That's good to know," Kilmer replied, trying not to sound too excited. He probably wouldn't get to meet Whitman this time either, but it was exciting to hear that the president of the United States had made the ask.

"Thank you, Professor. I've gotta run, but Joana, my chief of staff, will text you with information about the driver, the flight, and what to expect when you land. Let's see… what am I forgetting… oh yeah. As you probably already guessed, you can't mention this to anyone. Not even the fact that you're going to DC."

"Understood. I'll be ready in ten minutes. And I'll see you soon."

"Bye, Prof."

Nielsen hung up.

Kilmer changed into a pair of pants and threw on a sports coat, packed a carry-on, and equipped his laptop bag with the essentials. *Anything else? Yeah, why not.* He ran back to his closet and grabbed a tie. Just in case. He wore a tie about once a year, and only on special occasions. This might end up qualifying.

On second thought, he really hated wearing a tie. He tossed it back. It slipped off the rack and fell to the floor. He left it there.

A few minutes later, he saw headlights outside. He had just grabbed his keys and opened the front door when his cell phone rang. *Zack Nielsen.*

"Hello?"

"Professor?"

"Yeah. I just walked out the door. The car's here. What's up?"

"Sorry, I forgot to tell you something."

"What's that?

"President Whitman wanted you to know that she read your book. And that she loved it."

Well… that's something.

"Wow. That's nice to hear. Please tell her I'm glad she liked it," Kilmer said as he got into the car.

"You can tell her yourself when you meet her. She just told me that she'll swing by at some point while you and I are chatting tonight."

The car pulled out of the driveway.

Damn it.

I should have worn the tie.

17

As the car raced to the airport, Kilmer decided to get some rest. He closed his eyes and let his mind wander—and was unsurprised by where it chose to go. He was going to meet *the president of the United States*—so, naturally, he thought about the two people he would most want to tell.

Kilmer thought about his parents—the ones who had raised him since he was six years old and formally adopted him at the age of seven. They had no children of their own and were already in their forties when they took him in. He had very few memories of the life he'd lived before he met the Kilmers— and none of them were pleasant. He came to them broken—no ability to read or write, no capacity to trust, no desire to ask questions, no sense of identity, and no understanding of his own history. Patiently and painstakingly, they changed all of that. They gave to him—a complete stranger, to whom they owed nothing—everything that was theirs. A name. An identity. A home. And the chance to make something out of his life.

His father was a public-school teacher whose first love was mathematics. He taught Kilmer to play chess and cultivated his love of puzzles. *Every problem wants to be solved, son. Just remember that.* They created secret codes and passed notes to one another at the dinner table, annoying Mom to no end. As a boy, Kilmer was an average student—more B's than A's—but he always made sure to do well in math. It was the closest thing to solving puzzles that school had to offer, and he knew that his father cared more about that grade than any other.

His mother was a nurse at a local hospital, but she donated much of her time to an NGO that delivered medical care to conflict zones around the world. As early as third grade, he was following her adventures. He would read about the countries she visited and try to understand why the people in those places were fighting. By the time he was eleven, he could identify over a hundred countries on the globe. By the time he was sixteen, he was devouring two history books per month.

When he was seventeen, everything fell apart. His mother, along with three of her colleagues, was captured and killed in Sudan. The insurgents who took responsibility for the attack showed neither mercy nor remorse. Kilmer was devastated—and filled with even more rage than grief. He made plans to join the military after graduation, hoping to exact some measure of revenge against the kinds of people who had carried out the attack. It took his father five months to convince him that he needed a better reason than anger to go down that path—and he waited until his son graduated from high school to show him the letter that his mother had left for him.

"She would write you a letter every time she left—just in case—and then throw it away when she came back. This is the one she didn't get to throw away. I'm sorry I kept it from you, but I didn't want you to read it until you were ready."

Kilmer cried even before opening the letter, and for many hours after reading it. One passage, in particular, he went back to repeatedly—and by dawn of the following morning, he had committed it to memory.

Don't let your sadness turn into anger, or your loneliness into hate. Channel what you feel into something good. Find ways to help people. Cultivate your gifts and use them to make the world a little bit better.

I know, I know… I'm lecturing, as usual. And I'm making it sound so easy. I know it's not. I know you're hurting, baby boy. And it will take a while to figure things out. So, don't be too hard on yourself. It's okay. Just keep trying. That's all that matters. That you do your best. That you keep moving forward, even if you stumble along the way. You're a good boy. You always were. And you're strong in ways that only your dad and I will ever know. You'll get through this, my love. I promise you.

Kilmer had planned to major in mathematics when he went to college, but he switched to history during his first month at school. After two years, he was ready to drop out. For all his hopes of making his parents proud, he had nothing to show for his efforts except bad grades and disillusionment. It was his father who helped solve the mystery. "You're frustrated because you think you're on the wrong path. But that's not it. The problem is you expect the road you're on to take you someplace it can never reach. You want your education to help you make sense of what happened to Mom, to put it in some larger context that gives it meaning. That's never going to happen, son. All you can hope to do with what you learn is make it a *little* less likely that others will have to suffer like we did. If that's worth trying to do, then stick with it. If not, let it go. But Mom's life will have had meaning no matter what you decide. No book is ever going to tell you how wonderful she was."

Kilmer decided to stick with it, and he revived his grade point average just enough to give him a shot at getting into grad school. He would go on to earn a master's degree from Rutgers, and then a PhD from Columbia.

Kilmer lost his father to pancreatic cancer during his first year in grad school. If there was a saving grace, it was that he was able to say goodbye. They held hands as his father took his last breaths, and for a long time after. Kilmer's grief would diminish over the years, but what never faded was the sense of indebtedness—the kind that only someone who owes everything to the kindness of strangers can possibly understand. He knew it was an impossible debt to repay—but just as impossible an obligation to ignore.

At the age of twenty-two, he was an orphan again. But this time was different. He wasn't broken anymore. They had fixed him up. They had given him a name. And, along the way, they had taught him a few lessons that he would not soon forget.

18

Heirs of Herodotus by D. Kilmer.
Excerpt from Chapter 2.

For at least the last 2,500 years of human history, kings, generals, statesmen, and presidents have made use of analogies to guide them in such moments. But which analogy to use? If the appropriate analogy is 'war against Germany' in the years leading up to World War II, then the lesson of history might be that **aggressive actions, taken early, can help to avert war**. But, if instead, the correct analogy is 'war against Germany' in the years leading up to World War I, perhaps the lesson of history is different: **aggressive actions, taken early, can lead to war**. Which is it? How do you decide? And what are the consequences of getting it wrong?

If you see Khrushchev as Hitler, you are tempted to take very different actions against him than if you see him as Kaiser Wilhelm II. If you are enamored by how well things worked out after the American occupation of Japan, or the Allied occupation of Germany, you are much more likely to endorse regime change and occupation in Iraq. But if you look at Iraq and see Vietnam, not Japan, you will want to steer clear of such commitments.

This raises four fundamental questions: How do you know if you are using the right analogy? Will decisions improve or degrade when you attempt to combine multiple analogies? Should we even inform policy decisions— especially in the context of war and peace—with the use of analogies? And, if not, how else might we learn from and apply the lessons of history?

~ 19 ~

Day 14. 11:50pm. Joint Base Andrews.

The black Chevy Suburban was idling forty yards from Runway 19L at Joint Base Andrews. The call had come in at 11:20 p.m., and the two agents were dispatched immediately—before they could even be briefed. But this wasn't the night shift. The entire idea of shifts had become obsolete two weeks ago, at least among Triad agents.

Triad had been informed about the alien spacecraft on Day 3—or, as Art Capella would describe it, "before the Chinese but after the French." Within hours, Art had activated eleven agents. They were tasked with gathering intel from space, intel on what other countries might know, and intel on existing threats to national security that might get exacerbated in the days ahead. By the time the aliens had attacked the Moon, the number of agents working on behalf of Triad was nineteen. Hours later, the number had ballooned to thirty-five. But only four of these agents, apart from Art, were in the loop. The others were provided just enough information to do their jobs.

All manner of work had to be done—but some tasks were more urgent, more important, and more exciting than others. Sitting in an SUV, waiting for a plane to land, was decidedly *not* urgent, *not* important, and *not* exciting. It was also not the kind of task to which you would normally assign two of the four Triad agents who were important enough to be in the loop. But there was a rationale.

The first order of business was to escort Professor Kilmer to a 12:30 a.m. meeting with Vice President Nielsen. After that, unless the professor decided to return to Boston, the agents were to stay with him until 7:00 am—or, if he wanted to get some rest, they would take him to a hotel. At seven o'clock, they were to hand Kilmer over to another Triad agent who would accompany him to an 8:00 a.m. meeting.

VP Nielsen was going to brief the professor on the events of the last two weeks, which meant that the Triad agents assigned to him had to be in the loop as well. Kilmer might have questions after his meeting with Nielsen. He might want to talk about it. He might want to run and hide. He might freak out. Anything was possible—so they had to be prepared for everything. Their orders reflected the entire spectrum of exigencies, from "be respectful" to "have your firearms accessible at all times."

The aircraft touched down in the distance.

"Well, Ren, this should be interesting."

"I know you're joking, but I don't think it will be that bad."

"Playing babysitter? Give me a break."

"He's hardly a baby, Mark. He's what they call a 'distinguished professor.' You know what that means?"

"Just that he's old. Maybe he laid the cornerstone for the university when it was being built."

"It means he's influenced multiple fields, and not just his own. It's considered a pretty big achievement. And yeah, it probably means he's as old as the university itself. But his work is interesting."

Mark laughed. "You actually know his work?"

"I've read a few of his books—or heard them, to be more precise. I go through a lot of audiobooks."

"And?"

"And… I think it's among the best stuff I've read in quite a while. Maybe a bit dry for some people, but I was a history major, so it's the kind of thing I like. You should check it out sometime. It may even change the way you think about things. Not just about history, or about war and peace. Even about the work we do."

"Maybe if we survive this encounter, I'll take a look at it. I mean the encounter with the aliens—not with the professor. But who knows, maybe this will be even worse." Mark gave a chuckle. "Anyway, right now, I'm a little more concerned about the future than about the past."

Ren didn't respond, and Mark started to wonder if he had been complaining a bit too much. Ren was his boss.

Mark tried to dial it back a notch. "I suppose if the president thinks this guy is important enough to bring into the loop, he can't be a complete loser. Then again, Agent Calloway is in the loop, so maybe that's not a reasonable inference to draw."

Ren laughed at that. Agent Calloway ran the Directorate of Operations at the CIA. He was categorically disliked, and not for any one reason. Everyone found something different to hate about Calloway.

The aircraft they had been waiting for, a modified Gulfstream, came to a stop about one hundred yards from the Suburban. Mark put the vehicle into gear and started driving. He pulled to a stop approximately fifteen yards from the jet, and both agents stepped outside to welcome their guest. The airplane's door opened and quickly converted into a 10-step staircase. The pilot waved from inside, and both agents waved back.

The first person to exit the plane was a younger man. He was carrying the professor's luggage, which consisted of a carry-on suitcase and a laptop bag. He reached the ground and brought the bags over to the SUV.

"Hello."

"Hi," said Mark. He took the bags from the man and went around to put them in the trunk. When he returned, the scene was unchanged. Ren was still looking toward the plane. The man was just standing around, like he was waiting for a tip.

"That will be all, sir. Thank you," Mark said professionally.

"Well, that was much less work than I expected."

Ren glanced at him. "Do you accompany the professor on all of his travels?"

"Pretty much."

Ren looked back at the plane. "The staircase is a bit steep. Does he need any help coming down the steps?"

"I don't know. Did it look like I was about to fall on my face when I came down? All this time I thought I'd handled them like a champ."

One, two, thr—

It took just under three seconds for Ren's and Mark's faces to register enlightenment.

Ren turned toward Kilmer, looking thoroughly embarrassed. "I'm very sorry, Professor. I didn't realize—"

"It's okay. It happens every so often."

"I'm sure it does, but in our line of work, we're not supposed to make such mistakes. Not a good first impression I'm sure. Although, in our defense, you don't really look like a professor." Ren paused. "And I don't mean that in a bad way."

"How could you mean it in a bad way? I spend a lot of time with professors. I know what they look like."

The agents laughed.

The professor held out his hand. "I'm Kilmer."

Mark shook his hand. "It's very nice to meet you, Professor Kilmer. I've heard a lot about you—although mostly in the last five minutes or so. My colleague here is a big fan of your work."

Ren flashed a no-point-in-denying-it smile, then shook Kilmer's hand as well.

"It's nice to meet you, Professor. Welcome to Washington. I'm Agent Renata Silla. This is Agent Mark Lane."

"Agent Silla. Agent Lane. It's a pleasure to meet you both."

~ 20 ~

Lane drove while Silla, sitting in the front passenger seat, responded to some text messages. Kilmer sat in the back, directly behind Lane.

"Do you come to Washington often, Professor?" Lane asked.

"I spend about eight weeks here every year. Other than that, maybe one trip every two months."

"How do you like it?"

"I like it a lot. But I don't think I could live here."

"Boston sports are a lot better," Lane conceded.

"People keep telling me that. I've decided that it must be true."

Silla looked up from her phone and smiled. "So, what is it that you don't like about DC? Why couldn't you live here?" she asked.

"Good question. I'm not sure. Haven't given it too much thought."

"I thought professors went around giving too much thought to everything."

"Only the good ones do that. I try to get by with as little thinking as I can without people finding out."

"Not true, Professor. I've read your work. And if you're going to tell me that you wrote those books without too much thought, I'll have to conclude that you're either a genius or you're not very honest. Is that a risk you want to take?"

"No, Agent Silla, it is not. I'd rather you think of me as neither. I'll confess—the books took a lot of work. But you must read a whole lot if something I wrote made it onto your list. What made you pick it up?"

"Good question. Haven't given it too much thought." She smiled again.

Kilmer grinned, but then got down to business. "So, as I understand it, the plan is for you to drop me off at the White House. Do you know what my meeting is about?"

"Yes, sir, we do," said Lane. "But we're not authorized to discuss it. Our orders are to accompany you to the vice president's office and to stay there until you're done."

"And then what? Back to the airport?"

"I'm not sure, sir. That will be up to you and the vice president."

"Is the situation as bad as I've been led to believe?"

Silla responded. "We can't discuss the details. And I don't know what you've been led to believe. But in all likelihood... yes. Things are probably even worse than you imagine."

"I study war, Agent Silla. I'm capable of imagining all sorts of terrible things. How much worse can it be?"

"I'm afraid I can't answer that. But you'll find out soon enough."

Kilmer leaned back and closed his eyes. "Let's just fast-forward to the end then. Is there anything either of you can tell me that I don't already know?"

"Actually, yes," said Silla.

Kilmer opened his eyes.

She shot him a quick glance. "DC isn't really a bad place to live."

He smiled, and then closed his eyes again.

Kilmer's mind drifted back to a memory. He was twenty-nine years old, and he was visiting Washington to participate in a small, invitation-only symposium to discuss US policy in the South China Sea. The event was organized by the DoD, and included professors, members of Congress, senior military officers, and some high-ranking officials from the State Department. Kilmer was the youngest person in the room, and no one seemed to pay much attention to his comments—nor did anyone have a problem speaking over him when he tried to share his thoughts. But at the reception that evening, he was approached by one of the attendees, Vice-Admiral Finley, Commander of the Office of Naval Intelligence. For the next hour, Finley peppered Kilmer with questions on just about everything that had been debated during the conference. Kilmer had made a decent impression after all—on one person, at least.

The only other conversation he remembered from that night lasted less than a minute. He was ordering a drink when a man in his late forties came up to the bar. "I'll have whatever this young man is having," he said, before introducing himself as Zack Nielsen, congressman from Michigan. Nielsen, it turned out, was the one who had asked the DoD to invite Kilmer to the symposium in the first place. "I read your book, Professor. *The Case for War.* I thought we could use that kind of thinking around here. And I really liked what you had to say today... although you're going to need to be a lot more assertive if you want to be taken seriously in this town. Good ideas don't win unless they're heard, Prof. Just keep that in mind."

Kilmer had been all smiles after those two conversations. Finley and Nielsen had given him the kind of validation that he liked to tell himself he didn't really need—even if the evidence, occasionally, proved otherwise.

Kilmer opened his eyes to find the Chevy Suburban making its way down Pennsylvania Avenue. He looked over at Silla, who seemed to be gazing out the window as they approached their destination.

"I don't want to give you the wrong impression, Agent Silla," he said, picking up the conversation where they had left off. "I really don't have anything against this city. Things always seem to turn out better than I expected when I come to Washington."

Silla looked back at him and smiled mildly. "Well, Professor, there's a first time for everything."

~ 21 ~

Kilmer, Silla, and Lane walked into the White House through the West Wing entrance, where they were greeted by Joana, Nielsen's chief of staff. She offered the Triad agents a few options for where they might wait while Kilmer met with the vice president. They graciously declined the offer to hang out in the Press Briefing Room and settled instead for a small unused office nearby.

Joana knocked on the door to the VP's office. When they entered, Nielsen was sitting behind his desk at the far end of the room. A dark blue carpet covered the length of the room, and two couches sat facing each other in the center. Neither couch looked very comfortable, although someone had tried to hide that fact from view. It occurred to Kilmer that anyone missing a decorative pillow in the White House might start by looking for it in Nielsen's office. A glass coffee table and two ivory-colored armchairs helped to brighten the room a bit, but the office was still darker, narrower, and less glamorous than Kilmer had imagined. He had somehow pictured a smaller version of the Oval Office.

Nielsen met Kilmer in the center of the room and shook his hand enthusiastically. "Great to see you, Professor. Was the flight okay?"

"Flight was fine."

Nielsen looked toward the door. "Thank you, Joana, I'll take it from here."

"Should I have them send the coffee?"

"Oh, yes. Please do." As Joana departed, Nielsen turned back to Kilmer. "Are you exhausted?"

"More curious than tired. The sooner I find out what this is about, the sooner we can figure out whether there's any point in me being here."

"Unless you tell me the situation is completely hopeless, I'm sure we can use your help."

"Things often look hopeless at the start, Zack—that's not especially diagnostic, in my experience. Anyway, let's not get ahead of ourselves."

Nielsen nodded. "Come. Let's have a seat."

Kilmer was glad that Nielsen had pointed to the armchairs, and not at the pillow sale taking place on the couches.

"Let's wait for the coffee before we get started," Nielsen suggested. "I don't think we'll want the interruption later. And, sorry about this, but would you mind turning off your cell phone?"

"Sure." Kilmer took out his phone, checked it once for messages, then powered it down.

A minute later, the coffee had been delivered, and it looked to be steaming hot. The cups were taller and narrower than standard issue—built to keep the contents hot for longer. A thermos with refills had been delivered alongside as well.

Kilmer picked up his cup and waited for the vice president to do the same. Nielsen hesitated, and then finally decided against it. Instead, he leaned forward and clasped his hands together, as if to convey, *Here's the thing, you see...*

"Do you mind if I ask you something, Prof?"

"That's why I'm here."

"Right," said Nielsen, nodding his head as he contemplated his opening move.

"Professor... do you believe in aliens?"

~ 22 ~

Mark Lane was thirty-five years old and had worked at the CIA for eight years. Prior to joining the agency, he had been the founding chief technology officer of a cybersecurity firm and had made just enough money to no longer lose sleep over how much he brought home in his monthly paycheck. Lane was recruited heavily by the CIA's Directorate of Science and Technology, and the agency was delighted when he said yes. It was a big cultural adjustment, but he decided to treat it like a startup—you work hard, knowing that you won't get to reap the rewards for a long time. He stuck with it and loved it. In his fourth year, he switched over to Operations. In his sixth year, he was invited to join Triad.

Renata Silla was a star. She was thirty-seven years old and had been at the agency for thirteen years, starting out in Operations and then moving to Analysis. Silla had double-majored in history and computer science at Princeton, a college she had been able to attend only thanks to their generous need-based scholarships. She graduated early, and then spent a year doing graduate work at the Center for Nonlinear and Complex Systems at Duke— mostly because it allowed her to be closer to her father. Silla's mother had left them when Silla was only two years old, and her father still lived in the rundown one-bedroom apartment where he had raised her. He was suffering from alcohol-induced cirrhosis and died during her year at Duke. He was only forty-nine.

After her father died, Silla cleaned out his apartment, finished her semester at Duke, and decided to travel the world on the little cash she had saved up while working part-time as a waitress during college. After two years of living on the cheap and working odd jobs across Africa and Asia, Silla came back to the U.S. to start over. The quant funds she interviewed with offered her the kind of money that would forever make up for the poverty of her youth, but when she imagined her life in those jobs, she realized she wasn't desperate to leave her childhood memories behind. She had never resented how little her father made; the only sadness she carried stemmed from the fact that her father had never managed to find any joy in his life. He would take whatever work he could get, but only to put food on the table and to make sure Silla wasn't embarrassed by the clothes she wore to school. Yet when he died, he managed to leave her an invaluable inheritance: a deep conviction that what was most important in life could never be purchased. So when it came to her career, she opted for purpose over paycheck.

Silla joined the CIA at the age of twenty-four. As early as her third year, people joked that she might one day lead the agency. By her seventh year, it was no longer being said as a joke. Now, with only five more years at the CIA than Lane, she was already three levels higher on the pay grade. She oversaw three separate teams—a total of twenty-two people—and co-chaired two of the international working groups that had been created during the present crisis.

Two years earlier, Silla had been the one to ask Art to bring Lane into Triad, and Lane had reported to her ever since. The two of them had gotten along well from the start. She was a boss, a mentor, and, increasingly, a friend. A year ago, Lane had married Silla's first cousin, making them family as well.

Lane put away his phone and looked up at her. "Don't bother wasting your time on it. The information they sent over on Professor Kilmer is totally useless, except for the one bit of data that would have helped protect our dignity when we first met him."

They had been sitting in the room—a few doors down from where Kilmer was meeting with Nielsen—for over thirty minutes. A short while ago, Silla had asked Lane to look through what the agency had finally sent them on the professor.

"Nothing I need to know?" Silla asked.

"Bupkis. Except that he's unmarried—in case that's of interest."

Silla ignored the comment.

"Doesn't even explain why he doesn't want to live in DC," Lane joked. "These profiles just get worse over time."

Silla stood up from her chair and walked a few steps. "Doesn't really matter. If the president wants him at the White House on the night before Armageddon, I'm sure he checks out."

"Actually, his resume is included as well. I don't have much to compare it to, but it looks impressive. You might be interested to know that he's written *four* books. You can add the others to your reading list."

"I've already read all four."

"Really? You didn't mention that earlier. Afraid he'll think you're his biggest fan?"

"Shut up, Mark. Just find something useful to do. Look over the DoD and NASA briefs for anything Director Druckman needs to know before the 8 a.m. meeting."

Lane gave a quick salute, entirely in jest, and then took out his phone again. He skimmed through both briefs and finished reading just as Silla was ending a call.

"Hey, Ren, how do you think it's going for the professor?" Lane asked.

"Depends on what you mean. Do I think he fell off his chair when Nielsen told him what was going on? Probably. I wouldn't blame him."

"I thought you might expect more than that from him."

Silla leaned against a wall. "It's not about that, Mark. Keep in mind, as shocking as all of this has been for us, we've had the opportunity to ease into everything over a period of two weeks. First the detection, then FERMAT, then Station Zero, then the lunar attack—one thing at a time. Only recently did things go terribly wrong. That's not how it's going to be for Professor Kilmer. Those two weeks are going to pass by in a single meeting for him. In less than an hour, he goes from *life as he knows it,* to *aliens exist,* to *we're about to launch a nuclear strike to deter an alien invasion.* It's a lot to take in. It would be for anyone."

"So, he takes it pretty hard. And then what?"

Silla thought about it for a moment. "And then we find out what the guy's made of. I don't mean that in a snide way—I just have no way of knowing. Maybe he sticks around, maybe not. Maybe he can help, maybe not."

"I think he stays. I bet he tries to help. What do you think?"

"I don't know Professor Kilmer enough to venture a guess." She paused. "I'm not sure what I think of him."

Mark smiled. "You sure about that?"

Silla raised an eyebrow, looking textbook inquisitive. "*Excuse* me, Agent Lane?"

"Sorry, Agent Silla. I retract the statement."

"You don't get to decide which statements you retract. Just finish what you were going to say."

Lane wondered whether he had crossed a line. They joked around often enough, but not so much at work—and rarely about topics like this. Lane's wife was always trying to set Silla up with eligible bachelors, but Lane stayed out of those conversations. All he knew was that Silla typically said no to a second date.

Lane glanced over. The look on Silla's face made clear she wasn't going to drop the issue while the insinuation he had made still hung in the air. *No escape.*

"Okay. I'm just saying, there are some facts we ought to consider," Lane began casually. "You've read all of his books. You think he's brilliant. And then, it turns out he looks nothing like we expected, and 'I don't mean that in a bad way.' He even has a sense of humor. So I think it's only reasonable to ask... what does it all add up to?" Lane paused before adding the flourish he had picked up from binge-watching *Columbo* reruns on late-night television. "Oh—and just one more thing, Agent Silla. This... Professor Kilmer of yours... the president of the United States has just called on him to help *save the planet*. Ladies and gentlemen of the jury, I think the implications are clear."

Silla offered Lane a slow clap for the performance.

"Okay, Mark. I'll play along. I'll give you the rebuttal, and then we drop it—for good. First, I didn't think he was as funny as you did. Second, I read a *lot* of books. Third, if I had been smitten by his work, I would have looked him up before tonight—which, clearly, I did not. And fourth, he hasn't saved anything yet. He might come out of there begging to be taken back to Boston. The jury would vote to acquit within seconds. Are we clear?"

"Understood," Lane responded candidly. "And... in all seriousness... I'm sorry if I said something offensive or out of line. I didn't mean for it to come out that way."

"Don't worry about it."

"Then again," Lane added, reviving his smile, "if I heard you correctly, it sounds like you might reconsider the matter if the professor really *does* help save the day."

Silla sighed, not hiding her exasperation. "Okay, Lane. If he ends up single-handedly saving the world, I promise to give him a second thought. Happy? Until that happens, let's focus on our work. I mean it. We can't afford any mistakes—none of us can. So get to it."

Lane got back to work.

Silla returned to her chair and tried to focus on a lengthy email that Energy Secretary Rao had sent. But after re-reading the same paragraph three times, she finally gave up. Silla put away her phone and leaned back. As she closed her eyes, it occurred to her that she was really hoping Kilmer would stay.

Damn it.

That's annoying.

Heirs of Herodotus by D. Kilmer.
Excerpt from Chapter 4.

An examination of the historical record points to several problems in how we strategize for "today's" crisis. First, policymakers tend to overweight episodes from the past that they experienced first-hand—both victories and defeats. Second, too little data is considered, with the same half dozen or so salient historical examples cropping up in discussions every time a new threat arises. Third, the depth of the analysis is dangerously limited—what are described as "lessons learned" from the past are usually little more than punch lines, loosely tied to an event that was much more complex, and whose outcome was multiply determined. When all three of these factors coincide, the probability of disaster shoots higher still.

If you enter Korea to avoid another China, and enter Vietnam to avoid another Korea, and enter Cambodia to avoid another Vietnam—at what point do you begin to worry that you are drawing lessons and inspiration from too shallow a pool of historical events? Has this analysis really considered more than racial or geographic resemblances, or a shared ideological threat? Policymakers must resist the urge to think so narrowly— especially when the surface similarities between events seem compelling. **The phrase "this is just like" strings together four simple words in a seemingly innocuous way, but it does so in a manner that might do immeasurable harm when strategizing in high-stakes environments.**

Should we really expect Napoleon III to get away with acts of aggression like those committed by his uncle and namesake, Napoleon Bonaparte? Of course not. It is imperative for us to recognize that the seismic changes that took place during the decades separating their reigns make it such that **even a Napoleon is not a good analogy for Napoleon.**

~ 24 ~

It took Nielsen fifty-five minutes to give Kilmer a detailed summary of the previous two weeks, starting with the detection on Day 1 and ending with the show-of-force proposal that Strauss had made a few hours earlier. Kilmer didn't fall off his chair even once—but that might have been only because he had the habit of leaning back when shocked, not forward. He leaned back on three occasions. First, when he realized that Nielsen wasn't joking about the detection of alien spacecraft... *astonishment*. Second, when he was told that communication had been rendered possible, and FERMAT was now in use... *delight*. Third, when he learned about the lunar attack and the spacecraft's subsequent return to its Earth-bound trajectory... *horror*.

"That's where we are, Professor. You can see why I wanted you here tonight. We will discuss the show-of-force proposal at 8 a.m., and the president will make her decision soon after."

"Yes... I see."

"So—what do you think about Strauss's proposal?"

"I'm not sure yet. I need to think about it some more. And I want to hear from everyone at the meeting. I don't mind making a call with too little information, but I do mind making it with less information than I can get."

"Okay. What additional information can I provide?"

Kilmer reached for his coffee. He had taken only a few sips of it over the last hour, and what remained in the cup was now cold. He took the extra cup that was sitting in the tray and filled it with hot coffee from the thermos.

"I do have some questions. I didn't want to raise them earlier because they might have taken us off on tangents."

Nielsen waited until Kilmer had taken a sip. "Go ahead, Professor. Ask me anything."

Kilmer was about to ask his first question when there was a knock at the door.

"Sorry about that," Nielsen whispered. Then he called on the visitor to enter. In the few seconds that transpired between the knock and the opening of the door, Kilmer found himself hoping it would be someone bringing them a bite to eat.

It was not.

President Whitman had barely stepped into the room when Nielsen got up from his chair. Kilmer hadn't *entirely* forgotten that the president might stop by at some point, but the thought of meeting Whitman had fallen into the dim recesses of his mind. Seeing her in the room now renewed the profundity of the moment.

He was at the White House. With the president *and* vice president of the United States. On the eve of the greatest crisis that the world had ever faced. The enormity of the situation was incomparable.

I should have worn a damn tie.

Whitman walked over to Kilmer. "I'm delighted to finally meet you, Professor Kilmer. Thank you for coming."

"It's a pleasure to meet you, Madam President," Kilmer said as they shook hands. "I hope I can be of some help."

"Zack speaks very highly of you, and I trust his judgment. But I'll be honest—we are not at a loss for smart people in this building. What we could benefit from is having someone who sees things differently, and who might catch some things we've missed. I understand that's your specialty, Professor. Or—at least one of them."

"You're being too kind, Madam President. I can only promise that I'll do my best and try not to disappoint you."

"Then you're in luck, Professor. No one who does their best can ever disappoint me."

Nielsen suggested that they sit. President Whitman looked around at the options.

"There's no way I'm digging through those pillows to find a few inches of couch, Zack. I'll take one of the chairs."

Nielsen's reaction suggested this was an ongoing joke between the two of them. Kilmer resisted the urge to laugh.

The president took Nielsen's chair, and the VP switched over to one of the couches. Whitman was about to reach for some coffee when she noticed that all three cups had already been used. "Seriously, Zack? No cup for me?"

Kilmer froze. *There had never been an extra cup.*

I'm an idiot.

Nielsen came to the rescue. "I'm sorry about that, Madam President. My mistake. We'll get another one right away, along with some more hot coffee."

He gave Kilmer a nod that seemed to say, *Don't worry, Prof, I'll cover for you.* Kilmer smiled back a *thanks.*

Then, with a grin on his face, Nielsen continued. "As you can see, Madam President, I ordered three cups, but Professor Kilmer felt that he deserved at least two of them for coming all this way to help us. I think it shows courage, actually—not too many people would have the guts to steal a cup from the person who has access to our nuclear launch codes."

What the hell? Thanks for nothing, Zack. Kilmer tried to think of something witty to say. He came up with, "Sorry about that."

Whitman laughed. "Zack—be nice! It's okay, Professor. If you can help us get out of this mess, I'll gladly send you every piece of china in the White House. I'll even throw in some of Nielsen's pillows." She gave Kilmer a pat on the shoulder, as if to make it clear that she was taking his side, and that she was not the least bit offended.

Kilmer found a bit of footing. "I'm happy to take on the aliens, Madam President, but asking me to take these pillows off your hands is a little much."

"*Et tu*, Professor?" said Nielsen.

As Whitman laughed, Nielsen looked over at Kilmer and gave him a wink.

That's when Kilmer realized that Nielsen had actually done him a favor by throwing him under the bus. It had broken the ice and engendered a more informal atmosphere. Nielsen had even managed to get President Whitman to come to Kilmer's defense. It was a small gesture on her part, and entirely in jest, but it created a moment of camaraderie—a basis for rapport between Whitman and Kilmer that would otherwise have taken much longer to build. Kilmer already felt more relaxed in her presence, which was essential if he was going to be of any help. He didn't usually have a problem with speaking truth to power, but it would be naïve to think that talking to the president of the United States would not lead him to second-guess himself.

Nielsen was older than Kilmer—and was now the vice president—but Kilmer had always viewed him as a student first, a friend second, and an advisee third. For the first time, he was seeing Nielsen as the skilled politician others knew him to be.

After some additional cups and more hot coffee had been delivered, Nielsen updated the president. "I've provided a summary of the last two weeks, and Professor Kilmer was just about to ask some questions. Should we continue that conversation, or would you rather we discuss something else while you're here?"

"Please carry on as if I hadn't interrupted, Zack. I'm here to listen."

Whitman and Nielsen turned to Kilmer in perfect synchrony, and he suddenly felt like the target of a high-stakes interrogation. It was unnerving—and problematic. *It helps no one if I'm too nervous to speak my mind.*

Kilmer rose from his chair as he mustered up the courage to change the dynamic. "I hope you won't mind, Madam President, if I walk around while I talk. Would that be okay?"

"By all means, Professor. Do whatever is most comfortable."

Kilmer walked toward Nielsen's desk as he recalled the words to his mind: *Every problem wants to be solved.*

By the time he had turned back around to face Whitman and Nielsen, he had a slight smile on his face—an expression not of joy, but of renewed self-assurance. Whitman smiled back. Nielsen nodded. But both of their faces registered the same emotion. And it seemed like a perfectly good place to start.

Hope.

~ 25 ~

Kilmer kicked things off. "Okay. First question: Do we know whether any aliens are on board the spacecraft?"

Nielsen and Whitman looked at one another, briefly, and then back at Kilmer. "I'd have to say the answer is… we don't really know," Nielsen replied. "But we've been working under the assumption that there probably are. Why do you ask?"

"It just seems to me that if *we* were the ones sending a spacecraft to explore a planet for the first time, it probably wouldn't have humans on board. Our unmanned vehicles have always taken the lead in space exploration."

"Would knowing the answer to this question change your view on things—on what we should do?"

"I'm not sure," said Kilmer. "I'm just trying to get a clearer picture of what we know and don't know. It might have downstream implications, but I haven't had a chance to think it through."

"Understood," said Nielsen. "We can come back to that. Let's keep going."

"Okay. My second question is about the lunar attack. When the alien spacecraft altered its trajectory to target the Moon—was that an efficient maneuver?"

"What do you mean?" Nielsen asked.

"Sorry, I wasn't being very clear. What I mean is, was the path they were on, initially, close to optimal for making a stop at the Moon—requiring only a slight change in trajectory—or did the spacecraft have to make a relatively large adjustment to its course in order to carry out the attack?

"I don't know, but that's something we can find out. The folks at NASA should have the answer. If not, they'll be able to figure it out. Is it relevant?"

"Maybe."

"How so?" asked Whitman.

"I'm only speculating here, but if the Moon was more-or-less on the way for them, given the path they had originally set, then the lunar bombing might have been part of their plan all along. On the other hand, if they had already passed the Moon and had to double-back to carry out the attack, or if they needed to radically change their trajectory to pull it off, then it begs the question: *Why?* What made them change their mind?"

Whitman crossed her arms. "So, we have two questions here. First, is their flight path consistent with the idea that they had planned the attack all along? And if not, what might have caused them to change their mind during the voyage?"

"That's right," Kilmer agreed. "And even if we can't answer that second question—if we can infer that they changed their minds, but we don't know why—we'll still have learned something important."

"Such as?"

"Such as the fact that they have minds *at all*, Madam President. And that these minds can change. I have no idea what life elsewhere in the universe is like—assuming life, as we conceive of it, is even what we're dealing with here. I think we need to keep track of even our most basic assumptions. Of course, the question of *why* is still paramount. Did they simply make a calculation error when they were charting their initial course, which they corrected later? Were they reacting to something *we* did—and if so, what? Or… perhaps…" Kilmer paused. "Perhaps, just like us, the aliens have been debating what they should do. It's a useful reminder—regardless of the real reason for their change in trajectory—that we shouldn't assume we're dealing with a monolithic entity. They might have differences of opinion on their side as well."

"Very good, Professor," Whitman agreed. "We'll have Dr. Menon look into it. What else do you have?"

"Just one more question for now. But it's probably the most important." Kilmer took a sip of his coffee as he tried to work out how best to raise the issue. "Madam President… regardless of whether you decide to proceed with a show of force tomorrow, is it accurate to say that you wish to engage peacefully with the aliens?"

"It is," Whitman answered. "Without question. We absolutely want to engage peacefully."

"Okay—peacefully," Kilmer acknowledged. "But for how long, I'm wondering. Over what timescale?"

Whitman narrowed her eyes, unsure of what Kilmer was driving at. "Forever, I would hope."

"That's the only reasonable answer," Kilmer agreed, returning to his chair. "But it begs the question: What is our plan for achieving that? How do we hope to *bring about* this forever peace?"

"I'm not quite following you, Professor."

"What I'm trying to say, Madam President, is that human beings are great at starting wars. We are also reasonably capable of ending wars, given enough time. What we struggle with is *avoiding wars altogether*. I'm afraid we have a pretty dismal track record when it comes to meeting strangers—whether they be distant empires, new civilizations, aliens, or whatever—and then living peacefully forevermore. It just never seems to work out that way. When ancient kingdoms came into contact with one another, no matter how many gifts were exchanged in the early days, wars of domination eventually resulted. The Romans learned a lot from the Greeks, and they appreciated them for their gifts of wisdom and culture, but they still went ahead and conquered them. The Europeans who came to the so-called New World did not set sail with the intention of committing genocide, but somehow that's what transpired.

"Whether they were initially motivated by a desire to explore, or trade, or educate, or proselytize, or loot, or civilize, or conquer—human encounters eventually led to war. Not all wars led to the annihilation of one side. Not all of them stretched across decades or centuries. But it's hard to find examples of distinct races or cultures or empires encountering one another and avoiding war altogether, for the entirety of their relationship."

Whitman's face betrayed a feeling of foreboding. She was beginning to see where this was going.

Kilmer went on. "What concerns me is that there's little in our history to suggest we've figured out the formula for creating 'forever peace.' I don't think we know how to choreograph our early encounters with a new civilization so that we avoid war altogether. Which brings me back to my question. What exactly is our plan, not just to avoid war when we *first* meet the aliens, but to avoid it for the decades and centuries to come?

Madam President, if a war with them does eventually materialize—as human history suggests is likely, regardless of how nice things look early on—I very much fear that *they* will be the Europeans and *we* the New World. They will be the colonizers and we the indigenous tribes. They will be the ones claiming to civilize, and we the backward people who should be thankful for it. They will be the ones who demand trade or fealty at the point of a gun, and we the ones who have no choice but to accept their terms."

Kilmer observed their expressions. President Whitman seemed deep in thought. Vice President Nielsen looked like the Earth had moved under his feet. Neither of them said a word.

Kilmer had saved this question for last, and it was for precisely this reason. He knew they wouldn't have a good answer, because it wasn't likely that they had even considered the question. And once he raised it, there was a risk that everything else the White House had been doing for the last twenty-four hours would seem small—almost irrelevant. That was not what he wanted.

Kilmer addressed the issue. "Your team is focused on the crisis at hand, and the people in the 8 a.m. meeting are tasked with saving the planet from imminent destruction. Their job is to make sure that we live to see tomorrow—and that task remains essential. But you, Madam President, will have to do all of that and much more. You will have to chart a course that ensures humanity survives far beyond the foreseeable future."

President Whitman did not answer. Instead, she took a prolonged breath, reached for the thermos, and refilled everyone's coffee. Then she lifted her own cup, slowly, and took a small sip. It was like watching a sacred ritual—as if Whitman was unwilling to say a word before she had mindfully completed all the steps. Only after she had set down her cup did she turn to look at Kilmer.

"Professor Kilmer, I didn't think it was possible for someone to make me see the situation as more dire than I already considered it to be. But you have done just that. And I'm glad—because I can't solve a problem that I don't recognize. You're right. My team is making sure there is a tomorrow. But we must do much more."

She leaned closer. "Now, I have to ask you something. You say that history gives us very little guidance here. That our track record as a species suggests we are in a lot of trouble. Does that mean *you* think the situation is hopeless?"

Kilmer shook his head. "All I can say, Madam President, is that history only exists because people that came before us *made* history. If we can't find guidance in what they did—if history refuses to give us answers, or if it fails to offer us advice we can live with—then we will have to make history as well. We will have to be the first to do something remarkable. It won't be easy. But is it *hopeless*? No. There's always a first. Always."

Whitman managed a smile. "So where would you propose we start?"

Kilmer had no idea—so he took a few sips of his coffee, and a few steps around the room, as he considered the question. Finally, he turned to Whitman and Nielsen.

"I think we have to start by figuring out what's really going on here. History might not give us the answers, but it can still provide us with inspiration. I'm reminded of what Churchill said, just after Poland was invaded by both Hitler and Stalin in 1939. Churchill gave a radio broadcast in which he spoke about the difficulty of predicting how things would play out. His words are as good a place for us to start as any:

> *'I cannot forecast to you the action of Russia. It is a riddle wrapped in a mystery inside an enigma; but perhaps there is a key. That key is Russian national interest.'"*

Kilmer took another sip. "So, where do we start? I say we start by looking for Churchill's Key. We start by worrying less about alien plans and intentions, and more about their underlying interests. We shift our focus from *what* they want, to *why* they want it. If we are to survive—not just through the night, but into the future—we will have to understand what drives them."

~ 26 ~

Heirs of Herodotus by D. Kilmer.
Excerpt from Chapter 5.

It has become a tradition of sorts to judge history's great leaders on how they handled themselves in moments of crisis. Were they able to weather the storm? Did they manage to keep the ship afloat? Did they succeed in addressing the grave problems of the day? These are important measures of leadership, but they are incomplete—like evaluating the skill of a general on whether he wins a battle but losing sight of whether the war was ultimately won or lost. There is nothing wrong with celebrating Hannibal's remarkable crossing of the Alps, and much is to be learned from how he amassed his many wins on the Italian peninsula. But we should not forget that he failed to deliver a decisive victory even after fifteen years of fighting, that he was ultimately defeated by Scipio Africanus, and that Carthage was not just defeated by Rome in the Punic Wars, it was wiped off the map. **That Hannibal is still remembered for his brilliance, but the empire he fought for is remembered only for its complete destruction, should give us pause.**

Crises are vain creatures, always insisting that our attention and energy be focused on them alone. The greatest of leaders reject this demand and vow not to lose sight of what comes next—after the battle has been won or lost. For this they should be rewarded, especially by those of us who feel we have professional license to pass judgment on our forebears. **We do humanity no favors by telling our leaders that they will be judged only on how they navigate moments of despair—and not for what comes after. If crises are a test of leadership, it is not because they show us who has the strength to fight and win, but because they reveal who has the wisdom and courage to do so without sacrificing their vision for the future.**

~ 27 ~

Whitman glanced at Nielsen and conveyed something with a nod. Then she turned toward Kilmer again.

"Professor Kilmer, I'm glad we met tonight. I would not have asked Zack to invite you here if I didn't think you might add some value. But I didn't expect to hear anything that would make me rethink the situation so fundamentally. I had planned for Zack to fill me in on what you had to say, and for you to return to Boston soon after. But I'd like you to stick around. Would you be willing to stay in Washington for the next few days?"

"Of course, Madam President."

"Thank you, Professor. Now, we should probably let you get some rest." Whitman turned to Nielsen. "Zack, please stop by my office before you call it a night."

The three of them walked out of Nielsen's office, and Joana went to fetch the two Triad agents. Silla and Lane arrived just moments later, but they hung back while Kilmer, Nielsen, and Whitman finished chatting. Lane had never seen President Whitman in person, but his excitement faded a bit when he realized he couldn't even tell his wife about it. Silla had met Whitman for the first time only three days earlier, when she accompanied Art Capella and Director Druckman to brief the president on Triad's work, so this scene was only slightly less surreal for her than it was for Lane.

Whitman noticed the two agents and walked over to them.

"Agent... *Silla*. Is that right?" Whitman asked.

"Yes, Madam President. We met at the Triad briefing." Silla tried to shake off her amazement at the president knowing her name.

"Of course. Your presentation was excellent. Please give Art my regards."

"Yes, ma'am."

"And who is this?"

"I'm sorry. This is my colleague, Mark Lane—also with Triad."

"Nice to meet you, Agent Lane. Thank you for your work."

Lane almost froze, but then eked out a "Delighted to meet you, Madam President." He also managed to avoid adding "I'm a big fan," which he would have regretted later with absolute certainty.

"Were the two of you assigned to accompany our guest today?" Whitman asked Silla.

"Yes, ma'am."

Whitman turned to Nielsen's chief of staff. "Joana, where is Professor Kilmer staying?"

"Just down the street, Madam President. At the Willard InterContinental."

"Change of plans. He's no longer Zack's guest—he's a guest of mine. Please arrange for the professor to stay at the White House tonight. I think a historian would much prefer staying in the Lincoln Bedroom than in the Willard." She looked over at Kilmer and smiled. "Perhaps we can send a few extra cups for your morning coffee."

Kilmer and Nielsen both laughed, and Nielsen gave Kilmer a friendly pat on the back. Everyone else smiled, not quite understanding the joke.

"Thank you for the invitation," Kilmer replied. "I'd be delighted, of course. But if it's an inconvenience for anyone, I'm more than happy staying at the Willard."

"It's no problem at all, Professor. I'm really glad you're here," Whitman said, shaking his hand.

Lane looked at Silla and gave her a goofy smile. *He could still end up saving the planet...*

Silla just turned away. *Shut up, Mark.*

~ 28 ~

President Whitman and VP Nielsen sat in the Oval Office.

"We'll move ahead with the 8 a.m. meeting as planned," Whitman said. "What the professor had to say is important, but we still need a decision on the show-of-force proposal. I've asked Strauss and Allen to have two operational plans ready for me to evaluate by noon. I want to minimize delays in case I decide to move forward with the proposal."

"Understood."

"We'll meet at 9:30 to evaluate where things stand. I want to keep it small. You, me, Salvo, General Allen, and Secretary Strauss. Let's also invite Professor Kilmer. I want to hear what he has to say about the discussion. And to be perfectly frank, I want to mix things up around here. I have a feeling he can help with that."

"So... asking him to stay a while longer is not just about helping us make the right call."

"It's never *just* about making the right call, Zack. You need more than the right answers to navigate a crisis like this. We might have the best people, but we also need to orchestrate the right dynamic. And I see Professor Kilmer playing a role in helping me do that."

"How so?"

Whitman smiled. "Well, let's see. He's an outsider. An 'East Coast elite.' He lives in an ivory tower. He has no military background whatsoever. And he hasn't done anything to deserve a seat at the table. It's not exactly the kind of profile that commands a lot of respect around here, especially when we're on the brink of war. It should be more than enough to mix things up."

Nielsen looked puzzled. "I understand the case for diversity of thought, but I don't see how it improves the team dynamic if the rest of the group doesn't even respect him. Maybe he'd be better off advising you separately."

"No. I want him in the room. It's okay if they don't respect him for those reasons. There's always more to people than the things we can rattle off about them. I caught a glimpse of that tonight—and it's what I'm counting on. If I'm wrong about that, we'll find out soon enough. But I want him in this room for the 9:30."

"Yes, ma'am. I have a Triad briefing at nine, but I'll keep it short. And I'll make sure the professor is here on time."

"What's the Triad meeting about?"

"I don't know—it was added late. I'll let you know if I hear anything that warrants your attention."

They chatted for a few more minutes, and by the time Nielsen left the room, it was 2:30 a.m. Whitman walked to the windows overlooking the Resolute desk and gazed into the night.

We will have to make history.

Kilmer's words drifted through her mind, as if looking for a place to settle. They landed on a memory—from the morning of her inauguration. Her husband, Jack, was there. He would pass away only three months later, but on that day, he looked as alive and handsome as she had ever known him. He wore a charcoal-gray suit that she had insisted on, and a navy-blue tie. His face registered only love, pride, and admiration—and none of the physical pain that she knew he was enduring every minute of every day. He held her hand and looked into her eyes. "People keep saying that you've just made history, Marianne. I keep having to tell them you didn't come here to make history. You came here to make the future. I couldn't be prouder of what you've accomplished already, sweetheart, but just remember—this is just the beginning. There are so many more tomorrows."

Whitman's eyes welled up thinking of Jack, and she leaned her head back to make sure a tear didn't materialize. He hadn't received his fair share of tomorrows. In one of their last conversations, he made her promise that she would never look back at their time together in sadness—only to find strength and happiness. And so, standing in the Oval Office now, Whitman reminded herself that the person who had known her best would have wanted her to be the one leading the country at this pivotal moment in history.

And Jack would have been the first to agree that she had to think about the dawning of a new era, not just the dawning of a new day. She couldn't allow herself to be overwhelmed by the crisis at hand, no matter how existential it appeared to be. Humanity had to prepare for what came after.

Whitman's offer to Kilmer posed a problem for Silla and Lane. The agents weren't supposed to leave Kilmer alone, so they had booked rooms for themselves at the Willard as well. But now, Kilmer was headed to the Lincoln Bedroom, and the agents could neither leave the White House nor ask for additional rooms. Joana seemed unaware of their dilemma. She told Kilmer that the Triad agents would coordinate with him for his morning pickup, and that she would show him to his bedroom when he was ready.

Kilmer could tell that something was amiss by the way Lane and Silla were whispering. "Everything okay?" he asked.

"Yes, Professor," answered Silla. "We're just working out a few details. Sorry for the delay."

"No problem. Please take your time."

The agents decided that one of them would have to stay at the White House. Asking for a bedroom wasn't appropriate but requesting a place to work seemed reasonable. Silla insisted that Lane go home to his wife. She would stay with Kilmer until seven, at which point Agent Liu would take her place. Silla would head home after attending her nine o'clock meeting with Art and the vice president.

Silla walked over to Kilmer and Joana. "Sorry to keep you waiting. Joana, would it be possible for you to find me a place where I can get some work done for the next few hours? Agent Lane is leaving, but I'd like to stick around, just in case something comes up that needs my attention. Any place that you can spare will be fine."

Joana assured Silla it would be no problem, and then she ducked into her office to make some arrangements. She returned a minute later with a smile that indicated good news. "If you'll accompany us upstairs, Agent Silla, I'll get you settled as well."

Joana, Kilmer, and Silla walked through a series of hallways, leaving the West Wing and entering the Executive Residence. Kilmer decided to use the time to get some more information.

"Agent Silla, do you mind if I ask you something about the situation?"

"Of course, Professor. And I'm sorry I couldn't answer your questions earlier. I hope you understand why."

"Completely. And you were right—it's worse than I had imagined."

"I don't think anyone could have imagined this. So, what would you like to know?"

"For one thing, I'm wondering if there's any reason to assume that there are aliens on board the spacecraft."

"No," Silla answered without hesitation. "It could be an autonomous spacecraft, like we might have sent."

Kilmer nodded, recognizing the point that he had also made just a short while ago.

"But I'd offer two caveats," Silla added. "First, we shouldn't assume this is a challenging mission for them. Just because it seems magical to us doesn't mean the aliens are pushing the frontiers of *their* capabilities. They might think of it like we think of driving between cities. We should avoid over-indexing on our own experience and abilities."

"Good point. And the second caveat?"

"That my assessment could change based on what they do next. For example, if they were to land at Station Zero, I would consider it more likely that there is someone on the spacecraft."

"Why is that?"

"Because hovering above a planet is easy, safe, and a good way to obtain all sorts of information. Why land? And why land where humans have specifically *asked* you to land? It seems more consistent with an interest in engaging with your surroundings—with getting your hands dirty, so to speak. It would still be possible that they just want to collect soil samples, or test their landing gear, but the probability that someone is inside certainly goes up."

"So, *if* they land, you think that little green men might actually come out of the spaceship."

"It becomes more likely, anyway. As for how they'll decide to play it, I don't know. Even if there are aliens on board, we can't be sure if they'll come marching out, flying out, or decide to stay inside. But I'd be willing to bet you a fancy dinner they won't be green."

Kilmer's mind raced to find some basis on which such a conclusion could be drawn, but he came up with nothing that would hint at their pigmentation. "Why would you bet they're not green?"

"Because, Professor, there are many more colors that are *not* green. I'm just playing the odds."

Kilmer laughed. "No bet, Agent Silla. But point taken."

Kilmer had saved himself a few dollars but immediately regretted not taking the bet. Having dinner with Agent Silla sounded like a great idea no matter who paid for it.

He was about to ask another question when they reached their destination: the second floor of the Executive Residence. On the west end of a long hallway was the president's bedroom; on the opposite end was the Lincoln Bedroom, where Kilmer would be staying. As they walked eastward, they came to the room that Joana had requisitioned for Silla. It was spacious and elegantly decorated, with portraits on every wall, a large mirror over the fireplace, and a long baroque table sitting atop an ornate Persian rug. The papers scattered on the table, and the single chair beside it, suggested that the table was used as a desk. Across from the table-desk was a more comfortable sitting area. The full spectrum of what the room might have witnessed over the years was captured by two pieces of technology that sat facing one another: an old grandfather clock stood against one wall; a large flatscreen TV was mounted opposite it.

"This is the Treaty Room," explained Joana. "For two centuries, American presidents have used it as an office. The desk you see there is called the Treaty Table—it's where the treaty to end the Spanish-American War was signed. President Whitman uses it almost daily. Agent Silla, would you be comfortable here for a few hours?"

Kilmer turned toward Silla just in time to catch the look of wonder on her face. It quickly turned to propriety. "Joana," said the agent, "I couldn't possibly impose on the president's personal space. You can just put me on a chair in a hallway somewhere."

"It's no imposition. I called the president's personal secretary before we came up here. She said the president will not be using the room until noon at the earliest. She also assured me there are no classified documents in here. She did ask, however, that you use the sitting area instead of the president's desk, so as not to disturb the papers. I hope one of the couches or armchairs will be comfortable enough."

"Of course. And if you're sure it's no trouble, I'd be happy to use this room."

Silla glanced at Kilmer, only for him to realize he'd been staring at her for the last thirty seconds. He quickly turned away, though not as smoothly as he would have liked.

"Professor Kilmer," Silla said, allowing him to look back in her direction. "I'll be in here while you get some rest. If you need anything, or if you have any more questions, just let me know. At seven, Agent Liu will take over for me; he'll be the one who takes you to the meeting." She paused. "So this is probably goodbye from me." They shook hands. "It really was a pleasure to meet you, Professor. I wish it were under different circumstances."

"I think if different circumstances had prevailed, we might never have met," Kilmer pointed out. "So maybe the alien threat isn't all bad." He quickly realized that, given the gravity of the situation, his words probably sounded more insensitive than charming. "Sorry. That was a bit off-key."

Joana came to the rescue. "A bit of dark humor is always welcome around here. I'd even say we've come to depend on it. It just means you're one of us now."

"No apology necessary," Silla added. "It was a nice thing to say." She smiled— but then her expression changed, ever so slightly, from happy to bittersweet.

Kilmer looked at her just long enough for it to be a measurable amount of time, and Silla didn't look away. Then he gave a slight nod that seemed more formal than their interaction had been until that moment. "Good night, Agent Silla."

He picked up his bags. Joana took the lead, and he followed her out.

"Good night," Silla responded softly, but only after Kilmer had already reached the door.

Kilmer and Joana stepped into the hallway and turned right. The Lincoln Bedroom was the next room over. Joana turned on the light and oriented him to the room. "I won't give you the complete White House tour version of the speech, but there are two things every guest who stays here needs to know. First, no, this is not where Lincoln slept. He used this room as his office. Second, on January 1, 1863—"

"The Emancipation Proclamation," Kilmer said excitedly. "Is this where he signed it? I didn't know that."

"That's right. It really is amazing to think he was in this very room," Joana reflected briefly. "Well, I hope you enjoy your stay. If you need anything, just press zero on the phone over there. You can also call or text me if needed."

"Thank you. I'm sure that won't be necessary. Good night, Joana."

She said goodbye and walked out of the room. Kilmer didn't move from where he was left standing for almost a minute. He just took it all in. The White House. The President. The Lincoln Bedroom.

The aliens.

That brought the delightful little highlight reel to an abrupt end. For the last few minutes—walking through the White House, hearing about the Treaty Room and the Lincoln Bedroom—he had managed to avoid thinking about the reason he was here in the first place. He considered sitting down at the desk to organize his thoughts, but the idea didn't survive long. He needed to sleep.

Kilmer turned off the light, sat on the side of the bed, and took off his shoes. He was too tired to change his clothes or remove the covers, so he just crawled onto the bed and put his head on the pillow. When he closed his eyes, memories of what he had experienced that night flashed through his mind. Some frightening, some pleasant. And then he arrived at an image that gave him pause.

It was Agent Silla—the smile on her face before he left the Treaty Room. Happy, but then bittersweet.

It wouldn't take anyone more than a glance to conclude that Agent Silla was extremely attractive. He had noticed it himself, right away, when he first saw her at the airfield. But she was suddenly taking up much more of his mindshare. Given how little time they had spent together, it wasn't clear why. Was it her intellect, which he had glimpsed just moments ago? Her wit and sense of humor, which he had noticed since the car ride? The poise, confidence, and strength with which she carried herself? Maybe all of the above. Maybe something else entirely.

These various qualities began to affix themselves to the picture he was holding of Silla in his mind. He studied the composite as it materialized—all the while getting drowsier. And when he saw the completed image, Kilmer realized that he had somehow missed the mark. Agent Silla wasn't just attractive… she was beautiful.

He couldn't help but smile. He had solved the puzzle, and the answer was something quite wonderful. Whether or not he saw her again, Kilmer was happy that someone like her was out there, and that they had managed to cross paths.

Still, the last thought Kilmer had before falling asleep was a tad more selfish—to put it mildly.

I hope those damn aliens don't blow everything up before I get a chance to see her again.

~ 30 ~

Agent Silla spent twenty minutes writing emails before deciding that she was too tired to keep working. But it was only 3 a.m., and she still had four hours to get through before she could hand things off to Agent Liu. The thought of going to the Willard for a few hours of sleep crossed her mind, but she quickly dismissed it. She wasn't the kind of person—and this wasn't the time—to break the rules.

She stood up from the armchair and stretched, hoping it would wake her up. It did not. She moved to the couch, removed her heels, and curled up against the corner. Her mind got the hint—*the workday has ended*—and it started to relax, allowing her thoughts to wander. She thought about her best friend, who now lived in Georgia and knew nothing about what was happening. What a gulf existed between those in the loop and those who were still just going about their daily lives. It didn't seem fair that her friends weren't even allowed to know about the threat their families faced at that very moment. Then again, it wasn't fair that those in the loop had to carry such a heavy burden. Maybe the two injustices balanced each other out. Maybe. She was too tired to calculate which was worse. And she felt drained… almost sad. *Why?*

At first, Silla thought it was because she had been thinking about her friend. But that wasn't it. Maybe the anxiety of the last few days was turning into despondency, or a sort of malaise was setting in? No, not that either.

She felt as though she had lost something—except she hadn't. At least, not anything she could think of.

She went over the events of the preceding day to see if she could figure out what was bothering her. When she arrived at Kilmer, the mystery seemed to unravel. For the last hour or two, she had only caught a glimpse of her feelings toward him, but now, with her guard down, they were more discernable.

Agent Lane might have been joking, but he had stumbled upon something substantive.

The professor was supposed to have been a nice elderly gentleman who needed help walking down the stairs. A wise old man with interesting ideas. He was supposed to have fallen off his chair and begged for a flight back to Boston after he found out what was going on. He had turned out to be none of those things.

The problem, Silla realized, was that she wasn't going to be seeing him again—probably ever. By the time he woke up, she would be gone. And events were unlikely to conspire to bring them together again.

So what? This is nothing real.

Silla knew what it took for there to be something real. She had been engaged once, when she was thirty-two, to a smart, attractive, kind, and successful man whom she had dated for almost two years. But try as she might—and Silla tried for longer than was fair to either of them—she could never imagine him being devoted to any cause far greater than himself. He supported Silla and her aspirations, but he never understood what drove her. She would have been willing to overlook that, Silla finally realized, but what she could not do was spend the rest of her life with someone who could never inspire her.

That, it turned out, was not a small problem to have. Many of the men Silla met were impressive. Almost none were inspiring.

Then there was Kilmer. Silla had dated enough to know that she was incapable of falling for someone so quickly. But there was a catch. On one crucial dimension, Silla had already known Kilmer for a long time. It wasn't often that you got to know someone's mind before actually meeting them, but in this case, that foundation had already been established. Even before he managed not to tumble down the stairs at the airfield, she'd felt a genuine intellectual attraction toward Kilmer—and it was allowing her to think about him in ways that would normally take much longer.

Silla reminded herself that she barely knew him as a person, and that what she was feeling, however genuine, could be completely undone in a moment. She might learn one unflattering thing about him, and the spell would be broken. He might say or do something unkind or bizarre or stupid, and it would be a deal-breaker for her.

The only problem: Kilmer kept saying and doing everything right.

Damn it.

It was all she could do to keep from walking out of the Treaty Room, heading straight into the Lincoln Bedroom, and—

And what? Confront him? Chat about the alien threat? Make small talk? Climb into bed with him? A part of her was convinced that it didn't much matter which of those things she did, as long as it offered her an opportunity to see him again—if only to find out whether he could live up to what she was making him out to be in her mind. The other part of her—the rational part, which she always trusted more—could list a dozen reasons why leaving the Treaty Room was a terrible idea.

Silla decided to stay put. She wouldn't even leave the couch for a stroll around the room. It was too risky; she might get tempted. She closed her eyes, still thinking of Kilmer. Thinking of the words he had said.

> *I think if different circumstances had prevailed, we might never have met. So maybe the alien threat isn't all bad.*

Kilmer had gotten it wrong. Never having met was sounding a lot better than what she was feeling at the moment. Maybe he wasn't so smart after all. That would certainly make it a lot easier to cast him aside.

Or maybe the world would end. Either way, problem solved.

Silla could tell by the dwindling quality of her logic that she was starting to drift off. She tried a little harder to find reasons to be upset with Kilmer, but she couldn't figure out how to make that work. Her last thought before she fell asleep was that she wasn't upset at all. She was glad they had met. Kilmer was a good guy. Good for him.

~ 31 ~

The sound of the door startled Silla awake. It took her a moment to remember where she was, and another moment before she started to panic about having fallen asleep in the Treaty Room. What time was it? And who had just opened the door?

"Agent Silla, I'm sorry to disturb you. I just wanted to check in to see how you were doing. If you were sleeping, by all means, please get some rest."

Was she dreaming? That sounded a lot like—

President Whitman stood at the door.

"Madam President! I apologize. I must have dozed off. This is really embarrassing. If you need the room, I can find somewhere else to sit."

"Agent Silla, not at all. Please relax. My secretary told me you'd be here, and I saw the light on, so I thought I'd just check in on you. I was heading to bed myself."

Silla looked at her watch. 3:30. She had only been asleep for about fifteen minutes.

"Thank you, Madam President. That's very kind of you. Agent Lane and I had expected Professor Kilmer to stay at the Willard, so we had to improvise when plans changed."

Whitman walked into the room, making sense of the situation. "I see. I guess we didn't consider that. You and Agent Lane had orders to stay with Professor Kilmer even after his meeting with Zack?"

"Yes, ma'am."

"Why is that?"

"It's our protocol to accompany outsiders who are newly brought into the loop for at least the first few hours. To help them acclimate. And for security reasons."

"Is that to make sure he doesn't go to the press, or turn out to be a Russian spy, or lose his mind and start calling everyone he knows?"

"Something like that. But if you saw the full list of things the agency worries about in situations like this, you would really wonder who's lost their minds."

Whitman laughed. "Do you mind if I sit?" she asked.

"Madam President, of course. It's your room. Your house. I wouldn't dream of saying no even if it weren't."

"Agent Silla, I like you. Most people just assume that I'm not *really* asking for permission when I say such things. But I think it's right to ask."

"And if I had said that I *do* mind? That I prefer for you to stand?" Silla asked in a moment of unfiltered curiosity.

"I would have sat down anyway. But I wouldn't like you nearly as much."

They both laughed. Whitman took the armchair closest to the side of the couch where Silla was sitting. Silla slid her feet off the couch and placed them on the floor.

"Agent Silla, you probably already know this, but Art speaks very highly of you. That's why I remembered your name. I hate to admit it, but with the number of people I end up meeting, it's hard to keep track of the ones I've only met once or twice. Anyway, I'm fully aware that you've been leading the international collaborations on communicating with the aliens. It's a lot to figure out, but it's some of the most important work that's taking place right now. And you're doing a great job."

Silla smiled. If only she could wake up to such praise every day. "Thank you. But I'm fortunate to have excellent colleagues. If you don't mind, I'd like to convey your sentiment to my team. It will mean a lot to them."

"Please do. Now, as to your more immediate concerns—having just spent some time with Professor Kilmer, I am confident that he is none of those things the agency worries about. In fact, I was deeply impressed."

Silla felt a pit in her stomach. The last thing she needed to hear right now was how great Kilmer was.

"You thought he was that smart?"

"I wouldn't say smart, exactly—although yes, he's obviously very smart. But it's more about how he puts things together. It's how he sees things. Quite remarkable. And his ability to convey it. You can't imagine how many bright people, even people much smarter than Professor Kilmer, will simply lose their ability to speak when the president of the United States is in the room. We didn't have that problem tonight."

"He wasn't nervous?"

"He was at first. But then it was like he flipped a switch. After that, no sign of it. Quite frankly, I'm a little annoyed that I didn't instill more fear in him." Whitman chuckled. "You know, I've read one of his books. *Heirs of Herodotus*. If you ever get a chance, it's worth reading. But he's even better in person."

Yeah, tell me about it.

"Actually, Madam President, I've read all of Professor Kilmer's books," Silla confessed.

"Is that right? Had you met him before?"

"No, ma'am. The first time was tonight."

"And what did you think of him?"

"I'm not sure how you mean."

"Well, I had always pictured him as being much older. I'm not sure whether Zack ever mentioned how old he was, but I certainly didn't expect someone close to my son's age!"

"I know what you mean." Silla told Whitman about the incident at the airfield—when they mistook Kilmer for a young porter—and it gave the president a good laugh. The scene in the Treaty Room seemed unreal to Silla; she was sitting with the president and chatting like they were childhood friends.

Maybe it was that feeling of unreality, or her lack of sleep, or the sense that Whitman would understand—or maybe it was just how badly Silla wanted to get her thoughts out of her own head—but for some reason, she decided to take a chance.

"Agent Lane was giving me a hard time about Professor Kilmer after that episode," Silla confessed.

"How so?" Whitman looked at Silla like a mother might—curious about what's going on in her daughter's life.

"Agent Lane and I happen to be related—so it wasn't out of line or anything. But he was just pointing out how Professor Kilmer is smart, funny, young…"

"Handsome?"

Silla looked away. "I don't think… I'm not sure I looked at him in that way, Madam President."

Whitman laughed. "Agent Silla, we can't have people with visual acuity problems working at the CIA."

Silla blushed. "I don't know what to say about that. Sure, he's handsome. But lots of people are handsome."

"That's true."

"Although, it's not always the case that you find so many qualities you like all in one place." Silla stopped herself, realizing she'd said a little too much. Everything up to this point had still been abstract, not personal. This had crossed that line. She wasn't sure how comfortable she felt having this conversation with herself, much less with the president of the United States.

But Whitman seemed unbothered. "Listen, sweetheart—you feel how you feel. No benefit in trying to deny it."

Silla let out the breath she had been holding. "I'm not really *sure* how I feel. Or why. It's probably nothing. I think I just need some sleep."

"You're a smart woman. You'll figure it out," Whitman said with a smile. "But I have to hand it to you, Agent Silla, you sure know how to pick the absolute worst time in history to start falling in love. Couldn't you have tracked him down earlier? Maybe after the first time you read one of his books?"

Silla laughed, even as she tripped over the word Whitman had used. She was sure it wasn't the right one. She didn't have the ability to start falling in love with someone she just met, even if there was a connection already in place. But whatever it was, Whitman was right about two things. First, Silla felt how she felt, and it wasn't worth denying it. And second, this truly was the absolute worst time in history to be feeling anything for anyone.

Whitman put her hand on Silla's shoulder, as if she were about to say something more—but she remained silent.

"Madam President, is everything okay?"

"I was just remembering when Jack and I first met. You know, it's amazing how little time it takes to tell someone how you feel, and how much time we spend agonizing over whether to say it."

Then Whitman stood, and Silla followed her lead.

"Thank you, Madam President. I know I took a lot of your time—I'm sorry about that. And I hope I didn't say anything that was out of line."

"Not at all. Now get some rest. If you're uncomfortable here, we can find you an extra bedroom."

"No, ma'am. I'm perfectly comfortable here."

"Well, if you fall asleep, don't worry. No one else will bother you now." Whitman procured a blanket from one of the cabinets and placed it on the couch. Then she turned out the lights and left the room.

Nothing had materially changed in the past few minutes, but Silla felt better about things; some of the fog had lifted. A thought came to her, and before she could second-guess herself, she took out her phone and typed out a message. Then she put her feet back on the couch, made herself more compact and comfortable, and pulled on the blanket. She had spent the last 15 minutes chatting it up with the president of the United States, but when she closed her eyes, it was once again Kilmer who was in her thoughts. She didn't mind it so much this time.

It is what it is.

~ 32 ~

Kilmer looked at his watch. 3:50 a.m. Twenty minutes earlier, he had awakened to the sound of a door being shut, and sleep had eluded him ever since. There was too much on his mind. The White House. The president. The aliens. The crisis. The upcoming meeting. Agent Silla...

He knew he was unlikely to see her again, and it was not a pleasant thought. A few minutes ago, Kilmer had considered walking back to the Treaty Room to strike up a conversation. If he couldn't sleep, he might as well get some more information and be better prepared for the meeting. Even if they only made small talk, the idea of spending more time with Silla was undeniably appealing. He caught himself thinking about how exactly he would start a conversation with her if he decided to go for it—and was both horrified and embarrassed to realize he was acting like a teenager.

The worst thing that can happen is she doesn't want to talk. That's not so bad compared to the possibility that we're all dead tomorrow.

Kilmer rolled off the bed, turned on the light, and put on his shoes. Then he looked himself in the mirror and moved some hair around. It would just have to do.

When he reached the door to the Treaty Room, he found it closed. He thought about knocking, but he didn't want the noise to travel down the hall to the president's room. Instead, he just opened the door as quietly as he could. The room was dark, save for some streetlight coming through the windows overlooking the Treaty Table. His eyes were still adjusting, but Silla was nowhere to be seen. It occurred to him that she had probably left; that must have been the sound he heard earlier. Kilmer was more than a little disappointed.

He was just about to leave when he saw something on the floor. Shoes? He took a few steps into the room—and then he saw her. Agent Silla was snuggled up in one corner of the couch, her eyes closed, a slight smile on her face, and a lock of hair resting on her cheek. She looked stunning. But his delight at seeing her was only momentary. She was fast asleep. They wouldn't be able to spend any time together after all.

Silla's blanket had slid halfway to the floor and was now covering only her legs. Kilmer pulled it up to her shoulders, as gently as he could, knowing full well that it would make for a strange scene if she were to suddenly wake up. Then he backed away, slowly, and headed for the door.

"You don't have to leave."

Kilmer stopped—still facing the door. "I'm sorry. I didn't mean to wake you. You should get some rest."

"Well, you probably should have thought about that before you treated me like a damsel in distress and fixed my blanket for me."

* * * * * * * * *

Silla had been asleep when Kilmer entered the room, but some slight sound had awoken her. She had opened her eyes only for a moment, but it was long enough to see him standing by the door—and for her heart to skip a beat. She was still trying to work out why she didn't just say hello when she sensed him moving closer to her. A moment later, he was lifting the blanket to cover her up.

Oh, no. A gentleman as well. She certainly couldn't open her eyes at this point. It would be too awkward for him. For them both.

And then he walked away. By the time she summoned the courage to open her eyes, he was already at the door. *It's now or never,* she thought. *As in, truly never.* That's when she found the words that stopped him in his tracks.

Kilmer turned around and walked back to her, still keeping his distance. "I'm sorry, I was just trying to make sure you were comfortable. I tried not to disturb you."

"And yet, here I am. Awake. I was a little bored earlier, so falling asleep was a nice change. But since you've decided I don't deserve to get any rest, I'm afraid you'll just have to stay and keep me company for a little while." Her boldness came as a surprise even to her. Maybe she had a switch that she could turn on, just like him.

Kilmer sat down in the armchair. She was slightly disappointed that he didn't join her on the couch. Then again, that might have been a bit of a turnoff.

"Okay, Agent Silla. What would you like to talk about?"

"How about we start with why you came here. I thought you were supposed to be resting."

"I couldn't sleep. So, I had a choice between talking to myself and talking to you. Talking with you seemed much more interesting—and I thought I might learn something that's worth knowing."

"Do you have more questions about the extra-terrestrials?"

"Yes. And… well, you know a lot about me, and I know almost nothing about you. Seems a bit unfair."

Silla thought she might be blushing and was suddenly glad for the darkness in the room.

"Then we might have a problem," she said. "I don't talk about myself to people who call me Agent Silla. My name is Renata. Almost everyone calls me Ren."

"And if I wanted to distinguish myself from all the rest?" Kilmer asked. "Silla is a beautiful name. Does anyone call you Silla?"

Silla was taken aback. Only one person had ever called her that—her grandfather. When she was a little girl, she was closer to him than to anyone. He always called her Silla—and sometimes Silly Silla, but she wasn't about to reveal that. He passed away when she was eleven, and no one had called her Silla since.

"Professor Kilmer, you would be in perfect company if you chose to call me Silla. I won't mind it at all. Does that make you Kilmer? Or do you enjoy being called Professor?"

"I could afford to hear it less often. Kilmer will do just fine."

"Just fine?"

"More than fine. In fact, if you ever go back to calling me Professor, I'll take it to mean that you've entirely given up on us."

"On… *us?* Is that suddenly a thing?" she asked casually.

"Well, here we are making all this progress. I'd hate to have to start all over. You know, it wasn't easy to walk all this way to come see you."

Silla could relate perfectly well to that sentiment, but she wasn't about to let on. "You must not walk very much, Kilmer. You were only about thirty feet away."

"Seemed much farther."

Kilmer's eyes hadn't adjusted completely to the darkness, but enough to catch her smile.

"Well," she said. "Now what?"

"Now we get to know each other."

She looked at her watch. "It's four in the morning, Kilmer. And you have a meeting at eight. How much can you possibly get to know me?"

Kilmer leaned just a little closer and looked into her eyes.

"Silla?" he said softly.

"Yes?" she whispered back.

"We have time."

They looked at each other in silence, neither of them wanting to disrupt the moment.

"Do we?" she finally asked.

"I'm sure of it."

"And what if the world ends tomorrow?"

Kilmer smiled. He reached for her hand and risked taking it in his. She could feel the butterflies in her stomach as she wrapped her fingers around his, but only very lightly. Just enough to let him know the risk had been worth it.

"We won't let it," he said.

"You can promise me that?"

Kilmer smiled. "I think I'm supposed to say yes to that. But I don't think I can."

Silla laughed. "Well, you're not much of a hero then. A hero would have promised me the Moon and the stars. You can't even promise me the Earth."

"I don't claim to be a hero. But I'm no villain either. I won't make promises that I'm not sure I can keep. As for saving the world, all I can promise you is that I would die trying—if that's what it came down to." He paused. "But it would be a real shame if it came to that. All that effort and I don't even get to see you afterwards."

Something in the way he said it... it wasn't just a good line.

She looked into his eyes. "Okay, Kilmer, I'm game. Let's chat a while longer. But on two conditions."

"And what might those conditions be?"

"First, I get to learn about you at least as much as you learn about me."

"Is that like a CIA special agent thing? Not wanting to give someone an information advantage over you?"

"Uh, no Kilmer. It's a decent human being thing. Not wanting to be so self-absorbed as to only talk about myself. Are you familiar with the notion?" She went from just holding his hand to interlocking her fingers with his.

He laughed. "Okay, I agree to your first condition. What's the second?"

"You have to come sit next to me."

Kilmer kept her hand in his as he moved to the couch—sitting close, but not too close. She turned ever so slightly toward him, as though she hadn't really meant to reduce the distance between them by doing so.

"I hope you won't read too much into the invitation to sit next to me," she said sternly.

"Don't worry, I won't. I don't really like to brag, Silla, but I'm sort of the world's expert on not making dangerous assumptions."

She laughed.

"So why am I really here?" he asked.

"I didn't want you to be uncomfortable. We have a lot to talk about."

She moved closer—again, almost imperceptibly.

"After all, you've convinced me... We have time."

~ 33 ~

Kilmer and Silla talked for almost three hours, without interruption, except for the one time when Silla needed to check a text message. The early morning brought daylight into the room, but they barely noticed. At some point— neither of them would have been able to explain precisely when or how—they had managed to eliminate the distance between them almost entirely. Kilmer's arms were now wrapped around her, and she was leaning back and snuggling into him. His chin rested lightly on her shoulder, which caused their cheeks to brush against each other at times—he had to resist the urge to kiss her whenever she turned and locked eyes with him. He held her close, his hands resting on her stomach, and he wondered how hard someone had to work to have abs like that. Her hands rested on top of his, and she occasionally doodled on them with her fingertips while they chatted.

They talked about everything they could think of, but without rushing through any of it. Silla felt herself come close to tears once—when she talked about losing her father—and she noticed that Kilmer held her just a bit more tightly then. She told him how hard her father worked to make sure her birthdays were special, how he always sat with her late into the night while she did her homework, even though he couldn't help her with any of it, and how he made her promise that she would never think ill of her mother, even though she had abandoned them.

Kilmer told her about his parents, his childhood, and what little he remembered about life before the Kilmers. He also told her something he had only ever told one other person. Eight years ago, in Central Africa, he had advised the president of Cameroon *not* to pursue a course of action that they both believed would save lives. Instead, Kilmer proposed an alternative strategy that, although costly in the short run, would ultimately protect many more. It was an opportunity to save a far greater number of people, but it was still not an easy decision to make. A lot of innocent people died in the weeks that followed—men, women, and children who would have lived if not for Kilmer's advice. But that wasn't nearly the worst of it. A few months later, when it came time to follow through on the rest of Kilmer's strategy, national elections were just around the corner, and the president was no longer in a position to take the political risks necessary to implement the rest of the plan. Kilmer pleaded with him, but to no avail. They had sacrificed all those lives for nothing.

"I screwed up," Kilmer told Silla. "I should have been able to see it—how things would play out, I mean. Seems obvious now—but even back then, I should have known enough not to make such a terrible mistake. After that happened... I didn't advise anyone for almost two years. I just wasn't willing to offer advice unless I was *sure* it was the right call. I know there's no such thing as being sure, but it took a long time to be okay with that again—to even trust my own judgment. It still doesn't change what I did. I know that. And I'm not religious, Silla, but for this... for the people who died... I still pray for forgiveness. It never leaves me—the guilt of it. I can't rationalize it away, no matter how hard I try. I know it's selfish to even *try* to rationalize something like that away. I know that. But I still try."

Silla had taken his hands in hers. "Making a call like that takes courage, Kilmer. And it only hurts if you have a good heart. I know it's not my place to say this, but I think your mom would be proud of you. You're using your gifts—just like she wanted you to. I think she would be glad that you didn't stop trying to help after that."

Kilmer couldn't remember ever having been so unguarded, but something about Silla made sharing even his most intimate thoughts feel entirely natural. She challenged him, but she didn't judge. She was inquisitive, but not presumptuous. She was a stranger, but only in name—she already knew him better than most people did. Nielsen was the only other person whom Kilmer had told about the Cameroon incident. When the vice president invited him to advise during the Gulf of Aden crisis, Kilmer thought he had a right to know what had happened. But telling Silla was altogether different. It wasn't out of a sense of obligation. It was in search of solace.

The daylight had been dropping hints for a while, but it was already 6:50 by the time Kilmer finally glanced at his watch. "I think you're going to have to leave soon," he revealed reluctantly. "It's almost seven."

"You're kicking me off my own couch?" she joked.

"No, I'm pretty sure Agent Liu is the one responsible for doing that. Is he going to meet me here or downstairs?"

"You seem very eager to meet Agent Liu. Should I be jealous?"

"I just don't want you to get in trouble if he walks in here."

"Kilmer, I have something to tell you... Agent Liu isn't coming. I texted him a few hours ago to tell him that since I need to be at the White House for a 9 a.m. meeting anyway, I'll take you to your meeting at eight. I'm sorry to disappoint you, but you're stuck with me."

Kilmer moved Silla's hair to the side so he could get a better look at her. "Are you serious?"

"Yup."

"So, what you're saying is..."

She smiled. "We have time."

Kilmer considered it for a moment. "Now, if my calculations are correct, you must have texted Agent Liu about this even before I came into the room. Which means you'd already decided that you wanted to be here when I woke up."

Silla bit her lower lip and smiled, all but admitting she'd been found out.

"I must say, this seems highly unprofessional," Kilmer complained, trying his best to sound indignant.

"Are you going to turn me in?"

"I'm not sure what choice I have—unless there was a legitimate reason for you to stay longer."

"Don't flatter yourself, Kilmer. Of course there was a legitimate reason."

"Let's hear it then. I'm listening."

"That's your problem, Kilmer. Always listening for one clue or another. Just stop listening for a moment—you'll be surprised by how much you learn."

Then she turned toward him, wrapped her arms around his neck, and kissed him—for a very long time.

~ 34 ~

~ Interlude: A different time ~

Kilmer looked across the field. The two soldiers who had stormed into the kill-zone were now on the ground, bleeding. Possibly dead. He looked farther out in the direction of the perimeter. Secretary Strauss and General Allen were both shouting orders. The soldiers around them were struggling to figure out which orders to follow. Perez was yelling into a phone, almost certainly talking to Whitman on the other end, trying to explain how all hell had suddenly broken loose.

Then he saw Silla—and his heart broke into a thousand pieces. He lowered the gun, now pointing it towards the ground. She had pushed her way through the crowd of soldiers and was shouting something in his direction. She was furious—and he could make out the tears on her face. He couldn't hear any of the words she was saying, but he was terrified. A soldier tried to grab Silla, but she pushed him off and the man stumbled backward. She was squarely in the kill-zone now and walking toward where the soldiers had fallen. He screamed for her to stop. She didn't hear him. Or she didn't care.

And then, suddenly, Lane emerged from the crowd and raced toward her. *Thank God, Lane.* He caught up to her and tackled her to the ground before she could move any further into the kill-zone. She screamed and punched at him, but he wouldn't let her go.

The sound behind Kilmer grew louder. It was almost deafening.

He knew that Silla would never forgive him. Never.

But—hopefully—she would understand.

Silla stopped trying to fight off Lane and turned toward Kilmer. He saw the look on her face. It was the look of someone who had experienced the ultimate betrayal. Someone who would *never* understand.

I love you, he whispered. He knew she might only be able to make out the movement of his lips.

We have time, Silla whispered back. *We do,* she pleaded. *Please, Kilmer!*

His eyes welled up.

He would never forgive himself either—but he wasn't about to break his promise to her.

He wasn't about to let the world come to an end when there was still a chance.

I'm sorry.

He dropped the gun.

There was a bright flash of light.

And then everything went black.

~ **End of interlude** ~

Part III

the strategist

~ 35 ~

Day 15. 7:45 a.m.

Kilmer and Silla entered the room fifteen minutes before the meeting was scheduled to start, the physical distance between them calibrated to be the absolute minimum acceptable by professional standards. A few others were already seated, and Silla made some introductions, including with CIA Director Druckman.

"I'll be honest, it always makes me a little nervous when a teacher walks into the room," Druckman joked. "I sure hope you grade on a curve."

Kilmer smiled respectfully. "Don't worry, sir. The person who knows the least about the subject doesn't get to do the grading."

Kilmer and Silla dropped their phones in the metal box and made their way to the two seats that were placed against the wall opposite the door. As they sat down, Secretary Strauss walked in. He was on a call, so Kilmer decided against introducing himself. If Strauss noticed his presence, he didn't show it.

Kilmer turned to Silla and whispered, "Do you think I should have worn a tie?"

"I don't think your attire is what people around here are worried about right now," she whispered back.

Kilmer nodded.

"But to answer your question: yes, you should have worn a tie. Who walks around thinking they don't need to wear a tie when they meet the president of the United States?"

Kilmer frowned as Silla stifled a chuckle.

The last to arrive were VP Nielsen, National Security Advisor Garcia, General Allen, and... *Trina Morgan?*

Nielsen left the group and made his way around the table, eventually reaching Kilmer and shaking his hand. "Glad you're here, Professor." Then he turned to Silla. "And nice to see you again as well—"

"Agent Silla," she said before Nielsen had a chance to stumble on her name.

"Yes, Agent Silla. I believe you'll be at my nine o'clock with Art. Is that right?"

"That's correct, Mr. Vice President."

"Good. I look forward to the update." Nielsen turned to face Kilmer again. "The president would like you to meet us in the Oval Office at 9:30. Joana will meet you here when this meeting ends; she'll handle the logistics. Does that work?"

"Sounds good."

Nielsen continued his journey around the table, shaking hands and making small talk.

Kilmer turned to Silla. "Wow. Another invitation from the president. I'm starting to think she doesn't really care whether I wear a tie."

Silla rolled her eyes.

Trina Morgan saw Kilmer and waved. When she came over, she greeted Silla warmly—they apparently knew each other—and then shook Kilmer's hand. "Professor! Ms. Garcia said you'd be here. So good to see you."

"How have you been, Trina?

"Quite well. Except, of course, for what's happening right now."

Someone walked toward them as if to say hello, but it turned out he only wanted to close the blinds on the window next to Kilmer. Trina, meanwhile, handed Kilmer a sheet of paper with her cell number. "Please reach out if you have time."

"I look forward to catching up."

Trina walked away and Kilmer put the number in his pocket. He looked over at Silla as they waited for the meeting to start. She caught him staring from the corner of her eye.

"What is it?" she asked.

"Nothing," he whispered. "I was just... admiring, I suppose."

"I'm pretty sure that's not the work President Whitman invited you here to do," she said without looking his way. "If I'm going to be a distraction, I can get Agent Liu to take my place."

"Don't worry, Silla. When the action starts, nothing in the world can distract me."

Silla turned toward him slowly, crossed her legs in a subtle but decidedly sultry fashion, moved a lock of hair from the side of her face, and looked him in the eye. "Is that a challenge?" she whispered.

Kilmer stared at the vision in front of him. "No, Agent Silla, it is nothing of the kind. I retract my statement." He turned away from her. "Now please stop doing... whatever it is you're doing."

Silla acknowledged the win with a gracious smile, and Kilmer tried to push the image she had painted out of his mind.

A few minutes later, Nielsen stood up to address the gathering. "Thank you, everyone, for being on time."

Kilmer leaned back in the chair and folded his arms. He brought the entire room into view, seeing not only Nielsen, but all the expressions and movements around the table. His breathing slowed, as it always did in such situations, and he narrowed his eyes slightly in concentration. All else faded away as he turned his attention to what was about to unfold.

~ 36 ~

Art Capella was headed to the White House. The report that he and Silla were about to share with Nielsen had been updated as recently as thirty minutes ago. The results were preliminary, but important enough to share.

Almost everyone who was in the loop was focused on *ET-1*. That was the name given to the spacecraft that had attacked the Moon and was now making its way to Station Zero. One of Agent Silla's teams, however, was tasked with collecting and analyzing data associated with distal activity, with "distal" loosely defined as anything happening farther away from Earth than where ET-1 was located at any given time. This team continued to track the other three spacecraft, which were now collectively referred to as *the reserves*.

ET-1 was estimated to be 110 yards long, roughly the length of the International Space Station, the longest spacecraft that humans had ever put into space. The reserves were at least five times larger than that. They had moved on a few occasions, but always seemed to revert to a location approximately 600 million miles from Earth.

The update for Nielsen was focused entirely on the recent behavior of the three reserves.

Art reached for his cell phone as he drove. He was tempted—and not for the first time that week—to call his ex-wife. He had never figured out what he would say to her if she answered. Would he tell her what was happening? Would he ask her to move in with family in rural Wisconsin for a while, just as a precaution? Neither of those was an option from a legal or professional standpoint. Maybe he could just apologize for how he'd screwed things up between them, and then leave her wondering why he'd suddenly become a more decent human being.

Art put his cell phone away, as he always did. And he felt terrible, as he always did. He thought about the life he had created for himself—or rather, the life he had destroyed. Estranged, not only from his wife, but also from his two children. He had convinced himself that it was the price you had to pay if you wanted to devote yourself to fighting for the greater good—to do the work of heroes. You had to be willing to lose everything else.

Art wasn't sure he believed that anymore. There were no heroes left. More likely, there had never been any heroes to begin with. In all his years, Art had certainly never met one. Everyone thought they were doing God's work, but when you put it all together, you ended up with something only the devil could be proud of.

Art almost laughed at the absurdity of it all. Humans didn't need an alien race to come over and screw everything up for them. They could manage that perfectly well on their own.

But at the end of the day, Art's cynicism, although profound, was of little significance. He would still do his job—not because it was all he had left, or because he was damn good at it, both of which were true. He would do it because he knew that if there was any chance of salvation for Arthur Capella, it was based entirely on his willingness to continue sacrificing everything in the hope that he might one day end up doing some actual good.

Heirs of Herodotus by D. Kilmer.
Excerpt from Chapter 1.

Society cannot afford to forget the lessons of the past—nor to learn the wrong lessons. But there is a third danger—and it is the greatest threat of all, if only because it is the least well recognized. **Humanity can no longer afford to have only a handful of its citizens and leaders understand the lessons of history.** We cannot count on a select few to be the caretakers of knowledge. **The elite guardians of wisdom will be rendered useless if the masses are incapable of understanding their language, unable to appreciate their concerns, or uninterested even in considering their advice. This danger is not new, but it is always magnified during those times when a population is empowered at a faster rate than it is educated.** And it is worst in societies where the value of any idea is measured only after it is filtered through the lens of politics, partisanship, or ideology.

Of the diabolically complicated Schleswig-Holstein affair—as pertained to Denmark and Prussia in the mid-19th century—Lord Palmerston is said to have remarked: "Only three people have ever really understood the Schleswig-Holstein business—the Prince Consort, who is dead, a German professor, who has gone mad, and I, who have forgotten all about it."

We can no longer rely only on princes, professors, and lords to understand the affairs of the world. The professors and Palmerstons of the world must educate—and hence enable—the rest. And they must do it soon. **The time will come when the masses no longer listen to their advice—when expertise is unrecognizable because the gulf between those who know and those who don't is too wide to bridge. That day is almost upon us.**

Silla had rushed off to see Art and Nielsen as soon as the 8 a.m. meeting adjourned, but Kilmer found Joana waiting for him when he exited the conference room.

"So, how would you like to spend the next twenty-five minutes?" she asked.

"I just need a place to sit. Anywhere is fine."

"Sure. We can put you close to the Oval Office. That will make it easy to grab you for the 9:30."

A few minutes later, they were back in the West Wing. They passed by the Oval Office and Joana peeked into a room to see if it was occupied. She gave Kilmer a smile. *Success.* They entered.

A minute later he was seated at an enormous table that took up most of the space in what he recognized as the Cabinet Room. He had seen the room on TV; journalists were occasionally invited inside when the president wanted a meeting to be publicized. Kilmer hesitated, but then decided to take the middle seat on the long side of the table—near the windows overlooking the Rose Garden. This was where the president always sat during those meetings. *Hey, why not, right?*

Okay, now think.

Kilmer had been impressed with what he'd seen in the meeting—an open and honest discussion, with good arguments made. But there were a few problems. Many of the analogies left out important details, and when the historical record was seen in its entirety, it told a slightly different story. It was also unclear why the aliens would announce their intentions if they planned to launch a devastating attack as their next step. If logic was at all relevant here, this should not be the endgame. There would have to be additional moves and countermoves before the aliens took that kind of action. That was good news. It reduced the need to launch a nuclear weapon that, as General Allen had warned, could be perceived by the aliens as an attack. Based on everything he knew so far, Kilmer believed that a show of force should *not* be the next step.

But it's what we don't know that should worry us.

He thought back to his conversation with VP Nielsen and President Whitman the night before—only a few hours ago, really. There had been far too many ideas, assumptions, and questions floating around in his mind, and in that room. It was the same during the 8 a.m. meeting. He needed to separate the signal from the noise. Kilmer took out a pen and found the piece of paper Trina had handed him earlier.

What does it all boil down to?

He started to write, cross out, reframe, reorganize, circle, connect, and scribble, his pace quickening as things started to fall into place. Ten minutes later, he had something. It wasn't exactly Churchill's Key—it didn't reveal the nature of alien self-interest or what was driving them—but it was, quite possibly, the key *to* the key.

And yet, it was the one thing no one else seemed bothered by at all.

~ 39 ~

Nielsen, Art, and Silla were seated in the vice president's office.

"The lunar attack definitely got our attention," Art explained. "And we started to focus all our efforts on figuring out what ET-1 might do next. That is, until Agent Silla asked us to consider another possibility: What if ET-1 wasn't trying to get our attention? What if they just wanted us to *stop* paying attention to everything else?"

Nielsen leaned back. "You mean, a distraction. Like an Operation Bodyguard. What we did in World War II."

Silla responded. "Exactly. Let's get Hitler to focus on Pas-de-Calais while the real landing is planned for Normandy. We don't have eyes everywhere in space, so we can't always track the reserves. When they move, we usually just wait for them to return, some hours or days later, to what seems like home base for them—600 million miles away. But this time when they disappeared, we decided not to wait. It took a lot of resources, but we found them. It turns out the reserves are only 3 million miles away now—and they're no longer hanging together. They seem to be approaching Earth from three completely different directions, as we might expect if they were planning to land at locations that are maximally distant from one another."

Nielsen considered that for a moment. "Like a three-dimensional pincer movement."

Art weighed in. "Whether they are in an attack formation, we can't be sure. It's one of many hypotheses. Of course, it's the possibility that concerns us most."

"If they *are* planning to attack—or to land—what locations might they be targeting? Is it possible to know?"

Art looked to Silla, who explained. "It's a multivariate problem. Even if we assume that they plan to make a direct, line-of-sight approach to Earth, their point of contact will vary as the Earth rotates—their target depends on the time of day that they make their move. We also need to consider Earth's movement through space. If the reserves don't reposition as the Earth travels in its orbit, their angles of approach start to converge. Imagine just two spacecraft, one hovering above the North Pole and the other above the South Pole. Their expected points of contact are maximally distant at that moment. But suppose the Earth moves away and the spacecraft remain stationary. The farther away the Earth moves, the closer the expected points of contact get to one another—again assuming a linear trajectory."

"So, if they want to stay positioned, relative to Earth, exactly as they are right now, they have to move as well."

"That's right. But they are in perfect position—at this time—for what you described as a pincer movement."

Nielsen exhaled audibly, and then looked at his watch. "What else do I need to know?" he asked.

"Just that we'll continue to monitor things," Art replied. "There's too little data to detect patterns. We're looking at one snapshot in time and making lots of assumptions. But we wanted you to have this information ASAP."

~ 40 ~

President Whitman, VP Nielsen, Chief of Staff Perez, General Allen, and Secretary Strauss were already assembled when Kilmer entered the room for the 9:30 meeting. Under normal circumstances, he would have taken in the scene—his first time in the Oval Office—and tried hard to stay calm. But Kilmer wasn't thinking about the room, or its history, or the people who had occupied it over the years. He was thinking only about Churchill's Key.

After Perez and Strauss introduced themselves to Kilmer, they all took their seats, Whitman and Nielsen on armchairs and the others on couches. Kilmer noticed a large carafe and some cups on the coffee table but decided not to be the first to help himself.

Whitman started immediately. "Gentlemen, I had an opportunity to observe the meeting. Thank you, Zack, for running things. Strauss, can I assume that you are still in favor of a show of force?"

"I am, Madam President. Only as a means of signaling our capabilities."

Whitman turned to General Allen. "And Casey, am I correct in surmising that you are against the proposal?"

General Allen nodded. "As things stand, that is correct. Unless there is new information to consider, I am not in favor of the proposal."

"Okay. Before I ask Professor Kilmer to weigh in as well, I'd like Zack to update us on some new information that Triad has just relayed. Zack, please tell everyone what you told me a few minutes ago."

As Nielsen shared Silla's analysis with the group, Strauss nodded along. He had an expression of unjoyful satisfaction on his face, as if he'd hoped for better news but was unsurprised that the report only reinforced the need to follow his advice.

Two minutes into Nielsen's report, Kilmer decided to pour himself a cup of coffee. He knew this might constitute a violation of White House etiquette, but it didn't look like an invitation was coming anytime soon. He was relieved when Perez followed suit, although the first cup the chief of staff filled was for the president. Whitman smiled at Kilmer, as though he had behaved no worse—nor any better—than expected.

Strauss took over as soon as Nielsen had finished. "Madam President, I think this only underscores the need to execute an unambiguous show of force. If the aliens *are* getting into attack formation, it's now or never."

Whitman looked to the others.

Perez weighed in. "How do we know this is an attack formation, and not merely an attempt at reconnaissance? How do we know they're not simply imaging the planet, or analyzing our atmosphere, or some such thing?"

"We can't know," responded Allen. "The formation is consistent with a certain type of attack, but we would have said the same thing if the three spacecraft were approaching side by side. That, too, is an attack formation—just a different kind."

"Are you saying this doesn't concern you at all?" Strauss asked General Allen.

"It absolutely concerns me. But it does not make a show of force any less risky than before. The aliens are just as likely to misinterpret our actions as an attempted attack. We might still trigger a war."

Perez contemplated Allen's point. "A show of force is still just as *risky*, but the new information appears to make it more *important* than before. All else equal, our inaction seems more dangerous now than it did earlier."

"Precisely," said Strauss.

Whitman turned to Kilmer. "Professor, I'd like to hear from you as well. What are your thoughts?"

"Of course, Madam President. If you don't mind, let me first address the narrower question that has just been raised. *Does this new information change anything?* I agree that it increases the risk of inaction—if we assume the aliens are getting into attack formation *and* if we assume it's because they plan to attack imminently."

Strauss looked mildly pleased—the professor appeared to be on his side.

"In other words," Kilmer continued, "there are two conditions that must be met before we conclude that there is now a greater risk of inaction. But I'd like to suggest—*strongly*—that at least one of the conditions is *not* met."

Strauss looked slightly frustrated, but curious.

Kilmer went on. "I won't pretend to know what a proper attack formation looks like in an inter-galactic war—or on Earth, for that matter—but let's just assume that the aliens *are* poised for an attack. The reason that doesn't raise my level of concern is that I don't believe that their next action, even if we fail to act, will be to attack."

He explained how presumptive it would be for the aliens to conclude that "no action" meant humans were weak or vulnerable, and why it made little sense for ET-1 to give fair warning if the goal was to annihilate Earth as the very next step. "Where I come out, ultimately, is that a show of force is probably too risky, and that it provides no obvious benefit," he concluded. "If they can destroy us and intend to do so, they're not acting like it. And if they have the capability to annihilate us in a first strike, a show of force will not help us anyway. I concede that a show of force *might* be helpful in deterring an invasion or occupation, if that's what they're planning, but I don't think we have to make that call yet."

Whitman looked to the others. To her surprise, Strauss didn't jump in to offer an immediate rebuttal.

Perez was the first to speak. "Professor Kilmer, your analysis is quite helpful. But something puzzles me. You've just given a somewhat optimistic assessment of the situation, but when I spoke to President Whitman briefly this morning—after she had chatted with you overnight—I walked away with the impression that the situation was *more* serious than we imagined. I'm trying to reconcile these two impressions."

Kilmer nodded. And then, without a warning, he stood up, coffee in hand, and started to pace. The looks of bemusement, especially from General Allen and Salvo Perez, suggested that his behavior was, at the very least, unexpected.

"You're right," Kilmer noted. "My sense is that the situation is not so desperate *at the current moment*—at least not in ways that we can control. But I think we're not worried *enough* about how things will play out if we survive in the short term."

Strauss jumped in. "I'm sorry, Professor, but if they are *not* planning to attack, as you seem to think, why is the situation worse *after* we avoid war?"

"To put it simply, Secretary Strauss, it's because as hard as it is for us to predict what happens tomorrow, it is much more difficult to imagine what will happen a year or a decade from now. We don't know whether they have three reserve spacecraft or three million. We don't know whether they are here to learn, to profit, to colonize, to feast, or to do something else entirely. We don't know when or why their intentions might change.

"If they have the technology to destroy us—as we all seem to consider highly plausible—then avoiding a war today provides only temporary relief. Because what hangs overhead is not an alien spacecraft, it is the Sword of Damocles itself. For how long, do you suppose, can we keep it from falling?"

Kilmer turned to Whitman. "Madam President, I continue to believe that humanity will not survive unless we understand what really drives them. There are countless unanswered questions, but the one that I would most like to get answered is the one that's nagged me from the start: Why would the aliens visit our planet *now?*"

He let the question hang in the air for a moment before continuing.

"Our planet has been in existence for over four billion years. What are the odds that they happen to arrive within a few decades of when we might be able to detect them? Maybe they visited earlier but no one was around to notice. Maybe it's pure coincidence that this happened in our lifetimes. But I suspect not. I believe that the timing of their arrival is an important clue. I think it could be the key to unraveling the entire mystery. Which means it could also be the key to our survival."

General Allen leaned forward. "Professor Kilmer, I want to understand why you think *this* is the most important question. I might have said the most important question pertains to their military capabilities. Secretary Strauss might have said the main issue is whether they are planning to attack. How are those questions less important?"

"I want to be clear, General. Your questions are not less important. They are only less *fundamental*. And in the long run, I believe the fundamentals are what win out. Whatever their military capabilities and whatever their intentions, the greatest threat to us—if we think in terms of generations— stems from their underlying interests. What they *can* do or *want* to do might change. What we must understand is the constant: *what drives them*. And I believe that figuring out what brought them here, at this time, might help answer that question."

After some further discussion, Whitman reined in the conversation, thanked everyone for their views, and then announced her decision: she would not be moving forward with a show of force—at least for now.

As the group disbanded, Whitman looked over at Kilmer. "Professor Kilmer, please stick around for a moment." Then she turned to her chief of staff. "You too, Salvo."

As the others departed, Perez and Kilmer used the opportunity to check their phones. Kilmer saw that Silla had left a message a short while earlier. *Heading home for a shower and a nap. Back to work in the eve. Text you later.* He smiled.

"Gentlemen," Whitman began, "I'd like the two of you to—" She stopped mid-sentence.

Kilmer looked up to see Whitman staring at Perez, who was eyeing his phone with grave concern.

"What is it, Salvo?"

"Madam President. Art sent a message five minutes ago. The reserve spacecraft have moved again. They are now only 100,000 miles from Earth."

"What about ET-1?"

"ET-1 appears to be on the move as well. It's headed straight for Station Zero."

Whitman turned to Kilmer. "Well, Professor, it seems to me that your theories are about to be put to the ultimate test. We're at the endgame."

Kilmer shook his head. "I'm not so sure, Madam President. I think the game has only just begun."

Heirs of Herodotus by D. Kilmer.
Excerpt from Chapter 3.

Before we lay blame on those who came before us, we owe it to them—and to ourselves—to understand why they failed. Chamberlain made only one crucial mistake—to accept less than he had portrayed as his minimum demands—and it had two fatal consequences: he lost credibility and left too strong an impression in Hitler's mind that England wanted to avoid war at all costs. This happened first at Berchtesgaden, then in Bad Godesberg, and only later in Munich.

Apart from that, Chamberlain was simply dealt a terrible hand. His countrymen were unwilling to go to war over Czechoslovakia—if he had threatened war over it, and Hitler called his bluff, he would have lost even more credibility. England also overestimated German strength; Churchill, too, believed Hitler was far stronger than he was. Finally, even before Chamberlain came into office, the world had failed to punish Germany, Italy, and Japan for their brazen violations of the Covenant of the League of Nations. Had their actions been checked earlier, Hitler would have had neither the strength nor the resolve to do what he did in 1938.

Chamberlain's mistake was not that he appeased Hitler, but that he did it in such a way that—even when the British were finally ready to go to war—Hitler couldn't believe England would really fight to the end. **The problem was not with the strategy, but with how it was carried out at the negotiation table.**

~ 42 ~

ET-1 was only 20,000 miles above Earth's surface and continuing to move toward Station Zero.

General Allen and Director Druckman were on their way to Joint Base Andrews where a helicopter was ready to fly them to Station Zero. 75 soldiers, all from US Special Operations Forces, were already deployed to the area. Allen mobilized another 120 before he got on the helicopter.

Defense Secretary Strauss was racing toward the Pentagon and taking a call from General Ramsey, whom Whitman had appointed to be the commanding officer at Station Zero.

Vice President Nielsen was in his office, communicating with Congressional leadership. His next six calls would be with leaders of the international alliance.

Art was calling Silla, who was rushing back to the office from her apartment.

NSA Garcia had just walked into the Oval Office and was waiting for Whitman, who was finishing up a call with Attorney General Kim.

Chief of Staff Perez and Kilmer were also in the Oval Office, still sitting across from one another. They were arguing—and not as quietly as they thought.

Perez was frustrated. "Professor, there's no way the president is going to allow that. It's unnecessary."

Kilmer kept pushing. "Don't you see? You can't phone this in. Things are going to start moving too fast."

"They won't move faster than the president allows them to move. And she will take your advice into account. Your voice will be heard. You don't have to worry about that."

"You think I'm worried about *my* voice being heard? I'm trying to make sure the *president's* voice isn't ignored."

Whitman hung up the phone and looked over. "Salvo, what the hell is going on over there?"

"I'm very sorry," Perez said, as both he and Kilmer rose to their feet.

Twenty minutes earlier, Whitman had asked the two of them to figure out how Earth-side might go about answering Kilmer's "fundamental" question about the alien visit: *Why now?* She'd agreed that Kilmer would be given whatever help he needed to pursue the matter. She'd even given the initiative a name—*Operation Churchill*—before leaving it to Perez and Kilmer.

"Don't apologize, just tell me what you're fighting about."

Kilmer petitioned first. "Madam President. You've asked me to approach Operation Churchill as I see fit—and now we might have a chance to actually *engage* with the aliens. If so, it offers the single best opportunity to learn. We can't afford mistakes and we have to exploit every opportunity. There's only one way to do that effectively."

Perez interjected. "Kilmer is asking that we send him to Station Zero so that he can advise on our engagement strategy from the front lines. I've told him that's out of the question."

Whitman frowned. "Professor, I buy into the importance of Operation Churchill. But what we're dealing with at this stage is still, above all, a military operation. If we find ourselves sitting down with an alien delegation to negotiate the future of our planet, you will have a seat at the table. But this is not a summit at Camp David. We have no idea *what* we're dealing with right now."

"That's precisely my point. We *don't* know what we're dealing with—and the aliens might not either. If we frame this as a military problem from the very start, that is what it will become—because once a military frame takes hold, it does not let go. But that is a dangerously narrow definition of the problem—at this or any stage. I don't think you want the people at Station Zero filtering your strategy through a military or intelligence lens."

"Professor Kilmer. General Ramsey is in charge at Station Zero. General Allen and Director Druckman will be there to advise him. But none of them are authorized to make strategy or to reinterpret strategy. Their only job is to implement the strategy that I craft. That's how it works. And I trust them to do that. I understand your point about making sure we look at this more holistically, from the start, but it is not your job to ensure people make the right calls at Station Zero. Not even close. Salvo's right about that. They will take orders from me. Your advice can help shape some of those orders, but you can advise me perfectly well from Washington."

Kilmer tried one last time. "Madam President, having an effective strategy is never enough. Having people who can carry out orders isn't either. You know far better than I do that when the action starts, split-second decisions need to be made. When the unexpected happens, judgment calls need to be made. If we were at war, I'm sure no one could make those decisions better than General Ramsey or General Allen, and I would not even pretend to be of any value. But we're not *at* war—we're trying to prevent it. And if all hell suddenly breaks loose at Station Zero, in ways that your strategy and your orders never anticipated, are you comfortable with the judgment calls they will make to avoid war?"

Whitman considered it for all of five seconds—far longer than Perez had expected. "I see your point—but I'm not convinced we have a problem. We'll revisit this after we know what's happening at Station Zero. Until then, you stay put. That's the end of it."

She turned to her National Security Advisor. "Where do we stand with support for Operation Churchill?"

"Art will free up as many Triad resources as he can to support the initiative," Garcia answered. Then she looked at Kilmer. "You tell them what you need—people, data, intel, whatever—and they'll figure out if there's a way to make it happen. Art is assigning Agent Silla to work with you on this."

Whitman nodded. "I think Agent Silla is a perfect choice." Then she looked over at Kilmer. "What do you think, Professor?"

For the life of him, Kilmer couldn't figure out why the president was smiling when she asked him that.

~ 43 ~

A small room situated between the Oval Office and the chief of staff's office was vacated and designated as Kilmer's workspace for the coming days. He had just settled in when Agent Lane arrived. Lane was to provide an overview of Triad's operations so that Kilmer would have a basic understanding of its capabilities and resources. Kilmer was impressed, and somewhat troubled, by what he learned—but he managed to keep himself from initiating a debate about civil liberties or about what might have led to the fall of the Roman Republic.

Across town, Silla had taken a shower but skipped the nap. On the way back to her office, she texted Kilmer. *Bad news, and I don't mean the alien invasion. Art just told me I've been assigned to work with some boring professor.*

Kilmer texted back. *I just spoke with the prof. Apparently, he thought boring was part of his charm. He seems open to ideas for how to be more exciting.*

Silla responded. *I have some ideas.*

At 3 p.m., she joined Kilmer in his office to discuss Operation Churchill. Kilmer peppered her with questions. Was it possible to look deeper into space to check for additional spacecraft? Could images captured by NASA or other agencies over previous decades be reexamined to see whether aliens had visited previously? Had humans conducted any space activities in recent weeks or months that might have attracted the attention of aliens? What did the government know about extra-terrestrials prior to Day 1? Was there any truth to the countless conspiracy theories that had been floating around for generations? What did Triad know about the materials from which ET-1 was constructed? Was there any way to estimate how far the aliens had traveled to reach the Solar System? Were there any theories on how they powered their spacecraft? Did Earth have any resources that were especially rare in the galaxy, and which could be of broad biological or technological value? Kilmer's questions led to a lot of discussion, and more than a few "we can look into it" responses, but a eureka moment was nowhere to be found.

Meanwhile, General Allen and Director Druckman had reached Station Zero and were meeting with General Ramsey, the commanding officer. The trio was going over Ramsey's plans for establishing a perimeter around the spacecraft—if and when it landed. They were linked via videoconference to the Situation Room, located in the basement of the West Wing of the White House, where Whitman, Nielsen, Perez, and Garcia were joined by the Secretary of Homeland Security. Also calling in were the chiefs of the Army, Marine Corps, Air Force, and National Guard.

Secretary Strauss was still at the Pentagon, coordinating with the FAA and other agencies to ensure that the air space over Station Zero was cleared. A no-fly zone with a fifty-mile radius was put into place. Only aircraft that were specifically authorized by President Whitman, Secretary Strauss, or General Allen were to be allowed.

At 3:05 p.m., ET-1 descended, suddenly and rapidly, until it was hovering over a clearing near Loft Mountain Campground at Shenandoah National Park. It was a mere 150 feet above the ground.

~ 44 ~

The troops at Station Zero sprang into action at 3:10 p.m., establishing a perimeter of radius 0.5 miles around the precise spot above which ET-1 was hovering. The encircled area was dubbed *Touchdown-1*. Soldiers surrounded the spacecraft from a distance, along the established perimeter. No weapons were drawn, and none were to be made visible. Artillery and attack helicopters were situated three miles away at five different locations. At all times, four F-35 combat aircraft and two B-2 bombers were to remain airborne, flying between 10 and 100 miles from Touchdown-1. Satellite imaging of the area was increased, and UAVs were directed to fly overhead at an altitude of no lower than 20,000 feet above ground level.

By 7:00 p.m., several two-person military delegations from across the international alliance were on flights to the United States. One member of each delegation would remain in DC while the other would go to Station Zero.

At 8:25, Whitman sat at her desk in the Oval Office. VP Nielsen, NSA Garcia, Chief of Staff Perez, and Professor Kilmer stood nearby. General Allen was calling in from Station Zero.

"Madam President, this is General Allen. Can you hear me clearly?"

"Yes, Casey," Whitman responded. "We can hear you. What can you tell us?"

"Madam President, we have established two field headquarters. Secretary Strauss arrived a short while ago and is meeting with General Ramsey at HQ-1, which is our larger encampment, 500 yards from the perimeter at zero degrees. Zero degrees corresponds to due south of the spacecraft. Director Druckman and I are at HQ-2, which is located 75 yards from the perimeter at 270 degrees—due east of the spacecraft. As you saw in the live feed, ET-1 landed approximately eight minutes ago. We have detected no movement since.

We don't know if they need light to see around them, but it's getting dark out here, so we have some lights shining onto Touchdown-1. There has been a persistent humming sound—perhaps some kind of engine—that can be heard even from the perimeter. No radioactive materials have been detected.

"We will need a spectrometer that can get close enough to figure out what this thing is made of, but it looks metallic—as if it were made of something like titanium, or tungsten carbide. The ship is approximately ninety-five yards across and thirty yards deep. Sixty-five yards of its length are in contact with the ground; the remaining fifteen yards, on each side, arc upward off the ground. At its center, the height of the spacecraft is roughly twenty yards, but the edges reach up to about thirty yards off the ground."

"Have we learned anything from the landing itself?"

"Only that we don't believe it uses any technology we're familiar with when it hovers. ET-1 did not appear to disturb what was on the ground as it descended. Our helicopters would have blown things around quite visibly. It did, of course, crush a whole lot of bushes, some small trees, and a few park benches when it set down."

"Okay. Let's wait another thirty minutes," Whitman announced. "Then we send in the drones to poke around a bit. No weapons, no sudden movement, and no humans go near that thing."

~ 45 ~

At 9:00 p.m., eight drones took off from different points around the perimeter and flew into Touchdown-1, capturing images as they went. By 9:05, they had come within one hundred yards of ET-1. Seconds later, seven of the eight drones had been rendered inoperative and fell to the ground. There was no indication as to what had caused them, almost simultaneously, to come crashing down. The eighth drone had been lagging, and its operator pulled it back as soon as she saw what had happened to the other seven. When the lone survivor returned to the perimeter, its image files were corrupted, along with various other parts of its software, including the GPS and navigation system. The drone had made it back, but just barely.

At 10:00, another attempt was made, this time with drones flying at a higher altitude. The result was the same—all three drones were lost. An unmanned ground vehicle suffered the same fate ten minutes later. Reconnaissance reported that while animals had been spotted inside Touchdown-1, none had been seen within a hundred yards of ET-1—an area now dubbed *the kill-zone*.

By 10:30, everyone in the Situation Room and at Station Zero was trying to make sense of what was happening. There were more guesses than guessers. Did ET-1 have some sort of shield that automatically disabled or destroyed anything that came close? Had weapons been aimed separately at each drone? Did the spacecraft use some sort of electromagnetic pulse, or perhaps something entirely alien? Whatever it was, would it impact humans as well? What about birds or dogs? Was this an act of aggression, a defensive measure, or none of the above? Did the aliens even know they were having an impact on what the humans had sent toward it? Were there even any aliens on board ET-1?

Director Druckman came up with the idea of sending something "non-electrical, non-mechanical, and non-living" toward ET-1. "We need something that can enter *and* exit the kill-zone, something that doesn't have a brain or an engine, and doesn't need to be controlled from the perimeter. The only option that I can think of is ballistic—something that will follow its own trajectory once we launch it. I suggest we have a sharpshooter fire a single bullet through the kill-zone and to the other side, so that it passes maybe fifty yards away from ET-1. We place the sniper's target on the far side of the perimeter and see if the bullet gets through and hits it."

This proposal was met with vigorous debate, but ultimately, Whitman approved the idea.

At 11:25, the shooter was in position and armed with a McMillan TAC-50 sniper rifle. Three minutes later, he took aim and fired. Approximately two seconds after that, a *clang* was heard as the bullet struck the target on the far side of Touchdown-1. Cheers immediately rang out at HQ-1, HQ-2, and in the Situation Room. No one could have articulated precisely what they had learned from this experiment, or even what they were celebrating, but it felt like progress. A lead. A ray of hope. A first step. There was no visible reaction from ET-1 or the reserves. The sniper's bullet had not precipitated war. ET-1 might not have even noticed.

At 11:55, Whitman told the team to keep their cell phones on but to go and get some rest.

"If nothing has changed by morning, we take another step. I will want your ideas on what that should be."

Silla accompanied Kilmer back to his new office so that he could gather some things and lock up. As they were standing by his desk, he reached for her hand.

"So, what do you think?" he said. "What's your read?"

"I don't think we can reach too many conclusions with such limited data. I think we need to wait for the aliens to make a move. I mean, they've come all this way—they must have planned to do *something* after they landed. Then again, maybe they're already doing something, and we just can't tell that they're doing it. How about you? What do you think?"

Kilmer frowned. "I hadn't really considered the possibility that they're already doing something to communicate or engage with us, and we just can't detect it. It's possible. But if that's the case, waiting around doesn't really work. The good news, I think, is that we can afford to be more proactive. I mean, they've already exchanged messages with us; would they really be offended if we went ahead and knocked on their door? Sure, they might not have doors—and maybe knocking on doors is how they declare war on their planet—so we would need to think this through. But they did land exactly where we told them to. It shouldn't be a complete shock to them if we try to engage."

"True. But can we do it safely? We don't even know if humans can *survive* the kill-zone. Although, maybe if we stop calling it the *kill-zone,* it won't scare us as much."

Kilmer smiled. And then his mind latched on to something. "I just had a thought. Tell me if this sounds crazy."

"Okay. Shoot."

"Think back to high school, when you went to your first dance."

"I went to my first dance in fifth grade."

"Oh—really? Wow… Did you go with a date?"

Silla let go of his hand, looking mildly offended. "I was ten years old. What exactly are you implying?"

"Huh? Nothing. No… What?"

"What are you talking about, Kilmer?"

"Sorry. My point is—" He took a deep breath. "My point is you *didn't* go with a date. Nobody did, right?"

"Right. Well, except for Michael Feldman and Kimmy Paxton. But that's a whole different story."

Kilmer was intrigued but decided not to inquire about the details of the Feldman-Paxton Affair.

"Did you dance very much that night?" he asked.

She thought about it. "Just a little. Later in the evening."

"Why just a little? Do you not like to dance?"

"I love to dance, actually."

"Me too," Kilmer said, smiling and reaching for her hand again.

She let him take her hand, but only half-heartedly. "Is this going somewhere?"

"Yes, sorry. So, you like to dance, but you hardly danced. Why not?"

"Because no one else was dancing."

"Exactly. Now describe the scene to me—at the dance. What did it look like? I bet I'm envisioning the same thing as you, and I wasn't even going to dances at the age of ten."

Silla rolled her eyes and then conjured up the memory. "Let's see. School gym. Dark, but not too dark. Some decorations, but not many. Strobe lights. A few tables with pizza and soda. Large, empty dance floor. All the boys on one side, all the girls on the other."

"Bingo."

Silla looked at him. And then she saw where he was going with this. "You know what, Kilmer? I don't think this is crazy at all. I think you're on to something."

He smiled as she gripped his hand more enthusiastically.

A few minutes later, they were walking toward the exit.

"Hey," said Kilmer, "do you think if I'd asked you to a dance—you know, back in high school—that you would have said yes?"

She considered it. "I'd like to think so," she finally answered. "But…" She hesitated.

"But what?"

"But… you really should have seen me back then. I don't think you would have had the guts to ask me out."

Silla looked over and gave him an *I'm-not-actually-kidding* wink.

Kilmer didn't feel too bad about it, though. She was holding his hand now—and that was all that mattered.

~ 46 ~

Kilmer walked Silla to her car, but when she leaned in to kiss him, he faded back just enough to avoid contact.

"Well, then," she said. "Is this about my comment earlier? I'm sorry. What I meant to say was that I would have leapt for joy if you'd asked me to the school dance." She grinned.

"No, it's not that. I just worry that if I kiss you goodnight, you'll think it's time for you to leave."

"I see why President Whitman keeps you around. The way you piece things together. It's incredible."

"You're not nearly as impressed as I would have liked."

"And how impressed is that?"

"Impressed enough to stay."

"It's really late."

"We have time," he reminded her softly. "Especially if you spend the night here."

She smiled, but then looked away. "You would have me do the walk of shame down the White House steps in the morning?"

"You're a CIA agent. Don't you always have a duffel bag full of clothes and accessories in your car? Isn't that in the handbook or something?"

"You don't know a thing about the CIA."

"That's only mostly true."

She put her arms around him. "Kilmer, I'd love to stay. But I think we should both get some rest."

"You don't trust me to let you sleep?"

"It's not you." She gave him a kiss on the cheek. "I don't think I would trust myself to be with you in any room that has a bed."

They kissed again, and for longer. And by the time it ended, she had decided to stay.

She reached into the back seat and grabbed a duffel bag. Kilmer was just about to make a joke when she cut him off.

"Not a word, Kilmer. You don't want to ruin this. Trust me."

Heirs of Herodotus by D. Kilmer.
Excerpt from the Introduction.

It is said that history is written by the victors. But like many aphorisms, this one does not stand up to scrutiny. In fact, the statement was rendered false from the very start. In the fifth century BCE, Thucydides—who many consider the first "historian of war"—gave a detailed account of the war between Athens and Sparta, an epic conflict in which Sparta ultimately triumphed.

Thucydides titled his book *History of the Peloponnesian War*, a name derived from "Peloponnese," the peninsula in Greece where Sparta was located. But wait... the Spartans could not have referred to the conflict by that name. For them, every war was "Peloponnesian." Only an Athenian would call this "The Peloponnesian War."

Thucydides was an Athenian, and it is his story that we have all read—and in it, he does no favors to the Spartans. **History, it turns out, is not written by the victors, it is written by the storytellers—and in most cases, each side has them, with each writing their preferred version of the tale. The versions might agree on many things, including who emerged victorious and who was defeated—but they will rarely agree on who was the hero and who the villain.**

We should always worry about bias, but the blame belongs, in equal measure, to all those who lift their pens, whether they write on behalf of victor or vanquished.

Even the defeated get to tell their story—and in it, they are the heroes. For a while, they might even look destined to win. But poetic license has its limits, and no true historian will ever promise a happy ending.

~ 48 ~

Day 16. 8:00 a.m.

General Allen, Director Druckman, Secretary Strauss, and General Ramsey were in HQ-2. They were videoconferencing with President Whitman, VP Nielsen, Chief of Staff Perez, NSA Garcia, Kilmer, Silla, and Art, all of whom were in the Situation Room. The chiefs of the Army and Air Force were on the phone as well.

Kilmer and Silla had both walked out of the Lincoln Bedroom that morning, but at different times. And they had arrived at the meeting five minutes apart. They shook hands when they saw each other in the Situation Room.

After Strauss reported that nothing interesting had transpired overnight at Station Zero, Whitman asked for suggestions on next steps. The ideas ranged from throwing a rock at the spacecraft, to playing music, to delivering a sample of technological and cultural artifacts for the aliens to study, to releasing animals into the kill-zone, to sending an armored vehicle toward the spacecraft.

Ultimately, five proposals were blessed—two on how to approach ET-1, another on how to engage with the aliens from a distance, and two for how to communicate with them.

Kilmer had kicked things off with his school-dance analogy. "It's not that you don't want to dance. It's that you're afraid to be the first one on the dance floor. Everyone is waiting for someone else to make the initial move, and the longer the impasse lasts, the harder it gets—more anxiety, more uncertainty. Now, we're on one side of the gym, and the aliens are on the other. It's possible that they came only to study us from a distance, but I doubt it. I think that if there *is* anyone on board ET-1, they came here to dance. Otherwise, why follow the coordinates we sent them? I think it's unlikely they came all the way to Station Zero only to get upset if we approach their vessel."

Whitman nodded. "I never hesitated when it came to dancing, but I see what you mean. What do you suggest?"

"That we enter the kill-zone and approach ET-1. Instead of a soldier who advances cautiously with his weapon drawn, we send a larger group that tries to act non-threatening. Like you're asking someone to dance—or welcoming them to your home. My hypothesis is that the aliens are more likely to respond aggressively if they see our soldiers in formation or hiding in the bushes. If we accept vulnerability first, maybe they reciprocate."

"And what about the safety of our troops?" asked General Ramsey, the commanding officer at Station Zero.

"We do need to think about that," Kilmer responded. "But we should at least get to the one-hundred-yard mark, the very edge of the kill-zone. Beyond that, perhaps we move a bit slower. Maybe we use guide dogs on long leashes to lead the way. Maybe we just start talking from there and hope they get the message that we came to communicate, and not to fight. I'd even advocate taking gifts, but I have no idea what that would look like to them."

"I can't even figure out what to buy for my wife," Nielsen joked. Everyone laughed.

General Allen asked a question from HQ-2. "Would our men be armed?"

"I would suggest not," Kilmer replied. "But I leave that to your judgment, General. It might be risky to go unarmed, but it does build trust. And if the aliens can detect a weapon, or if a soldier brandishes it under pressure, that could create a problem."

Strauss interjected. "I would *want* our soldiers to brandish a weapon if they were under pressure. That's why we arm our soldiers in the first place, Professor."

General Allen spoke up in favor of Kilmer's proposal. General Ramsey was less supportive. Ultimately, Whitman gave it the green light.

"General Allen," she said, "I want you to work with General Ramsey and Professor Kilmer to come up with a plan that all of you are comfortable with—and it should include what our people will do if they get close to ET-1. I want something by 2:30. Anything else to discuss with regards to how we might approach them?"

General Allen weighed in with another suggestion. "Madam President, I propose we make the scene surrounding ET-1 less chaotic. Sending in drones or troops or deliveries from all directions might confuse or overwhelm them. It might also obscure the fact that our intentions are benign—that we simply want to engage. I propose we streamline our approach so that we always advance toward the kill-zone from the same direction, and along the same path."

General Allen then made a specific proposal along these lines: Given the angle at which the spacecraft was parked, the point of departure for all engagement should be 300 degrees on the perimeter. This would allow a straight-line movement toward ET-1, orthogonal to the length of the spacecraft, and aimed right at its midpoint. "Imagine it's a castle and we're paving a straight path from the perimeter to the front gates." No one objected.

The discussion then shifted from how humans might approach ET-1 to other forms of engagement. Director Druckman jumped in from HQ-2. "I like the idea of sending care packages. We need to figure out what to put in them, but thanks to Strauss, we already have a way to make the deliveries."

Overnight, HQ-2 had solved the problem of safely delivering something close to ET-1 in the kill-zone. It was a non-trivial problem. Any delivery device, like a drone, would probably malfunction and fall apart as soon as it entered the kill-zone. You couldn't tie a care package to a bullet or an RPG and shoot it at the spacecraft. And parachuting something from a high-altitude drone wouldn't work either—the winds would carry the item off-target. That's when Strauss suggested a variation on the parachute idea. He proposed the use of a catapult to deliver items close to ET-1, with a parachute attached to the catapulted item so that even fragile items might be delivered. Over the next few hours, the defense secretary oversaw a design competition: four separate teams of soldiers and staff raced against the clock to create prototypes that could be field-tested by breakfast. The winning entry had been called the "Cata-chute" by its inventors. It was quickly renamed the "cat shooter" by Secretary Strauss—for absolutely no reason other than it was more entertaining.

With no one objecting to the idea in principle, Whitman asked Nielsen to lead a small working group that would propose a list of items to send to ET-1.

The conversation then switched to communicating with the aliens. Until now, the only successful messaging had involved the sending of coordinates, but that would hardly suffice now that the aliens had landed on Earth. The problem was not figuring out what to say, it was how to use FERMAT to convey the desired message. After various ideas for how to tailor FERMAT to deliver more complex messages hit a brick wall, the group concluded that the language they had used while ET-1 was in space just wasn't cut out for the task at hand.

"Maybe we're thinking about this the wrong way," Silla finally said. "It's clear that our language isn't rich enough to do the things we want it to do. But maybe that's okay. It reminds me of when my father was sick, and we had very little time left. There was a lot that I wanted to say, but I couldn't find the words. I wasn't even sure he could hear me. So, I just used the words I *could* find—simple ones—and I made sure to convey just enough for him to understand what I was feeling. And if even that was beyond his comprehension, at least he would know I was there—that I hadn't abandoned him.

"We keep thinking about what we would like to convey to ET-1: that we come in peace, that we would like to enter the kill-zone, or that we want them to reveal themselves or their intentions. Maybe, instead, we should just think about what our language *can* do and see if any of that can be used in a productive way. Maybe they just need to hear our voice. Maybe they just need to know we're trying to communicate. Maybe we start with that."

"Okay, let's try starting from there," Whitman agreed. "What *can* we do with FERMAT?"

Art jumped in first. "We're dealing with numbers. We've already used them to provide coordinates. They can also be used to count, to tell time..." And then the brainstorming took off.

"To measure angles."

"To measure distances."

"For binary signal communication—*yes* versus *no*, or *on* versus *off*, for example."

"To create patterns."

"To create secret codes."

"To color by numbers," Druckman offered.

Laughter.

"Am I the only one with grandkids?" he protested.

With a number of ideas on the table, the group discussed how these capabilities might translate into something functional. In the end, Whitman approved two proposals.

The first was suggested by Director Druckman: the creation of a FERMAT-based timer that could be used to signal the most basic of Earth-side intentions—the intention to do *something*. Before any approach toward the spacecraft was made, for example, the timer would count down from five minutes. Humans would initiate their movement when the countdown ended. ET-1 would hopefully figure out the pattern and understand that Earth-side was trying to reduce uncertainty for ET-1 by signaling its intention to act—even if the action itself could not be described in advance. "If nothing else," Silla suggested, "they might understand that we're struggling to reach out to them. Maybe they have better ideas. Maybe it inspires *them* to propose a way to communicate."

The second idea was significantly more ambitious. Others had laughed when Druckman said "color by numbers," but Silla explained that the CIA director had, in fact, hit upon something profound. "The reason children color by numbers is because it makes it easy to create something that is otherwise very difficult. Each number represents the same color for the entire project—a crude but effective technique to produce something that looks halfway decent. So, what if we teach them to paint by numbers—or rather, to talk by numbers—by associating basic words with numbers? One is a human. Two is their spacecraft. Three is walking. Four is standing still. Five is a gift. Six is a weapon. Seven is approach. And so on."

"Brilliant," said Strauss, and the group started to explore the mechanics and limits of such an approach. Once Silla explained what could be done with the use of machine learning, the possibilities seemed almost limitless—*if* it worked in the first place. All they had to do was build a language that did not exist, a technology with which to deploy it, and a pedagogy for teaching it to aliens. Fortunately, they weren't starting entirely from scratch. Research on how humans might someday communicate with aliens was not new; ideas had been proposed and debated for decades. But none of those ideas were tailored to the precise requirements, opportunities, and constraints that existed in the current situation.

Art was assigned the task of building a team with scientists from DARPA (the Defense Advanced Research Projects Agency), along with linguists, mathematicians, and machine learning specialists, to design the language system. The group would coordinate with the FERMAT team to ensure compatibility with its broadcasting methodology. If the idea worked, it could be deployed quickly, at least with basic words. But the aspiration was far greater—to build a practical, efficient, and scalable tool for facilitating ever more complex communication.

"Art, you tell your team that if they can execute on Agent Silla's vision for this, I will make sure every one of them is named a United States poet laureate," Whitman announced with a completely straight face.

It was 10:15 a.m. by the time the meeting ended. The group would meet again at 2:30 p.m. General Allen would report on plans for a human approach into the kill-zone, VP Nielsen would report on what should be delivered to ET-1 using the cat shooter, Director Druckman would update the group on how the FERMAT-based timer would be deployed, and Art Capella would provide an update on efforts to create a language with which to speak to the aliens.

And then, as everyone set off in different directions, Whitman returned to the Oval Office and shifted her focus to the *non*-alien parts of her job. She still had a country to run.

~ 49 ~

When the group reconvened at 2:30 p.m., Director Druckman reported first: the countdown clock was operational.

"Based on ET-1's ability to decipher our earlier messages, we believe it should be possible for them to figure out what the broadcast represents—once they have some data to work with. I have teams broadcasting one-minute, three-minute, and eight-minute countdowns, after which they take some innocuous but salient action. For example, they might shine a bright light in the direction of ET-1, launch a drone that's visible to the spacecraft, or turn on some loud music. All actions are being initiated at 300 degrees on the perimeter."

"How will we know if they understand our use of the timer?" Whitman asked.

"If they don't respond to it at all, we probably *won't* know whether they understood it. On the other hand, they might mimic our behavior, as they've done in the past. Or, perhaps, they'll take some action that coincides with the end of one of our countdowns. It's hard to know for sure."

"Okay. Keep at it. There might come a time when we have to count on the fact that they know what we're doing."

"Yes, Madam President."

VP Nielsen reported on the care-package proposal. "We're working with some assumptions and constraints. First, we're not sure anyone is inside ET-1—nor do we know whether they're able to retrieve what we send—so we've included some things they might be able to assess from a distance. Second, we obviously want to avoid anything threatening. And third, we don't want to give them a one-dimensional view of humanity, so we plan to send a wide range of items and make multiple deliveries.

"Our list includes the following: a collection of fruits and vegetables, some packaged foods, bottled water, a number of books, some art, an analog clock, a camera, a fully charged laptop, a battery-powered portable CD player with music playing, a radio that's switched on, a small battery-powered television that's also switched on, a telescope, a soccer ball, a baseball, some clothes, shoes, a flashlight, a guitar, a model airplane, a chessboard with pieces and pictorial instructions, some dice, some candies, and some flowers. That's everything. Let's hear suggestions and concerns."

A few people were apprehensive about revealing too much information regarding Earth-side science and technology. Others pointed out that the electrical equipment might not even survive in the kill-zone. The most serious concern was raised by Silla, who strongly advised against sending food items. "We know nothing about their immune systems. The last thing we want to do is send something that kills them. They might even think we were trying to poison them." Everyone agreed, and the food items were struck from the list.

Apart from that, the plan was approved, subject only to some further discussion on which books to send. The group decided against sending any religious texts. Fiction was also eliminated from the list, so as not to confuse the aliens about the reality of life on Earth. In the end, they settled on a world atlas, a dictionary, an abridged encyclopedia, two books on human history, a physics textbook, a mathematics textbook, a textbook on algorithms and another on computer programming languages, a book with sheet music, and three picture books—one with images of nature, one with images of space, and one depicting diverse human cultures. Before the discussion ended, Whitman decided to add a third history book to the list: *Heirs of Herodotus*. "It's as good a book on human history as any," she said with a smile.

Kilmer thought she was joking—and then quickly realized she was not. *Okay. Cool.*

The president then turned the discussion over to Art, who was calling in from Triad. Art informed everyone that his team was up and running and that they expected to have Version 1.0 of the new language ready for deployment within twenty-four hours. They were calling it *Hermes*.

Whitman saw the blank faces in the room. "The messenger god," she explained. "As well as the Greek god of language."

"That's correct, Madam President," Art responded. "The linguists are unanimous in their support for the name. The mathematicians hate it, but they like the idea of being named poet laureates, so they're willing to continue working on the project."

Whitman laughed.

"Okay. General Allen, you're up. What do you have in mind for the first dance?"

After a few tweaks from the group, Allen's plan was finalized as follows. HQ-1 would broadcast a five-minute countdown, after which eight soldiers would cross the perimeter and make their way toward ET-1. Only four would be in uniform. They would chat with one another and occasionally look over at the spacecraft—and not pretend that it wasn't there. The soldiers would wear light body armor underneath their clothes, but they would carry no weapons. They would have cell phones, two-way radios, and body cameras, although these would probably not survive the kill-zone. The group would move at a comfortable pace until they were 115 yards from ET-1, at which point they would cease forward movement, look at ET-1, wave, and do their best to indicate they were asking for permission to enter. HQ-1 would then broadcast a three-minute countdown. When the clock hit zero, the group would continue to move forward, more slowly, into the kill-zone. Unless something stopped them, they would continue until they were 20 yards from the spacecraft. At that point, one soldier would address the spacecraft with a spoken message that the aliens would probably not understand but might still assume was a welcome of some sort. The team would then wait for up to five minutes in hopes of receiving some response. If they did receive a response, the soldiers would have to use their own judgment on how to react, because communication with the perimeter would probably not be possible. If they were afraid, hurt, or unsure what to do, they were to simply return to the perimeter.

Whitman looked around the room. "If any of you think this is a bad idea, now is the time to speak. You're only in this room because I trust you to voice your opinions."

Secretary Strauss spoke first. He opposed sending unarmed soldiers. At the very least, he argued, the president ought to send a second team of soldiers—visibly armed and in formation—behind the first. "Let's make sure they know that the welcome committee has backup."

General Ramsey, Director Druckman, and the Army's chief of staff all supported Strauss's suggestion, to varying degrees. No one else saw the need to revise the plan that General Allen had articulated. NSA Garcia said that she had been expecting something closer to consensus and wondered whether waiting another day to decide would be wise.

Whitman issued her judgment. "We will move ahead with the plan as described by General Allen—there will be one group of soldiers, and they will go unarmed. No changes to that. But I understand the concerns some of you are raising, so here's what we're going to do. First, I am not going to leave our men out there to fend for themselves. Armed soldiers and combat medics will be on the perimeter and ready to move into Touchdown-1 if something goes wrong. General Ramsey, I also want artillery and helicopters ready to deploy on a moment's notice. But *nothing* that happens inside the perimeter—and nothing the aliens might easily observe—should give them reason to think we are being hostile or preparing for a fight. I don't want to send any mixed signals."

She did not invite further discussion. "How soon can we do this?" she asked.

General Ramsey answered. "We can be ready in thirty minutes."

"Okay. We'll send in the welcome committee at 6 p.m. Before that, we'll deliver a few of Zack's care packages and see if there's any response. Maybe we learn something. At the very least, I hope it signals our good intentions."

~ 50 ~

At 3:30 p.m., the cat shooter launched its first set of "care packages". Some books, a cell phone, and a telescope. At 3:50, 4:10, and 4:45, additional deliveries were made. In each case the launch was preceded by a three-minute countdown. Only one of the deliveries missed the mark completely, landing outside the kill-zone. Most landed within twenty yards of ET-1. All fourteen of the deliveries sat on the field, untouched.

The first few launches had been fun to observe, but with ET-1 not responding, the team disbanded to focus on other issues. They would reconvene at 5:50 p.m., ten minutes prior to the start of Operation School Dance.

At 5:00, Chief of Staff Perez asked Kilmer to come to his office for a brief chat. When Kilmer entered the room, he saw that they weren't alone. President Whitman was there as well.

"Thanks for joining us, Professor."

"Madam President," Kilmer responded—and then looked back at Perez. "Is everything okay?"

"Not exactly," Perez replied.

Whitman addressed Kilmer. "I'm afraid that I need to burden you with one more thing. It's not something you signed up for, but I hope you'll agree to help. Regardless of your decision, I ask for your discretion in the matter."

Kilmer nodded, but more so in acknowledgment than consent. He couldn't help but notice that both Perez and Whitman appeared to have been expecting a more emphatic *Of course, Madam President.*

Whitman looked at her chief of staff and gave a nod, as if to say, *Go ahead, we'll just take our chances.* Perez looked skeptical but complied.

"Professor Kilmer," he began, "are you familiar with Article II, Section 4 of the US Constitution?"

Kilmer had not seen this coming. "I am, Mr. Perez. Why do you ask?"

"Because there are at least a few people around here who think it's relevant."

"I don't see how—unless the president has been doing things that I'm not aware of."

"Professor Kilmer," Whitman interjected sternly, "there are many things I do that you're not aware of. But as to the insinuation you've just made, no, I have not been *doing things* that would be of concern."

"Then I don't understand. If all you've done is—"

Suddenly, Kilmer realized what this was about. "I see," he reflected. "October 23rd. 1962."

"Excuse me?" Perez said.

"That's the day President Kennedy signed the order to blockade Cuba during the Cuban Missile Crisis. The date isn't important. What's important is that JFK felt he had no choice but to take that action—even though he was worried that matters might escalate as a result. That night Bobby Kennedy told him that if he hadn't ordered the blockade, he probably would have been impeached for being too complacent. JFK didn't disagree." Kilmer looked to Whitman. "Is that what this is about?"

"I suppose it's comforting to know that President Kennedy confronted similar demons," Whitman confessed.

"He did, Madam President. But he also managed to walk the fine line—giving the hawks in his administration a voice without letting them control the agenda. And despite the pressure, he didn't choose to protect his presidency over doing what he thought was right."

"Nor will I, Professor Kilmer. But it *is* a tight rope we sometimes have to walk. I'm asking for your help in making sure that we can strike the right balance."

"If you tell me what's going on, I'll try to help. But I have to be candid: I can't help you if it means supporting a strategy or an agenda that I think is wrong-headed or unethical."

Perez seemed uncomfortable with the condition—or, perhaps, just with the fact that Kilmer had the temerity to impose conditions at all. But Whitman seemed unbothered.

"Two weeks ago," she responded, "I would have said with genuine humility that I'm not the only one who is fit to do this job—that if something happened to me, others could be trusted to take over. But I'm afraid things have changed. If the reins are handed over to one of our more hawkish colleagues now, it could spell disaster. I can't let that happen. You don't know me that well, Professor, so this probably sounds very self-serving to you. That's okay. Your skepticism is healthy—and I can live with it."

"Madam President, I've seen the way some of the people on your team think about the crisis. I can understand why you might worry if they were in charge. But I need more information about what's really going on here. What can you tell me?"

Perez explained that Secretary Strauss, Director Druckman, and General Ramsey—and possibly others—were hoping to remove the president from office. They believed that the president's handling of the crisis showed weakness and naivety, and that it put the country at risk. There was no indication that they were out to undermine her legal authority—they would still follow orders while she was president—but they had started to build coalitions against her, including reaching out to members of the opposition in the House and the Senate. They had planted seeds of fear and doubt that were beginning to take root. If things went wrong, they wanted to be in position to make their move.

"It's public knowledge," Perez continued, "that Strauss considered running for president in the last election. He only decided against it because he didn't think an incumbent could be defeated given how well the economy was doing. Strauss figured he'd wait another four years and run after President Conway's second term was over. He certainly didn't think *Marianne Whitman* would beat Tim Conway. You might remember that Strauss didn't even endorse her until mere days before the election. How much of that was resentment versus political calculation versus genuine disagreement on policy is hard to know, but all three have always been in the mix.

"Strauss was the only person we asked to join the administration who turned us down at first. He's also the only one who has discussed the possibility of running against President Whitman when she's up for reelection—and those conversations started even before the current crisis. Of course, we mostly knew what we were getting into when we brought Strauss on board—and we still wanted him—but what he's doing now goes too far."

"What exactly are you worried he'll do?"

"Best case scenario, he won't do anything," Perez answered. "He'll just wait to see if things go wrong and if the president loses support. Worst case scenario... well, for certain people there isn't *any* line they won't cross. But it's not the ambitious politician you have to worry about. The most dangerous people are the ones who have convinced themselves that their cause is a righteous one."

"Is that why you sent General Allen to Station Zero? To keep an eye on Strauss?"

"That's a very small part of it," Whitman interjected. "As you've seen, I continue to count on Secretary Strauss and the others. I still trust them to do their jobs and to do them well. If that were to change, having General Allen at Station Zero would certainly be useful. But I have seen no evidence to suspect such a thing."

"Something doesn't add up," Kilmer said. "How does removing you from office help their cause? Impeaching you would put Zack in charge, and from what I can tell, the two of you see eye to eye on most things. Strauss would end up with someone he finds equally unpalatable. What can they do? Impeach you both?"

Whitman and Perez looked at each other. There was some strain in what passed between them, but the president allowed her chief of staff to answer the question.

"Yes, they could try to impeach both the president and the VP. The more closely he's tied to her policies, the more likely he can be painted with the same brush. If that happens, we end up with the Speaker of the House as president—and Speaker Hunt is as perfect a combination of hawk and imbecile as you are likely to find in DC."

"I see," said Kilmer.

"However," Perez continued. "Double impeachment is President Whitman's theory about how this would unfold. I see it differently."

Kilmer was about to ask, but then he figured it out. *That doesn't seem right. Could it be?*

"That's right, Professor. I know he's your friend. But my sense is that Strauss and his coalition are working to bring Zack over to their side. It's very hard to impeach both the president and the VP. It's a whole hell of a lot easier to impeach only the president—especially if the vice president will come out and says she is unfit."

"Do you have any evidence to support your theory?" Kilmer asked.

"Not much."

Whitman took it from there. "Professor Kilmer, I'm not asking you to choose between Zack and me. I'm not even asking you to choose between *Strauss* and me. I'm just asking you to do what you came here to do in the first place—help us with this crisis—but do so with an awareness of these dynamics. Does that make sense?"

"It does," Kilmer replied, as painful memories of Cameroon flooded back into his mind. "You brought me here to advise on the crisis. Now you want me to advise you on how to make sure that my advice actually gets carried out—not just today, but in the weeks and months ahead. Believe me, Madam President, I understand the distinction being made. Giving you the best advice is no longer enough—we need to ensure that you stay in office long enough to follow it."

"Precisely."

Kilmer's mind raced to evaluate as many nodes in the decision tree as possible. After a few moments of silence, he had reached a conclusion. He would help Whitman—but sitting with her in the White House was not the best way to do it. He had to be where things might *really* go wrong. The divisions were deeper than he had imagined.

"Okay, I'm in. But I do have two conditions."

"What are they?" Whitman asked, as Perez looked on, clearly astounded by Kilmer's ability to conjure up conditions at a moment's notice.

"First, that you will allow me to work from Station Zero, if I ask to do so."

"That could be extremely dangerous, Professor. I might not want to put you in harm's way."

"I agree, it could be very dangerous. Which brings me to my second condition."

"Which is?"

"If things start to get ugly, you won't evacuate me from Station Zero—unless I'm willing to leave."

Whitman looked at Perez, who shook his head in response. *That's asking too much.*

"If all hell breaks loose—if we are at war," Whitman said, "I'm not going to leave you in the middle of it."

"In that scenario, Madam President, I won't even ask to stay, and I'll probably want to be on the first flight out. But there are other scenarios. If things start to spiral out of control, but they haven't *completely* blown up yet, I might still be of some value. We both know that it's always the peacemakers who get evacuated first. The men and women with guns get to stay. But in this situation, we need to try harder than ever to resolve things peacefully. Our Plan B is a Plan B in name only—we all recognize that. I'm just asking for the opportunity to do everything possible to avoid giving up on Plan A. You don't have to listen to my advice, but I want the opportunity to offer it. I don't want General Allen or Secretary Strauss shipping me off while my continued presence at Stations Zero might still be of help. That's all I ask."

"Professor, I'm not sure if I should be annoyed or impressed," Whitman said. "I'm asking you for help in saving the planet, and you are... well, you're using it as leverage. It hardly seems right."

"I'm sorry. I'm not trying to take advantage of the situation. I probably shouldn't have even used the word *conditions*. Please just consider these to be requests. Assertive ones, to be sure, but I'm not asking for anything that you can't afford to give, Madam President. And I'm not asking for anything that enriches me personally. Worst-case scenario, I go there, and I add no value. You can live with that, right?"

"No, the worst-case scenario is you end up dead. I don't want to live with *that*." Whitman took a step toward Kilmer. "Here's what I can offer. You will go to Station Zero whenever you want. And if things get out of control, you will only be evacuated if *I* insist on it. I won't relinquish my authority to call you back when I want—no way, Professor. But Allen, Ramsey, and Strauss will not force you out. If they want you to leave, I'll let you argue your case to me. That's the best deal you're going to get."

"I understand. And I accept. Thank you, Madam President."

Whitman smiled. "Good. Now let's put all of this aside and get back to work. We have aliens to encounter. And nothing that we've discussed here takes precedence over getting that right."

They wrapped it up and Kilmer left the chief of staff's office. They would meet again soon enough in the Situation Room.

~ 51 ~

Kilmer walked the halls and reflected on what had just transpired. It had been easy enough to say yes to Whitman's request. He'd learned a long time ago, and quite painfully, that elected officials, no matter how well-intentioned they might be, were always attuned to their political constraints. If Kilmer ignored those constraints, or if he gave advice that could only be implemented in an ideal world, he was just wasting everyone's time—or worse, as in Cameroon, he could end up with blood on his hands. The hard part wasn't coming up with good ideas, it was coming up with a coherent strategy that someone with limited political capital could realistically execute. If Whitman needed his help to do that, or to keep her job long enough to do what was right, he was willing to help. He didn't expect her replacement to be any wiser or more ethical than her.

But something was bothering him. What was it?

Did he feel like he was betraying Zack? No, the greater good was more important—and Perez was probably wrong about Zack anyway. Was he concerned that Whitman and Perez were manipulating him? If they were, he would figure that out eventually, and then just walk away. Did he fear he was on the wrong side of this fight? Could Strauss and Druckman be right to worry that Whitman would buckle under pressure? He didn't think so. She seemed like the most level-headed person at the White House.

So, what was it? What was bothering him? Nothing had really changed about his role. And, as long as Whitman was still in control, all he had to do—

As long as Whitman was still in control…

But she wasn't. At least not as much as they all liked to believe.

Kilmer decided he would need to start paying a lot more attention to what was going on—starting immediately.

~ 52 ~

Kilmer sat next to Silla in the crowded Situation Room. All eyes were toggling between the five screens that provided views of Touchdown-1. Three of the cameras were trained directly on the spacecraft, offering different angles and different levels of magnification. Another camera showed the path that led from 300 degrees on the perimeter to ET-1. The last one provided an aerial shot of Touchdown-1 and its surrounding areas, including HQ-1 and HQ-2.

Kilmer familiarized himself with what each camera angle did and did not capture. What exactly he was worried he might miss, he wasn't sure—which was precisely why he was afraid he would miss it. He slowed his breathing to lower his heart rate. His eyes narrowed. He was ready—to collect, filter, evaluate, rearrange, analyze, infer…

At exactly 6 p.m., Whitman gave the order. Operation School Dance was a go. Eight soldiers took to the field and crossed the perimeter. They walked casually and appeared to be chatting.

"Are we able to listen in?" Whitman asked.

"Yes, ma'am," said General Ramsey, who was overseeing the operation from HQ-2. "All of their mics are still functioning, and we're capturing ambient sound using various field devices."

"Can you feed one of their mics through to our speakers? I want more than the visuals."

"Just one moment. I'll put someone through… Okay, here we go."

There was a slight crackle, and then a voice could be heard.

"…and oh my God, she was so hot. I couldn't believe it, man. So, there I am, totally hung over, and—"

"Can you pick someone else, General?"

General Ramsey ended the feed. "Sorry, Madam President. We told them

185

to have a normal conversation. They are very good at following orders."

There were some chuckles in the Situation Room and at HQ-2. A moment later, another soldier's voice came through the speakers.

"...if we keep looking over. ... That's my point. Let's make it more natural, especially when we get into the kill-zone. ... Come on. ... No, I agree. They shouldn't call it a kill-zone. At least rename it before the operation. Like *We're sending you to the mothership* isn't enough, they gotta add *in the kill-zone* to justify the hazard pay or something. ... Nah, man, I'm just messin'. But I do think they could've come up with a better name. ... Like, I don't know. Vacation zone. Or hottie zone. Yeah man, every soldier in the whole joint would've signed up if they called it the hottie zone."

Whitman rolled her eyes. "I hope to God the aliens aren't listening. This is just embarrassing."

Kilmer glanced over and saw that Silla was finding it hilarious—and trying not to laugh out loud.

Whitman asked for the field audio to be patched through instead. Soon a slight humming sound, presumably emanating from ET-1's engines, could be heard.

Kilmer turned his attention back to the screen. The soldiers were approaching the 110-yard mark. They slowed down. And then they stopped. The fourteen deliveries that the cat shooter had made were easily visible, all but one of them situated at various points between the soldiers and ET-1. A few of them would be along their path as they moved toward the spacecraft.

"Madam President, we have initiated the three-minute countdown."

The soldiers were facing the spacecraft and standing in a small cluster. They were chatting with one another and occasionally waving at the spacecraft. They looked like trick-or-treaters waiting for someone to open the door.

The three minutes went by with no visible change to the scene. At least a few of the soldiers could be seen checking their watches. There was some conversation between them. Someone seemed to be adjusting his body camera. A few appeared to be testing their collar mics. Two of them reached into their jackets to retrieve what were probably their two-way radios. They both tested them. Then the group of eight began to move forward—slowly—their movements more deliberate now. When they reached what might have been the one-hundred-yard mark, a few hands went up to the earpieces.

"Madam President," Ramsey reported, "we're starting to lose sound… We've lost sound. We can't hear them. We have to assume they can't hear us either. We've also lost the body cameras."

On the screen, two other soldiers retrieved their two-way radios, fiddled with them, and tried to speak into them. By the looks of it, they were having no success.

It took another three minutes for the group to make it to the twenty-yard mark. They stood in two rows, four in front and four a few feet behind them—like a group of Christmas carolers. One of the soldiers in the front had a piece of paper in his hand—the welcome message. He appeared to be reading it aloud as his fellow soldiers stood at attention.

After the soldier put the paper away, the group began their five-minute wait. One of the other soldiers in the front row had his hands in his pockets and was swaying left to right. The other two soldiers in that row were waving, every so often, at the spacecraft. A soldier in the back was cracking his knuckles and looking every which way. Two others retrieved their two-way radios and held them close to their bodies. The fourth soldier in the back seemed most at ease; he was moving his head to some tune that he might have been whistling or humming.

Suddenly, a voice from the speakerphone shot through the Situation Room.

"Madam President, this is Noah!" Director Druckman shouted.

"Yes, Noah. What is it?"

"The aliens—they understand our countdown!"

"How do we know that? What are you saying?"

"Madam President, they just replicated our methodology. About a minute ago, they started broadcasting a four-minute countdown of their own."

"Counting down toward what? Do we have any idea?"

"None, Madam President."

Silla reached for her phone. "I'm going to check on the locations of the reserve spacecraft, Madam President. It could be anything."

Whitman gave her a nod and then turned back to the speakerphone. "HQ-2. Listen carefully. I want our soldiers to have the option of a quick escape. Move our support vehicles forward into Touchdown-1 but stay out of the kill-zone. The fact that they're giving us a countdown probably means that they don't intend any hostile action, but we can't take any chances—nor can we presume we know what they would consider to be 'hostile.' I'm going to put our F-35s and B-2s on alert. General Ramsey, I'm also putting your helicopters in the air, but they will be kept at a distance and low to the ground. We have our eyes on you and we have your back. However, if we lose contact with you for any reason, you are not—I repeat, *not*—to initiate any aggressive action of any kind against ET-1. We will make those calls from here. Is that clear?"

At least three *Yes, Madam President*s came back.

"I want HQ-1 and HQ-2 evacuated, except for essential personnel. The only people who can stay indoors are the ones making sure we have eyes, ears, communication, and coordination. I also want the four of you dispersed. Ramsey, I want you out there with your soldiers. Strauss, head to 300 degrees on the perimeter to keep an eye on things there. Noah, I want you out of the building, but keep us updated on the alien broadcast. Casey, I want you to remain at HQ-2 and stay on this call. Let's move."

The next few minutes went by slowly. The aerial camera showed soldiers and staff evacuating the field headquarters. The soldiers on the perimeter appeared to be taking cover or lying flat on the ground. Three vehicles started to make their way toward the spacecraft. The eight soldiers in the kill-zone remained unaware that ET-1 had initiated a countdown; they stayed at the twenty-yard mark.

The four minutes ended.

There was a collective gasp in the Situation Room.

Kilmer's first thought was that an explosion had just blown all of Touchdown-1 to smithereens. All five screens showed nothing but a blinding bright light. It had originated at or near ET-1 and then, within a split second, covered the entirety of the area.

But if this was an explosive or incendiary device, it functioned differently from human technology. The seconds ticked away, but the light didn't diminish in its intensity. It didn't turn into smoke, or fire, or scenes of devastation. There was nothing but continuous light—like staring directly into a powerful flashlight.

"This is the president!" Whitman announced loudly into the speakerphone. "Casey, do you hear me?"

There was no response from HQ-2.

"Zack, Salvo, Art, get on your phones. *Now!* Everyone—find me someone at Station Zero—I don't care if they're on the ground or in the sky. I want to know how widespread the blast is. Get me images from our UAVs."

Everyone was instantly on a cell phone—dialing, talking, or anxiously waiting for someone to pick up.

Kilmer had no one to call. He just sat there… thinking… watching… listening.

It was hard to hear over the commotion, but the humming of ET-1 continued. Then he heard a different sound—metallic, like someone dropping coins into a panhandler's tin cup. It stopped. He looked around, but no one else seemed to have noticed. He kept concentrating. But there was only more blinding light and more humming.

And then, suddenly, the light went away and the images on the screen returned. As if a switch had been turned off. There was no smoke, no devastation.

Seconds later, General Allen was on the speakerphone.

"Madam President."

"Casey! What the hell just happened?"

"I don't know. It was like a flash grenade—except it lasted almost two minutes. It felt like you were looking into the sun. But there was no blast, no sound of an explosion. I'm going to call for a headcount immediately."

Silla tapped Kilmer on the shoulder. He looked over and saw her staring at one of the screens—the aerial shot. Kilmer turned to the screen. The eight soldiers had been crouching or lying down on the field—and were now scattered around the 20-yard mark where they had earlier stood in two rows. They were starting to get up.

But that wasn't what had caught Silla's eye. She pointed. "Madam President, I think you need to take a look."

The president turned toward the screen. The image showed ET-1 parked in the center of Touchdown-1, with the eight soldiers still nearby. It also showed, at varying distances from the spacecraft, eight deliveries that the cat shooter had made earlier.

"Six of the deliveries are gone," Silla announced.

The conversation came alive with a barrage of questions. Did the aliens leave any tracks? Which ones were taken? Why only six? Did anyone see anything through the blinding light?

Kilmer wasn't part of the conversation. Something about the aerial shot had bothered him. He was now looking at a different screen—one that offered a better view of the soldiers. Most of them were now fully on their feet and looking only slightly disoriented.

Oh no.

Two of the soldiers were still on the ground—and they had not moved at all.

"We have casualties!" Chief of Staff Perez shouted before Kilmer could even find the words.

Whitman turned to the speakerphone. "Get our men out of there!" she shouted.

Everyone was back working the phones.

Within a minute, three vehicles arrived at the edge of the kill-zone. Three men jumped out of one of the vehicles and ran toward the six soldiers who appeared to be unhurt—and started to guide them out of the kill-zone. Four other men spilled out of second vehicle and removed two stretchers from the back. They ran off to retrieve the two injured—or dead—soldiers.

The two groups passed one another—nine soldiers returning to the vehicles and four soldiers moving toward the fallen men.

At that very moment—but without any countdown this time—the

blinding light reappeared, engulfing everyone on the field and all of Station Zero. The level of anxiety and activity in the Situation Room skyrocketed once again. But, just as before, the blinding light stayed on for only two minutes before it switched off again.

Everyone in the Situation Room stared in shock at the TV screens.

For the most part, everything looked the same as before—but there was one conspicuous exception.

The two fallen soldiers had disappeared.

Heirs of Herodotus by D. Kilmer.
Excerpt from Chapter 9.

Good leaders attempt to learn from their mistakes. They have the courage to acknowledge the consequences of prior decisions, no matter how terrible, so that errors will not be repeated. But in doing so, good leaders risk discarding even excellent ideas—simply because they failed, previously, to deliver the desired results. Great leaders, on the other hand, recognize that all outcomes—bad and good—are but noisy signals of the wisdom of their approach. Chance, error, and unknowns also play a role.

While good leaders exhibit the strength to learn from bad outcomes, great leaders show the wisdom not to overweight outcomes, whether they be bad or good. **Ultimately, outcomes are not what matter. Inputs matter—because only inputs can be chosen**. If your decision process was sound, if the strategy was wise ex ante, if you can find no fault in your approach despite extensive examination, then it is misguided to second-guess your actions simply because the outcome was rotten.

Those who blindly replicate what "succeeded" and abandon what "failed" do not only relinquish the mantle of leadership, they also risk losing their status as human beings. They reduce themselves to mere algorithms—and mediocre ones at that.

~ 54 ~

Thirty minutes had passed since the second blast of light, and Strauss, Druckman, Allen, and Ramsey were all back inside HQ-2. They were calling into the Oval Office, where Whitman, Nielsen, Perez, Garcia, Kilmer, Art, and Silla were seated around the coffee table. The mood was tense.

"*They attacked our men,*" Strauss argued. "I'm not asking you to declare war. But if we let them kill or abduct our men with impunity, we are on a slippery slope. We must take *some* action. And we must demand the return of our soldiers—or their remains, if necessary. I'm open to ideas, but I am *not* okay with doing nothing."

Director Druckman supported Strauss. NSA Garcia agreed. The aliens had made the first move. Earth-side had to do *something*, if for no other reason than to show some resolve or a willingness to push back.

"What do you think, Zack?" Whitman asked the vice president.

"If we don't want war, an aggressive response is not the next step. We need to find a way to communicate with them. We need to figure out what just happened, and why. And for us to get our soldiers back, we need some way to make that demand clear to them. Then we see how they respond."

Kilmer was so lost in his own thoughts that he was barely following along. *Why would they do that?* If they wanted to kill humans, they didn't need to wait until the soldiers were twenty yards away. Was it an abduction they were after? Did they need the soldiers to come closer before they could capture them? The other six soldiers had all been successfully evacuated, and all seemed fine, but none of them knew what had happened to the two who were taken. No one saw anything after the lights came on.

And what about the gifts? Why not pick them up earlier? Why wait for the soldiers to come into the kill-zone? It didn't make sense.

And yet, despite the long and growing list of unknowns, one thing was clear: ET-1 had just captured, and possibly killed, two human beings.

Kilmer suddenly realized that Whitman had called on him to speak.

"I'm sorry, Madam President. I was just trying to make sense of what we saw. It—it doesn't add up."

"No, Professor, I'm afraid it adds up pretty well," Strauss replied. "You just seem unwilling to face up to it. Your plan blew up in our faces. *That's* what it adds up to. If the president had listened to more experienced voices in the room, we might have avoided this."

Art tried to defuse the situation. "Mr. Secretary. Maybe it was a bad idea, but just because it failed doesn't mean it wasn't worth trying. We took a risk—we knew it had an upside and a downside."

Strauss countered. "Some of us could see the downside much more clearly. Others of us are a little too keen on seeing only the good in others, regardless of the context, and regardless of the evidence."

Kilmer tried to ignore Strauss's comments, but it was starting to feel like Cameroon all over again—except this time, he couldn't just walk away, hole up somewhere for two years, and feel sorry for screwing up. There were only two casualties at the moment, but that could change in the hours ahead.

Silla looked over at him. He could tell by the look on her face that she knew exactly what he was thinking—and why he was struggling. She shook her head: *Don't think about that.*

Nielsen caught Kilmer's eye and offered him a reassuring nod. *Don't worry, Professor. We'll figure it out.* Then the vice president addressed the group.

"We're not here to point fingers, Strauss. I'd like to hear specific suggestions that the president can evaluate. General Allen? We haven't heard from you."

"Mr. Vice President," Allen responded, "I'm obviously in favor of getting our boys back. But I don't want to lose sight of the other facts. Fact number one: they picked up some of our gifts. Fact number two: they didn't pick up the gifts right away. And fact number three: they did not attack *all* the soldiers, even though all eight were sitting ducks after the lights came on. How do we explain that?"

Druckman offered a theory. "Imagine you're ET-1 and you want to learn as much as you can about us. You don't want to start a war—not yet anyway—because you don't know what you're up against. You first want to study our technology *and* our species. So, you take a sample of the gifts, and a sample of our soldiers. But you're smart about it. You don't attack the armed soldiers on the perimeter. And you sit tight—even though the gifts are within reach. You wait until the humans get impatient and come closer. That's when you strike and take what you need."

Kilmer was impressed. It tied a lot of the clues together—although not quite all. For one thing, why did the aliens bother to use a countdown? Kilmer put his head down and tried to think while still tracking the conversation.

"It sounds plausible, Noah," Nielsen replied. "So, what does that mean we should do?"

"I'll tell you what it means we should *not* do," Strauss bellowed. "They've already hit us twice with those goddamn lights—we can't wait to find out what happens the third time they blind us."

Kilmer's head snapped up.

They've already hit us twice.

Strauss had just handed Kilmer the missing piece of the puzzle. Almost immediately, the mental cascade began.

Two flashes.

Three tasks.

Two-way radios.

Tin cups.

Kilmer almost cursed out loud. *I should have seen it sooner.* Even now—after racking his brain for so long—he had come dangerously close to accepting Druckman's theory of what had happened.

But Druckman had gotten it wrong—and it changed everything.

Kilmer leaned back and took a deep breath. His eyes narrowed, and something that could have been mistaken for a smile came to his lips. But the expression evinced more anger than joy. Silla turned to him just in time to catch the look on his face—and she knew it in an instant. Professor Kilmer had something to say.

~ 55 ~

Kilmer had been wanting to stretch his legs for a while. But until that moment, he had felt uncharacteristically timid. It was the guilt. Whitman had made the final call, but Kilmer was the reason those soldiers were in the kill-zone in the first place. It was his idea, and it had failed in spectacular fashion.

He no longer felt any hesitation—and he took to his feet. Everyone else must have assumed he was in the doghouse as well; they seemed surprised that he was choosing to draw attention to himself.

"Madam President, would you mind if I pose a few questions?" Kilmer asked.

"Go ahead, Professor."

"I'd like to go back to something Secretary Strauss said a few minutes ago. He reminded us that the aliens have already hit us twice. Isn't that right, Mr. Secretary?"

"That's right. And it's two more than I find acceptable," Strauss replied over the speakerphone.

"Two more than *any* of us enjoyed, Mr. Secretary. But it does beg the question: *why two separate flashes?* They took six packages *and* attacked our soldiers during the first flash. Why not abduct the soldiers at the same time?"

There was a brief silence before Druckman responded. "Maybe they didn't have enough time. Maybe they can only keep the light on for two minutes at a time."

"That's certainly possible, but is it compelling? They seemed to have three tasks: retrieve the gifts, injure the soldiers, and abduct the soldiers. If you had to divide this to-do list across two flashes, how would you do it? I'll tell you what I'd do. I'd *only* take the gifts in the first flash, and I'd leave the attacking and kidnapping for the second one. Why put humans on high alert by injuring two of their soldiers the first time around, and not even finish the job? Or, I'd attack *and* kidnap the soldiers during the first flash, and then take the gifts in the second." Kilmer looked at Whitman. "That's how I would do it."

"Well then," said Strauss. "I guess we've learned something important. These aliens are just like the rest of us. Not *quite* as smart as Professor Kilmer." The sarcasm was not lost in transmission. "Or... *maybe* they just made a mistake. Or—maybe they think differently than we do. Or maybe it's hard for them to attack and kidnap all within two minutes."

"Maybe," Kilmer agreed. "But it got me thinking. What *else* might explain their behavior?"

Whitman leaned back and folded her arms, her posture evincing a strong interest in where Kilmer was headed.

"I have a prediction," Kilmer continued. "If we replay the recording of what just happened at Station Zero, we will notice a few things that everyone here will find... *curious*. Is it possible for us to take a look?"

"Sure," said Art. "I can stream it simultaneously over here and on Director Druckman's computer at HQ-2."

Kilmer looked at Whitman, who nodded her consent. "Then I suggest we do that," said Kilmer.

It took one phone call and about three minutes of waiting.

"Art, can you please take us to the moment when our soldier reads the welcome statement?"

Art queued up the recording while Kilmer told the group what he wanted them to observe.

"After the first bright light came on, the soldiers scattered all about. But, at this point, the soldiers are still in two rows of four. I don't know these soldiers, so I can't tell you which two were abducted, but I would bet that they're in the front row during the clip we're about to watch."

Art started the tape. The only sound that could be heard was the hum of the spacecraft, but the picture quality was excellent. Art paused it after the welcome speech began.

General Allen spoke up from HQ-2. "I can confirm that the two soldiers who went missing are both in the front row. What are we supposed to infer from this? That they were at greater risk because they were closer to ET-1?"

"General Allen, I'd prefer that you not infer *anything* yet," Kilmer replied. "But soon."

"The next thing I want you to notice," he continued, "are the two men in the back row who retrieve their two-way radios after the welcome speech ends."

Art resumed the recording. The speech ended, and then a few more seconds elapsed.

"Here it comes," Kilmer called out. On cue, two of the soldiers reached into their jackets to retrieve their radios. One hugged his close to his chest. The other held his slightly lower, close to his belt.

Kilmer asked Art to pause the recording again. Then he looked around the room, but no one seemed to have a clue what it all meant.

Druckman broke the silence. "I'm impressed that you noticed these small details about what the soldiers did, Professor, but I'm afraid I'm completely lost. So what?"

"It's not about seeing what the soldiers *did*. Noticing what they *didn't* do is what will make all the difference."

There were blank faces all around.

"And what is it that they didn't do?" Nielsen asked.

"Why would you retrieve your radio at that moment?" Kilmer asked. "It doesn't even work in the kill-zone."

There was a pause.

"Maybe they wanted to check whether the radios had somehow started to work—in case they were needed," Perez suggested.

"I had exactly the same thought," Kilmer admitted. "But then I realized, that couldn't be why they did it. Notice, Mr. Perez, that neither soldier even glanced at his radio after taking it out—and they certainly didn't test to see if the radios were working. They just held the radios close to them. Nice and snug. Like they were safety blankets, not radios."

Kilmer saw Silla's reaction. Her curiosity was starting to transform, slowly, into understanding. The rest could only see that Kilmer had identified a few anomalies. They had no idea what tied them all together.

He voiced the frustration that was starting to grow. "Clearly, a number of things don't make much sense. So—what *does* make sense? One last hint should do the trick. It pertains to something that occurred during the first flash. It was easy to miss, especially given the panic we were all experiencing at the time, but if you pay close attention, I don't think you'll miss it now. Art, can we please watch the two minutes of the first flash?"

Art looked confused even as he started to queue up the recording. "Professor Kilmer, there's really nothing to see. It's just blinding light. We all saw it when it happened—and I've re-watched the recording since. What exactly do you want us to look for?"

"Nothing at all," Kilmer answered.

There were some looks of confusion in the Oval Office—and some expressions of annoyance at HQ-2.

"What I want you to do *instead*," Kilmer clarified, "is to *listen.*"

The replay started a few seconds before the flash of light. Then everything went white. The only sound was the humming of ET-1. A few more moments passed. And then came the sound. Art looked up at Kilmer as soon as it happened. Kilmer nodded, and Art stopped the recording.

Kilmer looked at President Whitman and Chief of Staff Perez. "I have to confess this is not my area of expertise. When I first heard the sound in the Situation Room, I thought it sounded like someone was dropping coins into a tin cup. But there were no tin cups on the field. That sound, I now realize, was—"

"The sound of bullets," Perez finished. He looked shaken.

"Not just the sound of bullets," the president clarified. "That's the sound of bullets bouncing off of metal."

"Precisely," Kilmer agreed. He could see that both Perez and Whitman had pieced together at least half of the story. But did they understand the implication?

"Those bullets we heard in the recording weren't fired at our soldiers. They were fired *by* our soldiers. The two soldiers in the back had not been retrieving two-way radios. They were retrieving and concealing their firearms—which presumably had silencers, which is why we didn't hear the shots themselves."

Whitman clenched her teeth.

"*General Ramsey*. Is this accurate?" Whitman asked, with more patience than Kilmer thought he would have been able to muster in her position. "Did our soldiers… go into the kill-zone… with *weapons?*"

Ramsey came on the line. "Madam President, I'm not sure what—how this—"

Strauss jumped in. "Wait a minute. What the hell are you implying, Professor? Are you seriously going to play defense counsel for the aliens even *now?* Our soldiers were the ones who were attacked. Two of our men were abducted and are MIA!" he yelled.

But Kilmer was done playing games with the defense secretary. "That's right, Strauss. Our soldiers *were* the ones who were attacked. But our soldiers aren't made of metal. You know what *is* made of metal? A certain spacecraft the size of a football field that scared the daylights out of our men just moments before the shooting started. Those bullets were fired at *ET-1*, Mr. Secretary. They were fired by our soldiers. Now, I'd love for *you* to stop playing defense counsel for whoever fucked this up—and to start thinking about the implications."

"The two soldiers who were injured…" Silla started.

"That's right, Agent Silla. They were shot from behind. They were shot by their fellow soldiers."

Perez looked horrified. "Are you saying that they meant to—"

"No," answered Kilmer quickly, knowing where Perez was headed. "I don't think it was intentional. It was probably just the fog of war. But you don't have to take my word for it. The soldiers who did the shooting are still with us. I would take them into custody and test for gunshot residue. You'll find it."

Whitman was furious. "General Allen, as of this minute, you are replacing General Ramsey as the commanding officer at Station Zero. I want you to get to the bottom of what happened here, and not just in the kill-zone. I want to know who authorized the two soldiers to carry firearms in the first place. Attorney General Kim will get in touch with you and will coordinate with the IGs of the Army and DoD to ensure you have proper legal guidance. General

Ramsey will be reporting to you until further notice—at which point he will either be reinstated as CO, or permanently relieved of his command and removed from Station Zero."

General Allen acknowledged Whitman's orders. General Ramsey spoke immediately after and apologized for allowing this to happen under his command. He promised to help General Allen in any way he could. Druckman weighed in and thanked Kilmer for helping "clear up a grave misunderstanding." Strauss said relatively little except that the incident was "tragic," and that the outcome was "unfortunate indeed."

Whitman did not seem consoled in the least. She walked over to her desk as she addressed everyone, both in the Oval Office and at HQ-2. Her voice was only a few decibels below booming—and yet she somehow avoided the impression that she was yelling.

"Let me make something clear. I'm not out for revenge. I'm not even looking for justice. I can't afford such luxuries. The future of our country— and of *this planet*—is at stake. The only thing I'm looking for is the absolute *certainty* that once I make a decision, it *will* be carried out. That one of you will *not* screw it up simply because you think you know better." She paused to let her words sink in. "Everyone here has a choice to make. You can commit to doing your job, or you can resign. There is no third option."

She concluded with a piece of advice. "If you have something you need to tell me, I strongly suggest that you reach out to me before midnight tonight. You will not get a second chance. Is that understood?"

There were many *Yes, Madam President*s. General Ramsey's might have been the loudest.

~ 56 ~

Whitman called for a ten-minute break and asked Kilmer to follow her outside. They stepped onto the West Colonnade, overlooking the Rose Garden, and talked as they strolled in the warm breeze.

"Thank you, Professor. You brought us back from the brink."

"I almost missed it," was all Kilmer would say about it. Then he took a deep breath. "Madam President, I don't think what happened was simply a matter of someone disagreeing with you on whether to arm our soldiers, and then taking matters into their own hands. I think some people at Station Zero are willing to go much farther in undermining your authority—even if it risks serious escalation."

"Do you really think someone would risk all-out war with an alien race just to prove me unfit for the presidency? These people might be overzealous at times—maybe even insubordinate in this case—but they're not completely insane."

"That's just it," Kilmer cautioned. "Put yourself in their shoes and it doesn't seem insane. If someone genuinely believes you are unfit to lead, and that a more aggressive strategy is the right approach to dealing with this threat, what's to stop them from engaging in even more egregious behavior than what we saw today? If their actions save the day, they're vindicated. And if they lead to war, they'll probably just tell themselves that Whitman was to blame for not having been more aggressive from the start—or that war was anyways inevitable. Remember, we only figured it out a few minutes ago, but *someone* knew all along that our soldiers were armed—and they kept their mouths shut even after two of our soldiers were shot. Their silence on this crucial matter could well have pushed us toward war."

Whitman shook her head. "Not just a cover-up, but a dangerous gamble."

"Yes. But they would see it primarily as an act of courage—followed by a bit of bad luck." Kilmer paused. "I'm afraid we won't survive this crisis unless we get into the habit of examining—*constantly*—how things look from the other side of the table."

"It's disconcerting, Professor, that you're having to say this about people in my administration when we should be focusing on trying to understand the aliens."

"I'm talking about all of them, Madam President. I'm talking about seeing the perspective of everyone, on every side, of every table, in every room. Nothing could be more essential."

Kilmer had figured out what the aliens had *not* done—it was humans who were responsible for the shooting—but there was still no explanation for what the aliens *had* done. Why abduct the soldiers? When the group reconvened, NSA Garcia articulated a possible explanation. The aliens had seen the fallen soldiers and decided they might learn something from them. They hadn't *shot* the soldiers, but they *had* been opportunistic.

Art suggested something that seemed ludicrous at first, but which was nonetheless hard to dismiss: maybe the aliens thought the dead soldiers were some sort of sacrificial offering, or just another gift package they were supposed to accept. It was a ghastly conjecture, Kilmer thought, but then again, Art ran a super-secret group in an agency with a super-terrible past. They probably had a higher bar for what was considered dreadful.

The possibility that the soldiers had survived made retrieval an even bigger priority. How much they might suffer at the hands of the aliens, even if unintentionally, was impossible to know, but there were no limits to the imagination.

Druckman, who was coordinating with the FERMAT team, and Art, who led the Hermes team, were bombarded with questions about whether it was possible to communicate the demand that the soldiers be returned.

Art explained. "The problem is that we can't use the old playbook, which was to try a whole bunch of ideas and see if anything works. This issue requires much more nuanced communication than sending coordinates or broadcasting a countdown. The complexity vastly increases the risk of sending the wrong message. We also need to think longer term. The more signals or patterns we send now, the harder it will be for them to figure out how to put everything together once we start trying to teach them Hermes. My advice comes down to patience. Give us until tomorrow to launch Hermes 1.0. If it works, we can build on that. Hopefully, we can get it to the point where we can have complex conversations."

It wasn't a satisfying answer, but it was sensible. Nor were there satisfactory answers to other looming questions. Had the aliens come out of their spacecraft using the blinding light as cover? Did they use some other technology to extract the packages? Why hadn't they picked up *all* the packages? A list of what was retrieved by ET-1 showed no obvious pattern—except that every book had been taken.

"It's quite possible they have no clue what any of these things are," NSA Garcia cautioned. "And the packages were picked up pretty quickly. It might have all been impulse shopping."

Whitman moved to end the meeting. The priority, she announced, was to get Hermes up and running. "Art, I want something ready by tomorrow morning. Whatever it takes." She looked around the room. "It's not just about the two soldiers. There are a lot of questions we need answered."

They were back to square one—no information, no leads, no obvious next steps. The aliens had danced, but all too briefly.

"Madam President, might I raise one more issue?" Silla asked.

"Yes, Agent Silla."

"The aliens appear to be significantly more technologically advanced than us. But a curious pattern has emerged. Ever since the detection, *we* have taken the initiatives and they have merely reacted. We came up with a language to send coordinates. We created the timer. We sent care packages. We put our people on the dance floor first. I'm left wondering why they haven't launched any initiatives of their own. If they're so advanced, maybe *they* should be the ones looking for ways to communicate. Why aren't they proactive?"

No one had any good answers.

Silla turned to Kilmer. "Professor, do you think we risk seeming too eager in our overtures? Might they get the impression that we're desperate or subservient?"

"Yes, there is that risk—and we should be mindful. But there could be other explanations for their behavior as well."

"Such as?" Whitman asked.

"Well, fear, for example. And there is at least one fear that tends to afflict the strong even more so than the weak—the fear of losing everything. Whether ET-1's lack of initiative stems from a sense of superiority—or from a sense of vulnerability—we just don't know yet."

Strauss objected. "They're the ones who traveled all this way. They didn't have to do that, Professor. What could *they* have to feel vulnerable about?"

"I'm not sure. But even the coolest cat in town will hesitate before asking the prettiest girl in school to the dance. In fact, he might hesitate most of all. The cool cat has the most to lose."

"You think they fear...what? *Rejection?*" Strauss asked, with a hint of exasperation.

"No, Mr. Secretary. People don't fear rejection; they fear what rejection leads to. They fear *pain*. And the ones who fear pain most of all are the ones who have never felt it before." He paused. "Or those who have felt it so acutely that they will never allow themselves to be vulnerable again."

Heirs of Herodotus by D. Kilmer.
Excerpt from Chapter 10.

Greed, fear, and grievances—these have been the causes of war throughout human history. Across the centuries, across the globe, and across the many faultlines that have divided human beings since social constructs and social categorization took hold, the fundamental drivers of war have remained constant. Many other factors impact the duration and intensity of war—as well as how it ends—but if not for want, insecurity, and vengeance, humanity might have avoided the scourge of war.

Greed and grievance have fueled many a conflict, but it is fear that has contributed the most to human suffering. It is the hardest to root out. It is the most difficult to ignore. It composes the most alluring cry with which to rally citizens and soldiers. It provides the easiest moral justification for the killing of other human beings. No concession, no apology, no threat can put deep-seated fear to rest.

Those among us who hope to put an end to war—not only a specific war, but to war itself—must focus more of our effort, intellect, and creativity on the element of fear. **The greatest threat to security has always been—and remains—the perception of insecurity. We must find a way to resolve this paradox before it resolves itself through Armageddon.**

~ 59 ~

Secretary Strauss had butted heads with Whitman from the very start of her presidency, and his friends had been advising him to leave the administration for months. On at least two occasions, he had almost resigned, only to decide against it at the last minute. It was just a matter of time, he figured, before he called it quits—or Whitman asked him to leave. Yes, he had presidential aspirations of his own, but he was also tired of being the lone voice of dissent on too many decisions.

That changed—for Strauss, at least—when the aliens showed up. As a third-generation soldier and the son of a Navy Cross recipient, Strauss knew there were times in life when you were duty-bound to stay in the fight, no matter what the cost. This was one of those times. The president might not follow his advice, but she needed to hear it. They disagreed often, but Strauss knew that Whitman didn't give anyone a seat at the table unless she respected their opinion. Whitman could not be bullied, but she *could* be influenced. That meant he had to stay.

Despite what Whitman or Perez believed—and Strauss knew they believed it—he had never proposed that the president be impeached. He *had* been in the room when it was discussed—on at least a few occasions—and he had not denounced the idea. Strauss was smart enough to know that his silence could be construed as support—and he now realized it had been a mistake to leave that impression. Things had gotten out of hand. He had fought with Whitman publicly, failed to defend her privately, and made no secret of the fact that he believed he would make a better president, leading people like General Ramsey to surmise that he might support efforts to undermine the president's authority. It was supposed to have been a no-lose proposition for Strauss: put pressure on Whitman to shift her policies while laying the foundation for a future presidential campaign. *What's the harm?*

The events at Station Zero had answered that question in dramatic fashion. Not everyone understood that there were limits to how far you push your own agenda—and lines you should never cross. Those lines *had* been crossed.

This was what Strauss was thinking about when he received the call from Vice President Nielsen. The two had been close colleagues in the Senate, and Nielsen had played no small part in bringing Strauss into Whitman's administration, but there was no hint of friendship in the voice Strauss heard over the phone.

"If you had something to do with this, Strauss, I am going to personally make sure you pay for it."

"Zack, you know what I think of Marianne's policies and her approach. You also know that I would never do something like this. You need to make sure the president understands that."

"No, Strauss. *You* need to make sure of that. I've warned you before about playing with fire—that the sparks you let fly in every direction will someday burn down your own house. Whether you stay or go is between you and the president now. If she asks for my opinion on it, it will not go well for you, so don't let it come to that. And one last thing. We're friends, Strauss. But if you come after her again—while you're in the White House or from the outside—you're going to see a side of me that you have had the good fortune to never witness."

By 11:45 p.m., Whitman had received two phone calls and made three decisions.

General Ramsey called first and admitted to arming the two soldiers. He explained that he had done so out of concern for his troops. He apologized and told Whitman that no one else had participated in that decision.

The second call was from Strauss. He told Whitman that he had not been involved in any decision to arm the soldiers, but that it was possible Ramsey had gotten the impression that he would approve of such actions. For that, Strauss said, he was sorry. He acknowledged that he continued to see things differently from the president, and offered to resign if Whitman preferred a defense secretary who was more aligned with her thinking.

"Is that your preferred outcome, Strauss?" Whitman asked bluntly. "Do you wish to resign?"

Strauss responded candidly. "No, Madam President. I prefer to stay. And I want to help you succeed."

Whitman's first decision was to remove General Ramsey from Station Zero. General Allen would stay on as commanding officer. Her second decision was to reject Strauss's offer to resign. She told him that she still valued his counsel, and that his voice was important *because* he disagreed with her. She didn't mention her second reason for keeping him around: it was better for Strauss to do his complaining from inside the administration than from the sidelines. As LBJ had so eloquently said about J. Edgar Hoover: *It's probably better to have him inside the tent pissing out than outside the tent pissing in.* Whitman's final decision was to recall Director Druckman back to Washington. He had other responsibilities, ones that did not involve ET-1, and it seemed wise to separate Strauss and Druckman for a while.

Meanwhile, elsewhere in the White House, Kilmer had asked Silla to stay the night. She had just enough clothes left in her duffel bag to say yes. Their first hour in the Lincoln Bedroom was spent in silence. Silla sat working on the bed while Kilmer sat quietly at the desk, thinking.

Four big questions. What drives them? Why did they visit now? Why are they being so hesitant? How might humanity avoid disaster for the decades and centuries to come?

Something tied everything together—but what?

By midnight, Kilmer had reached a frustrating conclusion: no amount of cognitive effort would help him figure this out. He needed more information. *We have to talk to them.*

He looked over at Silla, who was on her laptop, fully immersed in her work. He knew that, sooner or later, he would make the decision to go to Station Zero. The idea of leaving her was becoming a less pleasant thought with every passing hour, but it had to be done.

He crawled onto the bed and snuggled up next to her. She gave him a quick kiss on the cheek and then went back to ignoring him. A few minutes later, he was asleep. Silla kept working, but in between calls and emails, she slept in his arms. It was the best sleep either of them could ever remember having.

~ 60 ~

Day 17.

By 1:00 p.m. on Day 17, human beings had taught the aliens five words. A human, a dog, a small tree, a stack of books, and a jeep had each entered the kill-zone after a brief countdown. A bright spotlight was shined on each object for five minutes, while a unique digital signature was simultaneously broadcast. After this was repeated for three rounds, the aliens started to broadcast back the unique signature—the "word" associated with the highlighted object.

By 11:30 p.m., the aliens had learned over one hundred words—including *ET-1*—and were now able to add new words to their vocabulary with only a ten-second spotlight needed per word. The error rate was minuscule.

Day 18.

By 10:00 a.m. on Day 18, the aliens had learned verbs, including run, jump, throw, catch, fall, and eat.

By 5:00 p.m., they had learned thirty-five verbs, ten colors, and over two dozen adjectives and prepositions, including large, small, fast, slow, round, square, broken, torn, on, near, strong, weak, soft, and hard. Many of the lessons required the contrasting of two objects, two characteristics, or two actions. To teach "large" and "small," for example, two identical objects, one larger than the other, were introduced simultaneously, and the spotlight/broadcast was alternated between them.

The aliens also started to combine descriptors—without being taught to do so. Late in the day, when a table was spotlighted, the aliens described it as "table," "brown," "hard," "round," and "still." The rest of the night was spent teaching concepts such as *yes, no, and, or, going, coming, leader, follower, waiting,* and *choosing.* It was unknown whether the aliens could understand human emotions, but they quickly learned to differentiate between happy, sad, scared, and angry facial expressions.

Day 19.

By late morning of Day 19, the aliens were not only learning the digital language Hermes, but also English. Large letters were spotlighted, pronounced using a loudspeaker, and marked digitally. And then, complete words were spotlighted, along with the objects that they corresponded to—for example, a sign that read "chair" was placed next to a chair, while the word "chair" was announced. By nightfall, the aliens not only responded with the Hermes signals for *human, sitting, on,* and *chair* when presented with a human sitting on a chair, they also sent those same signals when the loudspeaker announced the phrase "human sitting on a chair" in English.

At 11:00 p.m., several more books, including some picture dictionaries, were launched by the cat shooter.

At midnight, after a three-minute countdown, ET-1 switched on its blinding light and retrieved the package.

Day 20.

On the morning of Day 20, President Whitman was informed that the laptop sent to the aliens was being used to surf the web. The aliens were spending time on government websites, YouTube, Wikipedia, Google Maps, Google Translate, Google Scholar, and various science, technology, news, and military websites. They had also discovered human pornography but seemed uninterested in it.

It was unclear how they had connected to the internet.

~ 61 ~

Day 20. Morning.

At 10:00 a.m. on Day 20, the aliens sent their first unprompted message to human beings. Because the only way ET-1 could broadcast messages to Earth-side was through Hermes, which entailed the use of numeric signatures for letters and words, ET-1 had been forced to spell out the words for which it had not been sent a digital signature. The message was nine words in length:

Humans two a.n.d. Alive a.n.d. Walking a.n.d. t.h.e. Home.

For Whitman's team—at the White House and Station Zero—the message elicited as much surprise as it did a sense of hope. At 10:30, there was a blinding light. When it switched off, the two missing soldiers were standing in the kill-zone. They were retrieved immediately. Doctors reported that bullets had been removed from their bodies, including one from the heart of a soldier. They appeared to have been sutured using some type of laser. There were no signs of torture or trauma. Neither soldier had any memory of what took place during their captivity. They might have been unconscious the entire time.

At 1:00 p.m., the president met with her team in the Oval Office. Strauss and Allen were calling in from HQ-2. Energy Secretary Rao and Dr. Menon were joining remotely as well. Now that the soldiers had been released—not only unharmed but mended—Whitman wanted to find some way to build on the positive momentum. ET-1's ability and willingness to communicate had also boosted the prospects for productive diplomacy, and the appropriate next steps needed to be worked out.

Only ten minutes into the meeting, Art interrupted the president with urgent news to share.

"Madam President. Almost five minutes ago we received another message from ET-1. I thought there was an error of some kind, so I had the Hermes signal retranslated. The initial readout appears to be accurate."

Art read the message aloud, carefully enunciating each word. As soon as he finished reading, all heads snapped toward Kilmer, as if he alone might have an explanation for what they had heard. He had no answers for them.

The message was longer than the first one and used slightly better syntax. But it made absolutely no sense. Whitman looked shocked. Silla looked terrified. But no one said a word.

Kilmer repeated the message to himself, looking for some way to figure out how in the world it could have been translated accurately.

Large d.a.n.g.e.r. for Earth. W.e. w.i.l.l. r.u.l.e.

Enter ET-1. Come two a.m.b.a.s.s.a.d.o.r.s.

M.u.s.t. come t.h.e. leader o.f. Earth.

M.u.s.t. come D. K.i.l.m.e.r.

Part IV

the ambassador

~ 62 ~

"The message said *what?* That doesn't make any sense."

Professor Kilmer sat in a conference room that had been named Apate 3 by a group of witty Triad agents. One such agent was sitting across the table from him. Her name was Renata Silla. Professionally, she was Agent Silla. To her friends, she was just plain Ren. And to a man who had once loved her, she was Silla. But that man no longer existed. Professor Kilmer wished, very much, that he could have known him.

Two hours earlier, Art Capella had shown Kilmer a video recording that had completely blown his mind. The video was of a meeting that had taken place on Day 15. He and Agent Silla had sat next to each other during that meeting. But Kilmer had no memories of the event—and no memories of her.

And yet…

He couldn't explain it any better than that. *And yet.* There were no other words. He didn't even know why he had felt so crushed when he saw the tears on Agent Silla's face. That they shared a connection was obvious, and not simply by way of deduction. There was something more profound that testified to a link between them.

He had almost reached out to her then, reflexively, when he saw her in anguish. *Almost*—until a slight hesitation from her as he moved toward her curbed his instinct. She had left the room to wash her face clean of emotions. When she returned, she apologized for having acted unprofessionally. Then she went back to being, once again, a total stranger.

And yet.

Art, Silla, and Lane had then spent the next two hours telling Kilmer as much as they could about what he had lived through during the time he'd spent at the White House. He had listened, patiently and intently, but with an unwavering sense of incredulity. The agents had narrated, with great precision, the events of his life—from Day 14, when Nielsen first invited him to DC, until Day 20, when the alien message came through. He had no memory of any of it.

To facilitate the briefing, Art consulted a large binder filled with notes from interviews with President Whitman and Vice President Nielsen. Whitman and Nielsen had told the Triad agents most of what had transpired during their time with Kilmer, so that the professor would have a complete picture of the events that he no longer remembered. President Whitman had left out a bit of sensitive material that she didn't want to share with Triad, but the record was otherwise comprehensive and extremely detailed.

The only person who left out more information than President Whitman was Agent Silla. She mentioned very little about the time that she and Kilmer had spent together, detailing only their professional meetings and conversations, but he knew there was much more to her story. He knew it not based on data, facts, or memories. He knew it like you know the feeling of home, or the sense of your own being, or the sound of your inner voice—like something that is profoundly familiar but still inaccessible for the purpose of rational examination. He recognized her at a level too deep to engage with consciously, much less put into words. That was both the magic and the curse of his sense of Agent Silla. She was a complete stranger, *and yet*, as if in some other dimension, he knew her intimately.

It wasn't until Art mentioned the message ET-1 had sent on Day 20 that Kilmer felt the need to interrupt. But now that he had done so, a barrage of questions came crashing into his mind. He tried to sift through the rubble and identify the most important ones.

"I'm sorry to interject, Art, but I have some questions that I need answered."

"Professor Kilmer, you've been sitting silently for close to two hours. I'm amazed that you haven't asked a question, demanded a cup of coffee, or taken a stroll across the room. By all means, ask your questions. You're entitled to as many answers as you want."

"Maybe I can start with the easiest one and work my way up to what really makes no sense to me."

"Of course. Go ahead."

"What's with all the transparency? This evening started in a shroud of mystery. You let me believe that the meeting was being streamed live. None of you would answer any of my questions. Now, suddenly, you're an open book—with, literally, an open book in front of you—telling me as much as you can. Why the switch?"

"Professor, I was under strict orders not to reveal anything related to the time you spent with us, until we were sure that your memory of those events was, in fact, completely erased. If you remembered even a few things on your own—if aspects of the meeting you observed, for example, had seemed familiar to you—that might have meant that there was a chance we could help you recover more of your memory. That's also why I insisted that you tell me how you figured out that the meeting had taken place in the past. I was hoping there was something that had triggered a memory. As you eventually revealed to us, however, it was simply due to your powers of observation and deduction. What we were trying to avoid, Professor, was to conflate in your mind what you might naturally remember with what we told you or hinted at. We had to keep you in the dark until we were sure about whether and what you remembered. I'm sorry about that."

"But why should it matter whether my memories return naturally, or through your prompting, or through some combination of the two? Or if I remember anything at all? I appreciate your desire to put me back together, but I suspect that you aren't just interested in this for my sake. What's so important about this? You already have your binder with all the data. Who the hell cares if I remember anything that happened during my time in DC?"

Agent Silla flinched at his last statement, and he could see that his words had been hurtful, albeit for reasons he didn't fully understand. He would have to be more careful. He didn't want to hurt her—that much he knew.

Art tried to explain. "It matters a great deal what you remember and how, Professor. We're still trying to avoid a war, and many of us believe—or maybe we just *hope*—that hidden away in what you've forgotten is the key to doing that. Parts of your experience that none of us can remind you of—parts of your memory that none of us share—might hold the secret to resolving this existential crisis. This will become clearer to you as we fill you in on the rest of what took place—on what happened after we received that message from ET-1."

"I see. And just telling me where things stand now, and asking for my thoughts on what you should do—that isn't good enough? My memory of what I experienced is *that* important?"

"Like I said, we can't be sure—but we think so. But let me be clear about something. Whether you can remember anything or not, President Whitman wants you back on her side. That will probably come as no surprise to you. Based on what I've told you so far it should be obvious that she's a big fan."

The whole thing was bizarre. To Kilmer's knowledge—or to be more precise, to the best of his recollection—he had never met the president of the United States. Now he was being told that they had a close relationship. And for the life of him, Kilmer couldn't figure out what bothered him more—that he didn't wear a tie when he went to the White House, or that this detail was deemed important enough to be included in the briefing.

Do they really track that kind of thing? No, of course not. They had added some of the smaller details of his visit to see if *anything* might jog his memory. Perhaps some minor, seemingly innocuous fragment of memory had survived within him, and it could be the seed from which the rest might be cultivated. That might also explain the small detail about him saying "fuck" in the Oval Office while arguing with Secretary Strauss, and the one about him expropriating the president's coffee cup when he first met her. He was starting to wonder how he had managed to leave a good impression on *anyone* at the White House.

Art certainly didn't seem to mind sharing the snippets of Kilmer's life that seemed most likely to make him cringe. But, for Kilmer, it was like hearing your own voice on a recording. You know it's you, but you still wonder—is that really what I sound like?

And then a pattern came to his attention. He had seen Agent Silla smile only a few times over the last two hours, and it was always during those silly, cringe-worthy moments of the story—when Kilmer was just a regular guy, not the caricature of a protagonist who was brought in to save the day. *She knew me in ways that others didn't.* That was what she had lost. And, presumably, that was what *he* had lost as well.

But there was a world of difference between Kilmer and Silla. Hers was the kind of suffering that is reserved for those who still remember—a pain made even worse by the knowledge that others have forgotten.

Kilmer took a deep breath. "Agent Capella, you can let the president know that I will do my best to help—and that I'm sorry for being unable to remember."

"I will let her know as soon as we're finished here tonight. Do you have any more questions before I pick up where we left off?"

"Yes, I'm afraid I do. I understand that the number of people in the loop was small to begin with. But by the time you're in your second and third week since the aliens were detected, there are people from various agencies, hundreds of soldiers, and delegations from multiple countries involved. It defies logic that they all could have kept the secret. Things leak with even just a handful of people involved. Here we're talking about scores of people, and then hundreds. How was this not picked up by the media?"

"I'm sorry, Professor—I didn't mean to imply that the world never found out. My Lord, *yes*, they certainly did. I just didn't get into it yet because it's not relevant to what we're briefing you on. As early as Day 4, there were rumors, but they were fantastic enough that we didn't have to worry about them too much. They sounded like every other conspiracy theory on the topic and they didn't make the rounds with serious journalists or news channels. They did, however, push us to create a plan for keeping the news from spreading before we were ready for it. The usual grab bag of agency tricks, to be honest."

"Such as?"

"Well, just to be clear, Professor, it wasn't *Triad* doing this stuff. But we're talking about things like muddying the waters by planting fake stories about aliens that could then be proven false. Getting some fringe 'experts' on the air—people who won't be taken seriously because they always go too far into crazy-town. I mean, it's one thing to say that the government is tracking an alien spacecraft, but some of these folks can't leave it at that. They feel the need to insist that the aliens have already infiltrated the White House or some such thing. Anyway, my point is, there are things that the agency can do to make the news go away for a while. And, of course, we took all the obvious precautions. Not a single soldier at Station Zero, for example, knew *why* they were there until Day 15—the day ET-1 began to hover over Touchdown-1. And by then, none of them had access to phones or the internet. The Europeans had fewer such problems because fewer people were in the loop. And the Russians and the Chinese… well, let's not get into how they make sure no one talks.

"But by Day 11, the chatter on social media was getting loud, and on Day 12, President Whitman had to ask both the *Washington Post* and the *New York Times* not to print three separate stories that were hitting too close to home. It wasn't until Day 15 that there were short stories on some news channels that reported on seemingly suspicious government activity and on a variety of other leaks. They didn't put it all together, but they were getting close. On Day 16, we went public with it. Not all of it, but enough. *Yes, aliens are real, and we are tracking them* is how it started—and it was, of course, the greatest news story in the history of the planet. The day after, we revealed that we were in communication with the aliens. By Day 18, it was pretty much all out there—not the classified stuff, but the fact that a spacecraft had landed on Earth. We didn't confirm or deny the specific location, but people figured out it was Shenandoah."

"Wait," Kilmer interjected. "Hang on. If the whole world knew about this, there would have been demonstrations—hell, maybe even riots. And every news channel would have reported on it. They would have covered it nonstop, every single day."

"Well, yes, Professor, that's right. That's what happened. Except riots didn't really materialize because we never made it known just how grave a threat we perceived. But you're right about all of that. It's been unbelievable."

"Then how is it possible for the world to have just moved on? I mean, are you telling me—"

Kilmer tried to organize his thoughts.

"Are you telling me that everyone on the planet has just... *forgotten* about it now?"

"No, Professor, I'm not saying that at all. It's on the news every day. I mean, people talked about O.J. Simpson for years—you think they would move on from *aliens?*"

"Then how the hell is this news to *me?*" Kilmer exclaimed. "I accept the fact that I don't remember the time I spent in DC, but you said that was a while ago. What about all the days *since* then? How is it possible I haven't seen or heard anything about aliens since this happened? I've been living a normal—"

And then he knew the answer. If the world was still talking about the aliens, there was only one explanation for why he had no clue.

He suddenly felt sorry for himself—like he was a crash victim, trying to learn how to walk all over again, struggling with every step, or trying to feed himself, and finding more and more things he couldn't do. He saw the pity in their eyes as well. Art and Lane looked like they hadn't quite realized that this, too, would be a shock to Kilmer. It just hadn't occurred to them. Without even thinking about it, Silla started to move toward him, looking very much like she wanted to console him. But she stopped herself, as if it would be to defy God's law if she so much as touched him.

Kilmer turned to Art. "All of the days since then... Those don't exist for me. Is that it?"

"That's right," Art said quietly. "When Agents Silla and Lane came to your home earlier today, do you remember the circumstances? Do you remember where you had just been?"

"Of course. I had just returned from the hospital. I had—" Kilmer stopped short.

He had been at his office this morning, at the university, when he suddenly fainted and was rushed to a hospital in Cambridge. When he came around, the doctors assured him that it was nothing serious, and that they had given him some IV fluids to make sure he was properly hydrated. Then they sent him home. He had just entered his condo when Agents Silla and Lane came to see him.

None of that was real.

"Professor, do you know what the date is today?"

"It's Friday. May 10th."

The looks on the faces of the three agents made it clear that it was not, in fact, Friday, May 10.

"I'm sorry, Professor," Art said as gently as he could, "but May 10th was when Vice President Nielsen called you for help. That was what we refer to as Day 14. You arrived in DC late that night. It appears that the last thing you remember—waking up to your daily routine on May 10—is the point after which all of your memories have disappeared."

Kilmer swallowed hard. "So… what is the date now?"

Art glanced at his colleagues, as if hoping someone else would volunteer to break the news. No one did.

"It's June 21st, Professor Kilmer. It's Day 56."

~ 63 ~

Art explained to Professor Kilmer that he had never fainted at work on May 10. That was simply what the doctors told him when he regained consciousness. It was the only lie they needed to tell him. The rest of the illusion was created by all the things they did *not* tell him. For over four weeks, Kilmer had been in an induced coma—a treatment sometimes used for patients with traumatic brain injury or intractable seizures. He had been brought out of the coma only once during those weeks, very briefly, to check whether he might have regained any of his memories. Agent Silla had been in the room at the time, and Kilmer hadn't recognized her. That was the first test. When he was asked the date, he said it was May 10. That was the second test. He failed the third, fourth, and fifth tests as well. The coma was induced again in order to facilitate his recovery. His daily regimen included nutritional supplements, extra protein, physical therapy, and the latest in neuromuscular electrical stimulation. All of this had taken place in a hospital in Washington, DC.

Finally, on Day 54—June 19—he was moved to a hospital in Cambridge, where he would have likely been taken if he really had fainted at work. On Day 56—today—the drugs used to induce his coma were gradually withdrawn. When he awoke, the doctors told him he had fainted, and that it was not abnormal for him to feel unsteady on his feet, or to be confused about what had happened immediately prior to his fainting. They assured him he would regain his strength over the next few days.

Art had devised the rest of the plan. Agents Silla and Lane were to approach Kilmer as soon as possible after he recovered, and they had to do so before he learned anything about the existence of aliens. That meant he could have no access to TV, radio, his cell phone, or to any strangers. All the TVs in the hospital lobby had been shut off. The path from his hospital bed, through the lobby, and to the exit, had been cleared of people, except for a handful who were instructed not to talk to him, nor to discuss anything other than hospital-related matters. His cell phone was drained of battery, rendering it unusable. He would not be able to check messages or connect to the internet, and he would not be able to call for a ride home, thereby eliminating another potential risk. The first taxi in the line outside was driven by a CIA agent who was under strict instructions not to turn on the radio or to engage in any conversation except for the minimum required to act the part of cab driver.

Agents Silla and Lane were already in Brookline, parked a block away from his condo, ready to knock on his door the moment he entered. They had to do it before he could try to plug in his phone or turn on the TV. As a precaution, just in case Silla and Lane mistimed their approach, the electricity to his home had been shut off. Once the agents engaged him, they were to convince him to come voluntarily, but without revealing anything of substance. And yes, if he had rejected the offer, they would have forced him to come along.

Now, sitting in Apate 3, Kilmer shook his head in disbelief. He remembered waking up this morning, *knowing* it was May 10—when in fact, it was June 21. He had awoken from his induced coma less than twelve hours ago.

Kilmer stood up to stretch his legs. "You're right, Art. I've been sitting and listening for too long. I could use some coffee."

"I'll get it," volunteered Lane, and headed for the door.

"Let's all take a five-minute break," Art said. "I'll send a quick message to the White House about where we are in the conversation." He left the room as well.

For the first time that day, Kilmer was alone with Agent Silla.

He was not usually at a loss for words, but he could think of absolutely nothing to say.

Silla helped him out. "You don't have to worry about what to say to me, Professor Kilmer. There's also no reason for you to feel uncomfortable. Please feel free to treat me exactly as was natural for you about three hours ago. I know you're somewhat aware that we... well, that we were..." She settled on a word that they both knew wouldn't hold up in court. "… friends." She had said it with some difficulty. "This is all new for you, but I've had a couple of weeks to come to terms with what happened. The awkwardness will pass."

"Would you be willing to tell me about it, Agent Silla? About… *us?*"

"No, Professor. I would not. As brief as our time together was, it was still a part of my life that I shared with someone very special to me. I've made peace with the fact that he's no longer with us. I think it's best left where it is—with me. As a memory."

"I'm sorry." Kilmer wanted to tell her that he still felt *something* for her— that he just couldn't describe it. But he could see no benefit in saying that. Whatever they had shared, she had decided to put it behind her. He would respect that. He didn't want to complicate things for her.

"Don't be sorry, Professor."

"I wish I could remember, Agent Silla. I'm trying. I just… can't."

Silla attempted a smile, but it conveyed only regret. "I understand. I just wish I'd asked you to promise me that you would remember."

"Why do you say that?"

"Because, Professor, as I very much learned the hard way, there was a time when you would have done anything to keep a promise to me."

Art reopened the binder he had been using to brief Kilmer. "Any more questions, Professor, before we pick up where we left off?"

Kilmer took a sip of the coffee that Lane had just delivered. "Just one more, if you don't mind. What happens after you catch me up? Are you taking me to DC? Are we off to Station Zero? Do I get to go home?"

"You're free to decide for yourself," Art said. "We prefer that you accompany us to Washington. The president will be waiting to meet you at the White House if you agree to come. But it's entirely your choice."

"Forgive me for being skeptical, but if this is so important—and if earlier today you were prepared to drag me here kicking and screaming—why would you allow me to walk away now?"

It was Silla who answered. "President Whitman made it very clear to everyone that we've already asked too much of you, and that you have every right to say *no more*. But she didn't want you to decide before you were fully briefed on the events that have brought us to today. If, after that, you decide that this is no longer your fight, or if you think you can no longer be of help, she will respect your decision." She looked at her colleagues. "We would all respect your decision."

Kilmer smiled. "You all seem to know me pretty well. And you're right to assume, as I'm sure you have, that I'm not likely to walk away from this. Is that why you and the president feel comfortable giving me the choice?"

Art shook his head. "I can understand your skepticism. And you're right, we do know you're not the kind of person who would leave others to fend for themselves. But you haven't heard the whole story yet. You might learn some things that will make you reconsider. You might very well decide to walk away."

Kilmer thought about that. *What would it take for me to say no to helping them?* The list was short. If Kilmer thought that his perspective was going to be ignored anyway, or if he thought the president would abuse his advice, he would refuse to go along. That was obvious enough. But would Art reveal anything that might make Kilmer feel irrelevant or exploitable? No. So what could Art possibly say that would make him walk away?

Then he remembered the message from ET-1—and he knew the answer. *Fear* would drive him away.

"Do you think I'll be scared away, Agent Capella?"

Art sighed. "To be honest, some people think exactly that. And not one of them would hold it against you."

"And you? Do you agree with them? Do you think what you're about to tell me will frighten me off?"

"It should, Professor. But I don't think it will," Art replied candidly. "I don't think so at all."

"And what makes you so sure?"

Art rose from his seat, walked over to Kilmer, and sat down next to him.

"I think it's because I've seen a lot of *everything* in life. More of it bad than good, unfortunately. I've come across every type of character you can imagine, and many of them have been villains. But in all my life, Professor, apart from the soldiers we send into battle, I've only ever met one hero. His name was Kilmer." Art paused. "And I would *really* like to have him back, Professor. Because I think we need him. And once he understands why that is, I know he won't walk away—no matter what."

Kilmer was speechless. Whatever Art saw in him, Kilmer was sure he did not see it in himself. The disparity was so great that he wondered whether Triad had picked up the wrong guy.

Art returned to his chair and eased himself into it. He put his hands on the binder in front of him and pulled it closer. "Okay, Professor. If you're ready, let's pick up from where we left off… on Day 20."

~ 65 ~

Day 20. 1:30 p.m. The White House.

All was quiet in the Oval Office. A copy of ET-1's message had been distributed to each person on the team, but Whitman asked everyone to sit quietly for the first ten minutes to reflect on its text. "I want independent and uncorrupted assessments of the situation before we put our heads together. No words. Just think."

Large d.a.n.g.e.r for Earth. W.e. w.i.l.l. r.u.l.e.

Enter ET-1. Come two a.m.b.a.s.s.a.d.o.r.s.

M.u.s.t. come t.h.e. leader o.f. Earth.

M.u.s.t. come D. K.i.l.m.e.r.

There was a lot to think about, but Kilmer couldn't help but start with the last statement. How had *he* ended up in ET-1's message? He tallied the possibilities and came up with only three. The first was that the aliens had somehow found him on the internet and decided he was important. This was highly unlikely. Even if they had found him online, they would have quickly learned that he was insignificant. The second possibility was much more realistic. The cat shooter had delivered his book, *Heirs of Herodotus,* in one of its launches. Had they taken that as a signal that Kilmer was important, or somehow relevant to the scenario that was unfolding? Whitman had just been having a bit of fun when she added his book to the list—a small gesture of gratitude toward Kilmer—but the aliens might have thought there was greater significance to the choice. For all they knew, he was a powerful leader—or the high priest of planet Earth. The third possibility was the most concerning. Had ET-1 or the reserves found some way to listen in on their conversations at the White House? Did they know he was advising the president? Even then, why would they think he was the second-most important person to meet?

"Okay," said Whitman, as she walked over to the group. "Let's get started. You go first, Zack."

After twenty minutes of discussion, it was obvious that almost everything in the message was open to debate. The most obvious interpretation, everyone agreed, was as follows. The first two sentences suggested that the aliens intended to rule over mankind, and that resistance by humans would endanger the planet. They were inviting two representatives of Earth to enter the spacecraft—presumably to discuss terms of surrender, cohabitation, or whatever was deemed negotiable from the alien perspective. The next sentence insisted that someone capable of speaking for all of Earth be sent as one of the two ambassadors. The last sentence insisted that the second representative, for whatever reason, had to be Professor Kilmer.

If accurate, it was the worst possible scenario short of war itself. The aliens were demanding surrender and subservience—at gunpoint. Whitman made clear that slavery would never be acceptable. "It would have to mean war. No matter the consequences."

But not everyone was convinced that the obvious interpretation was correct. *Enter ET-1* could simply mean that the spacecraft had arrived, not that they wanted anyone to come inside. *Come two ambassadors* could mean that two of *their* ambassadors would be coming to meet Earth's people. *Must come the leader of Earth* might simply be an acknowledgment that Earth did not have a leader—and that the aliens intend to change that. *Large danger for Earth* might be a warning that the planet faced some other threat, having nothing to do with the aliens.

"We keep coming back to the same problem with every part of the message," Nielsen concluded. "Too much ambiguity. Too little clarity. Why don't we stop trying to guess what they mean and just ask them?"

Art explained why that was easier said than done. "Project Hermes has worked better than expected in many ways. The aliens are using words for which we haven't even created a Hermes signature—those are the ones they're spelling out with letters. But we're not equipped for the subtlety of what's required in asking them to clarify their intentions. How do we convey something like *What do you mean by that?* We're wanting to look inside their minds, but we haven't even figured out how to ask a question yet—*any* question. We've been working on it, but interrogatives have proven difficult."

Look inside their minds.

Art had been trying to curb expectations, but for Silla, his words had the opposite effect. "I think there's a way to figure out what they really mean—even if we can't ask them," she interjected enthusiastically. "In all this talk about their message, I think we've lost sight of something more basic. We don't really care what their *words* mean. What we care about is the meaning they intended to convey *with* those words."

She looked around at the faces in the room. There were only blank expressions.

"In other words, we should be focusing on what they were *thinking* about saying, not on what they actually *said*."

"And how do we do that?" Garcia asked. "We're having a hard-enough time with their words—and the words are right in front of us. We have zero visibility on their thoughts."

"I'm not so sure, Ms. Garcia. I think we *can* observe their thinking. Let me explain."

Silla turned to Kilmer. "Professor Kilmer, if you fell sick and wanted to figure out what kind of disease you might have, how would you go about doing that?"

"I'd probably talk to my doctor."

"And if there was no doctor available? Then what?"

"I'd probably go to Google, or to a medical website. I'd type in my symptoms and see what options it generates."

Silla turned back to the group. "Art said that the aliens are spelling words that we haven't even taught them. How do you suppose they're coming up with those words in the first place? It must be from the books we sent them, or from the internet. Now, if you were struggling to find a word that perfectly captured a complex sentiment you wanted to convey to me, what might you do? We know what Professor Kilmer would do. He'd go online, describe that sentiment, see what options pop up, and then choose one of those words. All I would ever hear is the word he chose—not the meaning he intended. If he chose poorly, or if the word didn't quite capture the complexity of his thoughts, I would be left with an inaccurate or ambiguous sense of the message he was trying to convey. I could ask him to clarify, but if that weren't possible, what would be another option?"

The CIA director couldn't resist the easy layup. "Well, since you work for me, Agent Silla, you could probably find some excuse to stumble across his internet search history." Whitman gave Druckman a dirty look, prompting him to issue a swift clarification. "With the appropriate legal authorizations, of course."

"Exactly," Silla said. "We know the aliens have been scouring the internet. If we look at what they've searched for—the words and phrases they typed, the options they saw, and the definitions and use cases they examined—we might get a better sense of what they were *trying* to convey."

Art embraced the idea immediately. "The amount of searching and browsing they've done—it's already a big data problem. I mean that in a good way. There's a *lot* to play with here."

Whitman interjected. "Art, how fast would you say they're progressing? How soon do you think they'll grasp the English language enough to be capable of having a real conversation—a substantive back-and-forth?"

"Madam President, what they're doing is very impressive. We might think that a phrase like *Must come leader of Earth* sounds clunky, but a linguist will tell you that it's remarkable. They could have done much worse, like *Go for leader Earth on must.* We don't know how much intellect or technology they are devoting to this—it could be one alien with super-genius levels of intellect or thousands of aliens on their home planet using a mind-blowing array of machine-learning equipment—or something we can't even imagine. But at the rate they're going, I won't be surprised if they reach the level of proficiency required for efficient conversations in just a few days."

"But do we even have the technology necessary to conduct a conversation in real time?" Garcia asked. "Even if we were sitting face to face with them, wouldn't we need some portable device to broadcast and receive signals in

Hermes, and then have some way to translate them into to English? I'm trying to imagine how it would work."

"I'm sorry, Ms. Garcia. I wasn't being clear" Art replied. "I didn't mean to suggest it would be through some handheld Hermes broadcast and translation system. I meant that, by the time Sunday rolls around, they should be able to talk to us without needing any numeric broadcast signals at all. We would be speaking directly *in English*. I don't expect it will be oral communication; we don't even know if they can speak. But we should be able to send typed messages to each other. Let's remember, they're already using a laptop and typing in English to search the internet. If we send them another laptop, this one with messaging software, and provide some basic instructions, there's no reason to think we can't start having real-time conversations as soon as they've mastered the language itself. And that will happen very soon."

"Incredible," reflected Nielsen. "We need to start preparing for that conversation."

"Madam President," said Strauss, "I suggest we start thinking a few steps farther ahead. We can't just wait to see what happens in our discussions with them—we must acknowledge the possibility that negotiations will only buy us some additional time. Their treatment towards our fallen soldiers was more than commendable, but their recent message is difficult to construe in a positive light. We must begin readying for potential conflict. I'm not suggesting war is preferred or winnable, but we must nevertheless be prepared for it—if only as a last resort."

No one disagreed, and Whitman gave the marching orders.

"Art, I want progress on communication, and I want an analysis of ET-1's internet activity. Strauss, by tomorrow evening, I want an update on each of the six areas the DoD has been working on: possibilities for deterrence, defending the homeland, coordinating with the alliance, fighting in space, how to protect our citizens if they attack population centers, and guerilla warfare—if that's what it comes to. Be sure to talk with Secretary Rao and Dr. Menon about their latest estimates on the likely extent of alien capabilities.

"Plan A is to avoid a war, at *almost* any cost. But there are limits to what we will accept. Plan B is war—but I am still a realist. I don't like our chances against a technologically superior enemy that occupies the high ground and is willing to pick a fight. If we discover that winning is not an option, we will fight all the same—if only to survive—which is why we need to know the level of resistance we can sustain if they *do* take the planet. I'm not asking easy questions, and I'm not giving you much time, but some analysis is better than none. Come to me with options and tradeoffs.

"Salvo, I want to speak with Congressional leaders before 5 p.m. today—and with the international alliance right after that. I will make a statement to the nation later tonight or tomorrow morning.

"Now, let's talk about the elephant in the room. Assuming we understood them correctly, we need to respond to their demand that we send two ambassadors. We can inform them that there is no such thing as a 'leader of Earth.' And sending an international delegation at this stage would be a disaster. The way I see it, either the alliance agrees to let me represent everyone, or we explain to ET-1 that I am willing to talk, but that I don't represent the whole planet. Either way, I am the ambassador, and we need to figure out how I will communicate with them."

Everyone agreed that sending Whitman to ET-1 was off the table. The president could not be allowed to take such a risk. A better alternative would be to use whatever system Art created for real-time conversations from a distance. Earth-side could propose that such a conversation take place in a few days.

"And what about the second ambassador?" General Allen asked. "What do we do about the demand that we send them Professor Kilmer?"

"That one is easier," Whitman replied. "We all agree that there is a misunderstanding on their part, even if we can't figure out exactly why it happened. We can tell them that they picked the wrong guy—or we can simply ignore the request and see if they insist. Once they have access to me, it might not matter."

Kilmer spoke up. "That means we'll be rejecting both of their demands. They've asked for two ambassadors to 'enter ET-1'—if neither of us does, that might not go over well. We can't risk sending the president, obviously, but if they want me to come, whether as a misunderstanding or not, that's a demand we can meet. And it's a risk we should be willing to take."

Whitman rejected the idea. "I'm not sending you into who-knows-what just because they asked for you. You're not even a soldier, Professor. And I won't throw away anyone's life over a misunderstanding."

Kilmer tried again. "But we have to be willing to take *some* risks. And consider the potential benefits: it could be the best chance we have of learning something of value."

Whitman put an end to it. "I'm not ready to take that step, Professor. The plan remains as follows. We say no to both requests—but we explain why that is. There *is* no leader of Earth, and *D. Kilmer* is of no value to them. The American president will talk to them, but not inside ET-1. That's our response."

Kilmer was frustrated with the president's decision. Adding constraints when there was already so little room to maneuver was a bad idea. He would have to try and change Whitman's mind about it. Lucky for him, he had a bit of leverage on the issue.

He looked at Silla, and she responded with a smile. He could see she was relieved that Whitman had overruled his suggestion. He tried to smile back, but he couldn't do it. He had a secret—and she wasn't going to like it. The president's decision on sending him to see ET-1 notwithstanding, *D. Kilmer* was headed to Station Zero.

~ 66 ~

Whitman asked Kilmer to stick around after the meeting ended to discuss how things were going. Kilmer told her that he agreed with Strauss on the need to accelerate preparations for war. It was the approach Prime Minister Rabin had advocated during the Oslo peace process: fight terrorism like there is no negotiation, and negotiate peace like there is no terrorism. "There is a risk, of course. The more you prepare for war, the easier it is to find yourself at war. But it's a risk worth taking here."

"I'm heartened that Strauss, you, and I are on the same page for once," Whitman reflected. "That's a good sign."

"It is, although it's hard to know how long it will last. So far, the only line you've drawn is that you will choose war over slavery or annihilation. What happens if the aliens offer a deal that is less harsh than slavery, but still terrible? If the alternative is a war that kills millions or billions of people, will you and Strauss agree on whether to fight? And if we go to war, will the two of you agree on when to stop or surrender? We haven't had to tackle such debates yet, thankfully, but it might come to that. And if it does, it won't just be you and Strauss who disagree. We might have seven billion points of view on what to do."

"Then we better find a way out of this before it gets to that point," Whitman concluded.

"Yes, ma'am. Which brings me to a point I would like to raise."

"You want to go to Station Zero."

"Yes."

"Even though allowing you to go there doesn't mean I'm sending you to ET-1."

"I hope you'll reconsider that as well. Worrying about me when there's so much at stake is a bad idea. And it's exactly the kind of thing that Strauss or

Druckman might use to paint you as unfit to lead in a crisis. They'll say you're responsible for hundreds of millions of people, and you can't even stomach putting *one* of them at risk."

Whitman smiled at that—but the expression conveyed none of its usual warmth.

"I can do the math, Professor. Saving the many is more important than saving one. I'm familiar with the concept. And, excuse me for being blunt, but I would sacrifice you in a *second* if I really thought it would help save the country. But even then, I wouldn't do it before I was sure there was no other option. I believe I owe it to the troops under my command—and to the people I serve as president—to never forget that my job is to protect *each* one, and not just *everyone*. You're lucky if you don't understand that distinction, Professor—it means you've never had to send someone to their death. Be thankful for that. So, does this mark me as sentimental? Maybe. Is it a sign of weakness? I don't know. But does it matter what *Strauss* thinks about it? Absolutely not. It's either the right thing to do or the wrong thing to do. That's it."

Whitman moved a step closer to Kilmer and locked eyes with him. "I have asked people to lay down their lives for our country many times, Professor. And I'll do it again—many *more* times. But I will never be bullied into making such a decision. Not by Strauss. Not by Druckman. Not by ET-1. And not by you."

Kilmer stood frozen—and awestruck. He had misjudged Whitman on at least a few dimensions.

"I'm sorry, Madam President. I was being extremely presumptive. I was out of line and out of my depth."

"You were. But no apology is necessary. Now, let's get back to your request. When do you want to go to Station Zero?"

"As soon as I can. Tomorrow, if possible."

"Okay, Professor. We'll get you there by tomorrow evening. As for sending you to ET-1—I don't see the urgency. I'm not ready to give in to ET-1's every demand just yet."

"I understand, Madam President."

Heirs of Herodotus by D. Kilmer.
Excerpt from Chapter 8.

"Let us never negotiate out of fear. But let us never fear to negotiate." That was the counsel JFK gave to his fellow citizens during his inaugural address in 1961. His statement identifies two risks. First, that we might do absolutely anything to avoid war. Second, that we might do nothing at all to avoid war. Both extremes are problematic, of course.

But JFK was not giving two pieces of advice. He was giving only one. That becomes clear when the two statements are read together. Kennedy lived at a time where he felt the pendulum had swung too far in one direction—that there was too much resistance to the idea of sitting down with our enemies. Had he lived in different times—had he felt the pendulum had swung in the other direction—he might have said, instead: "Let us never fear to negotiate. But let us never negotiate out of fear." All the same words—but when inverted, they take on an entirely different meaning.

The thing with pendulums is that they swing in both directions. And the thing with leaders is that they do not always know how far pendulums can continue to swing in one direction before a correction will be forced upon them by the laws of nature.

The challenge of leadership often boils down to one simple question: Are we doing too much, or not enough? And every so often—albeit rarely— the future of humanity depends on answering this question correctly.

Kilmer walked into the Treaty Room and found Silla sitting on the couch, in the very spot where she had fallen asleep nearly a week earlier. This was where they had first talked for hours. This was where they had first kissed. He had known her for only a few hours when all of that took place, but he had been drawn to every aspect of her. Now, just six days later, they had spent more time together than he would have spent with someone over many months, in normal circumstances. And it felt like they had known each other for years.

As he sat down next to her, Silla reached for his hand. "Okay, Kilmer. You said you wanted to talk. What's on your mind? And how are you such a celebrity that people from distant galaxies are wanting to meet you?"

Kilmer shook his head. "I think it's ridiculous. And to be honest, it gives me pause. Maybe the aliens really have no idea what they're doing. They might be savvy technologically, but they're really floundering if they think I'm someone they need to meet. Makes you wonder what other mistakes they'll end up making—which is not a comforting thought when even a slight misunderstanding could blow things up. I take solace in the fact that they've also done a few things to suggest this isn't a completely zero-sum game for them. If we're lucky, it will be enough to carry the day."

"Is that what you want me to believe so I won't be upset about you trying to hand yourself over to ET-1?"

"Are you upset?"

"I was—but only because I thought you were being impulsive. It doesn't matter now. If you agree that ET-1 is making a mistake, it means there's no reason for you to go."

"I'm not sure that's true. As I said to the president, even if they've picked the wrong person, saying no is risky. Better for them to meet me and discover on their own that they made a mistake. Not to mention, there's a lot of potential upside to saying yes. We might learn something. That's what Operation Churchill is all about. Figuring out what—"

"Kilmer, I hope you're not seriously considering going into that spacecraft. That's just madness."

"No, it's not. I made you a promise, Silla—that I would do everything I could. I'm going to keep that promise."

"I don't care about the stupid promise."

"Fine. You don't have to care about the promise. But think about why I made it. Not just for you or me—but for everyone. If I have to walk into ET-1 to convince, threaten, or beg them not to blow us all up—if that's what it takes—I will do it in a heartbeat. I don't see any other choice. Wouldn't you do the same?"

"Let's just agree to disagree. Either way, I'm glad you're not shipping off to Station Zero."

"I'm sorry, Silla. But I *am* going to Station Zero. The President has agreed to send me there tomorrow."

"She *what*? She thinks it's a good idea for you to be there?"

"No, she doesn't think it's a good idea. She sees it more like you do, actually."

"Then why is she sending you? I don't understand."

"Well, I guess I can be quite convincing," Kilmer smiled. "Maybe that will come in handy with the aliens—if the president allows me to meet with them."

"This is ridiculous. Kilmer, you're not thinking clearly. It's a *misunderstanding*."

He took a deep breath. "Silla, whatever happens, I want you to know that I'll be careful. The president didn't need to remind me that I'm no soldier. I don't have their skills and I don't have their courage. And I won't pretend that this doesn't scare me… It does. A whole hell of a lot."

Silla shifted toward him, closing some of the distance that had crept in while they were arguing.

"But I still have to do this, Silla. You understand that, don't you? I need to get to Station Zero in case it becomes necessary to send me to ET-1."

"I'm not letting you go unless you promise that you'll come back to me—no matter what."

Kilmer smiled. "I promise you that I'll try—no matter what."

She put her arms around him. That, he realized, was what he needed to somehow bottle up and take with him—so that he might revisit this feeling whenever he was afraid. The danger was the same. The fear remained. But he knew he wasn't alone—and that made a difference.

"There's something I need to tell you," he finally said.

"More secrets? My lucky day."

"Don't worry, this one won't make you doubt my sanity. At least I hope not. It's just that… well, with everything that's going on, and all the craziness, it's… I think it's very easy to lose sight of what's right in front of us. And I just want you to know that I haven't. That I haven't lost sight of it. Of what's right in front of me, I mean… Of you."

He paused. Silla didn't say anything.

"Of *us*, to be more precise," he added.

"I see. And what exactly is *us?*" she asked.

"I don't know. But it's something extraordinary."

She nodded. "Oh. And that's what you wanted to say?"

"Well… yes. And that it's really hard for me to be leaving you."

She nodded again. "Okay. Is that it?"

"I… I think so," Kilmer said, feeling terribly unsure. "Do you… well, do you feel the same way?"

"What way is that?"

This was not going well at all. "The way I do."

"You mean, is it hard for me that you're leaving?"

"Yes."

Silla laughed. "Yes, Kilmer, it is. It's very hard for me to see you leave." Then she kept laughing.

Kilmer was perplexed. "Then why are you laughing?"

"Because," she replied, laughing even louder now, "you're just so unbelievably bad at this."

He frowned. "I'm just trying to tell you how I feel."

"I know. I'm sorry. I know." She tried to control her laughter. "It's just that you really suck at it."

"Well, you're not making it any easier. It's like you're enjoying this—watching me stumble through it."

"I am. And I shouldn't. But I'm just used to seeing you wordsmith everything so well. It's fun to watch you struggle with something so simple."

"Okay, have your fun. But it's not so simple. If it were, I would have figured out how to say it."

Silla looked into his eyes. "I know. And I'm glad you couldn't figure it out."

Then she pulled him close and kissed him on the lips. At first he thought he was getting a pity kiss. As it continued, he came to realize it was nothing of the sort.

"Now don't feel *too* proud of yourself," she warned. "You didn't say anything that deserved that."

"Then why—"

"Because it's not always about what you say, Kilmer. Sometimes it's what you didn't say that makes all the difference. You could have used some cliché and taken the easy way out. I know that. And I'm glad you didn't."

~ 69 ~

Day 21. Morning.

For Kilmer and Silla, the night had only gotten better once they moved from the Treaty Room to the Lincoln Bedroom. The one regrettable moment occurred early the next morning when Silla stepped out of the Lincoln Bedroom at the precise moment that President Whitman was stepping into the same hallway. Whitman said nothing except good morning. Silla muttered something in response that was unintelligible even to herself. Kilmer laughed out loud when she told him about it later. Silla laughed about it precisely never.

The team met in the Oval Office at 10 a.m. Triad's analysis of ET-1's internet activity had led to a few preliminary inferences. First, the phrase *must come* appeared to represent an ultimatum rather than a sense of urgency. Second, their browsing history suggested that ET-1 ought to know that there wasn't any *leader of Earth*—but it seemed they wanted someone whom everyone else would follow. Third, *we will rule* might not have meant "we will dominate," as had been widely assumed. It might have been used in the sense of "we will judge." Druckman wasn't sure this was good news. "You might prefer to have someone rule over you if the alternative is that they'll find you guilty and order your execution."

For Kilmer, it was still a ray of hope. *If they plan to judge, they haven't made up their minds—which means it might be possible to influence them.*

The last part of the discussion featured *D. Kilmer.*

"ET-1 has been studying you quite a bit, Professor," Art explained. "They've accessed your writings and downloaded much of your work. But we're not sure what that tells us."

"So we still don't know why they asked for me?"

"That's what we almost concluded," Art confessed. "Then, around two o'clock last night, Agent Silla called us with a great idea. I don't know why you never sleep, Agent Silla, but I'm not complaining."

Kilmer knew exactly why Silla had been awake late into the night. Around 1:45 she had finally ordered Kilmer to go to sleep. That's when she had left the room to make some calls.

Silla described the breakthrough. "All this time, we'd been analyzing what ET-1 had said and done. But sometimes, the most important thing is what is *not* said or done." She gave Kilmer the briefest of smiles. "So I asked the team to start looking for what ET-1 had *not* searched. Here's what I mean. If we see that they executed a combined search for *Kilmer* and *Whitman*, we might deduce that they're trying to understand the relationship between them. But what if they did *not* combine these search terms? Wouldn't that provide insights as well? It might mean that they don't care about this relationship, which has implications of its own. The key, then, is to think not only about the search terms they combined—which tell a certain story—but also the combinations that we might have *expected* them to make, but which they never actually did."

"Excellent," Druckman exclaimed.

Art explained that *Kilmer* and *Whitman* had, in fact, never been searched together. It didn't appear that the aliens thought Kilmer was advising the president. Nor did they seem to think he was a world leader. While *Whitman* had been searched in combination with various other world leaders, *Kilmer* had never been associated with any. Perhaps more interestingly, although *Kilmer* had been combined with terms related to war, history, diplomacy, and strategy, he had never been associated with other people or an organization of any kind. Not the US government, the UN, the CIA, the DoD, or any political or religious organization. All these things had been linked to other individuals—but never to *Kilmer*.

It seemed the aliens didn't think Kilmer had any power or authority whatsoever.

"That professors hold no influence over the affairs of the world appears to be a universal constant," Energy Secretary Rao mused. That got some laughs, with Dr. Menon, calling in from NASA, finding it especially funny.

Art continued. "A picture begins to emerge. They don't see Kilmer as close to the president. Nor do they connect him to any other leader or power center on the planet. They don't seem to care what he knows about our military or technological capabilities. So, you have to wonder, why is this guy so special?"

"The eternal question," Strauss noted, drawing laughs from everyone—including Kilmer and Silla.

"So the team kept digging, and some of the things they checked probably went a little overboard. You'll be glad to know, Professor, that ET-1 does not associate you with human sacrifice or entertainment, for example."

"Seriously? And why would entertainment have anything to do with this?" Kilmer asked.

Art shrugged. "Some people on the team thought it was worth crossing off the list. You know, to make sure they didn't think you were some sort of performer—like a singer or an acrobat. To make sure they didn't want you for entertainment value. Like a court jester. Or an elephant that dances. Or—"

"Or what? A stripper? Have the folks at Triad lost their minds?"

Kilmer shook his head, but the rest of the room was practically on the floor laughing. Dr. Menon sounded like he was having a hard time breathing.

When the room regained its composure, Art continued.

"Sorry, Professor," he said with an apologetic smile. "Our analysts are encouraged to think outside the box." Then he turned back to the group. "Let's get to what *does* seem meaningful. The question was why, given all this, they wanted Professor Kilmer at all. Based on our analysis, it looks less like a mistake than it did before. They know all about him, they're not curious or mistaken about how much power he has, and they're not confused about what his role is—yet they still want him. Why they'd want to talk to a historian—or to this one specifically—we don't know. But they do."

Silla looked at Kilmer, knowing full well what Triad's findings implied.

Kilmer knew as well. "Madam President, I don't see how we get around it now. If this isn't a case of mistaken identity, it becomes riskier to say no to their demand—and more likely that I'll learn something if I go there."

The rest of the group had just started to weigh in on the issue when Art interrupted the discussion. A new message had just been received from ET-1, arriving precisely twenty-three hours after the aliens had sent their last message.

M.u.s.t. come t.o. u.s. a.m.b.a.s.s.a.d.o.r. D. K.i.l.m.e.r.

A.t. 8 p.m. t.o.n.i.g.h.t. h.e. w.i.l.l. enter ET-1.

No more t.i.m.e. i.s. left f.o.r. E.a.r.t.h.

D.o. n.o.t. test ET-1.

ET-1's language skills had obviously improved further, but Art noticed something others had missed. ET-1 didn't broadcast the word *left* one letter at a time—even though humans had never taught them the Hermes signature for it. How? "What we *did* teach," Art explained, "is left versus right. They used our signal for that version of *left* and imported it into this context. It's a good sign that they're ready for conversations."

Art also singled out the use of *8 p.m.* ET-1 had taught itself how humans measured time. "What we consider 8 p.m. is based on a combination of how long it takes the Earth to rotate and our arbitrary decision to partition that time into twenty-four segments of equal length. There's no reason to assume that an alien civilization would also measure time—if at all—using this approach. So again, it demonstrates that they've done a lot of work on their end to get this right."

Something about what Art had just said nagged at Kilmer. A thought tried to manifest in his mind, but he couldn't grasp it.

Silla pointed out that ET-1 had clarified some things that had been ambiguous in the earlier message. "It suggests they know the earlier communication was unclear. They're trying to make sure we understand."

There was that thought again, Kilmer realized—struggling to be born. *What is it?*

No one had a theory for why *leader of Earth* was no longer mentioned. Everyone agreed, however, that the language was more threatening than in the previous message. Most of the group—everyone except Silla and General Allen—now supported sending Kilmer to ET-1. General Allen wanted to negotiate a middle ground, such as having Kilmer speak to the aliens remotely.

NSA Garcia pushed back on the idea of making a counteroffer. "ET-1's demand is very specific now, and we would be rejecting it quite conspicuously. They've asked him to enter ET-1, they've set a deadline, and they've made it clear that our time is up. How safe do we feel rejecting such a demand with so much at stake? Are we willing to bet millions of lives that they'll see our counteroffer as reasonable?"

No one seemed eager to make that bet.

Nielsen agreed with Garcia, as did Strauss. "Pushing back at this point risks escalation," said the defense secretary. "And it's not like they're asking us to surrender. They're asking only that we send an ambassador. This is something we should do—one false move could lead to war."

One false move could lead to war.

Kilmer had been nodding along in silent agreement, but Strauss's statement suddenly dislodged something in his mind—and he stopped nodding.

The mood in the room had turned somber. Everyone knew they had just agreed to send one of their own to face an uncertain fate. Whitman informed the group that she would make a final decision by the time Kilmer landed at Station Zero, but it was clear that she agreed with the majority.

Nielsen looked apologetic. Silla seemed anxious. Only one person was beginning to see a way out of the predicament. It was Kilmer—and he had Strauss to thank for it.

~ 70 ~

"No, I don't think you should wear a tie if you visit ET-1. I think they will shoot you on the spot for impersonating the real Professor Kilmer."

Silla was sitting on Kilmer's bed, watching him pack for his move to Station Zero. He had more clothes to pack than he'd brought with him to the White House on Day 14. Two days after his arrival in DC, an officer had gone to Boston to bring more of his belongings—including the tie he had left on the floor of his closet.

Kilmer walked over to her. "Okay, I want to run something by you. I want you to critique the idea before I share it with the president. I'm advising on things that directly involve *me* now, so I worry that I'm biased."

"You don't think *I'm* biased when it comes to you?"

"I know you are. But it might work in our favor. My bias usually pushes me to underappreciate the risk I face. Your bias tends to be overprotective of me."

Silla exaggerated an eyebrow raise. "Overprotective? You mean like a nag? Am I smothering you, Kilmer?"

"You don't smother me enough, actually," he said, joining her on the bed. She pushed him away immediately, almost knocking him to the floor.

"Just pack your bags and tell me what you're thinking," she said. "I'm eager to get to the part where I tell you that you're out of your mind. That's always my favorite."

Kilmer obeyed. "Okay, so here's my first thought. I think the aliens might agree to a compromise along the lines of what General Allen was proposing— that I speak with them remotely."

Silla looked skeptical. "Why do you think that? Pushing back could be risky."

"Remember when we discussed how the aliens wouldn't come all this way only to get offended if we knock on their door? Strauss reminded me of that when he said *one false move* could start a war. Well, that can't be right."

"I don't often agree with Strauss, but I think this is different. We would be rejecting a specific demand, *after* they've warned us that time is running out. It's not the same thing as saying hello when they first land."

"Yes, but I'm also thinking about what *you* said today—that the aliens are speaking more clearly now, as if they understand there's a risk of miscommunication. If so, they wouldn't just blow us out of the water the moment we say something that sounds disrespectful. They'd recognize that it could just be a misunderstanding. So maybe we start by asking them to meet us halfway. They might say yes. If they don't, they'll clarify that their demand is non-negotiable."

Silla considered it. "I see the point—but I still think it's risky. Their demand is pretty unambiguous."

"Okay, I see that," Kilmer admitted. "So let's add one last layer to all this."

"Go for it."

"Imagine you're going out to dinner—just you. How long will you take to get ready?"

"I don't know. Maybe five minutes."

"Now imagine that you're going on a date with me. How long will you take to get ready?"

"Maybe two minutes."

"Very funny."

"Okay, fine—longer."

"Why?"

"Kilmer—give me a break. You know why."

"Fine, let's try this instead. Think back to the toughest class you took in college. How long did you study for the final exam?"

"Maybe… six hours."

"Why so much?"

"Because it was probably worth half of my grade."

"Okay. And when you showed up to take the test, if the professor suddenly announced that it would only be worth five percent of your grade, how would you feel?"

"Pretty annoyed. All that studying for no reason."

"Hmm. That's actually a bit disappointing."

"Shut up, Kilmer. Get to the point."

"The point is, of *course* you'd be annoyed. Because there's no way you would study so much if your grades weren't on the line."

"I get it, Kilmer. I'm not as big of a nerd as you are. Is that it?"

Kilmer took both of her hands in his and pulled her up off the bed. "That's exactly it, Silla. *No one* is as big of a nerd as I am. In fact, I can't imagine anyone in the entire *universe* doing so much work if so little was at stake."

71

At 2:15 p.m., Kilmer and Silla joined President Whitman and VP Nielsen in the Oval Office.

Kilmer explained his idea. "Art kept telling us how hard the aliens seem to be working—how much effort they've been devoting to mastering our language and learning words and ideas that they can't possibly use in most conversations. Why are they doing that? You don't need to work so hard if you're just planning to blow someone up. You don't need that level of mastery if you just want to rob a planet of their resources, or torture them, or put them to work as slaves. I've had PhD students with careers on the line who did less work over six years than ET-1 has done in a *day*. It makes you wonder—how much do they have on the line?"

Whitman considered it for a moment. "What do you think it means, Professor?"

"I'm working on two ideas. First—maybe our situation isn't as desperate as we thought. Usually, when we think about who has more power in a negotiation, we think about who's bigger and stronger and can do more damage. If that's all that matters, we're in big trouble. But often, your real source of leverage is not how hard you can hit them, but how much value you can *create* for them. If we have something they need, we have power. Whatever is motivating them to work so hard—whatever problem they hope to solve by communicating with us—if it's something only we can address, it would give us some leverage."

"What could they need from us?" Nielsen asked.

"That's the second idea I wanted to share. Triad's analysis suggests that the aliens didn't pick me by mistake. So why pick a historian?"

"Maybe they want to learn about human beings—and our past," Nielsen suggested.

"If so, then speaking to me would be very inefficient. They can learn almost everything about our history on the internet. Moreover, they didn't say *send us a historian*. They asked for *me*—even though they can access most of what I've written online as well. How much more could I possible add? And the way they're going about this, it seems that they don't just want to talk to me, they're prepared for a serious conversation. Which reinforces the idea that they want something from us—or, somehow, from me—that they can't get by simply dropping bombs. And the good news is, we can test whether that's true right away."

Kilmer suggested they propose General Allen's compromise: Kilmer would speak to ET-1, but only from a distance. Given how hard the aliens were working to specifically have a conversation with Kilmer, it seemed unlikely they would attack just because Earth-side made a counteroffer—especially if it was made well before the 8 p.m. deadline. "And we keep it simple. We set up a table for me just outside the kill-zone. I sit there and communicate with them using whatever system Art sets up. If they say yes to doing it that way, it supports the notion that we have at least some leverage—which is useful to know. If they say no, then I go to ET-1, and we try to make progress that way."

Whitman agreed to the plan, and Silla said she would coordinate with Triad and Station Zero to get things set up.

When the meeting concluded, Whitman approached Kilmer and Silla.

"Thank you, Professor, for everything. We're going to miss having you here. Though I do plan to get you back soon—hopefully in just a few days. We'll talk this evening to go over the guidelines for your conversation with ET-1. We obviously can't script everything, so I'm glad I can trust your judgment. Just be safe."

"I will," Kilmer assured her.

"And as much as I dislike the idea of sending you to Station Zero," Whitman added, "I do take comfort in knowing you're not going alone." She turned to Silla. "Thank you, Agent Silla, for agreeing to accompany the professor. I know that we ask a lot of you these days."

Kilmer's head snapped toward Silla.

Huh? What?

She ignored him, but he was pretty sure he caught the hint of a smile on her face.

"You two take care of each other," Whitman continued. "If you need anything at all, please let General Allen know. You can also reach Zack or me directly. Any time."

Nielsen gave Kilmer a firm handshake and half of a hug. "Thanks, Prof. We owe you. *Please* be careful."

Silla and Kilmer left the Oval Office and were escorted to a car that would take them to Joint Base Andrews. Kilmer waited for Silla to say something, but she just kept walking in silence. Eventually, he ran out of patience.

"Why didn't you tell me you were coming with me?"

"I thought Sherlock here would figure it out on his own."

"How was I supposed to figure out that you were coming with me?"

"It should have been obvious."

"How? What did I miss?"

"I think you missed the part where I told you that it would be very hard for me to see you leave. So, I did something about it."

"Did what? Did you ask Art to let you come along?"

"I practically had to beg. But I've been at Triad long enough—I have some clout. And Art could see that I was desperate. I think he was worried that I might quit the agency if he said no to me."

"Are you serious?"

"No, you dummy. I'm not serious. You think I would beg my boss to let me come with you? We're talking about my job, Kilmer. And we're talking about doing what needs to be done to save the planet. Please try to be a little less full of yourself. I couldn't bear the thought of you leaving either, but give me a break."

Kilmer smiled. "Okay, you got me. My bad. Just tell me. What happened?"

"Nothing. When I spoke to Art on the phone last night, he told me the president was sending you to Station Zero and that he wanted me to go along. That's why I went home early in the morning—to pack."

"So you knew this from the time you came back to bed last night."

"Yes."

"Why didn't you wake me up and tell me as soon as you got into the room. Or first thing in the morning?"

"Because I was still pretty upset that you had decided to leave me—and I wanted you to suffer as much as possible by thinking you might never see me again."

"Seriously?"

"Jesus Christ, Kilmer. Of course not. You think I would be that petty? I just thought it would be more fun if I could tell you when you were saying goodbye. But the president spilled the beans before that could happen."

The driver opened the door to the SUV and they both got into the back seat. Silla reached over and took Kilmer's hand. "I think I got about three hours of sleep last night, and I feel exhausted. I'm going to close my eyes for a bit."

Kilmer moved over slightly so that she could lean on him if needed. A minute later, her head was on his shoulder and she was fast asleep.

Silla had said it only in passing, but her words were still ringing nicely in his ears. *I couldn't bear the thought of you leaving either.* He closed his eyes, still holding her hand.

You're a lucky guy, Kilmer. That was his last thought before he dozed off as well.

72

At 5:00 p.m., HQ-1 delivered its counteroffer to ET-1. The message, which was translated into Hermes before being transmitted, read as follows:

D. Kilmer will not come inside ET-1.

D. Kilmer will sit 110 yards away from ET-1.

D. Kilmer will communicate with ET-1 in English by typing on a computer.

At 7 p.m. we will send a computer to ET-1 with instructions on how to send and receive messages in English.

At 8 p.m. D. Kilmer will send the first message to ET-1.

Does ET-1 agree to this plan.

Kilmer and Silla had landed at Station Zero at 4:40. They were taken straight to a large bed-and-breakfast inside Shenandoah National Park that had been seized, purchased, or rented by the US government—the officer who drove them wasn't sure which. General Allen and Secretary Strauss had two of the rooms. Kilmer and Silla would each have one. They dropped their luggage at the house and then made their way to HQ-1, which was eight miles away by car. They arrived there at 5:30.

Allen and Strauss were already at HQ-1 and the White House team was on the phone. The group was discussing the response that ET-1 had sent a few minutes earlier. After it was written out in English, the reply from ET-1 read as follows:

Send the computer to ET-1.

We will talk to D. Kilmer in English.

But your method will not solve the problem for Earth.

Very little time is left. The danger grows every hour for humans.

The syntax was excellent, and it suggested that the aliens were ready for effective conversation. It was also good news that the proposal had been accepted. The only person more relieved than Kilmer was Silla.

Kilmer told the group that two other aspects of the message stood out to him. "They again say that time is limited, but they don't set a specific deadline. It could mean that they don't know, or haven't yet decided, how much time we have. We need to think about the implications of that."

"What do you think it might mean?" General Allen asked.

"I'm not sure. But the deadline is conspicuous in its absence. We just... need to keep that in mind."

Kilmer considered his answer. It bothered him that he hadn't managed to articulate a single theory, or offer even one potential implication. Was the anxiety already throwing him off his game? Was he losing focus? It was a disconcerting thought. He needed some time alone to clear his mind—to reset—before he engaged with ET-1. But things were moving too fast now.

"What's the second aspect that stands out?" Whitman asked.

Kilmer snapped back to attention. "I'm sorry, what?"

"You said there were two things you found notable about the message," Whitman gently reminded him. "The lack of deadline is one. What's the other?"

"Yes, the second issue," Kilmer said, trying to remember the other point he had wanted to make. "Their choice of words. *Your method will not solve the problem for Earth.* It seems to imply that the problem is potentially solvable—which is good news. But what aspect of our method stands in the way? That we are pushing back on their demands? That we have been slow to respond? That we won't enter ET-1? What are we doing wrong, according to them?"

"Do you think we ought to reconsider our approach in some way?" Whitman asked.

Kilmer's mind drew a blank. He turned to Silla and saw the look of concern on her face. She could tell he was struggling.

What the hell is wrong with me?

"Madam President, I—I'm not sure. But I think it's important to figure out why a solution would be possible under their methodology and not possible under ours. I think—I think it's something I could ask them."

That wasn't a bad idea, but Kilmer was horrified that it was the best he could come up with. There were clues strewn all about, and he seemed incapable of putting any of them together.

I need to get out of here. I need some time alone. Kilmer looked at Silla desperately, asking her to read his mind.

She came to his rescue. "I'm not sure how much more we can learn from this message, and Professor Kilmer will be talking to them in less than two hours. Maybe we ought to move on and discuss what he should and shouldn't say during that conversation. After that, I think we should give him some time to prepare on his own."

Kilmer nodded in appreciation.

The next thirty minutes were spent discussing guidelines. No, Kilmer should not discuss military or technology matters. If they ask about these things, he should tell them he's the wrong guy. No, he should not mention the president or anyone else that they might decide they want to see. If they bring her up, he should clarify that he does not speak for Whitman. No, he should not raise the possibility of war between humans and aliens. If they bring it up, he should do his best to suggest, as delicately as possible, that humans have peaceful intentions but are not weak—all while making clear that he is not authorized to speak for humanity. Yes, he should ask as many questions as he can. Yes, he should be courteous and non-threatening. Yes, he should talk for as long as possible.

It was decided that there would be no troop presence near Kilmer, but there would be soldiers and medics, in their vehicles, ready to move at a moment's notice.

"What if they shine their blinding light while he's out there? Or they try to abduct him?" General Allen asked. "What's the plan?"

President Whitman was the only one who had already decided what would happen in that situation: she would let Kilmer be taken. But she waited to respond. Kilmer was not a soldier, and he might freeze up if she made her intentions clear. She needed *him* to advocate for the idea. He needed to own that decision.

"We have to consider all possibilities," Allen continued. "For example, if they come for him, should he try to resist? Should we charge into the light and try to save him? We can't leave such decisions to the heat of the moment."

Everyone looked uncomfortable and anxious—except for Kilmer, who found that General Allen's questions hadn't even fazed him. That was when he realized that his fears had already advanced far beyond the possibility of abduction—and that he was by far the most nervous person in the room. It was a wakeup call.

He had somehow allowed it to get to the point where he was accepting defeat before even taking the field. He knew he had little chance of winning, but was this how he wanted his story to end?

No way.

He had to snap out of it.

"I can answer that," Kilmer offered. "If they try to abduct me, I go without a struggle. No one races in. No shots are fired. We don't send threatening messages. We just play it cool. I do whatever I can to figure things out on my end. And if I can't, you all figure out what happens without me. But we don't lose sight of what's important."

Whitman's little gamble had paid off—Kilmer understood what needed to happen. She endorsed his proposal. "He's right. Unless there's a better idea, that's the plan. If they try to take him, he goes."

Silla tried with all her might to come up with a better plan, but she couldn't. No one else could either.

"Okay," Kilmer announced. "That solves that. Now, if I'm not needed for anything else, I'd like some time alone to get my thoughts in order. Is everyone okay with that?"

"Go ahead, Professor," said Whitman. "We'll finish up here."

Kilmer left HQ-1 and walked over to a clearing that offered a partial view of ET-1 in the distance. It was the first time he was seeing the spacecraft in person. It looked exactly as it did on the screens in the Situation Room, but seeing it like this made for a wildly different experience. An alien spacecraft—*on Earth*—a short walk away from him.

But Kilmer hadn't come here to stare in wonder at ET-1. He had come with a very different objective in mind.

He had come here so that he could be afraid.

73

Kilmer didn't want 8 p.m. to be the first time he saw the spacecraft. He couldn't afford to be distracted—or terrified—when he needed to be at the top of his game. Once he had acclimated to the sight of ET-1, Kilmer made a mental checklist of all the other aspects of the situation he would face. Then he went about normalizing and getting comfortable with every one of them— from learning how to use the messaging system, to sitting in the chair he would later occupy. He thought about how it might get cold if the conversation went late into the night. Would he need a jacket? Would he get thirsty or hungry? If he were abducted, what would he want to have with him? One by one, he chipped away at every factor that might divert his attention or burden his mind.

At 6:30 p.m., he sat down on a park bench a few hundred yards from HQ-1. He called Silla and asked her to meet him there in forty minutes. He still had plenty of things to think through on his own. Most importantly, he wanted to organize his thoughts about the conversation with ET-1. It could go in a million different directions. How would he keep his bearings? What exactly was he trying to achieve?

It comes down to one thing—finding Churchill's Key. I need to figure out what drives them.

All the other mysteries—all the questions that had arisen over the last three weeks—were somehow tied to this one thing. To Churchill's Key.

Why now? Why did they visit Earth at this moment in history?

Why was Earth in danger?

Why would the methods that humans had proposed not solve the problem?

Why was ET-1 being so reactive?

What did they plan to judge?

Why had they worked so hard to understand and communicate with humans?

Why did they choose Kilmer?

Kilmer knew that the answer to any one of these questions might lead him to finding Churchill's Key—which meant he couldn't allow himself to get fixated on any particular line of inquiry. He would have to be flexible. And resilient.

When he felt he had his thoughts sufficiently in order, Kilmer took a deep breath. *Now for the hard part.*

He knew he was no match for the kind of fear he would be dealing with, so there was no point in trying to fight it. His only option was to outsmart it. *At the heart of fear is uncertainty.* If he could identify and accept even the worst possible outcome—without losing his resolve to act—he could eliminate uncertainty from the equation. He would strip fear of its power.

Kilmer closed his eyes and took a few more deep breaths, taking in the fresh air. And then he reflected, systematically, on every terrible possibility, allowing his mind to slowly climb the ladder of horrors. No self-deception. Just an honest assessment. The only way this could work.

The first fear—I might be abducted. Okay. Then what? Will I be able to stay calm? Probably not. Will I start to lose hope? Maybe. Will I be able to keep my wits so I can at least try to find a way to escape, or to negotiate for my freedom? I think so—at least after the initial shock subsides. If I fail, will I be able to withstand a long abduction? Everyone breaks eventually—I will too. But I will plan for that to happen. I'll start to acclimate to my surroundings even while I try to find a way out. I will go into it knowing it could be a very long time. So, can I accept the risk of abduction? Yes, I can. Am I sure?

He paused.

Yes. I'm sure.

Second fear—I might not make it back alive. All right, this is much worse.

How will I die? Will it be painful? Will I know it's coming? Let's take the worst-case scenario: I know it's coming and it's going to be painful. Will I fight back? Yes. Without a doubt. Will it matter? Almost certainly not. Will I be able to accept that I'm about to die? I don't know. Can anyone? No idea. Does that mean I shouldn't risk this?

He paused for longer this time.

No. I still choose to go. Everyone dies. And this is at least as good a reason as any.

Third fear—I might be tortured. Damn, this one is bad. What kind of torture? The worst kind. Will it be unbearable? Yes. Will I scream? Definitely. Will I beg for them to stop? Probably.

Be honest.

Okay, yes. I'm sure I will. Will I give them whatever they want to make it stop? What the hell could they possibly want from me that I wouldn't give them even without being tortured? Good point. So, a lengthy torture is the worst—but it's unlikely. But still. What if it happens? Maybe they just enjoy torturing humans. No, that can't be right—they fixed up our soldiers. There was no sign of torture. But what if I make someone angry? I need to remember not to do that. Do not make anyone angry. Okay. Problem solved? No. I'm not facing the fear. What if I knew there was going to be torture? What if they didn't even realize they were torturing me? Or what if they said, we will torture you when you come here, and in return, there is a very small chance you can save countless lives? Would I do it? I would have to say yes. Only an asshole would say no. Still… I could probably find a way to justify saying no. Does that mean I shouldn't do this?

Another pause.

No. It just means it's a good thing they're not telling me in advance that they plan to torture me. That might have made me change my mind. When I'm getting tortured, I'll remind myself that I did the right thing—I couldn't have known it would come to this, and there was a chance I might do some good. No regrets. I should also try to convince them not to torture me—to let me go or to kill me quicker. Remember that, Kilmer. That's the plan. Use your brain—everything you know—to convince them to kill you or let you go.

Anything else?

One last thing came to mind.

Fourth fear—I might never see Silla again.

Kilmer thought about this one for a long time. Finally, he had a realization.

This isn't a fear. I'm not afraid of this. It just hurts to think about… Although it hurts far more than I would have expected. Will I still go? Yes, without a doubt. I don't want to, but I made a promise—and I won't break it. Why? Because I don't make promises that I don't intend to keep. And what about her? She'll probably miss me, too. Does that change anything? No. I just need to try as hard as I can to make it back alive.

Okay. Remember both of those promises. You promised that you would do whatever you can to help. And you promised that you would try to come back to her—no matter what.

That's the plan. Do both of those things. Keep both of your promises.

"Hey there, Kilmer."

Silla walked up just as Kilmer, his eyes still closed, was finishing up. "Just one minute. Sorry."

"Sure, take your time."

Okay. So, are we good? You got this, right? Yeah. I got this. I can set it aside now. But remember—you will be tested. You'll be scared again, without a doubt. You'll be terrified. But that's okay. You know where to file things when you can't afford to be distracted. Just remind yourself that you've already thought all of this through. Understood? Yes.

Kilmer opened his eyes. Silla was sitting next to him. She looked… beautiful.

"How are you?" she asked.

"I'm a lot better. I really needed some time to myself. Thanks for getting me out of the meeting."

Silla smiled. "Thanks for asking me to come here. I thought I might only get a few seconds with you before you have to go."

"Did you really think I would go to the kill-zone without a proper goodbye?"

"I don't even know what a proper goodbye is," Silla confessed. "And I'm not sure what to think or how to feel right now… I'm scared, I suppose. And

I don't know how to stay optimistic and supportive—but to still be afraid. I can't reconcile it. And now I'm just rambling."

He took her hand. "I know how you feel. All of it. I've been working through it myself. I guess we have to ask ourselves whether what we're doing is worth it—even if things don't work out the way we hope. I think it is."

"I think so, too," she said. "I just wish it was a little easier. That's all."

Kilmer leaned a little closer. "Silla, I want to apologize for something that happened last night."

"What happened last night?"

"Well, you were very nice about it, but I know I didn't do a very good job of telling you how I feel about you. And you weren't wrong when you said I suck at it. I really do. I would hate for you to think that the reason I stumbled through it was because I'm conflicted about how I feel. That's not it."

"I know," she said with a wink. "You're not the only one who can piece things together."

Kilmer smiled.

It was 7:40 p.m. when they headed back. They had shared what they agreed would be their final kiss before Kilmer's rendezvous with ET-1—and which they both knew, but never said, might be their last kiss ever.

Silla let go of Kilmer's hand as they approached HQ-1. She went inside to fetch Strauss and Allen while Kilmer continued toward the perimeter. He narrowed his eyes and took a deep breath. Then he forced a slight smile.

Let's do this.

Heirs of Herodotus by D. Kilmer.
Excerpt from Chapter 7.

The myth of the pivotal event has done considerable damage to our understanding of cause and effect as it relates to human affairs. There is perhaps no greater example of this than Caesar's crossing of the Rubicon in 49 BCE, which is said to have heralded the end of the Roman Republic and the rise of the Roman Empire. We give so much deference to that singular event that "to cross the Rubicon" has itself come to mean the making of a fateful or pivotal decision—of passing the point of no return.

But what of Tiberius Gracchus, who began to undermine the institutions of the Roman Republic as far back as 133 BCE? What of Gaius Marius, a few decades later, who changed the very nature of the Roman army, turning it into a weapon to be wielded by generals rather than an instrument of the state? What of Sulla, who was the first to march on Rome and take power by force? What of Cinna? What of Pompey? What of Crassus?

Alea iacta est, Caesar is claimed to have said. "The die is cast." But who handed Caesar the die? What brought him to the river Rubicon? Who allowed him to even imagine the possibility of entering Rome with an army? What made him so sure that the Republic was ready to kneel? **Caesar only did what those who had come before allowed him to do. Caesar did not destroy the Roman Republic. The Republic destroyed itself—one episode at a time— by refusing to see where they were headed.**

Pivotal moments make for great theater, but terrible history. **For those who wish to predict the future—or avoid the mistakes of the past—pivotal moments are among the most dangerous of history's artifacts.**

~ 75 ~

At 7:00 p.m., a laptop and instructions were cat-shooted toward ET-1. In a bright flash of light, the aliens retrieved it minutes later.

At 7:30, Kilmer's communication station was established 110 yards from ET-1. He would have access to a table, a chair, a laptop, two power banks for the laptop, two bottles of water, some trail mix, a notebook, and two pens. The messaging system would allow the team at HQ-1 to monitor the back-and-forth as it unfolded.

At 7:50, Kilmer, Silla, Secretary Strauss, and General Allen were at the perimeter, standing next to the Jeep that would take Kilmer to his communication station. Kilmer shook hands with each of them. Secretary Strauss thanked him for his courage. General Allen told him to be careful. Silla leaned close to him. "You're coming back to me," she whispered. "No matter what."

Kilmer got in the Jeep and an officer drove him toward the kill-zone.

At 7:55, Kilmer was seated. The laptop was on and the messaging app was ready for use. The plan was for Kilmer to send the first message at exactly 8:00 p.m. He had brought only his cell phone, an analog wristwatch, and a jacket. He had left his wallet with Silla, but not before extracting one thing from it— a picture of Kilmer with his parents, taken the day he was adopted—which he now had in his pocket.

He slowed his breathing. He audited his emotions. He cleared his mind. He was as prepared as he was going to be under the circumstances.

He looked at his watch. It was almost 8:00 p.m. He readied himself to type, but just as he was about to begin, his laptop emitted a *beep*. He knew exactly what that signified, but it caught him entirely by surprise. This wasn't the plan. *He* was supposed to be the one to send the first message. ET-1 had beaten him to it.

As he looked at the screen, he couldn't help but smile. The first message that the aliens had chosen to send was only two words in length, but it carried multiple layers of meaning. For over half a century, it had been a tradition of sorts for computer scientists to display these two words as a test message when they wanted to check whether their code was working. By choosing to send this as their first message, ET-1 had shown that it grasped not only human language, but also human culture—and that someone inside ET-1 had a sense of humor. Or at least a sense of irony.

Kilmer glanced up and gave a slight wave to ET-1. Then he looked back at the words on the screen.

Hello, World.

~ 76 ~

Only two words into the conversation, ET-1 had already taken Kilmer by surprise. It was a pleasant surprise, but it introduced uncertainty. Should he engage with ET-1 more casually than he had planned, or should he keep the conversation more formal? Could he build rapport by trying to be charming, or would he simply hasten the demise of the planet with his attempts at humor?

He decided to play it safe.

Welcome to our planet.

Thank you, Ambassador Kilmer.

Do you have a name or title that I should use for you?

You can continue to call us ET-1.

Okay. I have been looking forward to our conversation. May I ask you some questions, ET-1?

Yes.

Where do you come from?

From very far away.

How far?

That is not important to discuss.

Are you from a world that is similar to ours?

In some ways it is.

How are you similar to us?

Like you, we think. We communicate.
We build things. In our own ways, we
are born, we become older, and we die.
Those are some ways.

Please tell me more about our similarities.

What more do you want to know?

Do you have families like we do? Do you have emotions? Do you have art?

Sorry, Ambassador Kilmer, we cannot
answer other questions about this.

Okay. Can you tell me how you are different?

That is almost the same question,
Ambassador. We cannot answer.

Can you tell me why you decided to visit Earth?

Like human beings, we like to explore.

How did you find us? Were you looking for us?

We cannot answer that.

Why did you decide to visit us now? Or have you visited us before?

We cannot answer that.

Why do you like to explore?

Why do humans like to explore?

We are curious. We want to learn.

Are those the only reasons humans
explore? Are there no other reasons?

Kilmer hesitated. That was not where he wanted this conversation to go.

Yes. There can be other reasons for humans to explore.

We have many reasons as well.

Can you tell me what you hope to achieve with your visit to Earth?

We cannot answer that.

Is that because you do not know the answer? Or because you do not want us to know?

It is neither of those things. It is not what you think.

The exchange had already lasted fifteen minutes, and Kilmer had learned very little. He still had no idea what the aliens wanted, what kind of danger Earth was in, or what he could possibly do about it. When it came to the important matters, ET-1 seemed unwilling to share. But now he saw an opening—and he decided to try something different.

How do you know what I think?

We cannot know for sure. But we know a lot about you, Ambassador Kilmer. And we know a lot about what you know.

You asked to speak with me. Is that correct?

Yes.

Why would you want to speak to someone if you already know what they know?

We are not interested in what you know. It is for another reason.

What is the other reason?

> *We cannot tell you that.*

And if I had not been available, would you have asked to speak to someone else?

> *Yes. But it does not matter now. We*
> *have chosen you.*

If I am going to help you, I will need to know what you need from me. How can I help you?

> *We do not need your help, Ambassador*
> *Kilmer. It is a mistake to think so. It is*
> *your planet that needs your help.*

Kilmer paused. He opened a bottle of water and took a small sip as he considered how to approach the subject that had just been broached. If he was too direct, ET-1 might refuse to answer. And if his questions were too open-ended, he might get answers that were of little use. He would have to strike a balance.

Your message said Earth was in danger. What kind of danger?

> *The worst kind of danger. The kind*
> *that will destroy human civilization.*

Will you be the ones to harm us?

> *That is not our intention, Ambassador.*

That is good to know, ET-1. But you did not answer my question. Will you be the ones to harm us?

> *That is not our intention. But it is true*
> *that humans will be harmed. And*

humans will blame us for what
happens.

Will you not blame yourself?

No. We will not deserve the blame. We
have no bad intentions. We are not the
ones who will have shot the first arrows.

And neither are we. We want peace. We do not intend to shoot first.
We do not intend to shoot at all if it can be avoided. Does that solve the
problem? Does that eliminate the danger we face?

No. It is too late.

Why is it too late? You just arrived. And we have not done anything
other than communicate with you.

You have done much more than try to
communicate.

Kilmer removed his hands from the keyboard. What more had humans done? Earth-side hadn't even reacted to the lunar attack. Could this be about the two soldiers who had shot at ET-1? Maybe. But ET-1 had returned the soldiers unharmed. What was he missing?

Had President Whitman authorized some other action that he was unaware of? Had Strauss? The Russians or the Chinese? Suddenly, Kilmer was unsure about the foundation on which he was making his case to ET-1.

ET-1, I am not aware of anything that we have done that should be
interpreted as hostile. Maybe this is a misunderstanding. Have you
considered that?

Yes, we have considered that very
carefully. But the verdict remains the
same.

Then please explain to me what we have done.

We cannot answer that.

You say you have no bad intentions, but that you will harm us because of what we have done. Then you refuse to tell us what we have done. Can you understand why humans might conclude that you do not really have good intentions?

Yes. Human beings might think that.

This could make humans angry or afraid. Do you understand those emotions? Does that not concern you?

It does not concern us.

If you have good intentions, then why does it not concern you?

> *Even if humans are angry or afraid, there is nothing humans can do about it.*

Can you be sure? Humans might surprise you. Is it worth taking the risk, even if you think it is a small risk? Is it not better for all of us to live in peace? That is what humans want.

> *Is that how humans live with each other, Ambassador? Do they live in peace?*

Not always. But we try to live in peace.

> *Tell us, Ambassador, do humans try very hard?*

Kilmer saw the trap. If he said *Yes*, it was to admit that even the best of human effort is not sufficient to achieve peace. If he said *No*, he would imply that humans were not sufficiently interested in peace.

Everyone should try harder. There is always more we can do.

> *Not always, Ambassador. There are limits to what you can do. Sometimes there is nothing more you can do to achieve peace.*

Are you willing to try harder to achieve peace with humans?

> *We have already tried very hard.*

Have you? How? What evidence is there that you have tried hard?

> *You are still alive, Ambassador Kilmer. So are your fellow human beings. That is the evidence.*

But you are still talking to me. I think that means you want to keep trying to achieve peace. Is it because you still have hope that this can happen? Or is it because you know that harming us would be wrong?

> *You must stop thinking in terms of right and wrong. It will not help you at all. Thinking like this will only get humans killed.*

Then how should I think about it?

> *We do not know the answer to that.*

Why did you agree to meet me even after I refused to enter your spacecraft?

> *Because it was the only way to be sure that you would come.*

Why did you need me to come? How does it benefit you?

> *We did not need you to come. It benefits only human beings that you came.*

But you still refuse to tell me how I can help solve Earth's problem. You share nothing. How does that benefit humans at all?

The moment he pressed *send*, Kilmer was reminded of what Silla had said about ET-1—about how reactive they had been. They had taken no steps to build bridges. Without waiting for a response, he sent another message.

What are you afraid of, ET-1?

We are not afraid.

You have secrets, ET-1. On Earth, people who have secrets either have bad intentions or they are afraid of something. Is that not how it works on your planet?

You are correct that we have not told you everything. But if you want to help your people, you should think about your fears, not ours. Your fear is what stands in the way of you learning what you need to learn.

I have many fears, but I am not afraid to hear the truth. I am not afraid to learn. I am willing to hear your secret, whatever it is.

You do not fear the truth. But you fear what you must do to learn the truth. You have to take a greater risk, Ambassador. You have to be willing to sacrifice.

Kilmer braced himself. He had to ask the obvious question. But ET-1 was right—he *was* afraid.

What is the risk I need to take?

> *You must come to us, Ambassador*
> *Kilmer. You will have to enter ET-1.*
> *There is no other option.*

No other option? Does that mean you will force me?

Kilmer immediately regretted asking that question. He did not want to put the idea into anyone's head.

> *We could have forced you already. But*
> *it is better that you enter without force.*

And if I refuse?

> *We will make it very hard for you to*
> *refuse.*

How will you do that?

> *Let us show you how.*

Kilmer's heart almost stopped, and he typed as fast as he could.

No. I don't need to see how. I would just like to kno—

It was too late. The blinding light enveloped him completely. Kilmer put his head down and covered his eyes. Within seconds, his shock had transformed into fear. He grabbed on to the table; if someone was coming for him, he wasn't going to make it easy. He wished he had a weapon—anything.

Then he remembered. *This is not the plan. I had decided I wouldn't resist.*

He let go of the table and tried to steady himself in his chair. But he was trembling. He tried to slow his breathing. Then he heard the sound, and he readied himself.

This is it!

The sound came closer.

No. That's coming from behind me. That's not ET-1, it's—

It was the sound of the rescue vehicles trying to make their way toward Kilmer. But they were driving blind. They could end up running right into him. "I'm over here!" he shouted.

Just then, the blinding light switched off. Kilmer was still on his chair. He looked over his shoulder and saw the two vehicles with soldiers and medics. They had slowed and were coming to a stop about thirty yards away. Kilmer looked around. Everything looked the same. *So why the light?*

Just as he looked back at the screen, a message popped up.

Cover your ears, Ambassador.

Instead, Kilmer typed frantically.

What have you done?

And then it happened. The explosions almost knocked Kilmer off his chair. On both sides of him—to his right and left, but what had to be nearly a mile from where he was sitting—colossal towers of fire, smoke, and dirt rose into the air. Each tower looked to be the height of a twenty-story building. The amount of Earth displaced had to have been massive.

Kilmer banged at the keys.

What have you done? Why?

We did nothing to provoke an attack.

Will there be more attacks?

Ambassador Kilmer, that was only a demonstration. It was the smallest one we could use to send the message. We hope it is clear to you and your leaders why you do not have a choice. You will come to ET-1. If not, the next attack comes from above. And it will not be small.

When? How? And will you stop all attacks if I agree to come to ET-1?

Ambassador Kilmer, please relax. You are in a very difficult situation and you are afraid. But try to remember that we do not have bad intentions.

Kilmer was no longer scared. He was pissed off.

Were those explosions meant to help me relax? Or were they meant to remind me of your good intentions?

You are being sarcastic. We understand that.

Kilmer fell back in his chair. *Of course you do.*

ET-1 had learned enough to understand complex language, human subcultures, and, apparently, even sarcasm. *Why are they working so hard?* Previously, Kilmer had thought that ET-1's hefty investments meant that they had a lot at stake—and that Earth-side might have some leverage. That was still a reasonable inference, but his confidence in it was waning. He just couldn't figure it out.

It seemed about as desperate a situation as he could have imagined, and he felt the fear creeping back in. He wanted to get out of there, to wash his hands of the whole thing. He was obviously in over his head. And this was not his responsibility alone. He wasn't elected. He wasn't even a soldier.

He stood up and looked at the vehicles behind him. He took a step in their direction, but then stopped.

No. When you were calm and thinking rationally, you promised yourself you wouldn't run away.

He took a deep breath and sat back down at the keyboard.

If it will help to avoid a war, then I will come. But you need to understand that I do not represent this country or the planet. I cannot speak for everyone.

> *Ambassador Kilmer, you will be representing Earth whether you want to or not. We understand that you cannot make that decision alone. We will give your leaders time to decide whether to send you. We will give them one week.*

And if they decide that someone else should represent Earth?

> *Then we will accept President Whitman. But she will not be able to solve Earth's problem. She will serve a different purpose for us.*

What purpose is that?

> *We cannot tell you.*

Can she talk with you from outside ET-1? Like I am doing?

> *That is not an option. There will be no more conversations like this one.*

Why does it have to be inside ET-1? Why does that matter?

> *Inside ET-1 is not what matters. What*
> *matters is that no one else can know*
> *what is discussed. For that we will have*
> *to speak to you inside ET-1.*

How does that help? Even if we have the conversation inside ET-1,
others will find out about it afterwards.

Kilmer had just hit *send* when the answer to his question—the only possible answer—presented itself to him. ET-1 had said he would have to take a risk, but they had also said something else. *You have to be willing to sacrifice.*

He felt as if a stone was pressing down on his chest, making it hard for him to breathe. ET-1's reply confirmed what he had already concluded.

> *We want to be clear, Ambassador Kilmer.*
> *Once you enter ET-1, you will never return*
> *to your people. There is no other way.*

Kilmer's fingers were trembling even as they rested on the keyboard. *Don't lose focus. You need to stay calm now. There must be a way. There's always a way.*

And if we refuse your conditions? If we send no representative?

> *Then we will have no choice. Humans*
> *will pay the price. Many will die. We*
> *give you seven days to decide.*

You will attack us even if we still want peace? Even if we take no
aggressive actions against you?

> *None of that will matter. You and your*
> *leaders must now decide what to do.*
> *This conversation will end now.*

Wait.

Kilmer didn't want the conversation to end, even though he was out of ideas for what to say. He felt powerless. And he was worn out. *Think. Come up with something. You need more to work with.* His mind raced. And then...

May I ask a few final questions?

Yes.

Do you really care if I accept your invitation?

There was a longer pause than before—just as Kilmer had expected. And then an answer appeared on the screen.

There are many who do not care at all what you do, Ambassador Kilmer.

Do you think it will be possible to avert war if I accept your invitation?

Another long pause.

Ambassador Kilmer, you have the right to know that even if you come to ET-1, nothing you do is likely to matter. It is like your story of the Greeks. Archidamus and Pericles tried hard to avoid war. But it did not make any difference.

Kilmer was stunned by the reference. They had obviously studied human history quite thoroughly. But he wondered—*how thoroughly, exactly?*

So, you are asking me to sacrifice everything in exchange for nothing?

> *Human beings often sacrifice for even*
> *less. We are at least giving you a*
> *chance. It is all you will get. There will*
> *be no more questions now.*

Then goodbye to you, Archidamus.

Kilmer looked at the screen to see if there would be an answer. He had almost given up when the response came.

Goodbye to you, Pericles.

Kilmer leaned back in his chair. Anger, frustration, fear, sorrow, confusion, guilt—it was all muddled together. He closed his eyes and just allowed himself to breathe for a minute. Then another minute. He needed all those emotions to settle down, to stop demanding his attention. There was something more important to think about.

Kilmer had noticed it—the one thing.

He was glad there would be a transcript of the entire conversation for him to look over; there were many items to revisit, analyze, and piece together. But the real breakthrough, he knew, had come only at the very end. In a sea of despair, the only real sign of hope.

Kilmer knew that hope was never the answer. *But it is a foundation. You can build from there.*

He rose from his chair and walked over to the two vehicles, but he told the drivers to return without him—he would walk back to HQ-1 on his own. He needed time to think.

And he needed to start getting used to being alone.

Kilmer placed a call to President Whitman on his walk back from the kill-zone.

"Professor Kilmer!" Whitman practically shouted into the phone. "Are you okay?"

"Yes, Madam President. I'm fine. Those explosions—was anyone hurt? Has there been any other activity?"

"Everything's okay. There was no one in those locations. I think it was just what they said—a display of their capabilities." Whitman paused. "I'm sorry you had to go through all that. I want you to know that we're going to find a way out of this mess—together."

"I'm not sure that's a good idea, Madam President. That's why I'm calling you. I think it's time for me to step aside. You should decide how to move forward on this without me."

"If you want to leave, Professor, I'll bring you back to DC immediately. No one will force you to do anything."

"Sorry, I'm not being clear. I don't want to 'step aside' in that way. I'm not asking you to get me out of this. It's the opposite, in fact. I'm convinced that you will have to send me to ET-1—and I think everyone on the team will agree. But it might be hard for them to discuss it if I'm in the room. We can't have them hesitating or worrying about my feelings when they advise you. There's no time for that now."

"Let's not get ahead of ourselves, Professor. I understand your concern about team dynamics, but I still value your perspective. I want you in the room. We're meeting to debrief at ten."

"I'll share my perspective with you, Madam President—and with the team—but I can do that without being in the meetings. Also… I think I need some time to reflect on what just happened—and I won't be ready by 10 p.m."

"We can delay the meeting," Whitman offered.

"Please don't. Go ahead without me. I think that's best." Kilmer hesitated. "Madam President, I'm... I'm really exhausted. And I need some rest. I don't mean sleep—I just need to be alone for a little while to clear my mind. To process everything. And to organize my thoughts. Please give me some time. I'm really sorry."

"Don't apologize. Take your time and get some sleep. Agent Silla can catch you up on what we discuss."

"Thank you, Madam President."

After they hung up, Kilmer called Silla.

"Are you okay?" she asked. "I'm coming to you right now. I just left HQ-1 and I'm walking to the perimeter."

"Silla, I—" He didn't even know where to begin. "I'm..."

"Don't say anything. Just wait until I'm there."

Kilmer hung up and kept walking.

They reached the perimeter at almost the same time. As soon as she saw him, Silla made her way through the line of soldiers and ran into Touchdown-1. Ten seconds later, she was in his arms. For that moment, anyway, she wasn't concerned who might see them.

"I wish I had better news to report," he said finally. "I'm sorry."

"You're here now. We're all still here. This is not over." She looked into his eyes. "Just remember, Kilmer. *We have time.*" She gave him a kiss on his cheek and then held his hand as they walked back toward HQ-1.

Kilmer told her what he had said to the president, and that he would not be at the debrief session.

"If you want me to stay with you, I will," Silla said. "But I think it's important for me to be at the meeting."

"I wouldn't ask you to miss it. They need you. And I think you need to hear what they'll have to say."

"What does that mean?"

"Silla, I'm not sure what you think happens next, but I know how this has to end. And everyone else is going to come to the same conclusion. There's no choice but to send me off. No matter what else we might do as part of our strategy, there's no way around it. You see that, don't you?"

"No, Kilmer, I don't. We are nowhere near the point where we—"

"*That's* why, Silla. That's why you need to hear what everyone has to say. You're going to see that I'm right—that everyone agrees."

"That doesn't make it right. And I don't think anyone is ready to hand you over as a sacrifice. Some people will want to fight. And everyone will look for other options. Don't you dare give up so soon."

"I'm not giving up. I know what it means for me if I walk into ET-1. Believe me, I do. But I won't be doing any of us any favors if I don't face reality. I need to look at this objectively. Rationally. And I need you to help me with that. But you can't help me unless you're also ready to face facts."

"Okay, Kilmer. Let's not argue about who's right or wrong. Let's just agree that we're going to try to do everything we can to deal with the crisis *and* to keep you safe. Not one or the other. Both."

"Fine." Kilmer nodded.

Silla entered HQ-1 to fetch a transcript of the conversation for Kilmer. She returned with it a few minutes later.

"Now get back to the house and rest. I'll come as soon as I'm done here. We can talk in the morning."

She made sure no one was nearby before kissing Kilmer on the lips. Then she said goodbye and ran off to the meeting.

~ 78 ~

Kilmer had been sitting on the front porch of the bed-and-breakfast for over an hour. The transcript in his hands was completely marked up—lines, arrows, circles, and notes were all over it. Scribbled on the very last page were four tentative conclusions he had drawn.

1. ET-1 has more at stake than it is letting on.

The aliens said they were unafraid and didn't need Kilmer, but that wasn't the whole story. Why had they tried not to harm Earth? Why did they invest so much in learning? Why did they insist on meeting in private?

2. ET-1 is divided.

Kilmer had set a trap: *Do you really care if I accept your invitation?* Answering *No* wouldn't have been credible given how much pressure they were putting on Kilmer to come to them. Answering *Yes* would have implied that ET-1 *needed* Kilmer. ET-1 had tried to split the difference—*There are many who do not care at all what you do*—but in doing so, ET-1 had revealed, for the first time, that there were differences of opinion on their side. It was unclear what precisely they were disagreeing about, but from Kilmer's perspective, this was good news.

3. I might have a friend on ET-1.

ET-1 had made a reference to Archidamus and Pericles, the leaders of Sparta and Athens. But why? Did ET-1 know that the two of them had been friends? On a hunch, Kilmer had called his interlocutor *Archidamus*—who had tried to avoid war with Athens. In response, Kilmer had been called *Pericles*. Was that meant as a signal?

4. They care how I think.

ET-1 was uninterested in what Kilmer knew, and claimed to want him *for another reason.* What other reason could there be? One possibility was that they wanted to share what *they* knew, but that was unlikely—he wouldn't

287

even be able to tell anyone about it. The only other possibility he could see was that ET-1 wanted him for the same reason Whitman did. *They don't care what I know. They care how I think.* It was a bizarre conclusion, to be sure, but it fit the facts. Most of what he knew could be found on the internet, but the internet could not reveal to them the workings of his mind. They would need *him* for that. To what end? He had no idea.

Kilmer looked over the four points. *Now what?*

The situation still looked awful.

The worst kind of danger. The kind that will destroy human civilization.

Humanity was in danger of annihilation. Kilmer still had no idea what the aliens wanted. And he would soon be asked to sacrifice himself for almost no chance of making any difference. And yet, somehow, he felt okay.

His four points added up to *something*. And something was infinitely better than nothing.

Day 22. Morning.

The next morning at breakfast, Silla brought Kilmer up to speed on the previous night's meeting. No one wanted to send him to ET-1, she reported, but no viable alternatives had been proposed. Shockingly, it was Secretary Strauss who had most strongly opposed handing him over to the aliens. He thought Kilmer had no chance of stopping what was coming—and at best, sacrificing him would delay things by a few hours or days. It wasn't worth kowtowing to the aliens for that.

"More importantly," Silla said, "a number of people are now wondering whether we're giving the aliens too much credit. Sure, they can blow some things up—but so can we. Have we overestimated their capabilities? Are they counting on us being too afraid to test them? Maybe their rhetoric and aggression are meant to scare us into submission without them having to fire a real shot."

The meeting had ended on two open questions. First, how would the international alliance respond to the recent developments—and to the idea of Kilmer representing everyone? Second, what actions might Earth-side take in the next week—before ET-1's deadline—to deter or prepare for war?

Silla's final update was that Chief of Staff Perez and Agent Lane would be arriving later in the day to join the team at Station Zero. Whitman wanted Perez on the front lines to make sure nothing went off the rails as tensions increased, and Art wanted Lane to oversee the communication side of things.

Kilmer then told Silla about his four tentative conclusions. She homed in on the point about disagreements among the aliens. "Maybe that's something we can use to our advantage," she suggested.

"How do we leverage their disagreements if we don't know what they're arguing about?" Kilmer asked.

"The fact that they're arguing might be enough. Maybe if we put some pressure on them, it will expose some of the rifts on their side. Until now, we've been relatively compliant because we didn't want to test their patience. But maybe some non-compliance is needed to test their cohesion."

"That's interesting. What kind of pressure?"

"If we push back—show them that we're willing to fight—maybe the more peaceful or sane voices on their side will get louder. It could backfire, of course, but given how desperate things are, maybe it's a risk worth taking. If the temperature rises, maybe they stop making threats. Maybe they stop demanding sacrifices."

Kilmer nodded. "I'm torn. On the one hand, I agree. The situation seems pretty desperate, so we should try to shake things up a little—there's more room for upside than downside. On the other hand, what if we have it all wrong? What if the sane and peaceful aliens are the ones who are demanding that I come to ET-1? Maybe Archidamus isn't leading me to slaughter... Maybe he's a friend."

Heirs of Herodotus by D. Kilmer.
Excerpt from Chapter 8.

War has always been a dangerous business, but the pursuit of peace can be even more hazardous. Warriors know that they risk death in every encounter with their enemies—the troops amassed on the other side of the battlefield, or the soldiers hiding in the bushes. **Peacemakers risk death as well, but they tend not to die at the hands of enemies. They are killed by their erstwhile friends—the ones who feel betrayed by the notion that it is time to end the bloodshed.**

Anwar Sadat and Yitzhak Rabin both gave their lives as they marched on that same road—that long, winding, obstacle-ridden path that only sometimes leads to peace. But Sadat was not killed by the Jews. And Rabin was not killed by the Arabs. Both were assassinated by the very people who once considered them their brothers in arms.

Waging war takes guts, but you have the comfort of knowing that your friends stand beside you. Fighting for peace takes even greater courage, because all too often, you stand alone.

~ 81 ~

By 5:00 p.m. that afternoon—Day 22—the three reserves had moved to within 25,000 miles of Earth's surface. They were now moving like geosynchronous satellites, maintaining their positions over fixed locations on Earth. One was stationed above the US. Another was over Central Europe. The third was near the Chinese and Russian border.

Conversations with the international alliance had not gone well. The Europeans were frantic. Chinese President Zhao and Russian President Sokolov were angry. They felt the Americans had mishandled things—and that Kilmer's conversation with ET-1 had been weak and ineffective. Neither of them was willing to allow Kilmer *or* Whitman to represent them in talks with the aliens. They demanded—and the Europeans and Indians agreed— that a message be sent to ET-1 making it clear that Americans do *not* speak for the whole planet. At the very least, this might buy time. And everyone— including Whitman's team—believed that such a message would signal to the aliens that it would not be easy for them to bully the entire planet into submission.

Day 23.

The Earth-side message was sent to ET-1 at 8:00 a.m. on the morning of Day 23. A response from ET-1 was received an hour later.

This changes nothing. D. Kilmer must arrive by May 24 at 5 p.m. If not, the consequences will be dire. We will attack Earth at 6 p.m. on that day.

Zhao and Sokolov told Whitman that this would not end their efforts to engage with ET-1. Whitman advised them against doing anything rash and asked that they coordinate their efforts with the Americans. But it was clear to all three leaders that the level of mutual mistrust was starting to rival the level of shared anxiety.

That afternoon, Secretary Strauss and General Allen briefed the team on military planning in the six areas that President Whitman had prioritized. *Deterrence*, it was agreed, would require a show of force, along with much more aggressive rhetoric than Earth-side had employed until now. Whether it would work remained unknown, but there was increasing support for bolder action. *Defending the homeland* would be very difficult if the attacks came from space, but there was no way to say more until it was known what kinds of weapons the aliens would use. Earth-side stood a greater chance if the aliens hoped to invade and occupy. *Coordinating with the alliance* was getting more difficult. The default was that each country would fend for itself, but discussions were ongoing. There was, however, significant international cooperation in one domain: a robust and multilayered global communication network was being set up in case existing systems were destroyed or disrupted. *Fighting in space* had been an area of intense focus. Anti-satellite weapons could be used against the reserves, but the likelihood of a hit was slim if the spacecraft could take evasive actions. A more effective approach might be to weaponize rockets and satellites, but there was limited progress to report on that front. One problem remained paramount: Earth-side vehicles could not move anywhere close to the speed of the reserves. *Protecting civilian populations* would be difficult if the attack came from above, but dispersing a population was an option. There were plans in development for managing refugee crises across the globe, and for addressing the likely shortage of food, water, and medical supplies. The international alliance had been cooperating effectively on these issues, but the potential scope of the problem was beyond anything anyone had ever imagined. Finally, Strauss and Allen updated everyone on the feasibility of a *guerilla warfare* campaign. If the aliens planned to subjugate or enslave humankind, they would presumably require a large terrestrial presence. Alien capabilities were unknown, but humans might stand a chance of maintaining—for years, even—strong pockets of resistance. Each country was developing its own plan for how to disperse its armed forces if Earth-side lost the war and the aliens attempted a terrestrial occupation.

It was, without exception, the most dreadful meeting any participant had ever attended. No one imagined they would hear references to the Pony Express or the telegraph during a twenty-first-century briefing. But they did.

Day 24.

On Day 24, a rocket was launched into space from a small town in Northern China—it came within 300 miles of the reserve spacecraft that was stationed above East Asia. The mission had two objectives. First, to see how close to the alien spacecraft an Earth-side vehicle could get. Second, to detonate a one-megaton nuclear bomb if the rocket made it to within 100 miles of the reserve spacecraft. The goal was not to destroy the reserve, but to demonstrate the possibility of doing so.

At approximately 10:00 a.m. EST, when the rocket was almost 280 miles from its target, it was destroyed—presumably by a weapon deployed by the alien spacecraft. The nuclear weapon did not detonate.

Secretary Strauss was the only American not to be shocked by what had happened. His counterpart in Russia, the minister of defense, had alluded to the possibility that some such action might be taken by the Chinese, though Strauss had been given no details. Strauss didn't try to dissuade the action, nor did he report what he knew to the president. Whitman was shocked and angered when news got out about what had happened. She had spoken to Zhao the night before, and he had told her nothing about the planned launch.

At 12:00 p.m., the Americans received a message from ET-1. *We do not know the intent of vehicles that approach our spacecraft. They will be destroyed. Do not attempt such an action again. This is a warning.* The Americans hastily relayed the message to everyone in the international alliance.

Unbeknownst even to Strauss, a second rocket was already scheduled for launch. Its mission was to detonate a one-megaton nuclear weapon *before* it reached the location where the first rocket had been destroyed. At 2:30 p.m., the second rocket came within 500 miles of the reserve spacecraft and successfully detonated its weapon. The blast was too far from the alien spacecraft to do any physical damage, but its effects might have been felt.

Whitman was on the phone with Zhao only moments after the blast. Zhao denied having launched the attack. Five minutes later, Sokolov denied it also. The Europeans said they had nothing to do with it. So did the Indians.

At 2:45, another message came in from ET-1:

We warned you against such action. Earth will now suffer the consequences.

~ 82 ~

Two minutes later, President Whitman was on the phone with HQ-2, talking
to General Allen. She told him to send an immediate response to ET-1. Earth-
side had to buy time. Allen typed on the laptop as Strauss, Kilmer, Silla, Perez,
and Lane looked over his shoulder:

> *I speak on behalf of President Whitman. Let's not escalate the situation.*
> *We do not know who made the decision to launch that weapon. We are*
> *investigating. Please refrain from retaliating. Let's talk first.*

Less than ten minutes later, at 2:55, Whitman, Nielsen, Garcia, Druckman,
Art, and the chiefs of the Army and Air Force were in the Situation Room. HQ-
2 was on the other end of the phone line. Whitman called the meeting to order.

"We don't know how much time we have, so let's get started. Do we have
any basis on which to predict where or how ET-1 might retaliate?"

No one had anything to offer.

"Do we have any more information on who launched that goddamn
nuke?"

Druckman promised that his people would figure it out very soon.

"Okay. What do we want to say to the aliens if they give us a second
chance?" Whitman asked.

Nielsen answered. "As I see it, ET-1 has an optics problem now. If they
give us a second chance, it might look like they backed down—and whoever
launched the nuke might conclude that they scared ET-1 into inaction."

"True," Kilmer said, "but let's play that out. Does ET-1 really care what
we think? If *they* know that they can annihilate us, why does it matter if *we're*
sitting here thinking they're weak? As I see it, if they really are as strong as
they pretend to be, they don't have to worry if we get the wrong impression
for a little while. It's only if they're *not* so strong that it should concern them—

because they can't have us knowing that. In other words, the more vulnerable they are, the greater incentive they have to follow through with some sort of retaliation."

"So, what you're saying," Whitman summarized, "is that we are now *hoping* that our adversary is strong enough to annihilate us. That's the best-case scenario suddenly?"

"In the short run, yes," Kilmer agreed. "Of course, in the long run, we hope they're weak."

Whitman moved on. "Okay. If they attack, what is our response? Is there any reason for us to escalate?"

General Allen was the first to answer. "I don't think so. We probably can't do too much damage unless we attack ET-1 itself. And that's a bad idea—even if we can nuke it in minutes. If we do that, we are at war. And before we declare war, we'd better be sure we stand a chance against them. I think we need to get them back to the table—no matter what they do."

"No matter what they do?" Strauss said. "What if they wipe out a city? What if they attack DC?"

"Maybe that gives us even more reason to talk instead of fight," Allen responded. "We may have to swallow our pride and tell them that while both sides have launched attacks, it's time for cooler heads to prevail."

Druckman weighed in. "I'm a bit uncomfortable with a situation where they do something so disproportionate, and we respond in a way that seems weak. Over the last day or two, we've been talking about whether we've fallen prey to a carefully curated illusion by the aliens. With only one attack on the Moon and a few bombs in Shenandoah—all things we could easily have done ourselves—they have us believing that they can bring the wrath of God down upon us. Maybe they can. But maybe they can't. It *might* be a bluff. And as the professor points out, if this is a game of poker and they have a weak hand, of *course* they will come in over the top and retaliate disproportionately to scare us into submission. That is exactly when we should refuse to back down."

"That's a fair point," General Allen conceded, "but there's a problem. You're suggesting that we can forgive a small retaliation by them, but that if they hit us hard, we must hit back. I get the logic—but I fail to see how we do this *practically*. Hit them how? I don't think we should attack ET-1, because it's the only spacecraft we can communicate with, and destroying it would shut down our ability to negotiate—which at some point we will have do in order to deescalate. And if we can't attack ET-1, what other options do we have? Launch another rocket at their reserves? We've seen how well that worked. And if we can't inflict any actual damage, we haven't hit back."

Nielsen nodded thoughtfully. "It seems like we would be stuck in a situation where we have a strong inkling that they're bluffing, but we don't have enough chips to call their bluff."

"Precisely," said General Allen.

"So how do we get more chips?" Nielsen asked. "How do we increase our options for hitting back?"

"We need more time," said Kilmer. "There's no way around it. As of right now, we have four days before I'm supposed to go to ET-1. After that, maybe we get another day or two? Let's imagine, for the sake of argument, that I buy us a few more days on top of that. Is that enough, General Allen? Secretary Strauss? Are we in a stronger position by then?"

"We're working on it, Professor," Strauss replied. "And we'll be in a slightly better position with each passing day. But ideally, we need months. And I'm not talking about the time we need to defend ourselves against an all-out attack. I'm saying just for us to be able to have a decent chance of hitting one of the reserves."

"Then I don't see how we can think about hitting back at all," Kilmer lamented. "General Allen is right. It's not practical."

"What I'm hearing," Whitman said, "is that the only way to hit back is to blow ET-1 to pieces. I understand the downside, but I want to discuss that option further. I also want to—"

They were interrupted by a message from ET-1, transmitted simultaneously to the White House and HQ-2. The aliens had decided not to attack—but they had also refused to give Earth-side a second chance. ET-1's response was more nuanced than expected:

If you wish for us to avoid attacking Earth in retaliation, you will have to send Ambassador Kilmer now. You cannot have four more days. Time is up. He comes now, or Earth suffers the consequences.

Silla clenched her fists. Kilmer noticed that he was holding his breath and forced himself to start breathing again. Then he closed his eyes just long enough to remind himself—*every problem wants to be solved.*

"General Allen… Madam President… Would it be okay if I respond to the message?" Kilmer asked.

Both agreed, and Kilmer took Allen's seat in front of the laptop.

This is Kilmer. Am I speaking with Archidamus?

> *Yes, Ambassador. We expect to see you very soon.*

Can we please have the four days? We still need to coordinate an international agreement on this.

> *We have already seen how well human beings coordinate. Have we not? Or did all of Earth decide to send that weapon into space?*

You are right. We have not managed to coordinate yet. That is precisely why we need more time.

> *The recent actions taken by humans have eliminated that option.*

How much time can you give?

> *Less than 4 hours, Ambassador Kilmer.*

What if it takes me longer? What if I need until tomorrow?

> *Then some places on Earth will suffer, starting immediately. And more will be*

attacked every hour. Even Station Zero
will not be safe.

And if I come to you now, you will not retaliate?

Correct.

And there is a chance we can solve this problem entirely?

I am sorry, Ambassador. There is
almost no chance of that now.

Then why would I come?

Because if you do not, the suffering
begins much sooner. And, you never
know, Ambassador Kilmer, maybe you
will surprise everyone. Our demand is
simple. You will come to ET-1 before 7
p.m. tonight. When you arrive, you will
see a platform on which to stand. If you
are not standing on that platform by 7
p.m., we will launch a devastating
attack. If you continue to delay, each
subsequent attack will be worse. That is
all there is for you to consider.

The communication ended—and Kilmer sat staring at the screen in silence.

No one at HQ-2 said a word. No words came from the Situation Room either. It was as if everyone on the team was respecting Kilmer's right to process what had happened and to overcome the shock.

Well—*almost* everyone.

Secretary Strauss walked over and put his hand on Kilmer's shoulder. "Don't worry, son," he said. "There isn't a chance in hell we're handing you over to them. No goddamn way."

~ 83 ~

The team was divided. Secretary Strauss, Director Druckman, VP Nielsen, and Agent Silla were against allowing Kilmer to enter ET-1. Strauss saw no upside to sacrificing Kilmer; the aliens had made clear that war was inevitable. Nielsen argued that sending Kilmer would mean losing not only a valued adviser, but also the only human being who had built some sort of relationship with ET-1. Druckman again raised the possibility that ET-1 was bluffing. He also worried that the aliens might extract intel from Kilmer regarding Earth-side capabilities and fears. Silla pointed out that if they had any hope of deterring ET-1, now or in the future, it would require pushing back and testing their resolve—and this might be the least costly opportunity for doing so.

The others saw it differently. General Allen reiterated that Earth-side was incapable of effective retaliation, and that if ET-1 ratcheted up the pressure, Kilmer would be forced to submit to their demands eventually. Perez and Garcia thought Druckman's notion that the aliens were bluffing was mere wishful thinking. Art was torn, but ultimately came out in favor of sending Kilmer. "I agree it's risky to hand over someone who knows so much about us, but maybe he can continue to help us once he enters ET-1. If there's a solution hidden somewhere inside, I can't think of anyone who's more likely to find it than he is."

Kilmer had been sitting quietly, preferring not to influence the decision. Unfortunately, Whitman seemed to be leaning toward keeping him *out* of ET-1, and Kilmer thought that was a mistake. "I'm sorry," Kilmer interjected reluctantly, "but General Allen is right. Not sending me to ET-1 only postpones the inevitable, and countless people could die in the interim. As for needing to stand up to ET-1 and calling their bluff, all of you can do that, if necessary, even after I'm gone. Yes, there is a chance that they manage to extract information from me, but as far as we can tell, they don't even know I'm working with all of you. Apart from that slight risk, the decision to send me costs us nothing—except perhaps one life. I don't think anyone here would think twice before sending a soldier into harm's way in a situation like this. You can't treat me any differently."

Whitman responded firmly. "No, Professor Kilmer, we *can* treat you differently. The soldiers will do their jobs, and you will do yours. And it's not clear that sending you to ET-1 is even the best way to *delay* an attack. If ET-1 is so desperate to have you, maybe we should inform them that they'll have to play nice if they want access to you. Either way, I haven't yet made my decision. Their deadline is 7 p.m., and I plan to wait until 6:30 to make the call. We might learn something more between now and then."

The discussion shifted to the situation at Station Zero. The aliens had threatened it directly, and everyone agreed it would be unwise to have so many high-ranking members of the administration gathered at that location. Apart from essential personnel, HQ-1 and HQ-2 would be evacuated at 6:30. Strauss, Perez, Silla, and Lane would be flown back to Washington—along with Kilmer, if Whitman decided to reject ET-1's demand. General Allen would remain at Station Zero, but he would relocate to the outskirts of Shenandoah National Park.

The meeting ended and the team dispersed. They would touch base again once Whitman had made her decision.

~ 84 ~

"What do you think President Whitman will decide?" Kilmer asked Silla.

"I think she'll make the right call," Silla replied. "Handing you over in the hope that it delays the war by a few days is a bad deal. And she's right—if you're our trump card, maybe we should hold on to you for now."

After the meeting, the two of them had returned to the bed-and-breakfast. Kilmer wanted to gather a few things that he might need if Whitman agreed to send him to ET-1. He took his computer out of the laptop bag and replaced it with some clothes, a few snacks, and a bottle of water. He grabbed a pen and some stationery off the side table and put them in the bag as well. Silla had lent him a duffel bag so he could take additional clothes and food, and he filled it with some of each. Kilmer wasn't sure he would live long enough to use any of the things he was packing.

How had it come to this?

Silla sat down next to him on the bed and held his hand. "Kilmer, we'll get through this. We're going to make it past today and then we'll figure out what to do tomorrow. One day at a time. Together. Okay?"

"That's the thing, Silla. I'm not sure we can get out of this mess thinking one day at a time."

"I don't see what other option we have."

Kilmer didn't have a good answer to that—but he knew that an incremental approach wasn't going to work. The trajectory they were on ended in disaster. They had to chart a different course—and that probably meant they would have to make some sacrifices.

"Silla, if something happens to me—and if you never see me again… I just want you to know that—"

"Stop, Kilmer. Don't. Please don't say anything more. I don't want you to have a sense of closure. Whatever it is that you want to say to me, you can say it to me after this is over. Trust me, I can't wait to hear it. And if that gives you even an ounce of additional motivation to make sure you're around to say it, then it's worth it."

"You're taking a big risk, Silla. It might be now or never," he said softly. "We might not get another chance."

"No, Kilmer. You promised me we would get through this. And you promised that you would come back to me. You're going to keep your promises."

"I only promised that I would try, Silla. No matter the consequences. And I still plan to do exactly that."

She put her arms around him. "I know you, Kilmer. You'll find a way. Just—don't you dare give up. Do you understand? No matter what."

"I won't," he assured her. "I understand what's at stake. And I don't intend to ever stop fighting for it."

Heirs of Herodotus by D. Kilmer.
Excerpt from Chapter 11.

The prophet Muhammed's death in 632 was followed by what, at the time, was simply a disagreement over succession. Would the next leader of the Islamic community be Muhammed's father-in-law, Abu Bakr? Or would it be his son-in-law and cousin, Ali? The rationale for the first was that the followers of Muhammed should decide his successor. The case for the latter was that the line of succession should go through the prophet's family.

There is no reason to think that the fighting that followed was meant to evolve into a conflict that would last 1,400 years—and counting. But that is precisely what happened with the Sunni–Shi'a split. Events of those early decades—the First Fitna (656-661), the assassination of Ali in 661, the Battle of Karbala in 680, the death of Husayn—these might have been minor footnotes in history. Instead, they remain, to this day, rallying cries for war.

What if those men could have seen the future? What if they had known that the divisions they were creating would last for millennia? That they were writing death warrants for children many centuries into the future? One can only imagine that they would have come to their senses and worked things out. Had they known the true costs of their war, they would have worked harder to settle things peacefully from the start.

But why do we think that? How can we be so sure? Who would have backed down? Who would have surrendered? Who would have sacrificed their values and beliefs, and the lives of their followers? That's when a truly horrific realization dawns: **it might have changed nothing at all.**

"If only they had known, they would have done things differently." These are the words we most associate with tragedy. But the greatest tragedies are the ones where we must say, "They **did** know—and they did nothing."

"I don't accept those orders, Secretary Strauss."

"What the hell does that mean, Professor? I just told you that President Whitman has ordered all of us to evacuate Station Zero—including you."

Kilmer and Strauss were standing eyeball to eyeball, as General Allen, Perez, Silla, and Lane looked on.

"I'm not leaving this place until I talk to the president myself," Kilmer announced.

"I'm sorry that the president isn't available to listen to your grievances right now, but she's a little busy," Strauss snapped. "And in case you think that evacuating you was *my* decision, Salvo and Casey were on the call as well. So get your ass in the Jeep—*now*. I'm not wasting any more time on this."

General Allen separated the two men. "That's enough, gentlemen. Professor Kilmer, Secretary Strauss is right. We were on the call. The president made it clear that you will not be going to ET-1. Not today."

"But that doesn't make any sense. It's the wrong call—and the president said she wouldn't decide until 6:30. It's only six!"

"Professor, she has made her decision. And she's thought it through. President Zhao has admitted that they launched the nuke, and President Whitman hopes that will allow us to go back to ET-1 with a better explanation and a different proposal. President Zhao has even offered to draft an apology to help placate matters. We now have a few different options for how to play it."

Kilmer grabbed his phone. *We had a deal. I was supposed to be able to argue my case.* He dialed Whitman, but she didn't answer. He tried calling Nielsen and got the same result. *Shit!*

Silla placed her hand gently on his arm. "I know you're unhappy about this. General Allen and Mr. Perez feel the same way. But those are the orders.

The president wants us airborne before ET-1 is told you won't be coming. Yes, it's a risk. *Every* option entails risk. But the game isn't over. We can reevaluate after we see how ET-1 reacts."

Kilmer looked around at the others. "*None* of you see how dangerous this is?" he yelled. "ET-1 has painted itself into a corner," he explained, trying to lower his voice. "They will *have* to act if we ignore the ultimatum. Don't you understand that?" He turned to General Allen. "General, we will have blood on our hands. You *know* this."

General Allen didn't answer. And no one was willing to disobey the president. The only person who might have done so—Secretary Strauss—happened to agree with her.

So be it.

Kilmer closed his eyes. His mind raced as he constructed decision trees, worked through scenarios, and evaluated options. No one interrupted. Giving him a few seconds to come to terms with the decision seemed only fair.

But Kilmer was doing something else.

"Fine," he said when he finally opened his eyes. "Let's go. If I don't have a choice in the matter, there's no reason to waste time. But I will be calling the president again."

No one objected, and the group headed out of HQ-2.

Two Jeeps were waiting for them. All around, soldiers and staff were in motion. Orders to evacuate had already been given, and people were moving and driving in all directions. Kilmer handed his duffel bag to one of the drivers but decided not to hand over the laptop bag.

"Sit with me in the second Jeep," Silla said softly. "And tell me what you're thinking."

"I don't think you'll understand," he replied.

"I'll try to. I know you're worried about what happens next. So am I. But we have time—and we'll figure something out. Right?"

Kilmer said nothing. He was re-running his analysis. Had he missed something? Were there other options? He took a deep breath. *No. Same conclusion.*

Closing his eyes, he summoned the words that had always given him comfort. His mother's words. The ones she had left for him twenty-five years ago. He could still hear them, as if they were being spoken to him in her voice.

You're strong in ways that only your dad and I will ever know. You'll get through this, my love. I promise you.

He opened his eyes and took Silla's hand. Then he moved close to her, as if he were about to whisper a secret. Instead, he kissed her on the cheek—long enough that she knew he didn't care if anyone saw them. Only then came the whisper.

"I'll keep my promises, Silla. No matter what happens."

Silla's confusion was replaced by terror the moment Kilmer turned away from her and broke into a sprint toward the perimeter. Before she could even find her voice—and before anyone else could register what was happening—he was already twenty-five yards away.

Kilmer heard the shouts—Silla, Strauss, Allen—and kept running. He didn't know how many people were chasing him, but the real difficulty lay ahead. Fifty yards to the perimeter. Then another half mile.

The problem wasn't the distance. It was the soldiers who stood on the perimeter. They had heard the commotion. Strauss and Allen were issuing orders from behind—*stop him, arrest that man, take him down*—but the soldiers looked baffled, not knowing whether to grab Kilmer, shoot him, or get out of his way.

That was when Kilmer saw that the soldier directly in front of him was holding a handgun. If Kilmer could have identified any other option, he would have chosen it, but he was all of two seconds away from the soldier and it was too late to change course now.

The soldier blocking his path had made no effort to plant his feet or prepare for a possible collision—as if he assumed Kilmer would come to his senses and stop running. But Kilmer didn't stop. Instead, he raised his arms to protect his head, lowered his shoulders so that they were level with the soldier's ribs, and ran straight into him.

The soldier flew backwards and onto the ground, the handgun tumbling from his hand. Kilmer thought he was going to hit the ground as well, but he caught his balance just in time. He scooped up the gun—knowing that he would be safer if the gun was not in the possession of the soldier—and kept running. It occurred to him that he had never used a firearm before. *That's okay. You don't plan to use it today either.*

The incongruity of holding a gun while racing off to beg for peace did not escape his notice. But he didn't dwell on it for more than a moment. The thought was replaced by a sudden realization that he was doing exactly what he had worried Strauss might do—disobey the president and take matters into his own hands. If it was to be considered an act of arrogance and betrayal when perpetrated by Strauss, it had to be equally reprehensible now. The thought was almost enough to slow Kilmer down—and its failure to do so meant that he had crossed more lines than he had intended.

Kilmer glanced over his shoulder and saw a crowd moving in his direction. Some people were chasing him, but most were merely drawn to the spectacle as it moved farther into Touchdown-1. Kilmer had somehow managed to get a lead of about a hundred yards after hitting the soldier, while everyone else was still trying to make sense of what was happening. But running wasn't his forte, and his lead was shrinking. He heard someone scream *Shoot him!* Or was it *Don't shoot him?*

He kept running, his legs burning. He was almost at the kill-zone now. The spacecraft loomed before him, its humming louder than ever. Then he saw the metal platform—almost ten feet across and two feet high—that Archidamus had mentioned. It was situated maybe ten yards from the spacecraft.

Kilmer had no idea what the scene he had created would look like to the aliens, and he didn't want to be mistaken for someone trying to attack ET-1. The moment he thought he had crossed into the kill-zone, he shouted at the top of his lungs. "Ambassador Kilmer! This is Ambassador Kilmer!" He kept running, unsure if his voice could be heard over the humming.

He looked back and saw that the two soldiers closest to him had slowed down, as if they were trained to be more cautious near the kill-zone. Seconds later, Kilmer leapt onto the platform.

Nothing happened.

"Please stop!" Kilmer shouted at the soldiers. "You don't understand. I have to do this!"

The soldiers, less than fifty yards away, were walking toward him now, their guns drawn. "Put the gun down!" one of them screamed.

Only then did Kilmer realize that his own gun was pointed at the soldiers. He quickly pointed it toward the ground.

"Come down from the platform, sir. You need to come with us. That's an order!"

Kilmer didn't move. Instead, he raised the gun again. "No! You need to stop. I can't come with you. Please. Try to understand. I'm on your side!"

The soldiers stopped moving, but their guns were still drawn.

Farther away, at the edge of the kill-zone, a large crowd had gathered—and there was chaos. Kilmer could make out Strauss, Allen, and Perez, but there was no sign of Silla. She should have been able to outrun all three of them.

One of the two soldiers moved forward and issued an ultimatum. "I'm going to count to five, sir. After that, I shoot you in the leg. But I might miss and end up killing you. So I strongly suggest you get over here… *now*."

Kilmer didn't move.

"One! Two! Three! Fo—"

A blinding light interrupted the soldier's countdown—and the sound emanating from ET-1 turned even louder. Kilmer braced himself for whatever was supposed to happen next.

But only a few seconds later, the light switched off.

That's when he saw what had happened.

~ 87 ~

Kilmer looked across the field. The two soldiers who had stormed into the kill-zone were now on the ground, bleeding. Possibly dead. He looked farther out in the direction of the perimeter. Secretary Strauss and General Allen were both shouting orders. The soldiers around them were struggling to figure out which orders to follow. Perez was yelling into a phone, almost certainly talking to Whitman on the other end, trying to explain how all hell had suddenly broken loose.

Then he saw Silla—and his heart broke into a thousand pieces. He lowered the gun, now pointing it towards the ground. She had pushed her way through the crowd of soldiers and was shouting something in his direction. She was furious—and he could make out the tears on her face. He couldn't hear any of the words she was saying, but he was terrified. A soldier tried to grab Silla, but she pushed him off and the man stumbled backwards. She was squarely in the kill-zone now and walking toward where the soldiers had fallen. He screamed for her to stop. She didn't hear him. Or she didn't care.

And then, suddenly, Lane emerged from the crowd and raced toward her. *Thank God, Lane.* He caught up to her and tackled her to the ground before she could move any further into the kill-zone. She screamed and punched at him, but he wouldn't let her go.

The sound behind Kilmer grew louder. It was almost deafening.

He knew that Silla would never forgive him. Never.

But—hopefully—she would understand.

Silla stopped trying to fight off Lane and turned toward Kilmer. He saw the look on her face. It was the look of someone who had experienced the ultimate betrayal. Someone who would *never* understand.

I love you, he whispered. He knew she might only be able to make out the movement of his lips.

We have time, Silla whispered back. *We do*, she pleaded. *Please, Kilmer!*

His eyes welled up.

He would never forgive himself either—but he wasn't about to break his promise to her.

He wasn't about to let the world come to an end when there was still a chance.

I'm sorry.

He dropped the gun.

There was a bright flash of light.

And then everything went black.

Day 57. 2:30 a.m. Apate 3 Conference Room.

"When the light came back on a minute later, Professor Kilmer, you had disappeared."

Kilmer sat in stunned silence as Art closed the binder in front of him. Kilmer looked at Lane, who offered a slight nod, confirming everything Art had just narrated. Finally, Kilmer mustered up the courage to look Silla in the eye. She looked back at him with a calm defiance that made clear she was not about to shy away from his gaze.

Art hadn't revealed to Kilmer what he and Silla had said to each other in the kill-zone. Apart from that, however, he had described the scene in detail, including the part about Lane tackling Silla to keep her from ending up like the fallen soldiers. And Art did not hide the fact that Silla had been the only one, after the soldiers were shot, who raced into the kill-zone—risking her life to try to stop him.

Kilmer looked back at Art. "What happened to the two soldiers?"

"They survived."

"And what about me, Art? What happened to me? And how did I manage to return?"

"I can tell you what we know, Professor, but it's not much. Fifteen minutes after you disappeared, we received a message from ET-1."

> *You will not see Ambassador Kilmer again, but you should know that his sacrifice was not in vain. Approximately one million humans would have died today if he did not arrive by 7 p.m. It would have been an American city.*

Kilmer dropped back in his chair as though he'd been shoved. "So, the attack they had warned about—what they threatened they would do if I didn't show up—it didn't happen?"

"No."

"And *since* then? They said war was inevitable. Have there been subsequent attacks? Are we at war?"

"Not yet."

"Okay. I can understand why they didn't retaliate on Day 24—I met their 7 p.m. deadline. But that doesn't explain why they didn't follow through on their other two statements. That I would never be allowed to return, and that Earth would suffer. Why did neither of those things happen?"

"We don't know, Professor. What we know is that two days later—on Day 26—there was another blinding light. Moments later, you were lying on the ground, in the kill-zone, completely motionless. We assumed you were dead, but when we recovered your body, we discovered that you were merely unconscious, albeit in pretty bad shape. The doctors stabilized you and scanned your body for anything discernible that the aliens might have done to it—or implanted inside you—and found nothing out of the ordinary. The only problem, which we discovered later, was that you had no memory of anything that had occurred during your time on the spacecraft."

"Did we ask ET-1 why they let me go?"

"We asked. And they refused to answer."

"Do we have any idea why they didn't attack? We thought we only had a few days, but it's been weeks."

"We don't know. There was almost no communication between ET-1 and Earth-side during the two days you were missing. The only person they could have talked to during that time was you. I don't suppose you happen to remember what was discussed?"

"I don't. But you seem to think I somehow convinced them not to attack us."

"That's our hypothesis."

"But I thought you brought me here today because there's still a threat of an attack—or an invasion."

"That's right, Professor Kilmer. There is."

Silla tried to clarify things. "We're hoping that what you learned about them—or whatever you said to them to dissuade them from attacking—might help us figure out what to do next. A war is still coming, Professor, and you might have the key to avoiding it. We need to figure out what happened in there."

Kilmer shook his head. "Except I don't remember a thing. And ET-1 won't even explain why they busted me up and tossed me out. Unless *they* tell us something, I'm afraid we don't have a clue about what took place in there."

Silla looked at Art, and he responded with a nod. She then turned back to Kilmer.

"Professor Kilmer. When you were a kid, you had a habit of doing something peculiar after you took a difficult exam. And, at least on one occasion, it got you in serious trouble. Is that right?"

Kilmer stared at her in disbelief. "How in the world could you possibly know that?"

"Because you told me that story on the very first night we met. But that's not important. What matters, Professor, is that old habits seem to die hard with you."

"Are you saying…"

"Yes, I am. So, when you say 'We don't have a clue about what took place' while you were inside ET-1… well, that's not *entirely* true. We do have one clue. And we're hoping it might be enough for you to… you know. Do your thing."

"What's my thing?" Kilmer asked.

Silla laughed. "Well, I guess we're off to a bad start. Your *thing*, Kilmer, is that you figure stuff out—especially when things look bleak."

He smiled. "Point taken, Agent Silla—although I don't think I'm entirely hopeless. For example, I did just figure out that you used to call me 'Kilmer.' Is that right?"

Silla realized that, for the first time since meeting Kilmer that day, she hadn't referred to him as *Professor*. "That's right," she said.

"And I probably called you something other than 'Agent Silla.' What was it—if you don't mind me asking?"

"I don't mind. And no—you didn't call me Agent Silla." She dropped her gaze. "Almost everyone calls me Ren."

Kilmer smiled. "Then I'm sure I didn't call you that." He paused. "Was that... some sort of test?"

Silla wasn't sure what it had been—or why she had tried to misdirect him. She had no answer.

"You don't have to tell me," Kilmer said, apologetically. "And I'm sorry for asking. It's none of my business."

"It's okay. I just meant that I don't mind if you call me Ren or Renata," she offered. "We might end up working together again, so you don't have to keep calling me Agent Silla—unless that's your preference."

Kilmer thought about it. "Does anyone call you Silla?"

Silla was sure her heart had stopped beating for a moment. She stared at Kilmer, trying to figure out if he had just remembered something.

No—it wasn't a memory. He was just *remarkably* consistent. He was still the same guy. He was *Kilmer*.

"You would be in perfect company if you chose to call me Silla. I won't mind it at all."

He smiled. "Now that we have that settled, might I see the clue, Silla?"

Art handed her an envelope. She walked over to Kilmer and sat down next to him. They were sitting shoulder to shoulder when Silla opened the envelope and emptied its contents onto the table.

She turned toward him. "This is it, Kilmer. This is everything. What do you think?"

Kilmer picked up the photographs and thumbed through them.

What the hell?

Part V

the negotiator

~ 89 ~

Day 24. 7:00 p.m. Inside ET-1.

It had felt like a jolt of electricity coming up from the platform beneath him. That was all Kilmer could remember. He had passed out immediately. The next thing he knew, he was seated in what felt like it had the shape of a reclining chair—but not quite. He had no idea what it looked like because it was pitch black. He also had no idea how long he had been unconscious. He would later find out that it was for just under thirty minutes.

He assumed he was in the spacecraft. And the fact that he was alive seemed obvious. Beyond that, he had no information about the situation. He felt around him, but he didn't dare try to stand up. His feet were dangling, and there was no way of knowing what he might land on, or fall into, if he left his seat. Behind him, the chair extended far above his head, higher than he could reach. It had no armrests. At approximately head height, on either side of him, were straps of some kind. Were they for securing his head? To keep him buckled during flight? Or to strap him down for other reasons?

Stop. Get a hold of yourself.

There was no way to be sure this was even a chair, and even less reason to think it was designed with a human body in mind. The aliens might be much larger, and this could be a seatbelt designed to secure their midsection. Or it could be something entirely different.

Be mindful of your assumptions, Kilmer.

He listened for noise. He could hear what sounded like the hum of an engine, but it was barely audible. He waited for his eyes to adjust to the darkness, but there was no improved visibility even a minute later. Now what? He was about to call out and announce that he was awake, but then decided against it. He wasn't ready to find out who—or what—would answer his call. And even if there were no monsters waiting to leap out at him, he needed to get his anxiety under control before communicating with anyone.

He slowed his breathing. Then he took a few minutes to come to terms with his new reality. It was a terrible situation. And scary. But still, it might be an opportunity to do some good. And if he could make even a bit of difference, it might be more than if he had lived a full life under normal circumstances.

He wondered how the aliens would respond to his call. Did they already know he was awake? Would they turn on a light? Would someone walk or crawl or fly toward him? Would he be grabbed? Would they flash a message on a screen? Would there be no response at all? For how long?

Only one way to find out.

He braced himself. And then, with his voice betraying none of the anxiety that he still felt, he made his introduction—becoming the first human in history to speak to aliens.

"My name is Kilmer. And I have come here willingly. I'm ready for what happens next."

~ 90 ~

The light did not turn on. No one approached Kilmer. Nothing grabbed him. No screen or message flashed before his eyes. The response he received was not among the ones he had expected.

It was a voice that answered him.

"Welcome, Ambassador Kilmer. I greet you on behalf of my race. We don't have names the way you do, but you know me as Archidamus."

The voice had a certain synthetic quality to it, but it did not sound robotic. It came awfully close to sounding perfectly human.

"I am no ambassador, Archidamus. And, unfortunately, I am unable to greet you on behalf of my race. I'm sure you can understand why that is, given the circumstances."

"I can understand. And I'm sorry. But there was no alternative but to ask that you come immediately."

"There is always an alternative, Archidamus. I would like to know what it was—and why you chose against it."

"You're right. And I will explain that—and much more—very soon."

"And once you've done that? What happens next?"

"Then I will have to ask you a question of my own."

"And if I answer it to your satisfaction? Will you let me go and leave Earth alone? This can end peacefully?"

"I do not want to give you false hope. You should proceed with the understanding that there is nothing you can do to change our plans. But you are invited to try. That is why you are here."

"And why are *you* here, Archidamus? Are you the leader of your people? A diplomat? A soldier?"

"I'm none of those. I was chosen because you were chosen."

"Why? Who are you?"

"I'm like you, Kilmer. I'm a historian."

~ 91 ~

For the next twenty minutes, Archidamus answered a flurry of questions.

Yes, they were still on Earth. No, Kilmer would not fall into an abyss or hurt himself if he got off his chair. Yes, it was a chair of sorts. No, he was not in a prison cell. Yes, it was more like a bedroom or an office. No, they had no such things as beds. Yes, he would be allowed to sleep when he needed to. No, ET-1 would not yet turn on a light for him. Yes, there were lots of aliens on the spacecraft.

Yes, the bright light they had used outside was designed to hide what and how ET-1 did things on Earth. Yes, ET-1 had attacked the soldiers who tried to stop Kilmer from entering ET-1. Yes, it was possible they had died. Yes, they would have attacked Silla as well if she had gotten too close to the platform. Yes, ET-1 was heavily armed. Yes, the reserve spacecraft could do tremendous damage to Earth. Yes, the aliens would have attacked Earth if he did not enter ET-1 by 7 p.m. Yes, many people would have died in the first attack alone. No, ET-1 had not been bluffing or lying about anything it said. Yes, Earth-side had tried to contact ET-1 after Kilmer entered the spacecraft. No, ET-1 had not answered any of Earth-side's substantive questions. No, Kilmer would not be allowed to send a message to anyone on Earth—not even to say that he was okay.

"Why not?"

"Because it is a rule. And as you will come to understand, there are reasons we cannot break such rules. As to why such a rule might exist—it is possible that you have a code with which to communicate the things you have seen, experienced, or learned on ET-1."

Kilmer had not thought of doing that—none of them had. It was the kind of plan someone should have proposed. What else had they failed to consider? What other opportunities had they missed?

Shake it off, Kilmer.

His questions to Archidamus continued.

Yes, ET-1 planned to stay on Earth for at least another day or two. No, they would not take him to their home planet afterwards. Yes, there was a home planet. Yes, it was in the same galaxy as Earth. No, it would be better for Kilmer if they took him elsewhere—to a colossal space station. Yes, it would be very far away. Yes, they would be able to keep him alive for years. Yes, he would be living alongside the aliens—but not among many. No, he would not be in prison.

Yes, he would be allowed to meet the aliens on board ET-1—but not yet. Yes, it was because it could scare or distract him. They needed Kilmer to focus on the conversation that Archidamus was going to have with him. There would be plenty of time—years, in fact—for Kilmer to get to know the aliens. No, not all aliens were friendly. Yes, he would be safe. No, the aliens did not plan to hurt him.

And yes, human beings on Earth were still doomed.

"I know you have many more questions, Kilmer. I would as well if I were you. But I suggest we set them aside for a while. There will be plenty of time later. We have to get started on the reason you are here."

"You have some things you want to explain to me."

"That is correct."

"Are you going to explain why you think it's okay to kill millions or billions of human beings? Because if so, I think you overestimate my capacity to empathize. I can't imagine anything that would justify it."

"I do not intend to justify it, Kilmer. I only intend to explain it. There may be no justice in what happens. But we want you to understand why."

"What's the point? Whether I understand or not, I can't do anything about it. If you're just trying to clear your conscience, then there are another seven billion people to whom you should explain things. Maybe one of them will tell you it's okay."

"We did not pick you because we thought you would tell us it is okay for us to attack your planet."

"Then why?"

"We were looking for someone who might convince us there was a way to avoid it. We have tried hard on our own to do that—and we have failed. We believe it is fair for a human to have the opportunity as well."

Kilmer considered the statement. ET-1 had already said he was unlikely to change the outcome. Was this just a formality? Had he entered a kangaroo court—a show trial with the verdict predetermined? If so, who was the jury? And what choice did he have but to go along with it—even if it was a charade?

But if there *was* a chance to convince them—no matter how small—then he had to get this right. He couldn't afford to miss a thing. Not one hint. Not one opportunity. Not one piece of the puzzle.

"You say that you've tried, Archidamus. How long could you have possibly tried? You've only been here a week. You've only just started to learn about us."

"You are working from a flawed assumption, Kilmer. Time works a bit differently in our world. The physics are the same—we cannot shrink or stretch or reverse time—but the *pace* at which things happen on our planet would be unfathomable to you. Think about how much faster humans can calculate, transmit data, process information, or acquire knowledge today, as compared to one hundred years ago. Now imagine the technology you will have one hundred years from now. You might accomplish in a few days what currently takes a year. You might find ways to augment your brain's storage and processing capacity, changing the very nature of learning. Can you imagine how fast things will move a thousand years from now? Ten thousand years from now? You cannot. But that is what you would need to do to appreciate how much work has already been done by us. You were probably impressed by how quickly I learned to speak in English. But this is not a difficult task—many others on my planet have already done so as well in the last week. And, as for human history—I probably know more of it than you do."

"Then why do you need—" Kilmer stopped himself. He already knew why. "You still can't think like a human."

"There is always a difference between natives and foreigners, no matter how much a foreigner has studied. Some elements of understanding lie in the spaces between what is said or written or debated. Some knowledge is implicit. Some of what is known remains out of the grasp of conscious awareness."

"So, I'm the native you've picked to fill that gap. Is it because our people sent you my book? I should tell you that it wasn't meant to be a signal of any kind. It was added to the list of things we sent only as an afterthought. No one on Earth would have picked me to represent humanity."

"We debated that—whether it was a signal or not. I was sure it was not. Historians are very highly respected on my planet, but I know how they are regarded on yours. Humans would not have sent us a historian."

"Then why still insist on me? Why not let humans decide who will represent the planet?"

"Because only we know the task that awaits Earth's ambassador. Humans are not sufficiently informed to make the right decision—whereas we have considered it carefully. You will be surprised to learn that your book, *Heirs of Herodotus by Earth Historian D. Kilmer*, has already been widely read on my planet. Its ideas have garnered much attention. A few dozen excerpts of the book, especially, are a source of tremendous discussion and deliberation among our policymakers and scholars. Some of your ideas will, I predict, influence political and military debates on my planet for years to come."

Kilmer was stunned.

"As I said, Kilmer, I probably know more about Earth's history than you do. And yet, I was surprised by some of the lessons and insights you gleaned from your study of human history. Some of your analyses I might disagree with—as is the right of any fellow historian—but much of it is quite profound. You see and say things others do not, Kilmer. And that is the point. That one quality is the only chance your planet has. Because unless you see something that I and others have missed, there is no hope. The problem is that we are very capable and very thorough. We do not think we missed anything that would change our conclusions. We are confident Earth's fate is sealed."

"What exactly do I have to convince you of? That you can get what you want from human beings without destroying us? That we deserve to be treated better? Or do I have to clear up some misunderstanding about our behavior over the last few weeks? What is it exactly?"

"I'm not the one you have to convince, Kilmer. There are others who are listening to our conversation. They are the ones who judge. They are your audience. As for what you would need to convince them of—that will become clear once I explain why we came here. It is time that I do that. Are you ready?"

Kilmer closed his eyes and took a deep breath. And then another.

Every problem wants to be solved, son. Just remember that.

"Yes. I'm ready."

~ 92 ~

Archidamus began his narration.

"Far from here, there is a planet whose name translates as *Origin*. Even 20,000 Earth-years ago, its inhabitants—we call them *Originals*—were more socially, politically, and technologically advanced than the humans of today. They had systems of government that were more efficient and effective than those on Earth. They had known war in the past, but conflict among the tribes of Origin was now exceedingly rare. A return to the bygone era of warfare was almost unthinkable. Between 18,000 and 12,000 years ago, the Originals colonized space, creating large and thriving communities on six different planets. They were comfortable and at peace.

There is only one domain in which humans are clearly more advanced than Originals. The breadth, complexity, and quality of human *art*—in all its varied forms—goes far beyond what the Originals ever created. The Originals developed and appreciated art, but they focused more on the sciences and engineering. No one in the galaxy could have matched the Originals on any aspect of technological achievement.

Or so they thought.

War came 9,000 Earth-years ago. For the first and only time in Origin's long history, it was not a conflict between the tribes of Origin. It was a fight against invaders from a distant planet. Originals gave their enemies the name by which they are still remembered: *Wanderers*. The inhabitants of Origin had long known that there was life—even intelligent life—elsewhere in the galaxy. But they had never imagined military capabilities of the kind possessed by the Wanderers. These would be decisive in what came to be known as the *Forever War*.

The first phase of the Forever War lasted almost 200 Earth-years—and it ended with the conquest of Origin.

The second phase of the war started soon after and lasted 650 Earth-years. The Originals fought in small groups and makeshift armies, trying desperately to rid their planet of the occupiers. The Wanderers did eventually reduce their presence on Origin, but not because of the resistance. Civil war had broken out on the Wanderers' home planet, and it demanded most of their attention. Unfortunately, by the time this diversion occurred, the Wanderers had already robbed Origin of its vast resources and killed or enslaved much of its population.

The third phase of the war started as soon as enemy troop levels diminished. It lasted 300 Earth-years. This time, the resistance—larger and more organized than in the past—routed the occupiers. The Originals were merciless when it came to exacting vengeance on the Wanderers who were left behind. It was a massacre.

The Forever War lasted 1,150 Earth-years in total—and it devastated the planet. The population shrank by ninety percent over this period, and the environmental harm rendered Origin incapable of supporting a renewal of the race. Five of the six planets where Origin had created settlements were also destroyed. After years of heated debate, the Originals decided to abandon their home planet. The survivors resettled on the one planet that had escaped ruin. They renamed it *Citadel*.

From that point on, only those who were born before Origin was abandoned were referred to as Originals—and they were looked upon with reverence. Their years of persecution, and their ultimate victory over the Wanderers, was as much studied by scholars as mythologized by the masses. The inhabitants of Citadel vowed never to forget the Five Lessons of the Forever War.

Lesson 1. You can abolish war, but you will never end it.

Lesson 2. There will always be someone stronger than you.

Lesson 3. Wars are not won by the most powerful; they are won by the most persistent.

Lesson 4. You cannot choose your enemy, but you can choose the battlefield.

Lesson 5. The stronger you are, the easier it is to live in peace.

Citadel was founded on these principles. They were the source code, you might say, for Citadel's government, its society, its military philosophy, its education system, and its culture. Scholars were allowed to debate these lessons, but few ever did. There was never anything akin to religion on Citadel, but if there had been, these five lessons would have almost certainly been included in its primary text and attributed to some god.

But Citadel did not become a warrior culture like your Sparta in ancient Greece. It continued to grow and innovate and flourish on many dimensions. And it never cultivated any desire to expand its dominion by ruling over others. However, there was to be no compromise when it came to matters of self-preservation and survival. There was to be no compromise when it came to the prioritization of military strength over all else. None. Ever.

The inhabitants of Citadel live, on average, for almost 200 Earth-years. It took four lifespans—800 Earth-years—for Citadel to recreate everything it had lost in the Forever War: technologically, militarily, and psychologically. After another two lifespans, Citadel was not only stronger than Origin had ever been, but stronger than the Wanderers could have anticipated.

On Citadel, there is something known as a *Consent Period*. It occurs once in almost 100 Earth-years. Only during this period can major decisions, such as war declarations, be authorized. When a proposal to declare war on the Wanderers was introduced during the subsequent Consent Period, the debate was the shortest in Citadel history. Citadel decided—without a single objection—to bring war to the Wanderers. This was 6,500 years ago.

The *War of Redemption* lasted less than a hundred Earth-years. The Wanderers were annihilated. They were erased from the universe. Nothing of them survives except for what the citizens of Citadel remember of it.

Kilmer, I am a proud inhabitant of Citadel. It is where I was born. My ancestors fought in the War of Redemption. And I believe the Wanderers did nothing to deserve mercy. But even I will say this: *To be remembered only by your enemies—to have no one left to tell your side of the story—is the worst imaginable fate for any people.*

But this was not the prevailing sentiment at the time. Not at all. It would be another 2,000 Earth-years before the inhabitants of Citadel even started to wonder whether they had been too harsh in exacting their revenge.

Instead, between 6,500 and 4,500 Earth-years ago, Citadel engaged in three other major wars—each of them against a different planet. Together, these became known as the *Wars of Survival.*

The First War of Survival was the result of rising tensions, over a century, between Citadel and a rival planet. It is hard to know who attacked first. In the next two wars, however, Citadel was clearly the aggressor. We attacked first, and the other side did not even see it coming. In all three Wars of Survival, Citadel was victorious. In all three, the enemy was annihilated. In all three, the outcome was never in doubt. Citadel had eliminated another three intelligent species from the universe."

Archidamus paused.

"So tell me, Kilmer, do you think Citadel had now become what the Wanderers had once been? Had Citadel become the scourge of the galaxy?"

Kilmer had been listening intently, trying to ensure no detail was missed. But he hadn't expected to be quizzed along the way.

"I think you'll tell me the answer is *no*—that Citadel was not so bad. But I'm not sure you can convince me."

"You're right, Kilmer. The answer is *no*—and for one simple reason. *Never* did Citadel do to its enemies what the Wanderers did to Origin. There was no plundering. No occupation. No torture. No slavery. No exploitation."

"There was only genocide. How generous."

"That there was utter devastation is undeniable. And you are right—it is terrible what Citadel did in these wars. But unlike the wars waged by the Wanderers, these were considered wars of necessity by Citadel. Citadel neither sought nor gained anything of material value from going to war. That is the difference."

"That is *a* difference. But it doesn't change the fact that Citadel is now the villain in this story."

"Must every story have heroes and villains, Kilmer?"

"No. It's possible that this story only has villains. But I'm not sure why you want to debate this with me. I don't even know what led to these wars. All I know is what you have told me about Citadel's actions. You're free to ignore my opinion on the matter, but you seem to be asking for it. So let me summarize it this way: It is sometimes possible to justify war, Archidamus. But it is never possible to justify genocide."

"Then we agree, Kilmer. It is *never* possible to justify genocide. But—as you say—it *is* sometimes possible to justify war."

Archidamus had rearranged Kilmer's words—preserving their literal meaning but upending the sentiment. Kilmer didn't bother to argue. He could debate things later, after he understood why any of this mattered.

Archidamus continued.

"So, it begs the question, what led to the Wars of Survival? Why did Citadel decide to wipe out three alien races? As you say in your book, there are only three *fundamental* causes of war. The inhabitants of Citadel were not greedy. They had no grievances against these other species. All that remains is—"

"Fear."

"That's right, Kilmer. Fear. Of the kind that only those who have truly suffered can feel. Of the kind that seeps deep into the culture and into consciousness. The inhabitants of Citadel *did* behave like villains in this story, but they were simply trying to ensure their own survival. They were merely picking the time and place of battle in what they feared would one day become another Forever War. In all three of these wars, Citadel faced an adversary that they knew could be defeated *today*, but who might become unbeatable *tomorrow*.

Did the inhabitants of Citadel have a right to go to war? They believed they did. Did they have the right to wipe out an entire race? *No.* You and I agree on that. And we are not the only ones who find it abhorrent what they did. They themselves were troubled by it—eventually.

The Third War of Survival was brief—shockingly so. It lasted less than one Earth-year, but the outcome was still the annihilation of a race. The fact that Citadel had wiped out all intelligent life on a planet in such little time sent shock waves through Citadel society. It was hard to reconcile such a swift and total victory with the idea that there had ever been something to fear.

For the first time in Citadel history, there was an opportunity for serious reflection—and the possibility of change. A *Reexamination Period* was invoked—a necessary step before any sweeping policy change can be adopted. Debates raged, studies were commissioned, and every manner of expert was called upon to weigh in on Citadel's war policy. The review lasted 25 Earth-years. Finally, a historic change to Citadel military policy was ratified during the following Consent Period. It was known as the *Necessary War Doctrine*.

The Necessary War Doctrine had two key provisions. The first mandated that Citadel devise a new mechanism by which to address its security threats— *without* having to resort to acts of genocide. The time allotted for this was two Citadel lifespans—almost 400 Earth-years. The second provision in the doctrine made it unlawful for Citadel to commit *any* acts of genocide after the new mechanism was instituted.

Citadel had never waged war for material gain. It had never sought to rule over others. And now, by making the annihilation of a species illegal, Citadel was giving up the option of waging total war. This might not seem like a heroic leap forward to *you*, Kilmer, but on Citadel, this law challenged thousands of years of political precedent, cultural acceptance, and—in the eyes of many—even the prerogative of self-preservation itself. It was the first time in 3,500 Earth-years that the Five Lessons of the Forever War had been contested or reimagined. Some even said they were tossed away entirely in order to make room for the Necessary War Doctrine. Most citizens supported the change, but plenty of vocal detractors remained—and still remain.

As soon as the doctrine became law, the scientific, military, and policy minds of Citadel went to work. Countless ideas were surfaced, but none seemed capable of accomplishing the two-pronged objective: *to eliminate the risk of a future war with an enemy, but without eliminating the enemy.* It was like Earth's 'moonshot' in the 1960s, when your President Kennedy declared that Americans would, within a decade, land a man on the Moon and bring him back safely to Earth. It was inspiring—and it focused attention and resources—but the pronouncement was made without much thought as to how the goal would be achieved.

But, like the Americans, Citadel accomplished its goal. 4,000 Earth-years ago a new approach to war was devised and adopted, and in the years that followed, the relevant technologies were perfected. Citadel now had a viable alternative to genocide. We would no longer need to resort to the kinds of behaviors we had engaged in during the Wars of Survival.

In the 4,000 years since the new approach was adopted, Citadel has explored many worlds. On six occasions, these explorations have led to war. Each time, Citadel has been the aggressor. Each time, Citadel has achieved its goal of safeguarding its security. Not once has it required the elimination of an entire race.

Many on Citadel now look back at the Wars of Survival with some combination of shame and horror. There are others, of course, who remain proud of the fact that Citadel did whatever was necessary during those dark and uncertain times—and that it managed to avoid a second Forever War.

But most of Citadel's inhabitants have stopped thinking about war altogether—how it was waged in the past or how it is waged today. As a fellow citizen—and as a historian—it pains me to acknowledge this. But it is not hard to explain why most of our citizens no longer struggle with questions of morality or strategy when it comes to war. They have not changed. Citadel has changed.

In its early years, Citadel was under constant threat, but its inhabitants had a clear conscience, because they had been the victims. After Citadel committed itself to the Five Lessons, our citizens gained strength, but the atrocities they committed in the name of security forced them to give up the moral high ground. The Necessary War Doctrine solved both problems. It heralded a third stage in Citadel's evolution—one in which its citizens could live *with* security and *without* guilt.

This is what makes your task so difficult, Kilmer. In the absence of both fear and guilt, there is no reason for a society to question its actions. It is not easy to change minds when people see nothing wrong with the status quo."

Archidamus paused, briefly.

"Do you understand, Kilmer? Do you see where I am taking you?"

Kilmer said nothing. His mind was working at a feverish pace, trying to organize everything Archidamus had just told him. *Wait. Give me a moment.*

He kept processing. Putting together what made sense. Keeping track of what didn't add up. Identifying questions that he wanted to ask.

And there was something else about what Archidamus had said…

In the absence of both fear and guilt, there is no reason for a society to question its actions.

This seemed important. But how? Kilmer wished he could grab a pen and paper to organize his thoughts. Or walk around the room. Or take a sip of coffee. Or discuss things with Silla or Whitman—or even Strauss. But he was too much in the dark—and too much alone.

Get used to it.

Finally, he spoke.

"I have some questions, Archidamus. May I ask them?"

"Yes. You may ask them."

"If Citadel is no longer wanting to wipe us out—if you aren't even *allowed* to annihilate our species—then why are we in danger? If you aren't interested in stealing our resources, occupying our planet, or enslaving our people, then why will human beings have to suffer? Why do you say that the human race is doomed?"

"The human race is *not* doomed, Kilmer. That is true. It will survive."

"Then why the threats? What problem am I even trying to solve?"

"Kilmer—"

Archidamus paused, but not as though he was searching for an answer. It was the kind of pause doctors might stumble into just as they are about to break bad news to a patient.

"It is not about the human race, Kilmer. It is about human *civilization*. That is what we plan to eliminate from the universe. Human civilization cannot be allowed to continue. It is much too dangerous."

Heirs of Herodotus by D. Kilmer.
Excerpt from Chapter 6.

Some scholars have argued that the worst is over—that humanity is moving, inexorably, toward a more peaceful future. Inter-state wars have become rare, war fatalities have steadily decreased since the end of WWII, and there has been no catastrophic global conflict for generations. Despite these recent trends, the argument is dangerously flawed. It ignores too much data. It conceptualizes war too narrowly. It rests on unsophisticated analyses. And it fails to consider history in its proper—and broader—context.

History has witnessed such eras before—including the century of relative peace for Europe (1815-1914) that followed the Napoleonic Wars. Ninety years into that period, **many were convinced that major wars were obsolete. War was passé—a curious habit of earlier generations, when people were not as sophisticated, rational, or enlightened as <u>we</u>.** When this belief was proven tragically wrong, it was at the hands of a conflict so ruthless, it looked as though the devil himself had sent War back with a mandate to make up for lost time. In just four years, WWI killed 20 million people—four times the number who had died during all twelve years of the Napoleonic Wars a century earlier. Then, less than thirty years later, WWII killed 80 million, making it the deadliest war in history. **War had not disappeared—it had merely bided its time. It had evolved. It had come back stronger.**

It was with an appreciation for this history—and with a deep sense of humility due to our newfound ability to annihilate ourselves—that JFK addressed the UN General Assembly in 1961 and warned: **"Mankind must put an end to war—or war will put an end to mankind."**

Kilmer had come hoping to find Churchill's Key—and Archidamus had delivered it to him.

All social entities—just like individuals—will fight for survival. But the survival instinct does not *define* the community any more than it defines the individual. Security is one of many goals—one of multiple factors to consider in any decision. Security can even be compromised, at times, depending on how much there is to gain by doing so.

Citadel was different. The desire to survive was not merely a functional trait, it was the defining characteristic of Citadel's social, political, cultural, and military fabric. Self-preservation was not *a* consideration—it was *the* consideration. No amount of reward could justify accepting even a smidgen of existential risk.

Kilmer's own words came rushing back to mind.

The ones who fear pain most of all are the ones who have never felt it before. Or those who have felt it so acutely that they will never allow themselves to be vulnerable again.

Kilmer had been sure that a solution to the crisis, if one existed at all, depended on the answer to one question: *What drives them?* That question had now been answered. The desperate need to ensure survival was not merely a constraint that Citadel's leaders had to consider when crafting policy or driving their agendas. It was the driving force itself.

The need for security was what had launched Citadel into the far reaches of the galaxy. It is what still propelled them toward continued exploration. And it was what would push Citadel's inhabitants—who wanted nothing more than to avoid another Forever War—into waging wars forever.

But Kilmer didn't have time to reflect on the irony of it all. His problem was of a decidedly less philosophical nature. Citadel's leaders believed that human civilization posed a risk—and risks were not to be tolerated.

He needed more information. How humans could possibly pose a risk, especially an imminent one, was hard to imagine. And what Citadel was planning—*how* it would eliminate human civilization—was still unknown.

"I have a hard time understanding why humans pose a threat to your people," he began. "You've studied our technological and military capabilities. We are no match for Citadel—neither now nor in any foreseeable future."

"A future in which Earth destroys Citadel is not foreseeable by you, Kilmer. But we can see it clearly. We have much greater experience in these matters."

"I understand that your people have suffered greatly, and that this suffering was at the hands of an alien race. But that doesn't mean every alien race is willing or able to do such a thing."

"We know what humans are *willing* to do, Kilmer. As do you. I could quote your own writings to make the point. Human beings do not have a good track record of meeting new civilizations or empires and treating them well. That history, Kilmer, is why your civilization cannot be spared. There is no reason to think that humans will do anything other than intimidate, rob, manipulate, subjugate, or destroy the aliens they meet—especially when the aliens possess something of value or when they look different or scary. As for Citadel, humans would judge us to be guilty of all these crimes. You would never spare us. You would justify our destruction with ease."

Kilmer pushed back. "Human society has evolved, Archidamus. You know that. And we continue to move in the right direction. We struggle, yes, but we are working toward putting an end to war. Is that what I must convince you of? That you won't have to fear the human beings of some distant future?"

"Yes. And you can try, Kilmer, but you will not succeed. Even if you were to give examples of human generosity or provide data to suggest humanity might be inching toward peaceful coexistence, the overwhelming evidence points in the opposite direction. And we are not willing to accept even the slightest risk. As I told you, there can be no compromise when it comes to our security.

"I can anticipate most of the arguments you will make. Unfortunately, they come nowhere close to addressing this problem. They don't eliminate the risk we face.

"You will point to parts of the globe where war is now rare. But so what if the nations of Europe have avoided total war for a few generations? What your people call the *long peace* is only a sliver of time in a much longer history of horrific continental wars. So what if Earth's democracies almost never go to war with one another? They are still brutal when dealing with governments and societies that are differently structured. So what if humans have attempted, time and again, to create institutions that are designed to prevent war? You still do nothing to resolve your underlying conflicts. So what if structural conditions—such as a balance of power, or mutually assured destruction—make it less likely that Earth's great powers will declare war on one another? There is no reason to believe that, when humans arrive at Citadel's doorsteps, it will be under such conditions.

"I could go on and on. Do you see the problem, Kilmer? By law, we must give you a chance to make the case for humanity, but there is a *so what* to every argument. It does not matter if you find some way to suggest we *might* be wrong in our analysis of what human beings will do in the future. You would have to prove there is *no chance* that we are right. You cannot simply poke little holes in the hull of this ship—you either sink the ship entirely, or it shows up on Earth's shores. And when it does, there will be nothing left to discuss."

Kilmer did not offer a rebuttal. Earth's track record was not easy to defend. And Archidamus was right—this was not the kind of debate in which the side that accumulated more points would be declared the victor. If the other side scored even a single point, Kilmer was defeated. Citadel would not take even the slightest chance. The fact that Earth *might* attack *someday* was enough. How could he possibly prove that this would never happen?

He closed his eyes and took a deep breath. He was using the wrong metaphor—and it could lead him astray.

This isn't a debate. It's a street fight—against someone bigger and stronger. You won't win a war of attrition. You can't let it go to the ground. You either strike a knockout blow or they pummel you to death on the pavement.

He decided to change his line of attack.

"I am curious why it even matters what our proclivities are. Even if I can't convince you that we will be peaceful in the future, why would you attack us *today*? What's the rush? We won't even be able to *find* you, much less defeat you in battle, for hundreds or thousands of years. Based on what you've described, Earth is ten thousand years behind Citadel in technological development. So why the urgency? Why not reach some type of near-term accommodation with us—and if you don't like how things are going, you can come back in a century or two and do what you must? Why not wait to attack?"

"That is a good question, Kilmer. Unfortunately, there is a good answer to it. First, although Citadel is far more advanced, the rate at which humans are progressing is staggering. We have never seen anything like what humans have experienced in the last 200 Earth-years alone. There could be many reasons for this—you are different from us in many ways. But if I were to guess, it comes down to one key difference. *Human imagination.*

"As I said earlier, human art is far more advanced, on every dimension, than what Citadel has ever known or encountered. I believe these two things—human creativity in the arts, and human innovation in technology— are intimately related. Every advancement in technology, including military technology, remains, foremost, a feat of imagination. This is where humans excel. It is an admirable quality, but it is also something Citadel must fear.

"What took us thousands of years to do might take humans only a few hundred years. There is already very little that human scientists believe is *theoretically* impossible. Engineering problems persist, but you are solving them at a startling rate. Might you be able to find us and wage war against us within the next 200 years? It is unlikely, but not impossible to imagine. Might you find a way to defend against our attacks in as little 50 Earth-years? That is also conceivable—and we cannot risk it."

An answer to the question that had bothered Kilmer from the very start was finally materializing.

"The reason you chose to visit Earth at this particular time in our history—

is it because of the progress we've made in recent years? You only came once we started to look like a threat?"

"We not only had no reason to come sooner, but also no awareness that you existed. There are too many planets in the universe, and many of them have intelligent life. But we do not go looking for life to destroy, Kilmer. We go looking for technology against which we must protect ourselves. Civilizations that reach a certain level of advancement eventually start to leak their capabilities. They begin to explore. They launch things into space. They emit signals—intentionally and unintentionally. Those are the things we look for. When we detected those elements around your planet, we came. And what we found was more impressive—and more dangerous—than we could have predicted. In less than 70 Earth-years, your species had gone from inventing their first crude aircraft—which flew only ten feet off the ground for a few seconds—to putting a human being on the Moon."

"And that is what sealed our fate?" Kilmer asked. "If it weren't for our technology, we would be safe?"

"It is not technology alone. It is not human proclivities alone. It is the combination. You might find it hard to imagine, but there are planets on which intelligent beings coexist peacefully—where there is no such thing as war, as you and I conceive of it. And there are planets on which wars occur, but where they are a rare exception. That is not the story of Earth, unfortunately. At least, it has not been Earth's story for the last 12,000 years."

12,000 years.

Kilmer made the connection. "That is what you meant, Archidamus, when you said to me that your people are 'not the ones who will have shot the first arrows.' You weren't referring to anything that we did in the last few weeks. You were referring to actual arrows."

"Yes. Almost 12,000 Earth-years ago is when humans made the first great strides in the journey that has led them to this day. The advent of agriculture allowed them to build sedentary communities. And the invention of the bow and arrow made it possible to kill at scale. It was the marriage of these two that allowed human beings to go from squabbling with other nomadic tribes to waging war against established communities.

"Your ability to wage war grew steadily for thousands of years, and then exponentially in the last two centuries. There are only two constraints, Kilmer, on the kinds of weapons that a civilization can create. The laws of physics and the limits of imagination. The laws of physics will place some bounds on your capacity to create war. But human imagination has no limits. It is like nothing we have seen before."

Kilmer interjected. "So, the reason you've been reluctant to show us *your* capabilities is…"

"Yes, Kilmer. This is why we have let humans take the initiative in all of our interactions. We are not allowed to show our capabilities to advanced civilizations. We do not want to give human beings any more ideas than they already have about what might be possible. This is why, for example, we waited for humans to devise a communication system rather than offer one of our own.

"What humans came up with, not surprisingly, was ingenious. The way your people developed a system for us to communicate was impressive in its efficiency and effectiveness. Ironically, Kilmer, even *that* human achievement only confirmed for us that we were correct to worry about the pace of human progress. How hard would it really be for human beings—once they knew our capabilities—to find ways to defend against them? How long would it really take for human beings to reproduce our technologies, or even improve upon them, once they caught a glimpse of what was possible? Can you see how this might exacerbate the threat that we—"

"We were just trying to *talk* to you!" Kilmer snapped, his anger getting the better of him and his voice suddenly rising. "We were just trying to welcome you to our planet! And even *that* you will hold against us? First it was our history. Then our creativity and our art. Then our imagination. Then the speed with which we made technological progress. Then the speed with which we *should* have created peace on Earth. *All of these* you deem to be punishable offenses. And now—simply finding a way to invite you into our home and to say hello—that *too* is a crime?" He was no longer shouting, but his voice conveyed both his rage and contempt. "How dare you say you've tried, Archidamus? How dare you tell me that your people have tried hard to avoid war with us? You've done nothing of the sort. You are simply looking for reasons to attack. You are looking for things to be afraid of. You are looking for anything that will help you justify the horrors you plan to unleash on yet another innocent civilization. Have you no *shame?* Do your people have no *conscience?"*

Kilmer waited for an answer, but none came.

"And what role do you expect me to play in this? You didn't bring me here to convince your leaders that Citadel has made a mistake. All this time it's been *you* trying to convince *me* that Citadel is justified in what it plans to do. Why? Do you think that if you can convince a student of human history that the people of Earth deserve such a fate, it will give you the license to pull the trigger? You won't get that from me, Archidamus. I reject the notion that Citadel has the moral authority to decide our fate. I will not concede that. *Ever."*

The outburst hadn't assuaged his anger. If anything, it had added a sense of hopelessness to the mix.

This is impossible. They don't want to even consider anything that might change their minds.

Finally, Archidamus spoke.

"I understand your frustration, Kilmer. It is a difficult situation. But I have not misrepresented your role here. You are here to help your people, precisely as I described. We are required by our laws to give an ambassador of the targeted planet an opportunity to make the case for their species. We are required to do this even in cases where there is almost no doubt regarding what the outcome will be. Nonetheless, your job is to see things we might have missed, and which might make us reconsider. You have not been able to do that yet—but it is a difficult task precisely because we have already given this a lot of thought. Because we *have* tried to understand the human perspective. I never hid from you the fact that you were not likely to change what happens. If you wish to give up now, I will understand. But if you would like to continue trying, we still have time to carry on the discussion. Do you wish to give up, Kilmer?"

Kilmer could feel his anger rising again.

"Do I *wish* to give up? Do I *wish* to get out of your way so that you can go ahead and destroy human civilization? Is that really your question? Fuck you, Archidamus. And *fuck you* to everyone else who is listening to this conversation! Have we taught you that phrase yet? If not, please look it up. And once you do, feel free to add profanity to humanity's list of crimes. It might help you pass a stricter sentence."

"I understand the sentiment, Kilmer. But the question still needs to be answered. Are we giving up?"

Kilmer felt exhausted. And he felt the situation was hopeless. But there was something else. He didn't have all the facts. He hadn't asked all of his questions. And that meant he could not be *sure* that things were hopeless— even if he could see absolutely no way out of this.

He thought of Silla. He had promised her he would die trying. He wasn't dead yet. He was just exhausted.

"No. I don't give up."

"Then tell me what you would like to discuss next."

Kilmer took a minute to calm down. He didn't mind that he had lost his cool—he didn't think they would punish him for it. And it was probably better than keeping the anger completely bottled up inside. But it was not the way forward. He could not think and hate at the same time. No one could.

He took a deep breath and organized his thoughts. *What don't you know? What are the missing pieces? Start with those.*

"Who decides, Archidamus? Who ultimately decides what happens? What is the process? Walk me through how we got here, and what happens next."

"As I mentioned earlier, Citadel has something known as a *Consent Period,* which occurs approximately once every 100 Earth-years. By law, all major decisions, including the decision to go to war, must be made during one of these periods. The only exception to this rule is if Citadel itself is under attack and needs to defend itself. There are few limits to what Citadel can do if it comes under attack first.

"The discussion regarding Earth took place during the most recent Consent Period. That was almost twenty Earth-years ago. The armed forces of Citadel, along with two oversight bodies, were authorized to explore Earth and to make a judgment about whether its civilization should be left alone, engaged peacefully, or destroyed."

"Are those your only three options?"

"Yes."

"There can't be *any* fourth option? Under any circumstances?"

"No. And we have already chosen not to leave you alone. So, there are only two options now. Unless we can make the case that Earth poses no future threat and deserves our peaceful engagement, the only remaining option is to destroy human civilization. But we are still not allowed to exterminate your species."

"And leaving us alone—even for a few years or for a few decades—why *exactly* is that not an option?"

"It is not obvious how that would help humanity. It would only delay the inevitable for a few years, which is very little time in the broad span of human history. But for us, postponing the decision poses a problem. Citadel devotes a lot of resources to defense, but we are far from perfect in our ability to detect and eliminate threats. Timing and luck always play a role. We have other issues on our planet, and around the galaxy, that require our attention. There might be decades, even centuries, during which we cannot attend to a problem like this.

"Could we leave human beings alone for twenty or fifty Earth-years? Perhaps. But we cannot take the risk that when the time comes to return, we find ourselves unable to do so—or that we are unable to amass the resources necessary to do so effectively. If we are unable to return to Earth for even longer—two or three hundred years, for example—it might be far too late. That is a risk we are not authorized to take.

"For that same reason, Kilmer, we are also unable to solve this problem by signing a peace treaty, or an agreement that allows us to limit and monitor your military capabilities. The agreement could unravel at a time when we cannot seek redress. We have to act now, or we might act too late."

No wiggle room at all. And no other options.

Another dead end.

"You said Citadel has done this on other planets. Has anyone ever convinced you to change your decision?"

"Citadel has had six such encounters in the past, and each time, we invited an ambassador to speak on behalf of their species. But we have never had to change our minds. It is a testament to how carefully we conduct our evaluations."

"And, compared to these other six, how strong does Citadel consider the case against human beings to be? Are we as threatening as the rest?"

There was a pause before Archidamus answered.

"I am afraid the case against humanity is far more damning than it was against the others. As I said before, what makes human beings exceptional also makes them exceptionally threatening."

Kilmer took a deep breath. The more he learned, the more hopeless the situation appeared.

Don't dwell on it. Just keep going.

"Why did you ask for two representatives? You asked for me *and* for a leader of Earth."

"We must eventually speak to both. Once our discussion with the ambassador confirms that a civilization must be eliminated, we then speak to the leader of the planet—or to someone who represents one of its dominant tribes. We educate the leader on what we plan to do and ask for their advice on how to do it least painfully for the planet's inhabitants. The leader becomes a steward who ensures that matters are handled smoothly but has no power to debate or negotiate the outcome. In the case of Earth, and at this moment in human history, the leader would likely be the American president."

"And if I convinced you *not* to destroy human civilization—what would happen next?"

"I do not see how any of the information you are now seeking will help you with the role you have been assigned, Kilmer, but I can answer whatever questions you have. Obviously, you would be setting a precedent if you changed our mind. But if it happened, we would issue an immediate halt to our plans for an attack. And we would have no right to keep you here, so we would send you back to your people—with our gratitude. The decision would be submitted to the appropriate regulatory bodies on Citadel, and that would end things—at least for a while. As a precaution, the decision not to attack would likely be revisited in the next Consent Period, which is eighty Earth-years from now. We would want to confirm that we did not make a mistake."

"So, if you can be persuaded that our future intentions will be peaceful, it will buy us at least eighty years of survival. And maybe a lot more than that, if things go well for us in the next Consent Period. Is that right?"

"That is right. We cannot revisit our decision, except during a Consent Period. That is why we must be sure we are making the right decision. That is why we study things so carefully. That is why we invite an ambassador. That is why we follow strict policies in all stages of the process."

"But your strict policies do not seem to prohibit you from answering any of my questions—or discussing topics that seem irrelevant to you."

"My advice to you, Kilmer, is very simple: focus on what matters. Try to convince us, if possible, that Citadel has made a mistake. But I am not restricted from discussing other matters, if that is what you choose to do with your time. I have read the transcripts from the previous six times an ambassador was invited to persuade Citadel not to attack. You are spending much more of your time asking questions than any of them did—and that is your prerogative. But when this process comes to an end, we will make our judgment based only on our strict guidelines. The only thing that will matter is whether you have changed *our* minds, not how well you understand what we do or why we do it. I would keep that in mind."

Kilmer nodded to himself.

"Thank you, Archidamus. I will surely keep your advice in mind. Although, I'm also having to keep in mind the fact that the other six ambassadors never managed to save their civilizations. In any case, I do have a few more questions, and I appreciate you answering them. I am curious about the strict guidelines on which you must base your ruling. What exactly are those guidelines?"

"We are tasked with assessing whether a threat might exist—and if so, whether and how it can be addressed. More specifically, however, the law dictates that our final decision must be made based on our answers to three precise questions:

1. *Might human beings pose a threat to Citadel in the future?*
2. *Will deleting human civilization eliminate the threat?*
3. *Can we destroy human civilization without committing genocide?*

"Only if the answer to all three questions is *yes,* are we authorized to attack. If you can convince us that humans do not pose a threat, then I hope peace between our planets will last much longer than eighty Earth-years. I would love to discover that it is possible for us to coexist peacefully with the people of Earth."

"But you do not see that happening."

"I am sorry, Kilmer, but the answer to all three questions is *yes.* And we cannot consider any other factors. You might find this comparison offensive, but to us, human beings look a lot like the Wanderers did thousands of years ago. Highly advanced and impressive in many ways, but always wanting more, even at tremendous expense to others. They, too, were explorers, but somehow never managed to explore without causing harm to those they met. They, too, behaved as if the strong have an intrinsic right to dominate the weak. And, just like human beings, their creativity gave them the ability to easily justify such behavior to themselves."

"I wonder what the Wanderers would have said about Citadel," Kilmer responded.

"Believe it or not, I wonder that myself," Archidamus conceded.

"And yet you continue to believe they were evil—and that they deserved to be punished."

"No, Kilmer. Only that they were dangerous—and they deserved to be stopped. I advised you earlier not to think in terms of *right* versus *wrong.* I say that because our decision criteria do not allow for those considerations. We will issue our judgment based solely on the answers to those three questions. If you can convince us that we are wrong about the threat human beings pose, we will certainly reevaluate. Do you still want to try to do that?"

Kilmer didn't respond. Instead, he just closed his eyes.

He had hit yet another dead end. And to make matters worse, he couldn't even be sure he was thinking clearly anymore. A growing feeling of despair was weighing on him. The darkness was disorienting. He had no idea what time it was. His body ached from sitting on a chair designed for aliens. His mind was exhausted from trying to keep track of the countless details Archidamus had provided. His spirit was almost shattered.

347

"I need a minute, Archidamus."

"You can have more time if you need."

I can't convince them. Even if I can create doubt, it won't be enough. So what am I doing here? Am I just going through the motions? Just delaying the inevitable so that I can feel like I tried my best? Have I?

Silla's words came back to him.

I know you, Kilmer. You'll find a way. Just—don't you dare give up. Do you understand? No matter what.

He took a deep breath. Then he opened his eyes and looked out into the darkness, as if he could lock eyes with Archidamus by doing so. He forced a smile to his lips. It took more effort than he expected.

The toughest races are only won on the last lap.

He was not going to give up. He would keep pushing until he solved the problem. Or until they pulled the trigger. Whichever came first. No more despair. No more frustration. No more anger. No more exhaustion.

Let's try this again, Kilmer. Every problem wants to be solved—even the seemingly impossible ones. This is not a beast to be slayed; it's a puzzle to be solved. It wants to be solved. It's giving you clues. And it might give you more.

So… what do I still need to know?

Let's start with the thing I've avoided asking.

"How exactly do you plan to destroy human civilization, Archidamus? I want the details."

~ 95 ~

"It is not an easy task to eliminate a civilization, Kilmer, especially if you want its inhabitants to survive. This is why it took us a few Earth-centuries to develop the tools to do so—and millennia to perfect them. To eliminate a society's military capability is not enough. We must do away with the technology, artifacts, physical structures, rituals, language, art—even the imagination—of civilization. It is the only way to allow a race to start anew.

It begins with an occupation, and it can be relatively bloodless. We make our intentions clear from the start—there is no deception and there are no false promises. There is simply a choice: accept what will take place or be subjected to war of the likes the planet has never imagined. There are always pockets of resistance, but they eventually give up or are defeated. No one is ever killed if they agree to our terms.

In the case of Earth, the first few years will be devoted to preparing for the transition. All electronic technology will be disabled. In the following years, machines of every kind will be collected and destroyed, and all digital and physical repositories of information will be wiped clean or incinerated. The same will be done to anything else that could testify to what humans did, achieved, or resembled over the last 12,000 years—no books, no servers, no photo albums, no art, no maps, no music. This might take up to ten Earth-years. Compliance will be incentivized, including individual and collective punishment for efforts to resist or undermine the effort.

Human populations will be relocated as needed and transitioned to a form of agricultural living. We will ensure that farming will be able to feed the entire population. Humans will be allowed to live in small huts and use simple tools, but there will be no electricity or other luxuries, such as goods made from any type of manufacturing or those that would require distant trade. A barter system will be instituted, and money will be eliminated from society.

Cities will be evacuated and incinerated.

There are many other issues to address in such a transition, but only one that merits mention here. We must ensure that *memories*—ideas, information, knowledge, and stories—are not passed down to future generations by those who are alive today. When we first tackled this problem, thousands of Earth-years ago, our occupation had to last three or four lifespans for us to get this right. Draconian measures were instituted to ensure that memories were not discussed or transmitted to descendants. Think of how extremely repressive regimes on Earth, such as North Korea, might solve this problem. Now imagine a similarly brutal but much more effective campaign. If we had to do that on Earth, we would need 150 to 250 Earth-years to ensure that memory itself was deleted from human societies. What was left in memory, if anything, would be indistinguishable from mythology—like humans today might talk about Hindu or Greek gods.

But we now have tools that are much less harsh and much more effective. We are capable of targeting and erasing memories very efficiently, much like humans might do on a digital storage device. There are relatively few ways to store and organize information, even when it comes to complex data such as memories. Data structures can vary, but the organization, recall, and deletion of memory is not so complicated, conceptually, even in organic storage devices such as the human brain. We have spent many millennia perfecting the technology that allows us to identify memories—and delete them—efficiently and at scale.

We will delete everything related to human civilization, and to our time on Earth. Nothing that interferes with basic human functions or relationships will be deleted. Cognitive ability will remain, but what has been learned in specific domains, such as mathematics and science and history, will be wiped out. All of this can be done in less than ten years, and it is painless, so long as people do not try to resist.

Altogether, we should be able to finish the entire transition in less than twenty Earth-years. After that, we will maintain a small and unseen presence, for one additional human generation, to monitor how things unfold. If no issues arise, we will depart entirely. Earth will be allowed to chart its own course. Human beings will be allowed to start again and create something new.

We have every reason to believe, Kilmer, that human history will unfold differently the next time. That has been our experience with the other civilizations that we have reset. We have come to understand that civilizations do not become like the Wanderers because they are evil, or somehow predestined. Chance plays a role in how things unfold. Civilizations are complex systems, and their emergent characteristics are highly sensitive to initial conditions and events. Positive feedback loops perpetuate and strengthen societal tendencies and cultural traits that might have never existed had the dice rolled differently at the start, or if certain events and eras had not unfolded as they did. That is our hope for Earth. That is our wish for all of you.

I hope this answers your question. I have tried to be comprehensive without getting too deep into the details.

I will not ask you how you feel about what I have said, because I can predict your reaction. You are horrified. You are angry. And you are scared. All of that is to be expected. But you must try to remember, the alternative for your planet would have been the immediate and total annihilation of your species. This is far, far better, in ways that you are probably not even considering yet.

I will not pretend that we are motivated by goodwill toward human beings. No, we are doing this because of *our* needs. Nonetheless, in taking these actions, we will be giving humanity a second chance that it should have given itself. Most of what is good will survive. Much of what is bad will be eliminated. Partners will continue to know and love each other and their children. They will be able to eat and play and build small communities. They might even be happier in their new, natural environments, than they are in their crime-ridden, poverty-ridden, and stress-ridden cities where they have no time for themselves or their family, no sense of belonging or security. The reset will also put an end to war, poverty, and famine as it currently exists on Earth. We won't just take away weapons, we will erase all specific memories and beliefs regarding hate, grievance, and fear aimed at other groups. There will be no memory of any social constructions that have divided human beings. Some things humans seem to cherish might be lost along the way. For example, religions and national identities will be washed away. That will be hard for many of your fellow human beings to accept, at first.

Then again, if your gods truly exist, I am sure they will return—no matter what we do.

I am not trying to convince you that human beings should welcome the steps we are about to take. I would not want it done to Citadel. But it is not as bad as it seems. The current generation of human beings will mourn what they are about to lose, but future generations will have no memory of what they lost, and they might be better off with the future *we* give them than the future their own ancestors had planned for them.

Ask yourself, Kilmer. Do you really think human beings can avoid another great war among the nations of Earth? For how long? Will it really destroy less than what we will destroy? Will it provide any of the accompanying benefits? Think of the condition your planet is in. We have seen the state of your natural environment and your inability to protect it. Think of the passion with which large swaths of your species are embracing and encouraging tribalism and ignorance, even as these forces rip your societies apart. It is not why we are here, but we might end up saving humanity from itself.

You will still be horrified, angry, and afraid. It is still a tragic situation. But it is better than the alternative of annihilation. And strange as it might sound, it is probably better for humans than the alternative of leaving Earth alone. It is certainly better for all *other* species on Earth.

In any case, you have no choice. Maybe that is for the best."

Heirs of Herodotus by D. Kilmer.
Excerpt from Chapter 5.

If there was a prize for the most unapologetic speech to ever extol the privileges of power, it would go to the Athenians for what they said to the Melians during the Melian Dialogue, a historic "negotiation" that occurred just before they lay siege to the island of Melos.

"...we shall not trouble you with specious pretenses—either of how we have a right to our empire ... or are now attacking you because of wrong that you have done us—and make a long speech which would not be believed. And in return we hope that you, instead of thinking to influence us by saying that you ... have done us no wrong, will aim at what is feasible ... since you know, as well as we do, that right, as the world goes, is only in question between equals in power, while the strong do what they can and the weak suffer what they must. ... Of the gods we believe, and of men we know, that by a necessary law of their nature, they rule wherever they can. And it is not as if we were the first to make this law, or to act upon it when made. We found it existing before us and shall leave it to exist forever after us. All we do is make use of it, knowing that you and everybody else, having the same power as we have, would do the same as we do."

The Athenians never entertained **the possibility that the strong, instead of exploiting the existing system, might use their power to change it—while they still can**. It is not easy to do. To choose not to exploit is hard enough, but to ensure that others will follow your example when *they* come to power requires you to reimagine the world, upend norms, and build mechanisms that will secure a new equilibrium. Neither the weak nor the strong can do this. **Only the truly powerful have a shot at bending the arc of history in this way. But the truly powerful exist as a paradox: they live in constant fear of losing their status but are somehow incapable of imagining a future in which their empire has crumbled.**

Kilmer was horrified, angry, and afraid. But more than anything, he was shocked. He had certainly never tried to imagine how someone might eliminate a civilization without annihilating a race—but this was not what he would have imagined if he had.

Archidamus had made clear what the future held. But would the likes of Whitman, Strauss, Nielsen, or Druckman accept it? The Indians, the East Asians, the Europeans—and the nations of the Middle East and North Africa—all had histories that were much longer than those of the Americans. They might resist even more strongly. But would it matter? Archidamus seemed convinced that resistance would be useless. Would people still fight to the end? Or would the nations of Earth surrender after a few million—or a few hundred million—human beings were slaughtered?

Kilmer didn't envy the position Earth's leaders would find themselves in. They would face an impossible choice. He wasn't even sure what advice he would give to Whitman if he were around when the time came.

It hardly mattered. It was almost irrelevant whether humans fought to the end, or not at all. Either way, human civilization was about to meet a terrible end.

Unless Kilmer did something about it.

But the only thing he could think to do was keep shaking the tree in the hope that something of value might shake loose and fall into his hands. He had to ask more questions. There had to be *something* he had not yet considered.

He tried again. Another question. Another angle. Another chance—no matter how small.

"Do you expect resistance from Earth?"

"Yes. But we do not expect a long war. We will quickly demonstrate that we can kill many millions of human beings without suffering casualties on our side. A few demonstrations should be enough to make the point. Guerilla resistance will likely continue for a few years, and it will be able to inflict some casualties, but it will not slow down the process to any significant degree. The loss of life on our end will be limited and acceptable."

"And if humanity decides it will fight to the end? Will you kill us all? Isn't that genocide? Isn't that illegal?"

"We are not allowed to attack with the *intention* of genocide, but there is nothing to stop us from wiping out an alien race if it refuses to accept the alternative we are offering. But again, I do not think human beings, of even a single nation, will choose to fight to the end once they see our capabilities."

Archidamus was probably right about how things would play out. There would be fighting, rioting, looting, vigilantism, countless attempts to skirt compliance, and much more—maybe even mass suicides—but none of these were likely to change the outcome. At best, they would add a few years to Citadel's process.

Another dead end.

"What happens to me during this time?" Kilmer asked. "Am I returned to Earth, eventually, to have my memories erased as well? Do I at least get to say goodbye to the people I care about before you do that?"

"No. From this moment on, your path is separate from theirs. You will not see the people of Earth again, and in exchange, your memories will be spared. You will remember everything."

"Is that my reward for playing the role you have assigned me in this show trial? What if I prefer to return to Earth, even if that means my memories will be deleted? What if I wish to be there with my friends, if only for the final moments before you destroy our civilization? Do I have that option?"

"No. You have no choice in the matter. And it is not a reward, Kilmer, but our obligation to the people of Earth. I said earlier that we never wish to repeat what was done to the Wanderers—and the genocide we committed was only *one* of the tragedies in that war. Do you remember what else I told you about it?"

To be remembered only by your enemies—to have no one left to tell your side of the story—is the worst imaginable fate for any people.

"I do," said Kilmer. "So, now you hope to lessen your guilt by keeping one man alive who remembers what existed before you destroyed it all?"

"No, Kilmer. We hope to keep one *historian* alive who can tell the story of humanity. Your perspective on what led to human civilization's unfortunate end—your memoirs as the last historian of planet Earth—will be read not only by the inhabitants of Citadel, but far beyond it. Your people will be remembered, not as *we* saw them, but as they saw themselves. That is the reason you must keep your memories. Whatever we might say about Earth and its people, nothing will be as important as what is written by Earth's last historian. Your remembrance of Earth's forgotten past—the good, the bad, the heroic, the tragic, the spectacular, and the mundane— will outlast us all."

Kilmer was just starting to grapple with the gravity of what was being said to him when he forced himself to stop.

No. I can't divert my attention to how things will play out after I fail. We're not there yet. There must be some way out of this. But what?

"I need a few minutes, Archidamus. May I have them?"

"Of course."

In the silent darkness of the alien vessel, Kilmer went through the questions he had listed for himself before coming to ET-1.

Why now? Why did they visit Earth at this moment in history?

Why was Earth in danger?

Why would the methods that humans had proposed not solve the problem?

Why was ET-1 being so reactive?

What did they plan to judge?

Why had they worked so hard to understand and communicate with humans?

Why did they choose Kilmer?

He had thought that an answer to even one of these questions might help him resolve the crisis. He now had answers to *all* the questions—he had even found Churchill's Key—but he was no closer to a solution.

Churchill's Key.

He flashed back to Churchill's words.

> *"I cannot forecast to you the action of Russia. It is a riddle wrapped in a mystery inside an enigma; but perhaps there is a key. That key is Russian national interest."*

The Key was never supposed to be the answer. It was merely a reminder that interests drive behavior.

Their interests would help explain everything... even the inexplicable.

Citadel's interest was self-preservation. Not aggrandizement, not status, not dominance, not growth, not exploration, not happiness. *Survival*—at all costs. *Fear* was why its citizens did what they did. Why they explored. Why they attacked. Why they committed genocide. Why they deleted civilizations. Why they came to Earth. Why they would do whatever they did next.

Whatever they did next...

The idea gave Kilmer pause, and he delved deeper into it. Was it profound? Maybe not profound, exactly, but it hadn't been obvious to him. What was it that Archidamus had said?

> *In the absence of both fear and guilt, there is no reason for a people to question their actions.*

Fear. Guilt.

All this time, Kilmer had assumed that fear would motivate Citadel to attack—and that guilt, if heaped on high enough, might get Citadel to back off. And so, Kilmer had tried to do two things: reduce Citadel's fear by explaining that humans were not a real threat, and increase Citadel's sense of guilt by portraying an attack on the Earth as unconscionable. If he could reduce fear on one side of the equation and increase guilt on the other side, he might convince Citadel to reverse its decision.

This strategy had been doomed from the start. You could never reduce the level of fear to zero, which was what Citadel required. And guilt—the question of right versus wrong—wasn't even part of their decision criteria.

It would have to come down to Churchill's Key.

It's fear that motivates them to attack. And only fear can make them change their mind.

Not guilt. Fear.

Kilmer could already see another dead end ahead. After all, how could fear stop Citadel from attacking when human beings had no chance—*zero*—of winning the war? Earth-side couldn't impose any significant costs on Citadel's forces. There was nothing for Citadel to fear.

Don't you dare give up...

Kilmer pushed aside the doubt. There *was* a dead end ahead, but he wasn't at the end of the road yet. There might be some small alley he could duck into and still make his way around to the other side. *Just keep going.*

"I need more time, Archidamus," he said after almost ten minutes of silent deliberation.

"Take your time, Kilmer. I know it's a lot to accept."

Kilmer wasn't planning to use the extra time to accept anything. He was still fighting. It was the last round of the bout, and he hadn't won a single round. There was no way to win on points. He needed a knockout.

He held his breath, as if preparing to leap into a pool, and jumped off his chair. The floor was only about three feet below where his feet had been dangling. He stumbled a bit when he landed because he had not known when the impact would occur.

Kilmer reached out in every direction and found nothing other than the chair. Then he walked forward, slowly, his hands stretched out in front of him, until he reached what felt like a wall. He moved just as cautiously in every other direction, and found another wall, a counter, and then some sort of metallic structure or piece of equipment. In all, he had carved out an area—approximately 15 feet by 20 feet in size—that was free of obstructions.

He took a moment to stretch and get rid of the stiffness. Then he walked back and forth in the space he had mapped out in the dark until he no longer had to think about how far he could move in one direction before needing to turn around. All he was missing now was a cup of coffee in his hand.

Kilmer slowed his pace and issued himself a directive. *Think.*

No way to convince ET-1 we have peaceful intentions.

No way to convince them we will never be a threat.

No way to eliminate all doubts in their mind.

No way to delay their decision. No wiggle room to negotiate with them.

They have only two options: either destroy human civilization or engage peacefully. No third option.

A third option would require a Consent Period. There won't be another Consent Period for eighty years.

What else?

They don't care about right versus wrong.

They will answer only three questions. Is there a threat? Can it be eliminated? Can genocide be avoided?

Self-preservation is the Key.

Fear... not guilt. It must be fear. Only fear will drive them away. But what could they possibly have to fear?

Kilmer again asked for more time—and then continued to pace.

There is a solution. It's in front of you. It's hiding, but it's there. You just need to look more carefully.

They have strict guidelines. Only three questions to answer.

They have limited options. Destroy our civilization or engage peacefully. If only there were a third option. The problem is that they have no third option.

The problem... is that they have no third option.

They have no third option.

Suddenly, an image of Silla flashed before his eyes—their first night in the Treaty Room. And he heard her voice.

We have time.

Kilmer stopped walking. His heart was pounding. He closed his eyes and went through the logic again, slowly, disassembling the puzzle and then putting the pieces back together again to see if they still fit.

They did.

And he knew, with certainty, that this was it—his one chance. His only chance.

All or nothing. Do or die.

He opened his eyes and looked out into the darkness as he spoke.

"You've made a mistake, Archidamus. And it changes everything. I'm afraid you're in a lot more trouble than you could have possibly imagined."

~ 98 ~

"What do you mean, Kilmer? "What is the mistake?"

"You missed it, Archidamus. You missed it completely. Not because you weren't careful, but because you weren't looking for it. And I don't blame you. I almost missed it myself. All this time you were trying to find some way to persuade yourself that humans wouldn't pose a danger to Citadel. I was trying to do the same thing—to convince you that humanity would never be a threat. But we were looking for the wrong thing. I see that now. And you're going to see it as well—soon enough."

Kilmer interjected a pause. "Are you ready?"

"Yes. Please continue."

"Good. Then let's start with a pop quiz. But don't worry, I think it will play to your strengths. Here's the opening question: What was the first human civilization on Earth?"

"I suppose that would be Mesopotamia."

"Why do you *suppose,* Archidamus? You've studied this. Why are you not sure?"

"Because we cannot be certain. There were other contenders around the same time."

"That's right, Archidamus, there were other contenders. There was Mesopotamia. There was Egypt. There was the Indus Valley. Maybe in that order—but maybe not. All between 3500 BCE and 3000 BCE. Does that sound accurate to you?"

"It does."

"Three separate civilizations, Archidamus. Arising at roughly the same time. In three different parts of the world. Do you know what they all had in common?"

"They shared some necessary conditions. The climate. The land. The water."

"Right. All three were in temperate climates. All had flat and fertile land that would be suitable for farming. And all three had access to rivers that could provide the fresh water necessary for agriculture. It's what allowed them to create the first large cities. Now… do you know what they did *not* have in common?"

"I am not sure what you mean. There would have been many differences."

"That's true. Let's get back to that question in a few minutes. Let's talk about something else. Do you know which human civilization invented writing?"

"That is what you call a trick question, Kilmer. Writing was invented multiple times on Earth. By different civilizations. Not just the three civilizations you mentioned earlier, but also in China. It was probably invented in other places as well."

"Right again. And how about the crossbow? Where was that invented? I'll give you a hint. This is also a trick question."

"I do not know where it was invented. But I assume you mean there is more than one correct answer."

"Indeed. Variations of the crossbow were invented, independently, on four different continents. Now, let's get back to my earlier question. The one we skipped. What *don't* the three earliest civilizations have in common?"

"I think I understand the point you are making, Kilmer. One thing these civilizations did not have in common was a founder or ancestral tribe—they have no shared progenitor. The civilizations developed independently, just like the inventions you named. And I am sure there are other examples that you could have named as well."

"There are. Too many to remember, in fact. From the discovery of oxygen and magnetism to the invention of calculus and photography. All happening, independently, in different parts of the human world. It's really quite remarkable, Archidamus. It's almost hard to imagine that these are mere coincidences."

Kilmer paused—deliberately—and the silence lasted for almost twenty seconds.

"It is… difficult to imagine," Archidamus finally conceded, albeit with some hesitation.

"You're beginning to see the mistake, Archidamus. And you're beginning to understand why Citadel has a much bigger problem than you and your friends had imagined. And to make matters worse, you don't have any way to solve it. At least not any *legal* way, I should say."

Archidamus was quiet. Had he understood the implications? Was he working through the logic? Was he conferring with others?

Kilmer let the silence settle for another thirty seconds before he continued.

"You have good intentions, Archidamus. I believe that. You just got it wrong. You brought me here to help convince our audience that humans are not so dangerous after all. To somehow prove, beyond a shadow of a doubt, that humans of the future would not, or could not, attack Citadel. But you've done your homework, so you *knew* there was no way I could succeed. You were honest about that. You warned me I would fail.

But you still gave me a chance. You invited me here and you educated me. You answered my questions. You told me everything. You allowed me to make my case—even to scream into the darkness. You let me try, again and again, to prove that we are harmless. That we are no threat at all.

But it's simply not true. I see that now. It would be disingenuous to say that there is *no way* that humans could pose a threat to you in the future. All I can say is that I *hope* we will not. I pray we will become a more enlightened species long before we are able to travel to alien planets. But I can't promise you that. I can't promise that if you leave us alone, you will be safe. And given your aversion to any such risks, that creates a big problem for us.

But we're not the only ones with a problem, Archidamus. Citadel also has a problem. Because your rules dictate that you must answer *three* questions, not one.

Might human beings pose a threat in the future? Let's agree that the answer to this first question is *yes*. I concede the point that we might pose a threat.

But what about the second question? *Will deleting human civilization eliminate that threat?*

The answer to that, I'm afraid, is a resounding *no*.

Your solution to dealing with potential threats—tested though it might be on six other planets—will not work on Earth. You cannot hope to eliminate the risk posed by human beings by simply pressing *reset*. You can delete our civilization, but we will *not* come back so different. Our civilization, as you have witnessed it, with its incredible art and its horrific violence, is not the emergent outcome of a random draw from a wide array of initial conditions. We are not stuck in some tragic feedback loop. *This is who we are*, Archidamus. Not good. Not evil. Trying to find our way. Trying to be better. And making some progress. Moving forward shockingly fast in some ways. Advancing tragically slowly in other ways. Pretty smart. Very creative. And *highly* imaginative. More imaginative, in fact, than any species that Citadel has ever encountered. It's what makes us so dangerous, you said. But that danger will *not* go away.

Will you be able to set us back a few thousand years with your methods? Yes, you will. So what? Do you remember what you said about our gods, Archidamus?

> *If your gods truly exist, I am sure they will return—no matter what we do.*

I don't know if our gods will come back—they probably will, in one form or another. But there are some things I can *guarantee* will return. Cities will rise again. Competition and conflict will resurface—as will developments in coordination and control. Social identities will be reborn. Wars will resume. Art will flourish. Technology will advance. Weapons will become more deadly. And the *next time*, Archidamus, it won't take nearly as long.

Written language developed two thousand years earlier in some places than in others—that amount of variation isn't going away. And the size of the human population today—it's almost 200 *times* what it was in 5000 BCE. You can send us back to that date, or even farther back, but how rapid will our return be? How much faster will we innovate and discover and experiment and advance?

With so many of us on the planet—asking questions, tackling obstacles, imagining the impossible, and exploring the unknown—how much more likely is it that someone, somewhere, makes a new discovery, creates a new technology, builds a new weapon, or stumbles upon an innovation? You can run the numbers if you want, but I think you already know the answer. We will be back in the blink of a human eye.

We might be slightly better than we were the first time around, or we might be slightly worse. But what happens if we return slightly *better* in capabilities… but slightly *worse* in intentions? And what if we do it in a few hundred years—not a few thousand?

I'm not trying to scare you, Archidamus. But you should be afraid. As should everyone else who is listening to us. Because the answer to your second question—*Will deleting human civilization eliminate the threat?*—seems exceedingly clear. *No chance in hell.*

I'm not going to tell you what you should do about that, but I know what you *can't* do. You can't do the one thing that would eliminate the threat you perceive. You can't kill us all. You're not *allowed* to commit genocide. Not today, and not for at least another eighty years. When you decided not to leave us alone, you were left with only two options: destroy our civilization, or engage with us peacefully. Well, now you are down to only *one* option.

Once you examine the evidence for yourself, you will agree that it's overwhelming. Deleting our history will *not* eliminate the threat we pose. In fact, a reset of our civilization might make matters even worse for you. If you don't like humanity as it exists today, I strongly recommend that you not take any chances with a Version 2.0."

Kilmer closed his eyes and took a deep breath. He had nothing more to say—and nothing left to give. He could feel the adrenaline, but beneath that, he knew he was completely spent. Every part of him. And he was trembling.

This was not the argument he had come here to make. He had wanted to talk peace, not war. He had wanted to make concessions, not threats. And he had wanted to invoke goodwill, not fear. But Citadel hadn't allowed any of that.

And so, Kilmer had washed his hands of everything he had planned, and everything he had assumed, and looked for another way. He had told Archidamus that Citadel's only hope was to annihilate the human race entirely.

He knew it was a gamble. He was standing on the banks of the Rubicon and rolling the die. The best-case scenario was that it would postpone an attack by eighty years. By then, Earth-side might be better prepared. And who knows—maybe it would give humanity the time it needed to change its ways and prove that it wouldn't be a threat.

We have time.

If that time was squandered, however, then when the attack finally came, it would be even more vicious than what had been planned for today.

There was also a worst-case scenario. If Kilmer had miscalculated or misunderstood—or if he had simply overplayed his hand—Citadel might find a way to authorize a genocide immediately. If so, he had just sentenced Silla and everyone else he cared about, along with billions of innocent people, to a death that they would have otherwise avoided. It would be the greatest mistake in human history.

He wasn't sure what would come next. He was only sure that he had reached the limits of his abilities, and that he was too drained to throw even one more punch.

Kilmer dropped to his knees on the cold, metallic floor of the spacecraft. Then he took the picture of his parents out of his pocket, knowing full well that he would be unable to see their faces. He stared at it anyway, through the impenetrable darkness that surrounded him, as tears began to roll down the sides of his face.

Heirs of Herodotus by D. Kilmer.
Excerpt from Chapter 11.

Innovation, throughout human history, has been **non-linear**. For over 3,000 years—from the introduction of horse-drawn chariots to the invention of railroads in the 1800s—there was almost no progress in the speed at which a soldier could travel. But then, little more than a hundred years after railroads first came into use, humans were flying faster than the speed of sound and landing spacecraft on the Moon.

The pattern is not confined to technological or military progress. Monarchs ruled for millennia before giving way to the republics we suddenly take for granted. The Westphalian state system, the basis for international law, emerged only in the last 400 years—after the end of the Thirty Years' War (1618-1648). The inhumane treatment of civilians was made illegal only after the Geneva Conventions of the nineteenth and twentieth centuries—even though this idea had been debated and negotiated between warring nations for thousands of years.

The future of humanity will not be a linear progression of its past—but the **type** of non-linearity that will emerge remains to be seen. Our progress might accelerate, stall, or reverse. Our story might go on for countless millennia— or end suddenly. **Uncertainty abounds for one reason above all else: we have reached a level of scale and complexity in our societal evolution that allows us to do more and more—but control less and less.**

Humanity now finds itself hosting a high-stakes competition. It is a race between technological progress and societal progress—between our ability to create and destroy, and our ability to govern, manage, and coexist. What the graph of our time in this universe will ultimately look like, when drawn by future historians, will be determined by who wins that race.

~ 100 ~

Archidamus did not provide a rebuttal—nor give a lengthy response.

"We will need some time to evaluate what you have said, Kilmer. And we will need to discuss this matter on our end. You can rest in the meantime. There is something that can be used as a mattress in one corner of the room."

The room remained dark, but Kilmer was told how to navigate to the mattress. It was low to the ground and softer than he had expected. He sat down on it.

"Is there something we can do to make you more comfortable while you wait?"

"You wouldn't happen to have any coffee, would you? Just black would be fine."

"I am sorry, Kilmer. We do not have coffee. And if I am not mistaken, it is an unhealthy choice of beverage. I would not recommend it."

Are you fucking serious?

"Then can I have my bag? I have some water in it."

"Your bag is underneath the chair you were sitting on. You should be able to find it. Get some rest if you need. I will return to you in a few hours if there is an update."

Kilmer retrieved his laptop bag and sat down on the mattress. He drank some water and took out the pen and paper. These would have been useful earlier—if there had been any light by which to see. He put the pen in his pocket and the paper on the floor next to him. Then he lay down.

He wondered what time it was. He wondered what was happening at Station Zero and in Washington. Had everyone evacuated? Was Silla still nearby? Were they meeting right now? What were they discussing? What was Silla feeling? Had he managed to keep at least one promise—to help stop the attack? Would Silla get to live out the rest of her days in peace? And what would happen to him—even in the best-case scenario?

If Citadel ever let him go—and if humanity survived—Kilmer knew exactly what he would do first. He would take Silla in his arms and not let go. At least, not until she told him it was getting awkward. He smiled at the thought. It felt like an eternity since he had seen her, or held her hand, or kissed her. But only hours had passed.

He imagined all the ways in which they might see each other again for the first time. Just outside the spacecraft? At HQ-1? At the White House? He imagined what they would say. How he would apologize for leaving the way he did. How she would forgive him. How it would feel to look into her eyes again.

A few minutes later, still thinking these thoughts, Kilmer fell asleep.

101

"Kilmer. Are you awake?"

Kilmer woke immediately to the sound of his name, but it took a few seconds for him to realize where he was.

He sat up. "What time is it?"

"It is 7 a.m. where we are," answered Archidamus. "At Station Zero."

"What did I miss? What happens now?"

"A few things, Kilmer. I will go through them quickly, as I need to return for further discussions. You have made a shocking, but compelling case. It has been thoroughly examined by many of our experts, and it has caused a lot of excitement and anxiety on Citadel—to put it mildly. This is not the situation we expected to confront. As pertains to the consequences for Earth: First, you are right that genocide is not an option. It is strictly forbidden, at least for now. Your actions will probably force us to reconsider that position, but we cannot reconsider it until the next Consent Period. Second, the experts and regulators agree that we are not likely to eliminate the threat we face by destroying human civilization—and more importantly, that there is a risk we could make matters worse. That means we cannot follow through with the planned deletion."

"Does that mean you'll leave us alone? For at least eighty years?"

"It is more complicated than that. Questions pertaining to our second and third guidelines have never been raised before. Those guidelines were meant to impose strict moral constraints on the actions we could consider, but because our deletion methods were always so successful, the guidelines never had any practical relevance. Over the years, they drifted into the background. We were not trying to ignore them—we simply never had a reason to examine them so carefully. This is the first time an ambassador from a targeted planet has picked apart our process in such detail and forced us to consider potential implications of those guidelines. As it turns out, the implications are quite serious here, because the very factors that make human beings so threatening to us also make it highly unlikely that our methods will eliminate the threat.

"The situation we face is unprecedented. We know what we *cannot* do, but there is not yet consensus on what we *can* do. There can be no deletion and no genocide—not yet anyway. According to one logic, the only remaining option is to engage peacefully with human beings until a new authorization is debated and issued in eighty years. But there is a different perspective as well. There are those who say that ignoring a civilization that is this dangerous—whose own ambassador has confirmed its innate violent proclivities—would be negligent in the extreme. It cannot be allowed. That something must be done."

"What would that something be?"

"That depends on whose voice carries the day. On one end of the spectrum, it has been suggested that a delegation of ambassadors and technocrats be stationed on Earth, as guests of the human race, to monitor how things develop in the coming years. This would help reduce anxiety, build a relationship between the two planets, and serve as an early warning system if the threat posed by humans started to rise. On the other end of the spectrum, what is being proposed sounds like war and occupation."

"I thought you only had two options: delete our civilization or engage peacefully. Where was this kind of creativity when I was begging for it?"

"I will not deny there is hypocrisy, Kilmer. I am simply reporting to you the situation."

"And for the record, Archidamus, I never said human beings have 'innate violent proclivities.' That is a gross misrepresentation."

"Technically, you are correct. But you also cannot have it both ways, Kilmer. You cannot scare the inhabitants of Citadel into changing course the way you did—through fear—and then tell them they have nothing to fear. You have managed to stop the imminent destruction of human civilization, which is truly remarkable—and perhaps even commendable—but the way you have done it has complicated matters. You should be able to understand that."

"So, what happens now? How long before a decision is made? Do I get to participate in the discussion? Does President Whitman get a voice? Can this be negotiated now?"

"There might be a negotiation with your president when it comes to coordinating on specifics, especially if we proceed with the milder option of sending a delegation. But at this stage, there is no scope for negotiation. Citadel will decide what to do, and Earth will have to accept the decision. This will take time. A few Earth-weeks at least."

"Is there any way I can influence the decision?"

"You will not be allowed to weigh in on this decision. Neither will your president. Like your fellow human beings, you will simply have to wait to find out what is decided."

"Does that mean I can go home now?"

Archidamus did not respond.

"Can I leave now? You said that if I convinced Citadel not to attack, I would be allowed to go home. You said you would have no right to keep me here."

"I remember what I said. But the circumstances were different. We did not think—"

"You didn't think I would succeed. You were making promises you never thought you would have to keep."

"No. We just did not think you would convince us in this way. As I said, this is a complicated situation."

"I understand that. But what does that have to do with *me*? You say I'm of no more use to Citadel. And if you don't plan to destroy humanity or delete human civilization, why can't I go home?"

"We have no interest in keeping you here, Kilmer. Like many on Citadel, I think that you deserve to go home. But others are convinced we cannot send you back safely. You know too much about us. About our society. About our plans and our capabilities. Our way of thinking. Our fears. We cannot put you back in the hands of our enemy—not when we are still worried about a future war."

"We are *not* your enemies, Archidamus. That is what people like you should be reminding your fellow citizens. We have done you no harm. Let's not forget that fact just because things have suddenly become 'complicated' for Citadel. They are only complicated because Citadel's plan to launch an unprovoked and unjust war was derailed. Somehow, I don't feel like I should have to apologize for that.

"You have criticized my race plenty, Archidamus, but how many thousands of years has it been since your people reflected on what *they* have become? You can't spend your lives categorizing everyone you meet as a future enemy or a future friend. It causes you to do immeasurable harm. You should be finding ways to improve the social environments in which you exist—not to live in perpetual fear of them. Your people are at the height of their power, but they use this power only to destroy what they cannot control. That same strength could be used to transform relationships, to encourage cooperation where it might not otherwise take hold, and to underwrite a policy of generosity and goodwill rather than suspicion and hostility.

"I never said there would be war between our planets in the future. My only argument was that the *risk* of war can't be eliminated by deleting our civilization in the way you described. I believe we can and should live as friends. I think it is not only possible, but probable that we will find a way. Why not work toward that? I'm willing to play a role in that—even if Citadel no longer cares what I think.

"If you will no longer allow me to represent Earth in my discussions with Citadel, then send me back to my people so I can represent Citadel in my discussions with Earth. Let me help bridge the divide that exists. I can help them see that there is more to your people than what we fear, and that you are not driven by greed or malice or the desire for glory. If I can't be an ambassador *from* Earth, let me be an ambassador *to* Earth."

"Kilmer, I agree with you. But many are convinced that returning *D. Kilmer* to his people is too dangerous."

"Too dangerous? I'm a *historian*, Archidamus. On *Earth*. I have no power to do *anything*."

"You have proven otherwise."

"Okay. So, what would they have me do? How much longer do they want to keep me here? A few more weeks?"

"I don't know, Kilmer. But it could be forever."

Kilmer felt like he had been kicked in the chest.

He had come to ET-1 assuming he would never go back. But after his discussion with Archidamus the night before, he had allowed himself to hope. And that hope was being ripped away.

"I will not accept that, Archidamus. There must be another way. You said I could go back. That means it's possible. And I'm no longer of any use here. All I did was stop a war. You will imprison me for *that*? I understand that you don't like to talk about right versus wrong, but is there no such thing as *justice* on Citadel?"

There was a long pause.

"There is... one way, Kilmer. It is a possibility that has been discussed—but we have not yet reached a conclusion. Some on Citadel think that even this should not be permitted."

"What is it?"

"If we decided to send you back, we would have to delete your memories."

Kilmer felt a jolt of fear go through him.

"What does that mean? Delete *all* my memories? Or just your conversation with me? Is it dangerous?"

"It is only dangerous when someone resists, which will not be an issue if you are doing this willingly. As for what we would delete—it will probably be more than just our conversation. The way human minds are organized, we would need to dismantle some more... infrastructure... to ensure no memories are later revived. We will only know with certainty what needs to be deleted after the process begins—but we will remove as little as possible. If we delete a little more than you like, you can relearn that information after you go home."

Kilmer considered the implications. Not remembering his time in ET-1 would limit his ability to help President Whitman in the days ahead. Earthside would be completely in the dark, once again, about what was happening and why. All the questions he had learned answers to would be lost. But it was worth it. He was of no use here, and there was a lot waiting for him at home. The possibility of continuing to help Whitman. His career. Silla. He would have no memory of what he had accomplished—or how much worse things could have been—but that was okay. Humanity would still have avoided a terrible fate. He might lose additional memories as well, but it was far better to be home, filling in the details a little at a time, than to be whisked off into space for eternity.

"Is that the only way I'm going back?"

"That is correct, Kilmer. If you wish to go back, I will petition for you to do so under these terms. As I have said, there are those who consider it too dangerous to send you back even without your memories. But there is a chance that the request will be granted."

"Then let's do it."

102

Kilmer spent the next few hours in continued darkness. Thinking. Stretching. Exercising. Meditating.

And taking notes—which he couldn't even see—to help organize his thoughts. Thoughts that he would be forced to forget if they allowed him to go home.

He had been told that they would feed him when he was hungry, but he had resisted asking for anything to eat. He still had some food left in his bag— and if he was lucky, it was enough to hold him over until he returned home. Nor, as yet, had Kilmer felt compelled to use the bathroom, but he was assured those arrangements had also been made.

Archidamus returned at 1 p.m. to inform him that his petition had been granted—irreversibly. The process would go forward, and there was no way to overturn the decision.

Kilmer didn't mind that at all. "Any other updates?"

"Yes. But there are strict limits on what I can share with you now—even though you will forget what I reveal to you soon enough. I can tell you that most citizens are unwilling to declare war on Earth, and they prefer to simply monitor things in the coming years. Others—who are fewer in number, but much more influential—want war to commence immediately. They are afraid of what human beings will achieve in the next eighty years. The only thing that will restrain them is the law."

"They will follow the law?"

"Yes."

"That means Earth is safe—at least for now?"

"Not exactly, Kilmer."

"I don't understand. Your law doesn't allow—"

"There is nothing more I can say about it, Kilmer. I can only tell you, fellow historian, the things you already know. That laws cannot end war. Laws can only tell you how to start wars."

"I'm not sure I follow."

"I am sorry, but I cannot continue this conversation. I would have loved to spend more time discussing history and philosophy with you—debating what a Thoreau or a Lincoln might have said about the problems that your planet faces. But our time is up, my friend."

Kilmer hesitated. "Is that right, Archidamus? Are we friends?"

"I am your friend, Kilmer. You will forget that very soon... but I will remember."

With that, Archidamus left Kilmer alone again.

Kilmer sat down on the mattress and grabbed his pen and paper, ready once again to scribble and contemplate in the dark. What had Archidamus not been able to tell him? Why was Earth still in danger?

Laws cannot end war. Laws can only tell you how to start wars.

The first statement was easy enough to understand; Archidamus appeared to have quoted back to Kilmer something he had written in one of his books.

Laws cannot end war because wars exist in Hobbesian environments— political contexts in which, by definition, there is no higher authority that has the power to enforce laws.

But what did Archidamus mean by his second statement? How did laws tell you how to start wars?

Kilmer wished he could have talked with Archidamus for longer. Not about philosophy, or about what Thoreau or Lincoln or anyone else might have said about Earth's predicament. Kilmer wanted to know what Archidamus had been unwilling to reveal. He wanted to know why Citadel might still decide—

I can only tell you, fellow historian, the things you already know.

And suddenly, Kilmer understood exactly what Archidamus had said. *Thoreau...*

Lincoln...

Archidamus had told Kilmer precisely what he wanted to know. But he had done it in a language that others—who might still be listening—were unlikely to understand. But why Archidamus had taken such a risk was not entirely clear...

I am your friend, Kilmer.

The crisis was not over. The worst *might* have been avoided, but a war was still coming. And it could arrive at any moment.

Laws can only tell you how to start wars.

Kilmer knew what was going to happen.
And he knew how to stop it.
But he would remember none of it.

~ 103 ~

After another two hours or so, Kilmer was told to return to his chair. He did so, leaving his bag behind. Moments later, the chair was on the move. He was being rolled, or perhaps slid, to another location. It took almost two minutes to get there. It was like being on an alien-themed roller coaster. Except that the ride was slower. And the aliens were real.

When they reached their destination, Kilmer was told to lie down on what felt like a tabletop made of smooth concrete. He was strapped into place and then asked a series of questions. The questioner's voice sounded like the one Archidamus had used, but it was still distinguishable. The questions pertained to Kilmer's time in ET-1, and to the events that had led up to it.

A few minutes later, things started to unravel in his mind.

At first it felt like he was slightly drunk. He knew where he was and why he was there, but his memory of how he had gotten there was starting to fade. One moment he was in HQ-1, and the next he was talking to Archidamus. He tried to access a few more memories, but they slipped away as soon as he tried to engage them—like trying to remember a dream after you wake up. You see the memory disappearing and you can't hold on to it despite your best efforts.

Kilmer started to get anxious. He was beginning to lose memories not only of his time in ET-1, but of events that had preceded it. Why had he decided to come here? Had he been abducted? Had he been sent by Whitman? How long had he been here?

The deletions continued, reaching farther back in time.

"Wait!" Kilmer shouted. "You're going too far back!"

He felt a shooting pain in his skull.

"Ambassador Kilmer. Please do not resist. It could be dangerous. We are only going as far back as is necessary to ensure the deletion is robust. This will be over very soon."

The memories continued to fade. Kilmer still knew where he was and what the aliens were doing to him, but he could not remember most of the details of his conversation with Archidamus. His time at Station Zero consisted of only snapshots now. His time in DC was starting to disintegrate as well, losing its narrative structure. His memories of Whitman began to fade. His conversations with Nielsen started to feel like a dream—mere impressions. His anxiety was giving way to panic. How far back would this go?

"Stop! This isn't necessary—"

The pain was so sudden and so severe that his body jerked in response. Kilmer stifled a shriek, but only barely.

Resistance wasn't helping. He could hold on to memories slightly longer by fighting, but they still eventually vanished. And the pain was too much to take.

He took a deep breath and tried to clear his mind. *Stop fighting, Kilmer. It's okay. This will be over soon. You can rebuild your memories later. It's too useless and too painful to try to fight this.*

And then they came for Silla.

He could sense it immediately, and his heart raced as he took stock of his most recent memories of her. Had she been with him at Station Zero? Had they said goodbye? They had come on a helicopter and—wait. How had they traveled? Had she come with him at all? Where had he seen her last?

Oh God... not this...

"No!" Kilmer shouted at the top of his lungs as he tried to hold on to the memories. "Please! This has *nothing* to do with—"

The pain that followed was intolerable. Kilmer's scream filled the room and echoed off the walls.

"Ambassador Kilmer. Do not resist. This could be extremely dangerous for you. We are doing our best to keep you safe and to delete as little as possible. But you have to let go of these memories."

Kilmer tried to slow down his breathing, but he was hyperventilating from the pain and anxiety. He could still see her. He could still remember her voice.

...come back to me—no matter what.

He clenched his fists and strained against the straps that were holding him down. The pain surged down his spine as he screamed—but this time, his voice carried more rage than pain.

"Kilmer, this is Archidamus. I beg you to stop resisting. You are turning this into torture, and that is *not* our intention. If you keep this up, it will kill you. I'm your friend, Kilmer. Please trust me when I tell you that we are trying to delete as little as possible. But we cannot stop now. Let this go."

Kilmer tried to find the right words. Words that might convince them. A logic that might compel them to stop what they were doing. But the pain and fear and anger made it difficult to say very much at all.

"Don't… Not her, Archidamus… I don't have enough memories…"

"I'm sorry, Kilmer. But you must stop fighting. No memory is worth risking your life over. You still have work to do. Your people still need you."

Kilmer didn't want to die. He knew he had work to do. But he couldn't stop fighting.

The deletions continued. The resistance continued. The pain continued.

His memory of Silla's face was starting to fade, but he could still hear her voice.

Whatever it is that you want to say to me, you can say it to me after this is over.

Kilmer called out to Archidamus again, but his voice was little more than a whisper.

"Just one memory… That's all… *Please…*"

He could sense only her presence now, and he tried frantically to find another memory that would evoke that same feeling. That same sense of belonging. A sentiment too complex to describe with words.

A memory flashed into his mind. He was in the Treaty Room and she was in his arms. She turned toward him, so he could see her one last time. And for a moment, it was enough to make him forget the pain.

I should have told you when I had the chance. I'm sorry…

She told him to let her go. To come back and start over. To just come back—no matter what.

We have time…

Her image started to drift away. But he didn't let go.

The pain returned with a vengeance, and he could feel the tears streaming from his eyes. Kilmer no longer knew why he was fighting or what he was trying to remember. He knew only that he was about to lose something precious—something he could not replace. He gathered whatever strength he had left and launched a last, desperate effort to salvage his memories of her.

Kilmer felt one final surge of pain—like something detonating inside his head.

He was unconscious before the rest of his body could even react.

Part VI

the historian

Day 57. 2:45 a.m. Apate 3 Conference Room.

Kilmer placed the photographs Silla had just shown him back on the table. Then he closed his eyes, shutting out the scene that surrounded him in Apate 3.

His mind flashed back to when he was 14 years old, pleading his innocence. *I didn't cheat. It's a misunderstanding,* Kilmer tried to explain. He was punished anyway: one week in after-school detention.

Kilmer's teacher had caught him with his sleeves rolled up when he handed in his exam. This was not a punishable offense, of course—unless you had answers to some of the exam questions written on your arm. Looking back, Kilmer couldn't blame anyone for thinking he had cheated. But his arms had been clean when the exam started. He had written the answers on them during the test. He explained to his teacher how he hated to wait a whole week for his grade, so when he was unsure about an answer, he made a note of it on his arm and checked it after class. He wasn't cheating—he was just obsessed with finding out how he had done.

The habit stayed with him for a few more years, though he did it much more carefully after that. His subsequent notes were written in an ever-evolving code for which Kilmer's mind—his unique blend of thoughts and experiences—was the only key.

When Kilmer had told this story to Silla in the Treaty Room, the first night they met, he attributed his quirky childhood habit to a lack of patience. Silla suggested that maybe the real problem was that he was too much of a nerd. They had agreed to disagree.

The doctors at Station Zero had noticed the writing on Kilmer's arms soon after he was picked up from the kill-zone. They had taken the photographs. And when Silla saw them, she knew exactly what Kilmer had done. Why he had done it remained unclear until after they discovered he had no memory of his time on ET-1.

Did Kilmer know he would lose his memory? Had he left those hints for himself? Or did he expect to die, and had left messages for Earth-side to decipher? Had he written in code to keep the aliens from getting suspicious?

Kilmer had written what looked like four separate messages—or one message in four parts. Three of the messages were on his left arm. The fourth message, on the right arm, was harder to read because he had used his left hand to write it. Neither Silla nor Druckman's team of cryptologists could figure out what he had meant to convey with any of it.

Four hints. All undecipherable. Except, *perhaps,* by Kilmer. And he had been in a coma… until now.

He opened his eyes and took another look at the messages he had written.

GermanYin14

HDT/AL46

RWE2NRM4MJW

GALWAY4/3Kingdoms/21

Kilmer could make some sense of them, but what he had pieced together so far wasn't very insightful or actionable. The problem was that too much time had elapsed. The technique had worked when he was young because he would interpret his notes only hours after writing them, when the reason he had chosen a certain word, a particular reference, or a specific acronym was still fresh in his mind. That was not the case here. To make matters worse, he had lost a lot of memories. The Kilmer who had written these notes might not have known how much time would pass before he saw them again, or how much context would be missing.

Damn it.

He took a few deep breaths, and his frustration started to ebb, the words of the homicide detective from Chicago—Gerald-something—came back to mind.

You can't solve mysteries through guesswork. You start with what you know, and continue adding in more of what you know, until there is nothing left of what you know. Only then do you even begin to add logic, reason, and speculation.

Kilmer was ready to try it.

What do I know? I know that I would only write things if they were important—and if I expected to forget them.

Add logic and reason. If I expected to forget these things, I might also worry that I would forget the code I used. So I would adjust for that by making the code easier. I would make it much less ambiguous.

But it doesn't look like I did. This is all too ambiguous.

Or... maybe it isn't.

Add speculation. I would *make it unambiguous—but only after you read the clues properly. The wrong answers might look right. But the right answer would not look wrong.*

Kilmer looked across the table at Art. "I need more time to think about these clues. How soon does the president want to see me?"

"We can fly to DC tonight, and the president can meet you right away. She wants to brief you on recent events herself, and to explain why we're still in danger. Some of that we can't share with you unless you agree to join the team again."

"I'm going to see this through to the end, Art—no matter what. I'm pretty sure that the Kilmer who went through everything you've described to me would be extremely pissed-off if I just walked away now. But I want to wait until morning before we go to DC. I'm exhausted, and I need some time to process everything. To sleep on it, if only for a few hours. Would that be possible?"

"Of course," Art said with a nod. "And thank you, Professor. I will inform the president of your plans."

The meeting came to an end, and as they prepared to leave the conference room, Kilmer asked whether he could speak to Silla in private. She stayed back as Art and Lane exited into the hallway.

She walked over to him. "What is it, Kilmer?"

"It's a few things, actually, but I want to address just one of them right now."

387

He paused to collect his thoughts, and to gather the courage to look her in the eyes as he spoke.

"I know that when I go home tonight, Silla, all of this—everything from the last few hours—is going to weigh on me. It's completely overwhelming, to be honest. And I know that tomorrow, when I get to the White House and see even more people that I'm supposed to know, it will be even worse. I feel lost... and scared, to be perfectly honest. These aren't things I'm used to feeling, but—and here's what I wanted to say... That having you here...it really helps. It makes me feel less alone. And a little less afraid. I know you're someone I can trust. So, thank you for that. For being here. And for your patience. And just... for everything."

Silla stood quietly for a moment, meeting Kilmer's gaze, unsure what to say. She didn't want to say too much, nor regret having said too little.

"You're not alone, Kilmer. Not anymore. Whatever else might have happened in there, you found your way home. I knew you would. I never stopped trusting you either. Maybe some things are not so easy to erase."

They looked at each other a while longer. Silla could feel her heart beating faster. But it was joy, and not anxiety. There was nothing left to feel uncertain about—she knew exactly where things stood. She just hadn't felt this happy in a long time. The aliens had said Kilmer would never return. And when he did come back, the doctors said he might never recover. Now he was standing in front of her. He had no memory of her, but he was still *Kilmer*—in every way. They could talk. They could work together. And they still trusted each other. It was far more than she had allowed herself to hope for during the last many weeks.

She brought the moment to a close. "Okay, Kilmer. Let's get you out of here so you can get some rest. Tomorrow will be a busy day."

And then—before she could think twice about it—she took a step towards him and gave him a light kiss on his cheek. The look of shock on his face almost made her laugh.

"I hope you won't read too much into that," she declared as she stepped back into proper formation. "That was only because you kept your promise and came back. Don't get used to it."

Kilmer was trying not to read into it—but found himself struggling. It felt... *familiar?*

No. *Comforting.* Like a helping hand. Or a light at the end of a tunnel. Or the feeling of coming home to a warm fireplace after being outside on a stormy night.

Maybe some things are not so easy to erase.

"That was sweet of you, Silla. But don't worry—I won't expect anything like that again. I also know I didn't really deserve it. I didn't come back the way you would have wanted—or the way everyone needed me to."

She patted him on the shoulder like a commanding officer consoling a young recruit. "Trust me, Kilmer," she said with only a hint of a smile. "I already took that into account. If you had come back with your memories intact, that would have been an entirely different kind of kiss."

~ 105 ~

It was after four in the morning when Agent Lane drove Kilmer back to his home in Brookline. They discussed all sorts of things along the way, but only one of them rendered Kilmer speechless—and it had nothing to do with aliens.

"I think I should probably apologize to the president when I see her," Kilmer had said. "You know, for going to ET-1 without her permission. What do you think, Agent Lane?"

"It's not for me to say, Professor. But I know that she's very fond of you. I can't imagine she would hold it against you. The way I hear it, she was furious—and felt extremely guilty—about what they did to you in ET-1. She visited you in the hospital every week. Vice President Nielsen visited even more often."

"It's hard to believe I was in a coma for so many weeks. It went by in a blink of an eye."

"Well, then you're the lucky one, Prof."

"Lucky? And how is that?"

"I'm sorry. That was callous. I didn't mean you were *lucky*, exactly. I can't even imagine what you had to endure inside ET-1. I just meant… well, the last few weeks…they went by for you in a flash. You didn't have to see yourself struggling every day. You didn't have to worry about whether you would ever recover." Lane hesitated, but then decided to just say what was on his mind. "It wasn't like that for Ren. It wasn't so easy for her. That's all I meant."

"Oh…" said Kilmer, almost in a whisper. "Did she visit me in the hospital… pretty often?"

Lane glanced over at him. "I guess you could say that. You could also say that she never left your side. As far as I can tell, if she wasn't at work, she was in the hospital with you. Every day, and just about every night. Even after she found out you had no memory of her. She'll never tell you that, of course. But it's only right that you should know."

Kilmer had no words. Even after a minute, he found only a few. "Thank you for telling me, Agent Lane."

When he arrived home, Kilmer found that Triad had restored his electricity. He turned on the TV to find sporadic news and talk-show coverage devoted to the aliens. But whatever President Whitman planned to tell him was apparently classified, because he didn't hear anything that even hinted at an impending attack. He spent the next hour organizing his thoughts about what he had learned in Apate 3 and thinking about the messages he had written on his arm. By the end of it, he felt he'd made at least some progress on the clues.

Only when his head hit the pillow did he stop thinking about aliens and war. Instead, his thoughts found their way to Silla. He could feel the kiss on his cheek. He could see her smile. He could hear her voice. His last thought before he fell asleep was practically juvenile.

I get to see her again tomorrow—how cool is that.

106

Day 57. Afternoon.

Kilmer was wearing a tie when he arrived at the airfield, but Silla suggested he take it off.

"It's a nice tie, Kilmer, but you look like you're trying too hard. Remember, these people already know you. No one expects you to have discovered professional standards while you were in a coma."

Kilmer frowned and looked over at Art, who weighed in with a squint and a nod as if to say, *She's right. Lose the tie.*

At 2:30 p.m., the plane landed at Joint Base Andrews, and an hour later, Kilmer walked into the White House for what felt like the first time. Knowing that it wasn't made the experience even more surreal.

He had noticed the looks. The first was from the officer who greeted them when they exited the plane. He saw the same expression on the faces of their driver, the guard who waved them through, and the agent who opened the door at the West Wing entrance. They all looked at him the same way. As if he were a ghost. Or a celebrity. Or a starving child. Shock. Awe. Pity. All combined into one.

Kilmer wasn't the only one who noticed. Art turned to Silla as they entered the building. "It's like the Beatles are holding a reunion tour and John Lennon just came back from the dead to perform the encore."

"Does everyone know what happened to me?" Kilmer asked.

"Not out in the real world, Professor. But around here? Yeah. Rumors spread. None of these people know what *actually* happened, but they all have some version that gets the sentiment mostly correct."

"And what sentiment is that?"

"That you gave much more than you had been asked to give. Beyond that, there's no limit to the stories one hears. My favorite is the one where you went into the alien spacecraft with guns blazing and brought them to their knees. That's why we have peace on Earth."

"But we're still expecting a war."

"We are. But these people don't know that."

They walked past the offices belonging to National Security Advisor Garcia, Vice President Nielsen, and Chief of Staff Perez. Silla pointed out the office that had belonged to Kilmer; it didn't look at all familiar to him. As they neared the Oval Office, his heart started to beat faster.

Why am I so nervous?

Oh yeah... Going to see the president... who's supposed to be my friend... whom I can't remember at all... and whom I disobeyed.

Silla put her hand on his arm. "It's okay, Kilmer. They're your friends. You're going to be just fine."

He was surprised that she had sensed his anxiety. "Was I this nervous last time?"

"According to President Whitman, yes—but only for a little while. Then it was like you flipped some switch and felt completely at ease."

"She told you that?"

"She did."

"Well, that's encouraging. Did she happen to mention where that switch is located?"

107

Nielsen rushed over to Kilmer the moment he stepped into the Oval Office. Kilmer was just about to say hello when the vice president put him in a bear hug and almost lifted him off the ground.

"Hi... Zack," Kilmer said, struggling to breathe. But he was relieved to see him—Nielsen was the only person at the White House that Kilmer had known before he came to Washington on Day 14.

"It's really great to see you here, Professor. I'm so sorry about what happened."

"It's okay, Zack. Don't apologize. I have no memory of what took place." Kilmer stole a glance at Silla. "It was harder on the rest of you."

As President Whitman walked toward them, Kilmer's mind went blank. He tried to recall how he had planned to start the conversation with her—and couldn't even remember whether he had intended to introduce himself again.

"Madam President... I'm... uh... this is a little awkward, as you might imagine. I'm not sure where to begin. Maybe I should start by apologizing for what I did. I know I went against your orders... when I ran off, and—"

"Please, Professor Kilmer. Allow me to start. Hopefully, it will make this a little easier."

"Yes, ma'am," Kilmer said, very much appreciating her offer to take the lead.

"I know you don't remember meeting me, or any of our conversations, but I hope you'll believe me when I say that we had a close relationship. I can't speak for what was in *your* mind during the time you spent here, but to me you were a trusted adviser. If we were closer in age, I would consider you an old friend. As it happens, your age puts you closer to the age of my children. And when we lost you, I felt like I had lost one of them. Zack will attest to the fact that I'm not one to exaggerate.

"I don't expect any of this to jog your memory, and I don't expect you to suddenly see me as less of a stranger. Our relationship will remain asymmetric for a while—and maybe forever. But I want you to know that nothing you did requires forgiveness. You ended up saving a lot of lives that day; we owe you a debt of gratitude that is not easy to repay. And I'm afraid we're not going to try to repay it. Instead, I'm asking you for the same thing I've asked of everyone else—to give even more. I'm grateful that you've agreed to do so."

Kilmer wasn't sure how to respond. He felt like a specter, floating high above the crowd, playing both audience and actor in the dream-like sequence that was being enacted below and in front of him. He reminded himself that he needed to say something—to play his part—even if he'd never been handed the script.

"You're being very kind, Madam President. Whatever impression I made on you the first time around, I can only hope to match it again. But please don't feel like you owe me anything. I'm sure I knew the risks before I did the things I did. And given what was at stake, anyone else would have done the same thing."

"I'm not so sure about that, Professor. And even if they tried, not just anyone would have been able to pull it off. We expected a war. We were told that Earth was in imminent danger—that we were doomed, no matter what. Thanks to whatever you did in there, we're still around. At least for now."

"Then there's more work still to be done. Just let me know how I can help."

Whitman smiled at Silla. "Well, Agent. He looks like the same guy to me. What do you think?"

Silla didn't miss a beat. "I'm not sure we have much choice in the matter, Madam President. He's the only Professor Kilmer we could find on such short notice. He'll have to do."

As the others laughed, it occurred to Kilmer that Whitman and Silla had a personal relationship. There was a degree of informality between them that he hadn't expected. He wondered why that would be.

They moved to the sitting area, where two carafes and six cups were already on the table. He noticed that Whitman looked at him warmly when she asked everyone to take a seat, and that Silla, who had many options to choose from, chose to sit right next to him.

The meeting was off to a fine start.

~ 108 ~

After a few minutes of banter, Whitman brought the meeting to order. She told Kilmer that decisions would need to be made very soon, and she wanted his thoughts on the situation, however preliminary they might be.

"There's a reason I'm making time for this discussion, Professor. Anyone can give you an update, but I need us to get back to the working relationship we once had, as soon as possible. You have to feel comfortable with me, and I need to know that you'll speak your mind openly and without hesitation—the way you used to."

Kilmer nodded, then poured himself a cup of coffee, feeling uncertain about doing so before it was offered.

"Not bad," Whitman announced as he finished pouring. "It could have been worse. I was wondering how long it would be before Professor Kilmer helped himself to a cup. Looks like we need to knock about five minutes' worth of hesitation out of him. Other than that, he seems to be his old self. The aliens didn't do anything that should be *too* hard to undo—like teach our boy here some proper etiquette."

Kilmer had decidedly mixed feelings about the president of the United States using his lack of decorum as a way to measure the extent of his healing, but he didn't let that get in the way of taking a good long sip of his steaming hot coffee.

Whitman started the briefing by picking up where Art had left off the night before.

"You went into ET-1 on Day 24 and came out two days later. We tried, multiple times, to ask the aliens what had happened, what they did to you, why they sent you back, and what they were planning. They answered none of those questions. All we have are the bits of information and hints as to their intentions that we've gleaned from their subsequent behavior.

"The most notable change in their behavior, after you came out of ET-1, was the sudden absence of threats. We were no longer being told we were doomed, or that our days were numbered, or that we would suffer. It was like that entire chapter had suddenly ended—which is why we think you had something to do with it. We asked them why their tone had changed and what we might expect in the days and years ahead."

Art handed Whitman a document, from which she then started to read.

"Here was their answer:

You are correct to note that some things have changed. There is no additional information that we can provide at this time. You will wait to hear from us as to what happens next.

"We asked how much time they needed—but they wouldn't say. We asked whether the two sides could meet and jointly decide what happened next—but they rejected the offer. All this time, ET-1 was still parked at Station Zero, and the three reserves held their positions in space. Over a week went by in this way.

"We had known from your first night at the hospital, when you regained consciousness for a short while, that your memories had been severely damaged, and possibly wiped clean. Nine days later, on Day 35—which would be May 31—we brought you out of your induced coma just long enough to see if you had recovered your memories. It was clear that you had not. We reached out to the aliens again, demanding an explanation. They responded on Day 36 with the following.

Whatever the fate of Earth, or the future relationship between our two races, we are pleased to hear that D. Kilmer has survived. He served admirably as your ambassador. We wish that he could have avoided all harm. We harbor no ill will toward him. Consistent with our laws and values, nothing was undertaken in relation to Ambassador Kilmer without his approval.

"Their complete disavowal of responsibility for what they did to you was noteworthy—but so was their acknowledgment in this message that there was more than one way our relationship might develop. Day 36 was a day of hope, Professor. We weren't out of the woods yet, but it looked as though we might be moving in that direction. That night, Zack, Perez, Strauss, and I came to visit you in the hospital and raised a glass for what you had accomplished. Agent Silla was there as well, of course.

"On Day 39, the reserve spacecraft retreated to a distance of 600 million miles from Earth—as far away as they were when we first detected them. The following day, we received another message:

> *ET-1 will depart Station Zero today. When we return, we will again land at this location. In the interim period, our good wishes to Planet Earth, and to its humans. Every civilization has a story, and every story must end eventually. May your humanity flourish until that date arrives.*

"We tried to engage them again. I asked them to send a representative to meet with us before they leave, or to suggest some way for us to continue communicating after they depart. Their response was brief:

> *There will be no more communication until we return. It is not known when that will be.*

"By Day 41, we could no longer detect ET-1 or the reserves. For all we knew, they had returned to their home planet. After a few days, it began to look like a new normal, but tremendous anxiety remained. The last few messages weren't as threatening as what they had said prior to your encounter with ET-1, but they still hinted at possible trouble ahead. So, despite the respite, we continued to prepare for what might come. The level of resources—time, money, people, and expertise—devoted to military and defense planning increased tenfold around the time you disappeared. That continued even after the aliens departed. It was like the height of World War II, when, we were spending over forty percent of our GDP on national defense.

"Three days ago, the aliens returned. That would be June 19th—Day 54. Not coincidentally, that is the day we moved you from DC to the hospital in

Cambridge. We needed your help, and we knew we had to bring you out of the coma earlier than the doctors had advised. My apologies, Professor, but we felt we had no choice.

"We had three reasons for bringing you back. First, you might remember something important—which is why we went through the elaborate exercise of trying to test and jog your memory last night. Second, I wanted you back on the team regardless of what you might remember, and the sooner the better. And third, we thought you might be able to make sense of the messages you had scribbled on your arm.

"Day 54 started with the detection of five alien spacecraft, spotted 250 million miles away from Earth. They are smaller than the reserves that visited us earlier, and possibly smaller than ET-1 as well. We worry that the smaller size makes them more suitable for combat operations.

"Early morning on Day 55, the day before yesterday, we received the first new message from the aliens.

> *Leaders of Earth. We will visit your planet soon. Our laws permit us to explore all regions of the universe, and to take whatever action is deemed necessary in pursuit of our legitimate interests. This includes the right to inflict harm, if necessary, on the structures, habitat, and species of the planets we visit. We ask that you not interfere as we exercise these rights, established as they are on just laws that we conscientiously proclaim and faithfully follow. Our advice is for human beings to accept the consequences of our arrival and our actions, and to do so without resistance or belligerence of any kind.*

"Needless to say, this was extremely alarming. We put some contingency plans into action, but there was not much we could do other than wait and see what happened next. We didn't have to wait long. Early yesterday morning, ET-1 returned to Station Zero. We immediately started the process of bringing you out of your coma and sent Agents Silla and Lane to Cambridge."

"Yesterday afternoon, we sent a message asking the aliens what they considered to be their "legitimate interests," and what it was they were planning. We made it clear that we would not sit idly by and allow them to act with impunity, but we did not make any specific threats. We suggested that the two sides discuss matters to avoid unnecessary harm and unintended consequences. We also suggested that *you*, Professor Kilmer, might be willing to speak to Archidamus—remotely, of course—if a continuation of that dialogue would help resolve any remaining problems. My apologies for volunteering you, but we were running out of options.

"We received a response yesterday evening.

> *I am Archidamus. Now is not the time for discussion. When a conversation is deemed useful or necessary, humans will be informed, but we will speak only to the leaders of Earth's nations. Ambassador Kilmer and I have nothing more to discuss—now or in the future. He is no longer relevant to what we do, or to the future of Earth, or to the fate of its human civilization.*

"There have been no more messages since yesterday evening. Our immediate concern, however, is not the lack of productive conversation with ET-1. It's the behavior of their spacecraft. As of this morning, the fleet has moved to within one million miles of Earth. And there are now more than *two hundred* of them. We don't know what they plan to do—or when—but their rhetoric, the size of their fleet, and their refusal to engage diplomatically are all very concerning. Put simply, the situation is about as bad as it's been since you managed to bring us back from the brink last time."

"That's where things stand, Professor. Any questions or observations?"

"Just a few—but may I take another look at the messages you read out to us?"

Whitman handed Kilmer the document, and he skimmed through it.

"Their statements appear to have become more aggressive over the last few weeks," Kilmer reflected. "But none of them are quite as threatening as what we received before I went to ET-1. Is there agreement on that?"

"There is, Professor. But we could still be facing an existential threat."

"I agree. Which gets me to my second point—regarding the two hundred spacecraft. We were terrified when there were only three of them. Two hundred spacecraft should worry us much more. On the other hand, it makes me wonder: why do they need a larger force than last time if their threat is now of a *less* devastating nature?"

"And how would you reconcile that?"

"I can see two possibilities, Madam President—and there might well be more. First, if they need this large of a fleet to carry out a more limited mission, maybe we were more worried than we had reason to be when they brought only three spacecraft. Their spacecraft might be less powerful than we thought. On the other hand, and as you would well know, there isn't always a positive correlation between the size of the force and the damage it can do. If we wanted to annihilate an entire nation, we might just need a few bombers capable of dropping nuclear weapons. But if we wanted to do *less* damage—and we wanted the country to survive our assault or invasion—we would need ground troops, along with hundreds of aircraft that were armed with conventional weapons. Choosing to do less damage can sometimes require more equipment and personnel. If either of these inferences are correct, then there is a silver lining here. I'm not suggesting that the sudden arrival of two hundred spacecraft is good news, especially given their rhetoric, but it might mean they are not quite as powerful as we had assumed, or that they have a narrower agenda than to simply annihilate us from outer space."

Whitman nodded. "Secretary Strauss suggested earlier today that the smaller size of these spacecraft is more consistent with an attack that requires them to get closer to Earth and conduct more targeted operations. We can't be sure, of course, but your conjecture seems consistent with his. This is something we will need to evaluate further. What else do you see, Professor?"

"Just one more thing, if I may. I'm struck by the legalistic tone of the message in which they warn us not to interfere with their plans. It certainly doesn't sound like Archidamus speaking. Could it be some sort of bureaucratic protocol they're following? Maybe it's something they have to announce before they attack?"

"Maybe," Whitman replied. "But when they've warned us in the past, they haven't used language like this."

Kilmer nodded. "And it's not only the tone that's striking. The substance of the message is also very different from what they've conveyed previously. They're asking us not to interfere. They're warning us not to resist or strike back. Why is that suddenly necessary for them to say?"

"It sounds a bit like they're worried we *can* fight back," Nielsen suggested. "Which would be consistent with the notion that they're more vulnerable than we've been led to believe."

"That's true," Kilmer agreed. "But it doesn't quite add up. Why would they admit that? They would have to know—or at least consider—that a message like this will signal vulnerability? They've spent weeks portraying themselves as invincible, so why not just continue to scare the hell out of us? And if they *are* vulnerable, there's even more reason to hide that fact from us."

"Maybe they believe we can inflict *minor* harm, and they don't want to suffer it needlessly," Nielsen proposed. "In which case it's a legitimate warning. They just want to minimize unnecessary losses on both sides. That might align with the idea that they have a narrower agenda than we initially feared."

"Maybe," Kilmer acknowledged mildly. "Maybe that's what it is."

~ 110 ~

Whitman called for a break until 5:30 p.m., at which time Secretary Strauss, General Allen, and Director Druckman would join the meeting. Kilmer would then update the team on his interpretation of the four messages he had scribbled on his arm.

Kilmer was given the keys to his old office, and Silla walked him over. He saw her looking at him expectantly as they entered the room.

"Sorry," he said. "Nothing in here looks familiar either."

She smiled gently. "Just thought I'd check. So, how are you feeling now?"

He thought about it for a moment. "I'm not really sure. But the gravity of the situation certainly takes my mind off the unreality of everything else. So, I'm just trying to stay focused on the problems that need solving."

"And how's that going? Have you been able to make much progress on the four clues?"

"Some—at least when it comes to the first three messages. But I'm completely lost on the fourth. Then again, my handwriting is messy in that one, so maybe we're just reading it wrong."

Silla shrugged. "Ambiguity seems to be a recurring theme when it comes to dealing with the aliens. Nothing is ever quite clear. Why they wanted you to come to ET-1. How you got them to back down. Why they've changed their tone. And of course—the ultimate question."

Kilmer raised an eyebrow. "The ultimate question?"

"Churchill's Key," she explained. "Finding out what really drives them. You used to call it the ultimate question. *The why. We have to understand the why.* You used to say that all the time."

"Sounds like it would have gotten pretty annoying after a while."

"No comment," Silla responded with a smile.

Kilmer narrowed his eyes.

"Come on, Kilmer. I'm just kidding."

The why. We have to understand the why.

"No… it's not that. I just…"

I would make it unambiguous—but only after you read the clues properly.

"It's the first clue, Silla. I think you just helped me figure out what it means."

111

Strauss was the first to walk over to Kilmer when he entered the Oval Office. "I'll be the first to admit it, Professor. I didn't think you had it in you. What you did took serious guts." He paused. "It's good to have you back."

Kilmer didn't know what to say. He was saved from having to respond by General Allen and Director Druckman, both of whom shook his hand and added their own sentiments. As everyone moved to the sitting area, Kilmer was glad the reunion had been quick. Everyone was extremely nice, but he felt awkward throughout, as though he was being hailed a hero for things he had never done. It was like being called on stage to accept an award on behalf of someone who couldn't be there in person.

Once they were seated, everyone was handed a copy of the photographs with the four clues.

GermanYin14

HDT/AL46

RWE2NRM4MJW

GALWAY4/3Kingdoms/21

Whitman turned the meeting over to Kilmer, who warned everyone not to get their hopes up too high. He would interpret the clues as best he could, but he wasn't sure what they added up to. More work was needed.

"In that case," Art interjected, "it would be helpful to my team if you also tell us about the interpretations that you considered, but ultimately rejected. That way we know which leads are more and less worth pursuing."

Kilmer nodded. "I'll try to do that as efficiently as I can. So, let's start with the first clue: *GermanYin14*. That's the one written above the other two on my left arm. '*Germany in 14*' is what it looked like to me. The most obvious explanation was that I was referring to Germany in 1914—at the start of

World War I. Maybe I was saying that the aliens are like Germany in 1914—instigators in a war that others were trying to avoid. But we already knew that the aliens were the aggressors here, so why would I have bothered to leave a clue about that? And why leave that clue in particular?

"Then I thought about what had actually triggered World War I—and the role Germany had played. There's a lot there, but the most promising lead was Germany's attack on Belgium—a neutral country. The Germans invaded Belgium because it allowed them to invade France more effectively, which was their real objective. But this led the British to enter the war, because the Brits were committed to protecting Belgian neutrality, and they were worried that control of Belgium would make it easier for Germany to launch an attack on England itself. I started to wonder whether we are Belgium in this story. Are we just pawns in a game between the aliens and someone else? If so, I'm not sure what we can do about that right now. But it might be worth keeping in mind.

"Then there was the capital *Y* in the message. Maybe I just wrote it in haste. But it *might* be meaningful. Was the message *'Germany in 14'*, or was it *'German Yin 14'*? And what could *that* mean? The *yin* character in Chinese philosophy denotes the negative, or the passive element in duality. Maybe this was not about German *aggression*, but about German *passivity*. Maybe it was about what they failed to do—which was to rein in Austrian belligerence against the Serbs. Their unconditional support for Austria was what had led things to spiral out of control in the first place, forcing Russia, Germany, France, and Britain to all enter the fray. So maybe we should be thinking about what the aliens are *not* doing, but which could lead to further escalation.

"That was all I'd managed to come up with—until just before this meeting, when Agent Silla mentioned how focused I used to be on Churchill's Key. And how often I reminded everyone that *we have to understand the why.* That's when it struck me. The aliens weren't meant to be the Germans in this clue. They are the *British.* The letter *Y* is not a letter at all. It stands for a word: *why.* The clue is meant to be interpreted as *'German Why in 14.'*

"All this time, I had been thinking about what the Germans had done in 1914 from the perspective of the Allies—the story as told by the French,

British, Russians, and Americans, all of whom blamed Germany for the war. But the clue that I wrote down was reminding me to think about the *German* why in 1914. How the Germans explained what had happened. Why *they* thought the conflict had spiraled out of control. Not surprisingly, the Germans did not blame themselves. They blamed the British.

"When the British declared war on Germany, they said it was because Germany had invaded neutral Belgium. But the Germans never considered this to be true. If this were *really* the case, they argued, England could have warned Germany earlier that such an act would lead them to declare war. And the British never did that, despite many opportunities. From the German perspective, the British had not made their intentions clear because *Britain had wanted war all along.* Why? Not because they were out for blood—but because they were afraid. Germany had only unified forty years earlier, but it was already developing and strengthening at an incredible pace. The British knew they would eventually have to confront an even stronger Germany. War was inevitable, the British thought. And so, they decided that it was best to have it sooner rather than later—while Germany had not reached its full potential.

"The invasion of Belgium was just an excuse, the Germans believed. This was a pre-emptive war staged by the British. It could have been avoided—if not for the fact that England was too afraid of an even more advanced and formidable Germany in the future. What the first clue does, I believe, is point us to that "German why" from the year 1914."

He paused.

"That is also, I believe, Churchill's Key."

General Allen reacted first. "You are suggesting that the aliens are attacking us because they fear we might go to war with them in the future—at a point in time when we would be harder to defeat. I have to say, that doesn't seem like it could happen anytime soon."

"Let me say two things about that, General. First, I'm only suggesting that old-Kilmer believed this to be the case. And, if he was confident enough in his assessment to write that down for me to read later, I need to take it seriously. But I understand that others might sustain doubts. Second, I agree—it's not clear to me why the aliens should be in a rush to attack us. It will be centuries, I assume, before we can even go looking for them. I don't have a good answer for you on that. But we also don't know enough about the current situation. For example, one could argue that the British should have attacked Germany even sooner than they did—when Germany was even *less* formidable. But you can't always time these things perfectly. It can be hard to amass the resources, build the support, and manufacture the justifications necessary for war. The opportunity isn't always there, and when it is… that's when you seize it. Maybe something similar is going on here. I don't know."

Silla chimed in. "If the aliens are playing the role that the Germans claim was played by the British, it explains not only why they're intent on harming us, but why they refuse to tell us what we've done to provoke them. If Professor Kilmer is right, the answer is we haven't done *anything* yet. It's the fear of what we might do in the future that's driving them. Fear of our future capabilities could also explain why they seem unwilling to share or reveal *their* technology."

"If true," Nielsen added, "it would shed light on a question that you raised, Professor, the very first night we discussed all of this. *Why now?* Why didn't they come when we were living in caves or when dinosaurs roamed the Earth? *We* might wonder why they don't wait a few more centuries before attacking us, but from another point of view, they have already waited for millions of years. Life on Earth is far more advanced now than would even have been conceivable just a short time ago."

"That's a good point," said Art. "We look pretty weak if we do a *static* analysis of our capabilities compared to theirs. But a *dynamic* analysis might be worrisome. Our rate of growth has been exponential in recent years. Maybe we're gaining on them in ways that they don't like."

"Strauss? What do you think?" Whitman asked.

The defense secretary pondered a moment before answering. "The idea that this is a pre-emptive war is certainly interesting. Do I think an alien race could be motivated by the fear of what humans will do in the future? Yes—it's plausible. Human beings are bastards. You spend enough time thinking about it, and you can almost understand why someone might just want to kill us all."

Whitman sighed. "Thank you, Strauss, for reminding us once again why you were never considered for secretary of state. And I think we should all take a moment to thank our lucky stars that you aren't the one the aliens asked to serve as our ambassador."

There was a round of laughs, with Strauss leading the crowd.

"Which raises a question, Professor" Whitman added. "What could you have possibly said to them to get them to back off?"

"I really don't know. I assume I would have tried to convince them that we weren't likely to be a threat. But that could be a hard case to make—especially if they have a decent understanding of our history. Not to mention, they still look like they're ready to attack. I might have asked them to leave us alone for a few hundred years—what's the rush, as General Allen pointed out. But I can't imagine that would have convinced them either, because they wouldn't need me to point that out to them. They can probably see for themselves that we are a long way off from matching them in capabilities."

"Okay," said Whitman. "Let's move on to the next clue."

Everyone turned to a photograph that zoomed in on the second message Kilmer had scribbled on his left arm.

HDT/AL46

Kilmer offered his analysis. "I think I know what this clue is saying, even if I haven't figured out the implications for us. The first three letters appear to be initials, and they are not hard for me to decipher. The only *HDT* that I would expect to know immediately is Henry David Thoreau. *AL* might be many things, including Alabama, or aluminum, or the Arab League—but it stands to reason that I'm referring to another person—a contemporary of Thoreau's—who did not have a middle name: Abraham Lincoln.

"The *46* could mean a lot of things. It's the number of human chromosomes, as well as the number of books in the Catholic Old Testament. More directly relevant, perhaps, the number 46 just happens to be the secret code that allowed someone to take control of a spaceship in the sci-fi series *Stargate Universe*. Although, if I meant to say that there's a way for us to take control of ET-1, I have absolutely no idea what it is. Maybe Triad can investigate whether they can be hacked, although I assume that has already been tried.

"So, there are a few possibilities, but given the context of those initials, I believe that 46 *probably* refers to 1846, which has significance for Thoreau. It's the year he was inspired to write *Civil Disobedience* after spending a night in jail. But what about Lincoln? As far as I know, the only thing of potential relevance that happened to him in 1846 was his election to Congress—but I didn't remember that until I looked it up this morning, so that probably wasn't what I was thinking when I wrote the clue. As for putting the two of them together—I don't even know whether Thoreau and Lincoln were friends, enemies, or strangers. So I'm not quite sure where that leaves us... I'm still working on it."

Art responded. "This actually narrows things down quite a bit. You have no idea how many different possibilities have been associated with this clue. I will pass this information along to the analysts who are working on it."

"How about the third message?" Whitman asked. "Is that a reference to me at the end of it?"

RWE2NRM4MJW

"I believe it is, Madam President. You're the only *MJW* I know."

"And the rest of it? Our people were completely lost on this one."

"I think I can add a lot of clarity here. What we have are another two sets of initials. *RWE* is Ralph Waldo Emerson and *NRM* is Nelson R. Mandela. The message says:

'*Ralph Waldo Emerson to Nelson Mandela, for Marianne Josephine Whitman.*'

"There is only one thing that connects Emerson and Mandela in my mind. It's the lineage of an *idea* that has evolved and been adapted for two centuries. Let me explain. In 1837, a young Emerson gave an extraordinary speech, entitled 'The American Scholar' at Harvard College. In the audience was an even younger man, a student by the name of Henry David Thoreau. The two became close friends, and Emerson's ideas in *Self-Reliance* shaped Thoreau's ideas in *Civil Disobedience*. A half-century later, an Indian lawyer in South Africa read Thoreau's work, and it influenced his views on political action.

This lawyer, 'Mahatma' Gandhi, as he was later known, credited Thoreau for inspiring some of his ideas on *Satyagraha,* and on passive political resistance against British rule in India. Then, a few decades later, Martin Luther King, Jr., found inspiration in Gandhi, and deployed the tools of nonviolence and civil disobedience in his fight for civil rights in America. MLK in turn inspired Mandela, who embraced non-violence and reconciliation as a remedy to hostility in South Africa.

"From Emerson to Thoreau to Gandhi to MLK to Mandela. One idea, in many forms, passed along from one giant to another. Perhaps the greatest relay race in the history of inspiration."

Whitman steepled her fingers. "That would imply, Professor… or are you in fact *suggesting*… that we *not* fight back? To instead initiate a campaign of passive resistance and civil disobedience in the face of an alien invasion?"

"I'm not sure I would advise doing that knowing what I know now. But I do believe that it could be the message old-Kilmer was sending."

"So why wouldn't you support the idea now?"

"Because things have changed. The behavior of the aliens is different from what it was before I went to ET-1. We have reason to believe that they might be less formidable than we originally feared. As we discussed earlier, if they find it necessary to come close to Earth, in large numbers, to do the kind of damage they are planning, it might even be possible for us to defend ourselves. And if that's true, I don't see how I could advise against that. But old-Kilmer might not have known any of that."

Silla provided an alternative perspective. "It's true that we know things now that you couldn't have known when you wrote that clue, Professor. But let's not forget—you also knew things inside ET-1 that we don't know now. I'm not sure which information is more crucial—what we know now, or what you've forgotten."

"You're right about that, Agent Silla. I'm only saying that, as things stand, I'm not sure we can justify doing nothing."

Strauss leaned forward. "I would like to echo that. I don't see *any* circumstance in which I would advise not fighting back, if doing so effectively were a possibility. For example, if they need to enter our atmosphere to launch an attack, we stand a decent chance of being able to hit them. And if so, I don't see how we can allow them to kill Americans without fighting back."

Druckman agreed. "At the very least, we would want to test their capabilities and resolve. If we fight back, and matters escalate beyond what we can withstand, then we reassess. But we cannot allow them to just do as they please—especially after a war has begun."

Whitman pulled the discussion together. "As I hear it, the first clue gives us a sense for why the aliens might be doing what they're doing: it could be a pre-emptive war. As for the second clue, we don't yet know what Thoreau and Lincoln have to do with the situation, but we're going to keep working on it. The third clue appears to offer advice, but we're beginning to doubt its relevance to the situation as it exists today."

There were nods all around the room.

"So, what about this fourth clue? What does it mean, Professor?"

GALWAY4/3Kingdoms/21

Kilmer shook his head. "Madam President... I'm sorry, but I don't have any idea what this one means."

"None?"

"I'm afraid so. Whether *GALWAY* is a set of initials, an acronym, or some phrase, I just don't know. The numbers could have all sorts of interpretations, but none worth thinking about unless we have some idea what the words mean. The *3 Kingdoms* could refer to a few different things. The British Civil Wars in the 1600s were known as the Wars of the Three Kingdoms, referring to England, Scotland, and Ireland. And China, around two thousand years ago, had three famous kingdoms—the Wei, Shu, and Wu. Even farther back than that, Ancient Egypt had three eras known as the Old Kingdom, the Middle Kingdom, and the New Kingdom. I'm sure there are other candidates as well. But I don't know where I was going with this at all. It's almost embarrassing."

Art offered some help. "Galway is the name of a small city in Ireland. Does that help?"

"I don't think so," Kilmer said. "Is it significant in any way?"

"There's only one thing about it that seems potentially relevant. Do you know what a Claddagh is, Professor?"

"Yes. It's an Irish ring. It has a heart, a crown, and a pair of hands—signifying love, loyalty, and friendship."

"That's right. It's sometimes given to a loved one—offering love, loyalty, and friendship—but it can also signify loyalty and friendship to another entity or power. For example, to a king or a ruler. The Claddagh originated in the city of Galway, in the 1600s. Does that ring any bells?"

Kilmer considered it. "Not to my mind. I suppose there's a potential overlap in dates with the War of the Three Kingdoms. Is there any connection between the two?"

"None that our research has uncovered. We looked at the War of the Three Kingdoms as well."

Kilmer turned to the rest of the group. "Sorry, everyone. I still have absolutely no idea why I wrote that. I'm completely lost."

112

After the meeting, Whitman invited Kilmer to move back into the White House. When he was shown to his room, Kilmer became the only person in history to enjoy a first visit to the Lincoln Bedroom twice in his life.

After one-on-one meetings with Nielsen and Whitman, Kilmer entered the Treaty Room. It was nearly 10 p.m., and this was the last meeting on his schedule. Silla was already there, sitting on the couch. Kilmer took the armchair, and they chatted about aliens and war and history and clues. They had talked for over an hour before they even grazed a topic that might be more personal than professional.

"How does it feel, Kilmer? People telling you about the things you said and did. Or explaining to you what your relationship with them used to be."

Kilmer shrugged. "I'm not sure how to describe it. But I'm starting to accept it. The way you might accept the loss of a loved one. It's not as sad—but it's a lot more complicated. I feel a bit like a phony. And I feel like I let people down. That I let myself down, too—for not having the strength to remember. I wonder what people think about that—do they think that if it were them, they'd be able to remember? And are they right?

"Most of all, I suppose, I'm just trying not to think about it too much. It's one of those things where there isn't a silver lining. When you lose someone, at least you can think about happy memories, even if they make you cry. Here, I just draw a blank—and it's frustrating. You feel guilty, even though everyone tells you that you don't have to apologize. You feel alone, but you don't know why, because in your mind, these are not people you're supposed to know anyway. So you just try to ignore it—but it's not so easy. Especially when everything you've forgotten is still the most important thing that's going on in your life. All day, you're having to face the fact that you can't remember things. It's probably…"

Kilmer stopped talking. It suddenly occurred to him that Silla might have just been making small talk—and he had recited an entire thesis on the topic. "You don't need to hear all of this. I think the short answer is, it's complicated."

"You're right, Kilmer. I don't need to hear any of this. But if you want to talk about it, I want to hear it. That's why I asked. I already figured it was complicated."

"And… this isn't hard for you? I don't mean working together. I mean talking about these other things."

Silla laughed. "No. Hard was when I thought I'd never see you again—or when I thought you might never wake up. This is a walk in the park in comparison."

Kilmer was silent for a moment. "I might be betraying someone's confidence when I say this, Silla, but… I know what you did for me. That you were there. When I was in the coma. That you were always there."

"I see. Well, I think a certain CIA agent will be taking a hit on his performance review for this. We have an entire section on being able to keep a secret, you know."

"Agent Lane said that it was only right that I should know—even if you didn't want me to. I thought it was an interesting choice of words. But I think I agree. I think it *is* right that I should know."

"And why is that?"

"For the same reason you asked me how I felt. Because there's only so much pain a person should have to bear alone."

"I can handle pain, Kilmer. And the reason I didn't want you to know is because I thought it would only make you feel awkward—or guilty. Or maybe something else, but certainly not anything good."

"You only think that because you don't know how it feels, Silla. You don't know how it might feel to find out, suddenly, that heaven spared one of its angels just for you, to look over you, while you were at death's door." He paused. "So, yeah—it's complicated. It's awkward. There's guilt. All of that. But it's also the first time in decades that I've had reason to feel like maybe I was blessed."

Silla didn't answer. He could see that she was biting her lip. In the dim light of the room, and with the moonlight floating in through the window behind her, she looked every bit the angel he had just described.

"You're wrong about that, Kilmer. I know exactly how it feels. Because when *everyone* was at death's door—when the world looked like it was about to end—you ran off to stop it from happening. Do you want to know what your last words to me were?"

Kilmer nodded, but only barely.

"You said, *I'll keep my promises, Silla. No matter what happens.*" Silla paused, visibly reining in her emotions. "I'm no angel, Kilmer. Hell, I work at the CIA. You know the kinds of things we do. But what you did—I had never been so hurt in my entire life." Silla paused again. "Nor had I ever felt so lucky to have known someone."

Silla took a deep breath. "So, yeah. It's a little complicated."

Kilmer managed a smile. "It is. But you know what's *not* so complicated?"

"What's that?"

"That I'm here now. And that means all the days that came before today somehow conspired to allow me to be sitting right next to the person I most want to spend time with at this moment. I feel pretty lucky."

"I feel lucky, too, Kilmer. Although... *technically*, you're not sitting right next to me."

Kilmer tried to play it cool, but he couldn't stop himself from grinning—like he was in middle school, and the smartest and prettiest girl in class had just asked him to sit next to her on the bus.

He rose from the armchair and sat beside Silla on the couch.

"Don't worry," He said. "I won't read too much into the invitation to sit next to you."

"I'm glad—because I didn't actually invite you to."

Kilmer realized she was right about that.

"You used to be a lot better at not making dangerous assumptions, Kilmer."

"Well, in my defense, I did take a blow to the head recently. Do you want me to go back to my chair?"

Silla sighed in faux exasperation. "You're already here, so you might as well stay. And after all, how often does someone get the chance to sit next to their angel? It wouldn't be right to take that opportunity away."

"Good point. I don't think I've ever had such an opportunity."

She turned toward him and moved just a bit closer. Then she locked eyes with him and whispered.

"I was talking about me, Kilmer. *I'm* the one who finally gets to sit next to my angel."

~ 113 ~

They talked for four hours. Only in the last hour did their hands even touch. They spent the next few minutes pretending to be unaware of how their fingers had become intertwined. When they said goodbye at 2 a.m., they did so with barely a hug—but still holding each other's hand.

Kilmer set his alarm for eight o' clock, but it was a phone call that woke him up. It was Nielsen.

"Sorry to wake you, Professor. But there have been some big developments, and we're meeting in the Situation Room at seven—that's in thirty minutes. Can you please join us? Joana will show you to the room."

When Kilmer entered the Situation Room, most of the attendees were already seated. He already knew Whitman, Nielsen, Strauss, Allen, Druckman, and Silla. National Security Advisor Garcia and Chief of Staff Perez introduced themselves to him, but there was no time for anything other than *hello* and *good to have you back*. The atmosphere in the room was tense.

The half dozen or so people calling in from other locations included the chiefs of the Army, Navy, and Air Force, as well as the chief scientist at NASA, Dr. Menon.

Secretary Strauss began the briefing.

"Three hours ago, at thirteen different locations around the globe, squadrons of alien spacecraft entered Earth's atmosphere. There were eight spacecraft in each contingent, hovering approximately 40,000 feet above the ground. There is a squadron stationed close to, but not directly above, each of the following cities: New York, Moscow, Shanghai, London, Paris, Berlin, Toronto, Mumbai, Jerusalem, Tehran, Riyadh, Baghdad, and Caracas. What do the countries involved have in common? Every one of them is among the strongest militarily powers on the globe, or one of the largest oil-producing countries, or both. These spacecraft—104 in total, as of our count—look identical to one another. Each vessel is about sixty yards across. They are smaller and of a different design than ET-1.

"The spacecraft started to approach Earth's atmosphere approximately four hours ago. I was alerted of their movement immediately, and within ten minutes of that, many of you in this meeting were also informed. President Whitman and I quickly spoke to the leaders of most of the countries on this list, and we obtained their assurance that they would avoid taking any action that might be considered provocative. Correct me if you heard it differently, Madam President, but I thought everyone agreed—although a few of them made a point of saying that they would not commit to inaction if attacked. We did not push that point, because we ourselves are in the same situation. Still, everyone agreed that we should try to coordinate on Earth-side strategy and actions."

"That is a good summary of our calls, Secretary Strauss. Please continue."

"Yes, Madam President. Just over two hours ago, six squadrons initiated a further descent. Spacecraft over New York, Moscow, Shanghai, Jerusalem, Tehran, and Riyadh were suddenly hovering only 10,000 feet overhead.

"Ninety minutes ago, we sent a message to ET-1, asking them to explain their intent. We've received no response.

"Around 6:15 a.m. Eastern time, less than an hour ago, the Iranians sent a helicopter to get a closer look at the squadron located twenty miles east of Tehran. The helicopter flew to within five hundred yards of the alien spacecraft. It took photographs, while the soldiers on board held up welcome signs written in English and Persian. After a few minutes, we are told, the helicopter turned around and started to fly back to Tehran. Moments later, it was shot out of the sky, killing all the soldiers on board. We cannot independently verify what happened.

"Ten minutes later, the squadron near Riyadh made its way south and east toward the Al-Ahsa governate in Saudi Arabia, which is home to Ghawar, the largest oil field in the world. Ghawar accounts for over a quarter of Saudi Arabia's total oil production, but that number will have to be revised downwards now. Eyewitness and satellite accounts confirm that at 6:38 a.m. Eastern Time, an explosion destroyed five square miles of Ghawar. This is still only a small portion of the total oil field, but the attack appears to have targeted the main buildings and critical infrastructure. They're shut down, and the damage is likely to be in the billions. We don't know much more, but the Saudis are keen to keep us in the loop. They're scared out of their minds, quite frankly.

"No other attacks have been reported, but more squadrons appear to be on the move. The Russians tell us that some spacecraft have moved from Moscow to Saint Petersburg, and at least one is hovering less than 3,000 feet above the General Staff Building, which houses the headquarters of the Western Military District of the Russian Armed Forces. The Chinese have mentioned that some of the spacecraft from Beijing have moved to locations that might allow the aliens to target 'key assets' of the Central Theater Command of the PLA. They are not being terribly specific about exactly which assets or capabilities are threatened. We worry, of course, about nuclear weapons in this case. There is some movement in Europe and Israel, but the squadrons near New York, Toronto, and Mumbai seem to be stationary.

"As I understand it, all the alien spacecraft that are in the Earth's atmosphere are now less than 10,000 feet above the ground. But this could already be old news. General Allen, do you have anything you'd like to add?"

General Allen leaned forward with a pained look on his face. "We just got word of two more attacks, Madam President. Both were within the last ten minutes. The first was an attack on an oil field in Venezuela. The second involves some sort of explosion near Saint Petersburg. It's not the General Staff Building, but it *is* a military installation. The Russians are angry and anxious—but they're holding fire for now."

Whitman took to her feet. "So, what the hell is going on here? The Saudis aren't going to fight back—they're going to ask us for help and then go along with whatever we say. The Iranians might have the capability to shoot something down—and you know they want to fight back—but they won't dare either. Not with something this big they won't—they're going to look to Russia or China or us to make the call. Venezuela has no capability to do anything. The Russians will fight back if things escalate, but they can endure this level of pain easier than just about anyone. So, I repeat. What the hell is going on here? What are the aliens up to? What's the pattern? These are just pinpricks. They could do a lot more damage. Why aren't they doing it? And why haven't they come after *us*? What do they have to gain from a handful of such attacks against those who won't retaliate? Oil prices will be through the roof on Monday, but I doubt that's their objective."

The next twenty minutes of discussion were a mess. No theory seemed to explain the pattern, plus the magnitude of the attacks, plus the choice of targets. But everyone agreed on three things. First, the attacks were still small enough that Earth-side could choose not to retaliate. Second, while the attacks were economically costly—and terrifying—relatively few lives had been lost, and it was unclear what the aliens stood to gain from destroying a few energy and military installations. Third, the aliens had not attacked any of the countries that would be most likely to feel public pressure to retaliate. What did it all add up to? No one could say.

"Maybe they're just testing the waters," NSA Garcia suggested. "Starting out with smaller attacks to see if we comply with their demand not to retaliate."

"To what end?" Strauss asked. "Just because we didn't respond to small attacks doesn't mean that we won't fight back if they escalate and start killing millions."

"Then why not *start* with larger attacks?" Whitman asked.

After a protracted silence, Nielsen asked Kilmer to weigh in.

"I haven't reached any sort of conclusion, but I can tell you how I'm starting to think about it. The president has asked why the attacks have not been larger. What if we disaggregate that question into three separate questions: *can* they attack us, do they *want* to attack us, and are they *afraid* to attack us.

"Is it possible that they *can't* launch more aggressive attacks? That seems hard to believe. Based on the lunar attack, we know they can do more damage. So, do they not *want* to do more damage? I have no idea, but if *either* of these is the explanation, that they either can't or don't want to launch bigger attacks, that's great news. We can probably survive this.

"On the other hand, if they both can *and* want to do more damage, then we have to consider the possibility that they're *afraid* of how we might retaliate. That would also be good news. But there's a problem with this explanation. It doesn't explain why they would bother to attack at all then. If you're too afraid to do what you *really* want to do—to initiate a major military campaign, let's say—then what purpose does it serve to do so little?

"So, let's put that together. Any of those *could* explain their behavior— they can't, or don't want to, or are afraid to attack more aggressively. And we can expect to survive all those possibilities. None of those are the nightmare scenario."

"What *is* the nightmare scenario?" Whitman asked bluntly.

"That someone *can* hurt you. And *wants* to. And is not afraid to do it. And the only thing holding them back is *something else* that you still haven't figured out. That's the scenario that we need to be focused on. The other scenarios will more or less work themselves out. We need to figure out what *else*, if anything, might be holding them back—because there may come a time when that factor, whatever it is, is no longer there to stop them."

Whitman turned to Nielsen. "What do you think, Zack?"

"That helps clarify things," Nielsen responded. "Unfortunately, I think we *are* in the nightmare scenario. They're certainly capable of doing more damage. And I believe they're willing to hurt us—although I hope I'm wrong about just how far they're willing to go. I also don't see any reason for them to be afraid of our current capabilities—although we could probably do some damage to the alien spacecraft in our atmosphere.

"Let's remember, it's only been a few hours. They might only be warming up. Maybe they want to see how effective our defenses are before they go full force. I do agree that if something else is holding them back, we need to figure it out ASAP. But I would say it's too soon to even conclude that they *are* holding back."

"So how do we find out what's really going on?"

"Well," said Kilmer, "If you need more information to figure out what someone is up to, you can simply wait for them to *act*, you can force them to *react*, or you can *communicate*. Waiting for them to act is costly in this case; it means waiting for more attacks, more lives lost, and more damage. The second option is to test them—we retaliate, or nudge them in some way, to trigger a reaction—and see what we can learn from their response. Third, we can try to talk to them again and figure out what is going on and why."

"Waiting costs lives. Testing them risks escalation. And communication we've already tried," Perez noted.

"I agree," Kilmer admitted. "There are no good options. But I think there *is* a good place to start. I say we try to communicate again—but we do it differently. I think the next message should go from me to Archidamus."

Perez looked puzzled. "Archidamus made it clear that you have no role to play in what happens next. And I believe his message said, quite specifically, that he will have nothing more to do with you."

"The main reason is that he and I had a relationship once, however modest it may have been. And they seemed pleased, at least in the earlier message, that I had survived what they did to me. Maybe once they hear from me, they'll reconsider and decide to give it a chance. No downside, right?" Then Kilmer smiled. "As to Archidamus saying that he'll have nothing to do with me anymore... well, the tone of that struck me as a bit strange, to be honest. Maybe I did something that really pissed him off while I was in ET-1. But 'the lady doth protest too much, methinks'."

114

At 8:30 a.m., a message was sent to ET-1.

Archidamus… This is Kilmer. You once demanded that we speak, and I obliged. You insisted that I sacrifice everything, and I agreed. Now I ask a favor of you. Before more damage is done, let's discuss matters one more time. War is never the answer if you are asking the right questions. I hope we can try to do that again. To ask the right questions before we rush to answer them with violence.

At 9:00, Kilmer joined Secretary Strauss, General Allen, Director Druckman, NSA Garcia, VP Nielsen, and President Whitman in the Oval Office. There were three topics on the agenda: military preparedness, strategic options, and coordination with the allies.

General Allen led the first discussion. "Let me start with the good news. From everything we've seen so far—how fast their spacecraft move, the way they maneuver, and their infrared signature—we think we can hit them from the ground and from the air. We don't know exactly what they're made of, but we think we can probably do some serious damage. The bad news comes in two varieties. First, we don't know how fast they can move if they're under attack. Second, we don't know what kind of defensive capabilities they can deploy.

"The fact that they're flying so close to the ground when they carry out their attacks gives us some hope. If they need to do that to be effective, then our surface-to-air missiles can possibly take them out. They could be flying more than ten miles overhead and we could still hit them, but the farther they are the harder it is. If they launch themselves out into space, they're out of range for our SAMs and conventional aircraft. For that, we will need to rely on the work we've been doing with our anti-satellite weapons. The ASATs can get into space and hit targets many hundreds of miles above the Earth's surface. But they're not quite field-tested. And we don't know what we're up against out there. We have options, but we can't bet the farm on them."

After thirty minutes of discussion on the topic, Secretary Strauss outlined the strategic options.

"The questions we've been struggling with for weeks remain the same. Whether and when to engage? How aggressively? To respond proportionally or to hit back harder? How to project strength while conveying a willingness to negotiate? What is the exit strategy? How much damage are we able to sustain? Under what conditions do we surrender? What are our red lines?

"The situation at hand brings into sharper focus two of these: under what conditions do we fight back, and how aggressively? I believe, as I said yesterday, that we cannot allow them to act with impunity. If there is an attack on American soil, and if it is possible to fight back, then some response is necessary."

"By that logic," Nielsen said, "would you be comfortable with the Iranians or the Russians launching an attack right now? They've been hit—but we've advised them to be patient."

"I understand that," Strauss replied. "But I believe the United States is different. Not because American lives are more important than Iranian lives, or because we are exempt from behaving responsibly. It's the opposite, in fact—we shoulder a *greater* responsibility. If America fails to respond, it sends a signal. We don't rule the world, but we are first among equals. The aliens have done their homework, and they know that. They will weigh our actions much more heavily than those of other nations. We have a responsibility not to show weakness."

"It's like the difference between someone killing one of our soldiers and assassinating our president," Druckman offered. "We don't say one life is more important than another, but we make it clear that if you cross *that* line— if you come after our leaders—there will be a whole different level of hell to pay. I believe Strauss is just pointing out that the US is the leader here, and the aliens should know we will respond differently. And I agree."

"What is the threshold then?" Nielsen asked. "I don't imagine we go to war if they blow up a cabin in the woods. What's the line?"

"That's what we have to decide," said Strauss. "No, I will not go to war over one cabin. But a military installation? A small town? Yes—I would respond, hoping that it would get them to stop."

"The problem arises," said Kilmer, "when one side has a red line, but the other side doesn't know what it is. If we decide to draw the line at a small town, but they don't think we would retaliate unless a large city is attacked, they might inadvertently cross our line. And then we have to attack. And then they might need to respond to our attack to maintain *their* credibility. And then we are on the path to serious escalation. We might need to make sure that they understand our red lines, so that these might act as deterrents."

Whitman followed up. "So you would let the aliens know—announce it to them, even if they won't talk to us—that if they do X, Y, or Z, we will retaliate. Is that what you're proposing?"

"That is what I was suggesting, but it's not so simple. If you don't communicate your red lines, the other side might cross them by mistake. But there's also a risk in telling people what your red lines are. If we tell them we will go to war if they do X, Y, or Z, we have also told them, implicitly, that we will *not* go to war if they do something short of that. The challenge is how to let the other side know which lines they will be punished for crossing, without giving them the license to cross all sorts of other lines. It's not easy to do.

"This is perhaps why Chamberlain waited so long to give Hitler an ultimatum. If he had said that invading Poland was the red line any earlier, it would have made it even easier for Hitler to attack Czechoslovakia, knowing there would be no consequences."

"So, yes, there is a tradeoff. But what about in this case? What would you propose, Professor?" Whitman pushed.

"If our true red line is actually very aggressive, as Secretary Strauss suggests it should be, then we need to be transparent about it with the aliens; otherwise, there is a good chance they well stumble over the line unintentionally. But if we are unwilling to fight unless the aliens do *really* terrible things, then we want to avoid being transparent, because revealing our red line will allow them to do even more damage, with impunity, than they're doing now. Whether we reveal our red lines depends on how far they are from crossing them. We can't make that call until you decide what your line is, Madam President."

After fifteen more minutes of debating what the red line should be, there was nothing close to consensus. Strauss and Druckman favored a more aggressive threshold. General Allen and NSA Garcia saw it differently.

"We have to consider the full range of what's possible here," Allen advised. "We're saying that an attack on a military installation or small town is a big deal, but that's only because the aliens haven't done anything even *more* aggressive yet. I shouldn't have to remind anyone that, not long ago, we thought they would kill us all. *That* is the full range of what is possible. Will we risk an escalation that could result in complete annihilation just because they killed ten thousand people? Or because they blew up a base? I think that's madness."

"That's a fair point, General," Druckman conceded. "But what do you think happens after we *don't* retaliate? Do you think they stop with one town? Do they stop at ten thousand deaths?"

General Allen shook his head. "I don't know what happens after ten thousand deaths. Or after fifty thousand deaths. Maybe what happens is more deaths. But I would want to *see* what happens next. If they continue to escalate regardless of our restraint—or *because* of it, which is your worry—then we can always retaliate later in the engagement."

Just after 10 a.m., Kilmer's phone buzzed. He had asked Silla to message him if there was a response from ET-1, or if there was another attack. He assumed other phones would also be buzzing if there was any such news, and he didn't see anyone else react. He took out his phone and saw that it wasn't a text message at all—just an email. He was about to put the phone away, but then decided to allow himself a moment of distraction. He opened the email and started to read.

Then he read it again.

And suddenly, it clicked.

Whitman was in the middle of making a point, but Kilmer didn't bother to wait.

"I'm sorry, everyone. I don't mean to interrupt. Or, rather, I do mean to interrupt."

Everyone turned to look at him.

"I just got an email," he said. "It was sent to my university account. And I'm pretty sure it's from Archidamus."

115

Agents Capella and Silla were asked to join the meeting, and Kilmer showed everyone the message. There was no greeting or salutation of any kind. It said only the following.

> *A letter from you calls up recollections very dear to my mind. It carries me back to the times when, beset with difficulties and dangers, we were fellow laborers in the same cause, struggling for what is most valuable.*

"What the hell does that mean?" Strauss asked. "And what makes you think Archidamus wrote it?"

"Actually, Mr. Secretary, Archidamus *didn't* write it," said Kilmer. "Thomas Jefferson wrote it. What I mean to say is, Archidamus sent me this email, but he was quoting something Jefferson wrote over two hundred years ago. These words are from a letter he wrote to John Adams in 1812. Adams and Jefferson were close friends, but over time, as you probably know, they became fierce political rivals. When Jefferson defeated Adams for the presidency in 1800, their friendship seemed lost forever. They had no more correspondence for a dozen years. But then, in 1812, after both had retired from public life, Adams sent Jefferson a letter. That one act revived their friendship, and they exchanged over 150 letters in the fourteen years that followed. Those letters are a treasure trove for historians. The words in this email are from Jefferson's response to the first letter that Adams sent to him. It was Jefferson hinting that he, too, was ready to rekindle their lost friendship."

"And you recognized this as a quote from one of Jefferson's letters?" Nielsen asked.

"The words looked familiar, but I don't think I would have figured it out if not for the none-too-subtle hint: the sender's email address. It says *ThomJ1812@gmail.com*."

"What makes you think it's Archidamus?" Whitman asked.

"I can't be sure, of course. But what are the odds that I would receive an email like this, with these sentiments, within two hours of asking Archidamus to restart our correspondence?"

"Fair point," Nielsen agreed. "Still, why the subterfuge? Why not use our messaging system? And why not sign it?"

"The obvious explanation is that he's unwilling or unable to communicate openly. That might also be why he made it such a point to denounce our relationship earlier. Maybe I'm a *persona non grata* in his world. Or maybe the aliens aren't allowing anyone to communicate with Earth-side anymore. Or, maybe, he has a different agenda than those around him. He hinted during my conversation with him in Touchdown-1 that not everyone on their side was on the same page."

"So Archidamus is opening up a back channel with you," Strauss said. "To what end, do you suppose?"

"Maybe he wants to help. Maybe he's against the war. Maybe he didn't like what they did to me. Maybe it's something else. But I don't see any reason not to pursue this."

"I agree," said Whitman quickly. "We need to respond. Let's try to find out if it's really him. Let's cultivate the relationship. And let's learn as much as we can."

Kilmer crafted a response and—with everyone's approval—sent it via his email.

If this is who I believe it to be, I am delighted to renew our correspondence. Do you still consider us fellow laborers in the same cause? Do you consider it a lost cause, as you once did? Are you able to help?

The response came within a few minutes.

It is not yet time for you to give a Funeral Oration, friend. And I am willing to help—as I always have been. But I can do very little. I can only tell you what you already know.

Kilmer smiled. "It's him. And he's very good at this. He's answering two questions in one—identifying himself and letting us know there's still hope.

Funeral Oration refers to the famous speech that Pericles—leader of the Athenians and friend of Archidamus—gave at the end of the first year of the Peloponnesian War. It commemorated the dead, extolled the greatness of Athens, and inspired the survivors to fight on for their righteous cause. The Gettysburg Address is similar, in both content and structure, and Lincoln probably took inspiration from Pericles."

"What about the last line?" Art asked. "How does it help us if he can only tell you what you already know?"

"I'm wondering the same thing."

Kilmer sent a reply—again, with the president's approval.

Your help is appreciated, but my memory does not serve me too well these days. I think you expect me to remember more than I do. I don't quite understand what is happening or what to do about it.

The response came soon after.

You know enough. Potsdam is upon us. Tehran you know. Only Yalta is lost. But you have the means to decipher the three Ptolemaic decrees you issued there.

Kilmer sat looking at the message—utterly speechless. The others around him started to ask questions, but he ignored them. Instead, as if in a trance, he typed out another short message and sent it.

Four. Not three.

The noise around him stopped, as everyone turned to look at the screen. The response came back in seconds.

Only three. You did not issue a fourth.

"Please explain, Professor," Whitman said.

Kilmer leaned back in his chair. He decided to start with what was easiest to understand. "Archidamus and I must have spoken while I was in ET-1. He must have been there, or he was involved in some other way. The reference to those cities is clear. During World War II, the allies—the US, UK, and

Russia—met three times to discuss strategy and coordination. Once in Tehran, then in Yalta, and finally in Potsdam. The Tehran meeting refers to my first conversation with Archidamus—which was held remotely, and for which we have transcripts. Potsdam is the *third* meeting—that is what we are having right now. Yalta was the second—the one for which I have no memory. It must refer to what happened in ET-1."

"And the Ptolemaic decrees? Is that some reference to what the allies agreed to at Yalta?"

"No. It refers to something else entirely—the Rosetta Stone. It was found during Napoleon's campaigns in Egypt, sometime around 1800. Inscribed on the tablet were decrees issued two thousand years earlier, during the Ptolemaic dynasty in Ancient Egypt. The decrees were written not only in Greek, but also in two forms of Egyptian writing. The stone tablet allowed scholars to finally decipher hieroglyphics, which were mostly untranslated until then.

"I believe Archidamus is referring to the messages on my arm—those are the decrees. Those are the hieroglyphics. And he's right—only I'm supposed to have the key to deciphering them."

Silla spoke for everyone who had suddenly understood the implication. "He *knows* that you wrote those things?"

"Apparently... yes."

"And what's the debate regarding three versus four? Do you think he missed the one on your other arm?"

Kilmer shook his head. "No. I don't think that's it at all. I think he's right. I only issued three decrees, not four." Kilmer paused, feeling oddly vulnerable. "I don't think I wrote the fourth message. I think Archidamus did."

The silence that followed was palpable.

It was Kilmer who finally broke it. "That explains the handwriting. It was unrecognizable, but not because I wrote it with my left hand. It's because I didn't write it at all. That also explains why I can't make any sense of it."

Without waiting for approval, Kilmer sent another email.

Will you help me with the fourth?

Yes. But now is not the time. It is not important at this moment.

Can you say anything about the other three? I'm struggling with at least one—and it might be the key.

Certain risks even I cannot take, came the reply. *And I cannot say more right now. I will try to write again. In the meantime, I'm afraid the crossing of rivers is likely to continue.*

Everyone watched Kilmer, awaiting his interpretation. He looked back at them with an expression that suggested he was hoping one of them had an answer.

"Well, one thing is clear," said Director Druckman. "This Archidamus, if that is indeed who it is, is going out on a limb by doing things that are incriminating. He's trying not to write anything that might be *too* damning. If we found that one of our people had initiated a conversation like this with a Russian counterpart, we would know immediately that we were dealing with a spy. But could we prove that our agent had shared state secrets? That would be harder. We would be able to prove that laws had been broken, but it would be difficult to pin the highest of crimes on a traitor who engaged in a dialogue like this one."

"Of course, if a Russian or Chinese or Iranian agent did this for *us*, we would consider them heroes," Art mused.

"That's right, Art. Because we're the good guys," Druckman reminded him.

Art shrugged. "Maybe we should just agree that anyone who's trying to prevent a war is a good guy."

Whitman jumped in. "Let's get back to the message. The *crossing of rivers*—is that a way of saying that the aliens will continue to attack? Does it have some other meaning?"

Kilmer wasn't sure. Nor was anyone else. The discussion continued for another few minutes, but without much progress.

And then, just before 11:30, all the phones in the room started to buzz.

Heirs of Herodotus by D. Kilmer.
Excerpt from Chapter 12.

Every so often, history reveals that it has a flair for the dramatic. Or, perhaps, those are just the moments we remember. Mindful of that potential for bias, the historian is warned not to read too deeply into such episodes—or to look too closely into them for meaning. But none of this prohibits the student of history—or even a scholar—from marveling at the poetry of it all, or from finding in it some inspiration and joy.

The two Founding Fathers who outlived most others—Thomas Jefferson and John Adams—were both giants during the Revolution and icons of the decades that followed. They rekindled their lost friendship in 1812, and then sustained a storied correspondence until they died 14 years later. Adams was 90. Jefferson was 83. Remarkably, they both died on the same day. Even more remarkably, it was the 50th anniversary of the birth of their nation.

On Independence Day, July 4, 1826, when Adams lay dying in his home, he did not know that his friend had died earlier that same morning. Adams's last words were an homage to his friend—the person he hoped might carry on the remarkable legacy of the Founding Fathers a little while longer.

The final words he spoke offered a simple, yet eloquent tribute...

"Jefferson survives."

At 11:30 a.m., the team learned about two additional attacks. One was on a military installation of the Central Theater Command, located in China's Hebei province. The other was on an oil refinery in eastern Canada. Both the Chinese and Canadians had resisted retaliation.

At 2:00 p.m., there was an attack in India, at an air force facility of the Western Air Command, in the city of Chandigarh. The Indians did not retaliate.

At 3:00, the death toll, across all attacks over the two days, was estimated to be between 12,000 and 18,000.

At 5:00, Whitman gave her daily address to the nation, but this time with members of both political parties at her side. She announced bipartisan support for her administration's effort to forge a national and international strategy for addressing the crisis. She warned that attacks on the United States were possible and asked her fellow Americans to remain strong—and calm—even as they prepared for things to get worse before they got better. Whitman alluded to the idea that strategic patience might be a necessary component of Earth-side strategy, at least early on, but that neither the Americans nor their "brothers and sisters around the globe" would allow the aliens to act with impunity.

The speech went about as well as could be expected—which was not an especially high bar.

A nationwide curfew was considered, but Whitman decided against issuing one. The aliens had not yet targeted major cities, and it was far from obvious that people would be safer indoors in any case. In the attacks on military bases, even those soldiers who had been in basements had perished. Instead, the governors of all fifty states, in coordination with the National Guard, the Army, and the Department of Homeland Security, readied their emergency evacuation plans. The presumption was that *run* would be more effective than *hide* if the bombings spread to large population centers in the US, and that the de-densification of cities might become necessary.

Some restrictions, however, did go into effect. Drones and private aircraft were prohibited from flying within three miles of alien spacecraft. A plan to ration gasoline was implemented. Launching a projectile or aiming a laser at an alien spacecraft became a criminal offense.

Out on the street, people were terrified. There were mass demonstrations in most major cities, and riots in many, causing four US states and three dozen cities to issue curfews of their own. Protesters were demanding everything from greater transparency, to a declaration of war against the aliens, to federally mandated national prayer. Panic-buying and the hoarding of food and other essentials, which had started on Day 16 but had since declined, was now returning to peak levels.

From the start, Whitman's administration had worked closely with state and local governments, as well as the private sector, to prepare for the situation that now prevailed. For the time being, at least, the defense industrial base, as well as the broader supply chain, appeared secure. Whether these would hold up once the country was in a state of war remained unknown, but it was considered highly unlikely.

Gun purchases were at record highs, as was activity on social media and attendance in houses of worship. Airlines were still operating, but demand was at record lows; with an alien invasion on the horizon, both business and leisure had started to seem like irrelevant constructs. The market had been trading only intermittently since Day 16, the day of its first big crash; after a much bigger crash on Day 58, a three-week halt on trading was announced for all public securities.

At 6:00 p.m., Whitman had a conference call with the leaders of the twelve other countries that had been directly targeted by the alien presence. UN Secretary-General Nkosi, the president of the European Council, the secretary-general of NATO, the president of the World Bank, the United Nations high commissioner for refugees, and the director-general of the International Atomic Energy Agency were also on the call. The call lasted two hours, during which time there were additional attacks in France, Germany, and Israel, adding over 7,000 fatalities.

The recurring themes during the phone call were confusion, fear, and anger. But there were four things that everyone agreed to—eventually. First, no one would launch an attack against the aliens without first informing the others. Second, there would be no use of nuclear weapons unless there was something close to a consensus among the nuclear powers regarding their use. Third, all countries would devote more resources to gathering intelligence on the alien squadrons. Finally, if humanity survived, there would be a global effort to help rebuild the countries that were hit hardest in the war.

At 10:00, Kilmer and Silla met in the Treaty Room.

They sat across from each other, neither of them wanting to appear presumptive by trying to pick up where they had left off the night before. The conversation eventually shifted back to the four clues, and whether there was anything in them that might lead to a path out of this desperate situation. By now, most of the team had the four messages committed to memory.

German Yin 14

HDT/AL46

RWE2NRM4MJW

GALWAY4/3Kingdoms/21

"I'm comfortable with my interpretation of the first clue," Kilmer explained. "It tells us why the aliens are here in the first place—they're looking to wage a pre-emptive war. And the third clue is clearly my way of saying we should adopt some form of passive resistance—though I don't currently think that's a good idea. The fourth clue is a mystery—understandably—since I didn't even write that one. That leaves only the second clue, about Thoreau and Lincoln, which I'm still struggling to decipher. As for my conversation with Archidamus… well, it's good to know that he's trying to help. But I don't know what to make of his final message. About the *crossing of rivers.*" I suppose that's now the fifth clue in all of this.

Just then there was a knock at the door. It was President Whitman.

"I saw the light on. Thought I'd come by and crash whatever party

Professor Kilmer is hosting in my house."

"Madam President—by all means—please..." Kilmer stammered as he and Silla rose to their feet. He was glad that he hadn't been caught sitting too close to Silla or holding her hand.

Whitman sat down and shared what was on her mind. "I'm not sure how much longer anyone will wait before taking the fight to the aliens. The only thing holding some countries back is that they don't want to be the first to feel the aliens' wrath. And I don't blame them for wanting to fight. Even knowing what I know about what the aliens might be capable of—and even though the US hasn't been attacked—I think I'm ready to retaliate, at least in some small measure. What they're doing is unconscionable—attacking and killing innocent human beings without even allowing a dialogue or providing any justification."

"Is that your plan, Madam President?" Silla asked. "Are you planning to order an attack?"

"Not tonight. But if things don't start to improve, it will happen soon enough. Whether *we* want to or not, *someone* will cross that line. For now, we have bipartisan support in Congress for our policy of restraint, but rank-and-file members are all over the place on this. I'm told there will be at least a dozen speeches made on the House floor tomorrow that will not be very kind to us. I'm not worried about it, but I think it reflects the mood of our citizens. Anyway, enough about what I already know. What have you two been discussing?"

"We were just starting to talk about the message from Archidamus," Kilmer replied.

"The crossing of rivers. Have you made any progress on figuring out what he meant by that?"

"I keep thinking it has to do with Caesar's crossing of the river Rubicon—when he broke with precedent and marched his armies into Rome. But I don't know what to do with that. Sill suggested that it could refer to Washington's crossing of the Delaware River during the Revolutionary War."

The three of them discussed both possibilities, and what they might mean, until Whitman took her leave about twenty minutes later.

"Feel free to stay up and chat, kids, but remember that tomorrow's a school day—and you have to be up early."

Kilmer and Silla continued to talk until nearly 1:30 a.m. When she said goodbye, Silla considered giving Kilmer a kiss on the cheek, but decided against it at the last moment. Kilmer noticed the hesitation but tried not to let on—nor to show his disappointment. Silla caught it—and smiled.

"What are you smiling about?"

"I just noticed something about you, Kilmer."

"What's that?"

"That you notice things about me."

"I hear that's why I was brought here—I tend to notice things. It's what makes me special, apparently."

"No, Kilmer. Noticing things is what makes you valuable. It's not what makes you special."

"So… then… what makes me special?"

Silla forced a grimace. "Wow. This is kind of awkward, Kilmer. I didn't even say you *were* special. And now I need to come up with something just so you won't feel bad. What to do?"

"Before you try to answer, I should tell you that I'm on the verge of feeling really, *really* bad. So you might want to take that into consideration as you come up with something to make me feel better."

Silla made a show of thinking about it.

"Okay. I have an answer. About what makes you special."

"What is it?"

"First, close your eyes. And don't open them until I tell you."

Kilmer did as he was told.

"What makes you special, Kilmer, is that you are always you—no matter what."

He sensed her moving closer to him… and then he felt the kiss on his lips. It lasted only a second or two, but it left him feeling like he might lose his balance and fall over. He couldn't help the smile on his face.

Ten seconds later, he heard her voice, coming from the hallway.

"You can open your eyes now."

Kilmer opened them, knowing she would not be there. But his smile persisted.

There's always tomorrow.

~ 118 ~

Day 59.

On Day 59, an international task force reported on its preliminary findings regarding the squadrons.

According to the report, none of the spacecraft had ever moved faster than the speed of sound. If they continued to fly below Mach 1, they could be easy targets for SAMs and fighter jets. The spacecraft flashed a blinding light in all directions before they attacked, shielding them from view for up to three seconds. It was unclear what kind of bombs were dropped; nothing was detected hurtling toward the ground before the explosions took place. The spacecraft that attacked military installations moved significantly slower than those that attacked oil and gas installations, making them easier targets. It was possible that the aliens were trying to hit more precise targets on military bases, and they could not do so at higher speeds.

There were three additional attacks that day, all on military installations—in England, Israel, and Russia.

Day 60.

The first attack in the United States took place on June 26—Day 60. The target was a military base in Texas, and over 2,000 people were killed. Calls for retaliation ratcheted up significantly across the country. The governor of Texas demanded the impeachment of President Whitman if she refused to respond militarily. Three other governors, eight senators, and a few dozen members of Congress made similar demands. After lengthy discussions with her advisers, the international alliance, and Congressional leadership, Whitman decided against ordering an attack.

That afternoon, Kilmer sent another message to Archidamus.

Archidamus did not respond.

Soon after, Whitman sent a warning to ET-1, but she did not draw any precise red lines. "I am well aware," she told her team, "that failing to issue a clear ultimatum will reduce the credibility of our threat. But I don't want to paint ourselves into a corner when we're not ready to follow through with a retaliatory strike."

The message asked for there to be dialogue, and read, in part:

> *We have been patient in the belief that misunderstandings, grievances, and legitimate concerns are best addressed through dialogue, and not through retaliatory attacks. But there are limits to our patience, and to our ability to give the benefit of the doubt. We ask that you cease your attacks on all nations of Earth to avoid a situation—which draws nearer—in which we must fight back to defend ourselves.*

ET-1 rejected the request for dialogue and responded to Whitman's warning:

> *...As to the threat you have made, we refer you to the guidance we offered in our earlier message. We continue to act in accordance with our laws and consistent with our legitimate interests. We ask that you not interfere with these activities.*

Kilmer and Silla talked until 2:00 a.m. that night. Silla was sure that, by now, she had told Kilmer everything he had known about her life before he entered ET-1. It was strange to have done it twice, but Kilmer was just as fascinated the second time around. Kilmer's attempts to tell Silla about *his* life were becoming a bit of a joke. He would start a story, and then pause to see whether she could finish it. He was amazed to discover just how much old-Kilmer had told her—and what she already knew provided compelling evidence of just how close their relationship had been.

"I feel like the guy who tells the same jokes at every party, and people don't know how to tell him to stop. If this gets annoying, will you let me know?" Kilmer asked.

"Okay. Well. In that case—it got annoying a few days ago."

"Really?"

"No. I'm just kidding."

"Good."

"Well... maybe a little."

"Really?"

"No. Still kidding."

"Are you sure?"

"Yes, I'm sure."

"Good, because—"

"Well... *pretty* sure."

"Stop it, Silla."

Silla gave Kilmer a big hug. "It's not annoying at all, Kilmer. It's wonderful. It doesn't matter if I already know something about you. What matters is that you want to tell me."

Day 61.

There were six attacks on Day 61—including, for the first time, an attack on a military base in North Korea. Chinese President Zhao was asked to ensure that the North Koreans did not retaliate, and he assured Whitman that North Korea would not act unless the Chinese government gave it permission.

A second and third attack also took place in the United States—one in Florida and another in Colorado.

That evening, Strauss argued strenuously for a change in approach. "We *need* to respond, Madam President. Even if we shoot down only *one* spacecraft, it's essential that we let them know we have both the ability and the guts. And this isn't just about deterrence, either Think about what we might learn if we can get our hands on the wreckage! It could be a game-changer. Ideally, we get NATO to support us. Or we ask the Chinese or Russians to join. They will, I think. Or we just go it alone. After all the damage the aliens have done, we have not only the right, but the *responsibility* to act. At the very least, Madam President, you must issue an ultimatum. Let the aliens know that their next attack *will* lead to retaliation. If we can't even do that much… then with all due respect, I don't think I can support what this administration is doing much longer."

It was a heated conversation—but professional. Whitman seemed to take no offense. She saw the merits in Strauss's argument, and she asked Nielsen, Garcia, and Kilmer to draft specific language for an ultimatum. She then asked Strauss and Allen to draw up at least three separate operational plans for a military response.

She would decide how to proceed the following day.

119

Day 62. 9:00 a.m.

The team met in the Oval Office at 9 a.m.

"I am deciding between two options," Whitman announced. "Option one is to issue an ultimatum, warning the aliens that their next attack on a US target will lead to retaliation. Option two is to skip the ultimatum and move ahead with the least aggressive attack option that Strauss and Casey have proposed to me. This entails shooting down a spacecraft that is approaching a military installation. Either way, we're one move away from retaliation, and that means we need to inform the international alliance. I've already told our NATO allies where I stand. They will support us—but they're worried. The French, Germans, and Canadians don't believe we have passed the threshold of pain that would warrant a retaliation. They think we should wait. Strauss tells me the Russians are on board. The Chinese haven't rejected the idea, but they worry about what happens if we launch an attack and it fails. Do we look even more vulnerable?"

"Between the two options," General Allen said, "I support the ultimatum, because it has *some* chance of eliminating the need to follow through with an attack. But there is a tradeoff. We are more likely to actually hit them if we don't let them know that their next attack will lead to retaliatory measures."

"I agree," Strauss said. "And yes, the Russians are on board. They've even offered to launch a similar attack against a spacecraft in Russia. I don't think the Chinese will do that yet. They feel more vulnerable because they launched the initial nuke in space—which did not go over well with the aliens."

Nielsen preferred an ultimatum. Druckman preferred not to give warning. Art, Silla, and Perez didn't weigh in.

"Professor Kilmer?"

Kilmer was unsure. All he could think was that no matter which option they chose, everything was about to change. "Before we decide, can we go over the logic again? Let's revisit what we know and don't know. One more time."

Over the next twenty minutes, they reviewed the evidence. The aliens had attacked both military installations and oil fields without warning, and without any obvious provocation. The military installations were disproportionately those that were best equipped to carry out an attack against the aliens. This could mean that the aliens were trying to slowly chip away at Earth-side capabilities, and if so, it might mean the aliens were not as formidable as had been feared. Furthermore, either because of the limits of their technology, or because they believed they could act with impunity, the alien spacecraft weren't moving very fast. This could make it easier to take them out—unless they had defensive capabilities that had not yet been demonstrated. In their message advising humans not to retaliate, the aliens had given no indication what the consequences would be if Earth-side fought back, but that could simply have been because a bureaucrat, and not a military strategist, had composed the language.

"I don't see anything that makes me worry excessively about escalation," Kilmer admitted. "I agree with General Allen that *if* matters escalate, things could go terribly wrong. But nothing here suggests to me that shooting down one spacecraft that is on its way to launching another attack—*after* they've already killed tens of thousands of human beings—would be the kind of thing that would trigger significant escalation. That's especially true if we've first issued a warning. If the aliens stand to benefit from continued attacks, they'll launch them regardless."

"I'd take it a step further, Professor," Strauss added. "Their behavior suggests they might be worried. They ask us not to fight, but they don't issue a specific threat or announce what the consequences will be if we fight back. Their attacks are chipping away at our capabilities, but only a little at a time, as if *they* are the ones who are trying to avoid escalation. Maybe they know that if they attack too viciously, we'll be forced to fight back, so they keep things just below that threshold. Maybe they're hoping that when the damage is done—one base at a time, for however long they can keep it up—we really will be too weak to fight."

Silla entered the conversation. "I see your point, Secretary Strauss, but it bothers me that we're suddenly seeing them as being so weak. None of what we've seen recently changes the fact that they've traveled trillions or quadrillions of miles to get here, and that they have at least some types of technology that we can only dream of. I'd like to remain a bit scared. I don't think fear is necessarily our enemy here."

"Does that mean you're against an attack, Agent Silla?" Whitman asked.

"I still lean toward waiting, yes. But I understand it's not my call, nor my place to weigh in strongly. I can only suggest that we ask ourselves how many deaths, *ex ante,* would we have been willing to suffer before we felt that the risk of retaliation was worth taking. I thought about that after the first two attacks, and I came up with a number in the many hundreds of thousands, at least. Maybe even millions. We're not at that number yet. Perhaps others would have set a lower limit. But if not, we should stick with what we considered wise before stress, anxiety, frustration, and political pressures began to weigh more heavily in our judgments."

"It's not just a matter of the numbers, Agent Silla," Druckman counseled. "Perhaps the fatalities *are* lower than what we should be willing to endure, but there are now other factors—the fact that they seem hesitant, and the fact that they're trying to whittle away our capabilities. These are what increase my willingness to fight sooner rather than wait. What a major escalation would do is still terrifying, but the likelihood of escalation is lower if our analysis is correct. And hell, the way these guys are behaving—floating in at a leisurely pace to kill our people and take out our most defensible facilities—they're practically begging us to punch them in the face. I'm not saying we declare war. I'm just saying we throw a few jabs. And if not now, when? If we're going to inch toward hundreds of thousands of deaths anyway, and we'll eventually have to fight back, then I'd like to try to save those lives and employ that strategy sooner—before they do even more damage to our military."

Kilmer looked at the floor and furrowed his brow. Then he set his coffee cup on the table in front of him—a bit too loudly—and all heads turned toward him. But Kilmer's mind was already elsewhere. He didn't notice that everyone was staring at him, nor did it occur to him to apologize for banging the table, or to clean up the coffee that had spilled from his cup.

Someone said something—it might have been Nielsen. Everyone chuckled. Kilmer had no idea what was said, but he smiled, almost unconsciously, as if to reassure the assemblage that he was still part of the conversation. But he was not. He was somewhere else, grappling with something Druckman had said.

Whitman continued the conversation.

"You make a good point, Noah. Now, I want to hear more discussion regarding the ultimatum. Maybe it gets them to back down. Even if it doesn't, their response to it could provide useful information. And if they alter the way they fly or attack after our warning, that tells us something about their capabilities as well."

By the time others were weighing in, Kilmer had closed his eyes and completely tuned them out. If there were jokes being told, or new arguments being made, or missiles being launched, he was unaware of it.

...the way these guys are behaving...

Kilmer thought back to their earlier discussion about why the aliens had asked Earth-side not to fight back.

...why not just continue to scare the hell out of us?

His heart started to beat faster.

Lincoln...

Thoreau...

The crossing of rivers...

1846...

In a flash, the entire image snapped into focus.

How did I not see this? I'm sorry, old-Kilmer. My mistake. It was a good clue—I just wasn't thinking straight.

Kilmer jolted back to attention—he didn't even know who was speaking when he interrupted. "Wait!"

Everyone turned to look at him.

"Welcome back, Professor. You look refreshed," Whitman teased. "Zack thought you fell asleep."

"What? No, ma'am. I was—Madam President—please *listen* to me. Sorry. I don't mean—I just—"

"Slow down, Professor. Slow down. What's on your mind?"

Kilmer took a deep breath. He noticed the spilled coffee and wiped it away with a napkin. He could feel the adrenaline coursing through his veins. Whitman was right. He needed to get a grip. He refilled his cup, stood up to stretch his legs, and took a few steps.

"Shit," muttered Strauss. "Here it comes. The Sermon on the Mount."

Everyone chuckled.

"Madam President," Kilmer said, much more calmly now. "I think we're going about this the wrong way. I don't think we should launch an attack. And I don't think we should be issuing ultimatums."

"So, you're in favor of waiting?" Whitman asked. "For how long? How many more attacks—or deaths—before you would say it's one too many?"

"I say we wait for however long it takes. No matter the number of attacks. Even if thousands more are killed. Even if it's millions. I hate to say this, Madam President, but I don't think we should fight back. No matter what they do."

120

Strauss looked more shocked and confused than annoyed, but all three sentiments were clearly in the mix. "You don't want us to fight back—*no matter what?* A moment ago, you saw no reason for us to wait. Now you're proposing the precise opposite of that. Is this about the scribble on your arm? Thoreau and Gandhi? MLK and Mandela? I thought we had put that behind us?"

"Yes, Mr. Secretary. It is tied to that."

Strauss made no effort to conceal his exasperation. "Professor, you should know this better than anyone. Those were good people, but not one of them ever won a war—or even ended a war—with their approach. Thoreau spent exactly *one* day in jail, and had precisely zero impact on any policy, before he decided to write a whole book on civil disobedience. Gandhi did not defeat the British through passive resistance; they left because their empire was crumbling after World War II. MLK fought and won battles for civil rights and social justice—but he wasn't in a real war. And Mandela, bless that man's soul—he stood for reconciliation, but he only came out of prison *after* it was clear that apartheid had to end. He won no wars either.

"On what basis are you suddenly proposing that we adopt a strategy that has literally *no* track record? I understand strategic patience. I understand waiting to attack—for all sorts of reasons. But to suggest that we *never* fight? That's no strategy at all—not when you are at war!"

Kilmer nodded. "I understand your point, Secretary Strauss. And I won't argue with your description of what those men did. You're right, they were not trying to win wars or end wars. But sir, neither are we. We are trying to *avoid* war—and that makes all the difference."

"*Avoid* war? The war has already started, Professor. They have been targeting and killing human beings around the globe. They have been chipping away at our ability to function as a society and to defend ourselves. And they have made clear that they are unwilling to negotiate—that they expect us to sit back and take the hits. I'm not sure what definition of war *you're* using, but by any definition that I'm familiar with, they are *at war* with us."

"That is where we disagree, Mr. Secretary. This is *not* war. This is something else. It is the crossing of rivers."

Whitman interjected. "What exactly does that mean, Professor? You need to explain what's caused you to change your mind."

"The second clue, Madam President. I know what I was trying to warn us about." Kilmer reminded everyone what the clue had said.

HDT/AL46

"There's only one thing that would tie Thoreau and Lincoln to the year 1846, at least in my mind, and I now realize what that is. And it explains everything. 1846 is the year the Mexican–American War began—and it was a travesty of justice from the very start. President Polk *wanted* that war with Mexico, but there just wasn't enough support for it in the United States. So he decided that the only way to justify a war would be to get Mexico to attack American soldiers—and he did this by sending troops to stir up trouble in parts of Texas that were disputed territory at the time.

"This is what Archidamus was referring to. Polk sent General Zachary Taylor across the Neuces River, into the disputed territory that sat between the Neuces and the Rio Grande. Mexico took the bait and sent its own troops across the Rio Grande to attack the Americans. Polk got exactly what he had wanted. He told Congress that Mexico had invaded the United States and 'shed American blood upon American soil.' America declared war. And by the time the smoke cleared, in 1848, the US had conquered about a third of Mexico—all of what we now know as California, Arizona, Nevada, and Utah, along with parts of other states as well. We took it all.

"Both men—Thoreau and Lincoln—spoke out against this war. It was why Thoreau went to jail—because he refused to pay taxes to support a government that would launch such an unjust war. It's why Lincoln spoke out in Congress, calling Polk's claims about 'American blood upon American soil' a 'bold falsification of history.'

"That's what my reference to the Mexican–American War was about. It wasn't simply an immoral war against a weaker power, it was a war that is remembered—to those who know its history—for *how it was started*. The weaker power was suckered into behaving in ways that allowed the stronger power to declare war—and then to impose its will.

"The aliens are doing the same thing we did in 1846, Madam President. We think this is war. But it is *not* war. It is merely the prelude to war. It is the opening gambit of a game in which those who *want* war need the rest of us to play along. We should not make that mistake."

Nielsen leaned forward. "Are you saying that everything they're doing now—including their attacks—is designed to tempt us into fighting back?"

"I am. Think about it. All this time, we've been wondering what holds them back. If not their ability, or desire, or fear, then what keeps them from escalating their attacks? Maybe the answer is that there are limits to how much damage they are permitted to inflict on a planet that isn't even fighting back— a planet that's clearly not a threat yet. Maybe they need greater justification for a larger campaign. It would explain a lot. For example, why they backed off their earlier rhetoric about destroying human civilization. Why they sent a legal notice, as if to ensure they're doing things by the book. Why they refuse to engage in a dialogue that might de-escalate the conflict. Why they don't attack large population centers. Why they provoke us by attacking critical oil and gas infrastructure. Why they tempt us by flying slowly and low enough to be shot down with ease. And why they've been targeting those countries and those military installations that are most capable of defending against an incoming aerial assault.

"I think Director Druckman said it perfectly. *They're practically begging us to punch them in the face.* They want us to throw a punch so they will have a reason to unleash that concealed handgun they've been carrying. Let's not give them what they want. Let's *not* hand them a license for total war."

Whitman was nodding along. "This is persuasive, Professor. And a strong argument against retaliating or issuing ultimatums. But I won't embrace this theory before we've tried to poke some holes in it."

"I find it believable, Professor," said Nielsen. "And it ties a lot of things together. But I have one hesitation. Do you really think they would *need* to play such games?"

Kilmer gave this some thought. "As I see it, Mr. Vice President, we only have to believe two things. First, that they want to launch an aggressive campaign. That seems easy enough to believe at this point. And second, that they face certain constraints on their ability to declare war. Maybe they also have debates about what is ethical. Or arguments about what is legal. Or disagreements about what is wise. Once these two elements—their interests *and* their constraints—are properly in place, the explanation becomes plausible. Even then, I would be a bit skeptical if not for one other crucial point. This isn't some theory I hatched out of thin air, one that just happens to fit the data. Old-Kilmer wrote down certain things for a reason. And taken together, the three clues tell a complete and consistent story.

"The first clue tells us why they want war to begin with. It's a pre-emptive war, of the kind that Germany believed Britain was waging. The second clue warns us that their strategy is to bait us into war, like the US did with Mexico. And the third clue advises us not to fall into the trap, and to resist peacefully— however long it takes."

NSA Garcia raised another doubt. "If we were to accept this theory—that their objective is to provoke us—then why aren't they targeting religious and historic sites? Why not destroy Saint Peter's Basilica, or the Great Mosque in Mecca, or the Pyramids, or the Statue of Liberty? Those types of attacks would likely incite even more Earth-side anger than what we've witnessed so far. The cries for war would be deafening."

Director Druckman offered an explanation. "Bombing those targets might make sense from the point of view of what they *want* to do, but I can tell you from experience that what would be most effective is not always feasible. If we take seriously Professor Kilmer's idea that there could be limits to what the aliens can to do in the absence of a direct provocation from us, then it's not hard for me to believe that they can concoct justifications for bombing a military installation or an oil field, but they can't justify bombing religious or cultural targets. When you can't get away with doing whatever you want, you tend to do the most you can get away with."

More discussion followed. After another twenty minutes, Whitman had made her decision. Everyone, including Strauss, was on board with the approach Kilmer had suggested—albeit with varying degrees of confidence.

"As soon as we're finished here," Whitman announced, "I will update Congressional leadership. More importantly, we need to get the international alliance on board immediately. Many of them will be relieved when they hear the analysis and what it implies. But this will not be an easy journey for anyone. We have no idea how long the aliens will continue to attack while we sit quietly. We don't know how many rivers they're allowed to cross before they have to stop trying to provoke us."

"You're right," Kilmer said. "We could see a lot more death and destruction before they stop. But I don't think we have to sit quietly. We don't plan to send them an ultimatum, but we can still send a message. Passive resistance is peaceful, but it still calls for defiance. Civil disobedience is civil, but it permits insolence. We can't launch missiles, but we still have a target to hit: the conscience of what appears to be a powerful, but still reluctant enemy. We can still try to shame, energize, and empower those among them who know this war is unjustified—but who are waiting to see how we react to these provocations. That is what old-Kilmer would have advised, I believe. I think that's the message he left for all of you after he realized he wasn't coming back."

"Well, I trusted old-Kilmer," Whitman said. "And I think he was wise to put his trust in new-Kilmer."

Whitman turned to the group and asked whether anyone had any final thoughts to add. "I don't want anything that you think is important to have gone unsaid."

"I will speak for myself," General Allen announced. "This is extremely compelling. At the same time, it worries me that we're dealing with an entity that would stoop to such a level to justify war against a weaker power. It makes you wonder what else they're capable of doing."

"It's evil, plain and simple," NSA Garcia concluded. "But I believe the professor's argument is sound."

"What the aliens are attempting might be unconscionable, but it makes sense," Druckman added.

Strauss spoke last. "I support this approach, Madam President. And I'm ready to help make the case to Congress and to our allies. I also think we need to speak to the Russians *very* soon, as they could launch an attack at any time. But if Professor Kilmer is right, this is actually good news—even if it means we're dealing with darker stuff than even I had imagined."

Kilmer hesitated for a moment—*I should probably just let it go*—but then decided to wade back into the discussion.

"Madam President, if you don't mind, I'd like to add one last thing— about what I just heard. I say this with some hesitation, given the harm the aliens have already inflicted on us, but… maybe we should not be so quick to judge them. The reason they need to resort to such nefarious tactics seems to be that there are others on their planet who will *not* allow an unjust war. We lose sight of such things at our own peril. Maybe they have moral codes or laws that are not so different from ours. And they have people like Archidamus, who has put himself at risk to help us. He knew I was smuggling out information that could help stop this war, and he not only allowed me to do it, he contributed to it. We'll have to deal with these aliens for a long time, I suspect. We should stay open to the possibility that they are, *perhaps*, not so different from us. At least in some ways."

"Do you really believe that, Professor?" Strauss asked, sounding genuinely curious. "Or is that something your employment contract with an elite liberal university forces you to say?"

Kilmer shook his head. "My contract says only that I should try to provide evidence for the things I say." He looked around the room. "And in this case, there is plenty of evidence to choose from."

He paused, briefly, before addressing each person in turn.

"General Allen, you're familiar with Operation Northwoods, I'm sure. After all, it was the Joint Chiefs of Staff, in 1962, that proposed to President Kennedy that he authorize false flag attacks to help start a war against a weaker country. The JCS even proposed attacks on American soil, perpetrated *by* Americans, just so we could incriminate Fidel Castro and create a pretext for war against Cuba. Thankfully, JFK rejected that idea, even though other covert action against Castro continued.

"Secretary Strauss and Ms. Garcia. You both know that President Johnson used the infamous Gulf of Tonkin incident to justify the first major escalation of war against Vietnam, even though Johnson knew that his justification was premised on a complete fabrication. But let's not forget that it was his defense secretary, Robert McNamara—and later, Nixon's national security advisor, Henry Kissinger—who most helped their presidents perpetuate the war by lying to the American people about what they were doing in Vietnam, and about how well things were going.

"As to the past sins of the CIA—Director Druckman, you know that history better than I do. What the agency did in the 1950s alone could fill many bookshelves. And that was just the beginning.

"And we aren't even close to the worst offenders on this planet. We have done a lot of good along the way, but what we're now calling evil should not look alien to us. Every one of you in this room has predecessors who did precisely the things we find unconscionable here—and in many cases, they did so quite recently."

Strauss smiled. "Touché, Professor. All true. And you managed to hit every one of us. I suppose the only people who are still innocent are the historians."

"I didn't mean to suggest that at all, Mr. Secretary," Kilmer said, returning to his seat. "I think we deserve more blame than all the rest. Every leader has the power to do harm, but it's only when citizens know nothing of history that leaders find it possible to do *evil* on behalf of their people. My predecessors and I have failed humanity more often, and in more ways, than anyone else.

"But I don't say any of this to justify what the aliens are doing. My concerns are entirely practical. Because I don't think we can strategize against a player that we're unwilling to understand. We will neither fight effectively, nor negotiate successfully, if we are too blinded by fear or hatred to see what's really going on—or to consider how the other side justifies the things they do."

~ 121 ~

At 11:00 a.m., Whitman and Nielsen gave the international alliance a preliminary update. All leaders agreed not to retaliate and committed to establishing additional safeguards to ensure no attacks were launched by accident.

At 12:00 p.m., Whitman, Nielsen, Strauss, Allen, and Perez briefed members of Congress. There was palpable anxiety, as political pressure was expected to surge when the death toll mounted. But there was also relief—the strategy made sense and there was renewed hope that Earth might, in fact, survive this.

At 1:30, Kilmer sent a message to Archidamus, hoping he might validate the strategy Earth-side was adopting.

> *We have discovered the missing piece and the puzzle is complete. We find ourselves, suddenly, with nothing left to do. My friends and I just sit around now.*

At 2:00, Archidamus wrote back.

> *You deserve the rest. And sometimes, it is what is needed most.*

At 3:15, another three attacks were reported, one each in the US, Russia, and China. No one retaliated.

At 7:30, after a three-hour meeting of the international alliance, a message was delivered to ET-1. It was drafted by a group that included Kilmer, Silla, and Nielsen, and was then approved by an international panel. Written on behalf of the *Human Population of Planet Earth*, it included the following text:

> *From the very start, we welcomed you to Earth. Despite not knowing anything about you, we invited you to our planet. Even before you spoke a word to us, we offered you gifts so that you might understand our good*

intentions and learn more about us. When the gifts went unreciprocated, we sent more. Even after you started to threaten us, we implored you to consider peaceful coexistence. Despite your repeated rejections of our acts of goodwill, we continued to propose communication, dialogue, and engagement.

Now you have started to attack—without any provocation—the people of Earth. You have killed many thousands, including our innocent children, and you have scared and angered billions of us. Perhaps, given your strategic interests, you consider your behaviors to be appropriate. Perhaps these actions are technically legal according to your laws. We can only assume that you find some way to justify these acts, no matter how clearly immoral they are. At least by the standards of any human society on Earth, your actions fail to meet even the most basic requirements of moral conduct or justice. We would hope that a civilization as advanced as yours would hold itself to an even higher standard than we hold ourselves. And yet, your behavior suggests otherwise. The attacks continue. The terror campaign continues. The killings continue. And worse—the unwillingness to even talk of peace, continues.

How are we to respond? While we would consider ourselves morally justified to retaliate militarily, we wonder—how would that make our behavior any different from yours, which we condemn? Do you not also find ways to legitimize the damage you do and the pain you inflict? Retaliation will only fuel the cycle of mutual mistrust and enhance the perception of mutual grievances. That cannot be the way forward if there is ever to be a durable peace and genuine friendship.

So, we have decided—as one global community—that we will not fight back. We will stand, with the strength of our moral convictions, and face whatever it is that you claim you have the right to do. We will suffer until you are tired of making us suffer. We will endure until you are ashamed of having tested our endurance. We will show you what it means to be strong, even as you destroy, with little effort, all that we have built and known. We will bet our lives, and the lives of our children—even the very survival of our species—on the fact that, ultimately, it will be you, not us, who will have to say **enough of this... no more.**

We pledge never to say those words. We vow never to change course and draw our weapons. And so, it falls upon you to decide whether to put an end to this brutality and thus honor your conscience... or continue to attack until there is nothing left of our physical existence—or of your moral souls.

We are ready to face the worst. But we are equally prepared, even now, to welcome your best. One path leads to mutual ruin. The other path, however fraught with peril it might seem to you at the start, is the only one that leads to a destination worth reaching.

~ 122 ~

At 8 p.m., the team reassembled in the Oval Office. Whitman sat in an armchair, with VP Nielsen at her side.

"The die is cast, ladies and gentlemen. Now we wait to see how it lands. I have not said this enough over the last many weeks, but I hope you know that I feel fortunate to have had all of you by my side as we navigated this crisis. What happens tomorrow is unknown. Maybe things get worse before they get better. Maybe they only get worse. But we deserve to breathe a sigh of relief for this one moment. And to know that we did our best. Future generations might judge us differently—but if future generations survive to judge us at all, perhaps we will have succeeded at least in part."

Nielsen spoke next. "There have been many nights, Madam President, where I have thanked my lucky stars that we have you to lead us during this crisis. When your story is told, I believe it will be an inspiration to others. And that sentiment is shared by every one of us. I know that even Strauss here agrees—although he'll have a hard time admitting it in front of such a big crowd. But I have no problem outing him."

Everyone chuckled, and Strauss nodded along. "I only ask that you keep this off the record," he said wryly.

Nielsen continued. "Things might get worse after today, and we might have gotten it all wrong. But there is also another possibility—that what we've endured and achieved these last few weeks will be a catalyst for greater progress than humanity was likely to achieve on its previous trajectory. We have gone from fighting one another to standing shoulder to shoulder. We heard the Israelis and Iranians, this evening, refer to each other as *brothers in arms and brothers in peace*. Who would have seen that statement coming two months ago? We saw the North Koreans and South Koreans table every proposal and every question in one voice. It was just a symbolic show of solidarity, of course,

461

but who knows what more is possible? It's far too early to tell if any of this will stick, but if the aliens can nudge us toward a more peaceful Middle East, or to a peaceful reunification of the Korean peninsula, they might end up having done more good than harm."

Kilmer was breathing the sigh of relief that Whitman had recommended, and he was sharing in the hope that Nielsen was expressing.

Then he heard those words—and he tuned out of the conversation entirely.

...reunification of the Korean peninsula.

Kilmer started to search for an answer that he knew was stored somewhere in his mind.

Three kingdoms.

He tried to remember whether Korea had ever been divided into three kingdoms. It sounded vaguely familiar. He conjured up an image of the fourth clue in his mind.

GALWAY4/3Kingdoms/21

It was the second half of the image that grabbed his attention. *3Kingdoms/21.* He understood it differently now.

'Three kingdoms to one.'

Three kingdoms that had been united.

He didn't want to take out his cell phone in the middle of the meeting, but he couldn't resist. He was on to something. He took it out of his pocket.

Silla, sitting next to him, gave him a slight nudge. *Put it away, Kilmer.*

He gave her an apologetic smile. *Sorry, just one sec.*

Silla turned back toward the conversation. General Allen was speaking now.

Kilmer typed in the search terms, *3 kingdoms of Korea,* and hit *enter.* The results took a fraction of a second to appear. And it took Kilmer less than five seconds to realize that he was on the right track. And then, another thirty seconds later...

How in the world?

Kilmer had figured out exactly what Archidamus had wanted to tell him.

He flashed back to some notes Silla had shown him—the ones that old-Kilmer had written after his first conversation with Archidamus.

I might have a friend on ET-1.

He put his phone away and leaned closer to Silla. Then he whispered in her ear. "If they give us the night off tonight, can I take you out for a drink?"

"Give *us* the night off?" Silla whispered back. "I'm the only one who ever has to work. You just sit around waiting for me to finish up so I can spend time with you."

"That rings true, somehow. But can I still take you out for a drink?"

"Yes. Now stop talking and let me pay attention."

Kilmer smiled. He tried to focus on the conversation, but his mind was elsewhere.

They might have just saved the planet. He had figured out the fourth clue. And he had scored himself a date with an amazing woman.

Things were pretty good.

~ 123 ~

That night, Kilmer and Silla went for a walk. They strolled around a mostly deserted DC for almost two hours, and Silla explained to Kilmer why she had always considered it such a great place to live. Eventually, they stepped into a cozy bar for a drink. Silla ordered a red wine. Kilmer asked for a Guinness. They sat on either side of a long, narrow table in the far corner.

"So, what do you think about DC now? Have I convinced you that it's a wonderful place to live?"

"You have. But that's not saying much. If you spent two hours with me anywhere, I'd start thinking it was a wonderful place."

Silla smiled. "I want to tell you something."

Kilmer took a sip of his drink. "Okay. I want to tell you something, too. So, who should go first?"

She thought about it. "You go first. What is it?"

"It's about the fourth clue. I figured it out."

Silla's eyes grew wider. "When? Just now?"

"No. When we were in the Oval Office—a few hours ago."

"Why didn't you tell us then?"

"I thought I would tell you first. And then you can advise me on whether I should tell the others."

Silla looked confused as she took a sip of her wine. "Okay. Tell me."

"Art was right about the first part. Galway is the city in Ireland. And it does refer to the Claddagh, the ring signifying love, loyalty, and friendship. The *3 Kingdoms*, it turns out, refers to the three kingdoms of ancient Korea. I probably read about them years ago, but it wasn't something I would have recalled on my own—until Zack made the comment about the reunification of the Korean peninsula. That's when it hit me. *3Kingdoms/21* could mean *three kingdoms to one.*

So, maybe the clue had something to do with love, loyalty, and friendship towards that kingdom, or with how the unification took place, or what happened afterwards—I wasn't sure what. That's why I pulled out my phone. Turns out Korea had indeed been three separate kingdoms, for centuries. It was only united, for the first time, in the seventh century CE. Now, here's where it gets interesting. The largest of the three kingdoms was named *Goguryeo*, a predecessor to the name *Korea* itself. The second largest was named *Baekje*. But it was the smallest of the three kingdoms, it turns out, that eventually unified and ruled the combined entity. And what Archidamus wanted me to know, or remember, or reexamine once I returned, was that third kingdom. Do you know what it was called?"

"I have no idea."

Kilmer took another sip… and then he took a deep breath. "The third kingdom was named *Silla.*"

Silla felt the wine glass start to slip from her hands. She tightened her grip just as she caught her breath.

"I don't understand, Kilmer. How is that possible? How could… you didn't even write the fourth clue."

"I know. I have the same questions. And I hope to ask Archidamus about it. But I'm pretty sure I already know the important part. He wanted me to remember something that he knew I might otherwise forget. And it had nothing to do with war and peace. He did what he did so that I would remember that my love, loyalty, and friendship was for someone named Silla."

Silla sat quietly, and Kilmer didn't push her to tell him what she was thinking.

"Kilmer…" she finally said. "You might think you're telling me something I always knew, but which you happen to have forgotten. But it's a little more complicated than that. I always knew how I felt about you. And I knew how you looked at me, and how you treated me, and how we were when we were together. But we never put any of those things into words. But there was a moment, just before you left, when you wanted to tell me something. I think it was about how you felt about me. And I didn't let you. I told you to tell me after you came back. I have regretted that moment ever since. And now…"

She took a deep breath.

"Archidamus didn't just tell you something you'd forgotten. He helped you tell *me* something I'd never really known. Those three words don't hold the same meaning for you today—I understand that. Nor should they. But they still give me a kind of closure that I didn't think I would ever find. I don't know how you—or how old-Kilmer, as you call him—managed to get this message to me. But I love him for having done so."

Kilmer smiled as he took Silla's hand. "I suddenly feel like the third wheel in my own relationship with you."

Silla laughed. "Don't. It's all a little strange, I know. But let's put all of that aside. You're not sharing me with anyone. I'm here with *you*. Not with *new-Kilmer*, or *you-Kilmer*, or whatever it is you call yourself these days. I'm here with *Kilmer*. The real Kilmer. The one who asked me out on a date."

They both took a sip—a toast to Silla's sentiment.

"Okay, your turn," Kilmer said. "What did you want to tell me? Are you going to tell me what makes me special again? If so, I'm ready." He closed his eyes and grinned.

"No, I'm not. And you can open your eyes."

Kilmer obliged, and Silla locked her gaze with his. "It's along the lines of what I was just saying, actually. I wanted to tell you it no longer bothers me that you don't remember what happened between us. Not that I had a right for it to bother me earlier, but... it was hard for me. You know that. And... well, it's not hard anymore."

"Why do you think that is?"

"I'm not sure. But I think it's because I see things differently now. What they did to you... they erased me out of your mind completely, but they didn't erase *you* at all. Not one bit. And maybe that's all that matters. I don't believe in fate, Kilmer. I *know* things could have played out differently, and I might have never seen you again. Even after you returned from ET-1, a lot of events had to conspire for you to return to Triad, and then to DC, and for me to still be involved. I don't believe even for a second that you and I were destined to meet again.

"But here's the thing. After you and I *did* meet again—once we allow for that one piece of good luck—maybe the rest isn't so crazy. The fact that you and I would start to… well, look at each other the way we do now… maybe that isn't such a surprise. Because you're still you. And I'm still me. And maybe once you put us together, maybe there just *is* such a thing as *us*. They can erase the memory of us, but they can't change the fact that you and I, once we're together, will *always* make an *us*."

Kilmer had been nodding along, smiling, and listening intently as Silla spoke. It had given her the courage to keep saying what was on her mind. But at that moment, just as she finished her thought, she saw all of it disappear. Kilmer was no longer nodding along. No longer listening. No longer holding her hand. And there was no smile on his face. His eyes moved away from hers, as if to look at something off in the distance. Then he closed his eyes tight—so much so that she could see the intensity with which he was concentrating. Almost as if he were in pain. He lowered his head toward the floor, his eyes still closed.

Silla went from worrying about whether she had said something that bothered him, to worrying about his health. "Kilmer, are you—"

His hand shot up, as if signaling for her not to say another word. She stopped mid-sentence, now even more concerned. Her first thought was of the brain injury he had suffered. She grabbed her phone. "I'm going to call a doc—"

"No," Kilmer whispered urgently. "Please. No." Then his hands went to his ears, as if he couldn't stand the noise in the room.

As she waited for Kilmer to explain what was happening, Silla sent a frantic message to Art. She told him that Kilmer did not look well and asked him to send a car to their location.

Kilmer, meanwhile, was focusing his energies on controlling his breath. He knew it was the only way. He had been nodding along, listening intently, right until the very end. That was when he had heard the sound. Or was it a thought that had raced through his mind? Or a memory that had flashed past, ever so briefly? It was fleeting, to be sure, but it had managed to grab his attention, like an urgent tap on the shoulder.

If your gods truly exist, I am sure they will return—no matter what we do.

The statement was undoubtedly a strange one, but not *entirely* unfamiliar. And there had been a voice behind it, but not one that he recognized.

Kilmer tried desperately to hear the words again, just so that he might figure out where they had come from. And so that he might search for more. He covered his ears and slowed his breathing, trying to shut everything out. He let the phrase return to his mind, on its own terms this time. Slowly, like segments of a dream returning as you allow yourself to fall back asleep.

If your gods truly exist, I am sure they will return—no matter what we do.

Then came a second voice, but this one was intimately familiar.

I don't know if our gods will come back... but there are some things I can guarantee will return.

Kilmer searched for more—but it was all that he could remember.
...remember

These were memories. But how? He tried to stay in the fragile reverie he had constructed, allowing his mind to wander around in it, keeping it lightly tethered to the words he had just remembered. *What else is here?*

Then he heard Silla's voice. The words she had spoken only moments earlier.

They can erase the memory of us, but they can't change the fact that you and I, once we're together, will always make an us.

The stranger's voice. Then his own. And then Silla's. Only a few dozen words in all, but they had brought along with them something else entirely.

A *sense* of something. An understanding—albeit detached from any evidence or data. It was something to feel. Something to accept, without question—not based on faith, but on experience. A memory of sorts, but not of any event. *And yet...* unquestionably real. Undeniable.

Kilmer opened his eyes. He saw that Silla had moved next to him, to his side of the table. Her anxiety began to fade as she saw him recover, but the vestiges of concern remained on her face. He gave her a smile, letting her know he was okay. A tentative smile appeared on her face as well.

He took both of her hands in his own and looked into her eyes.

"What happened, Kilmer? Are you okay?"

"Yes, I'm fine. And I'm sorry. I knew I was worrying you. But—I had to do that."

"Do what? What just happened?"

"I'll explain that in just a moment. But first, I want you to know that I heard what you were saying. Before I turned away from you. I heard every word. And I think you're right. Maybe there just is such a thing as us. And if there is, it's not the kind of thing they would be able to take away. What makes *us* is not our memories; the building blocks are just you and me. And here we are."

Silla could feel the butterflies in her stomach. She smiled as she lightly bit her lower lip.

Kilmer stared at the vision in front of him. She looked perfectly...

No. Not perfectly anything. *Just perfect.*

Silla's expression turned more playful. "Is that what you were thinking about all this time? I came up with all of that with a lot less effort."

Kilmer smiled. "No. That's not what I was thinking about. It turns out, I *do* remember something. Something that I thought they had erased. It's not about the aliens, or about the war. It's about us. And I was trying to search for more—to see if there was anything else that I could retrieve. But I came back with just the one thing."

"Kilmer! That's amazing. What did you remember?"

"The memory... it's not a specific event, or about something that happened. It's about a feeling. I'm not even sure whether it's a memory about a feeling or a feeling about a memory. But whatever it is, I know it's real."

Silla bit her lip again, looking just a bit nervous about what he might say. "Just describe it however you can."

Kilmer smiled. "I'll do my best."

Then he pulled her close... and kissed her with the kind of passion that she thought was reserved only for fairy tales.

~ 124 ~

They didn't even bother to finish their drinks. For the next two hours, Kilmer and Silla did almost nothing but talk. Kilmer still had no specific memories of the time he had spent with her, but what she had meant to him was no longer a mystery—neither in his mind, nor in his heart.

"I don't know how it works," he confessed. "But I guess when you love someone, you're not constantly accessing all of the memories and reasons that make you feel that way. You just love them. There *are* reasons, but they don't stay top of mind. They're somewhere in the background—or maybe they no longer even matter."

"I'm not sure I paid too much attention to what you just said," Silla teased. "I do think I heard the word *love* twice. I don't think I caught much else." Then she kissed him.

They never discussed whether she would spend the night at the White House, but by the time they left the bar, it was a foregone conclusion. When she entered the Lincoln Bedroom with him, it was the first time she had been there since Kilmer's return.

When he woke up the next morning, he wondered how it was possible that he could have forgotten a single night like the one he had just had with her. *You're an idiot, Kilmer.*

"I have to tell the president about the last clue," he told Silla as they got dressed. "It's going to be awkward."

"Not as awkward as you think," she assured him. "The president already knows a few things."

Silla told him about the time Whitman had caught her leaving the Lincoln Bedroom. Kilmer found it just as funny the second time around. Silla rolled her eyes and punished him with an unenthusiastic kiss as they said goodbye.

As of 11:00 a.m., there had been eight more attacks—two in the US and an especially deadly bombing of a naval base in the UK. Earth-side did not retaliate. Instead, at military bases around the globe, large signs were raised. They shared a common slogan, translated across dozens of Earth's languages:

Our desire for peace is stronger than your need for war.

At 1:00 p.m., Kilmer told Whitman about the last clue. She was all smiles, but just as perplexed as Silla had been.

"Why do you think Archidamus did that?" she asked. "It's a big risk, and it doesn't even help us with the war."

"I'm not sure, Madam President. This will probably sound crazy... but I think he and I are friends."

At 2:00, Kilmer sent another message to Archidamus.

No more puzzles left. Just a few questions and a lot of gratitude. Can we correspond now?

The response was brief—and troubling.

I am not sure we will ever talk again. But it has been a pleasure, my friend.

Day 64. June 30.

A total of fourteen attacks took place on Day 64. Most military installations had been evacuated except for essential personnel, so the death count was significantly lower in those locations than it might have been. The aliens adjusted their tactics accordingly. They bombed three airports, all of which were used primarily for civilian purposes. Two were in Russia and one in China. The total death toll for the day was almost 25,000.

Earth-side did not retaliate. There was no communication with ET-1 or with Archidamus.

Day 65. July 1.

Twenty-three attacks. Over 48,000 killed.
No retaliation. No communication.

Day 66. July 2.

Six attacks. Over 11,000 killed.
No retaliation. No communication.

Day 67. July 3.

No attacks. No communication.

Day 68. July 4.

No attacks. No communication.

~ 126 ~

Day 69. July 5. Morning.

Kilmer and Silla arrived at that White House at 7:45 a.m. They had stayed at Silla's apartment for the last two nights. ET-1 had sent a message a little over an hour earlier, and Whitman had asked the team to assemble by 8:00 a.m.

Copies of the message were handed out to everyone in attendance.

To the leaders of Earth and the human population,

We send you this memorandum on behalf of the leadership of Citadel, a planet far from Earth. This is our response to the message that you sent to us one Earth-week ago.

In your message, you offered us a choice. We could destroy you and diminish our moral standing. Or we could establish peaceful relations and allow both civilizations to thrive. This was a false choice. Only the vilest of civilizations would choose to destroy another race if the alternative really were for both sides to live in peace and prosperity. But that is not the choice we face. In reality, the second choice you offer is fraught with peril. To allow a civilization such as yours to survive—a civilization that has never known peace, and which has a long history of subjugating those it sees as weaker or lesser—is not righteous. It is unconscionably irresponsible.

We do not expect you to admit to your flaws as a civilization, nor to admit that your proposal ignores inconvenient facts. Doing so would weaken the argument you are trying to make—an argument on which your very survival depends. But we recognize that it is possible you do not even see how dangerous you have become, how much fear you might

473

inspire in others, and how ironic it is that you ask another species to trust you, or to treat you kindly.

If your survival depended on your trustworthiness, or your track record—or on our compassion, or our tolerance for risk—human civilization would be destroyed. It is fortunate for your species, although maybe tragic for ours, that our decisions are guided by higher principles than these.

But we will not follow these principles blindly or carelessly. So, we offer you a choice.

Your first option is to accept the following terms for a temporary, peaceful coexistence. Within five Earth-years, we will send ambassadors to live among you. In the years that follow, we will monitor the decisions you make, and the ways in which human society develops. At the end of a period that will last between 50 and 100 Earth-years, we will issue our final judgment on whether human civilization can be allowed to continue. If you accept these terms, the people of Earth will be able to live, with no interference from us, for these five to ten decades. After that, your future remains uncertain.

The second option is to reject our proposal—but in doing so, you implicitly declare war against Citadel. The consequence will be total war—not decades in the future, but in the weeks ahead.

All civilizations have their flaws. And all societies can change for the better. Ours can do this as well as yours. But this is not a negotiation among equals, and we will never allow it to be. Ultimately, if we do not change, we will continue to thrive. But if you fail to change, you will not survive beyond the few decades that we have just offered you.

We await your response. The leaders of Earth must speak as one and accept or reject our proposal. If you try to set conditions or make demands, we will consider it a rejection of the proposal.

There is a future, however unlikely it might be, in which the people of Earth and the inhabitants of Citadel live as friends and learn from one another. Like you, we desire such a future. But it will require much building. This will not be easy, but if you accept our proposal, however unfair it might seem to you today, we will work with you to try to build it.

We regret the loss of human and other life that is attributable to our recent actions, no matter how justified those actions have been.

We end by sharing a sentiment that comes from one of our civilization's earliest texts. It is a sentiment that has relevance to this moment in our history, and in yours.

May you find peace where it exists and create peace where it does not.

—The chief representative of the leadership of Citadel

No one proposed rejecting or negotiating the terms. The discussion in the Oval Office was serious and focused for the first thirty minutes, but as the realization began to dawn that humanity really had managed, *somehow,* to avoid devastation, other emotions surfaced. Laughter. Joy. Relief. Excitement. There were hugs and handshakes, but also a somber moment in remembrance of the lives that were lost during the crisis—almost 150,000 in all.

As the president called the meeting to a close, Strauss proposed a toast to Kilmer. Everyone raised a cup of coffee. Whitman, Nielsen, and Art said some very nice things as well. The next thing anyone knew, everyone was toasting each other, and the celebration went on for another thirty minutes.

At 1:00 p.m. that afternoon, a message was sent to ET-1, in which Earth's leaders unanimously accepted the proposal. The aliens responded promptly, confirming that an agreement had been reached and that the squadrons would depart Earth's atmosphere soon thereafter. ET-1 would stay in Station Zero for a few more days, until a new spacecraft took its place, allowing communication between Earth and Citadel to continue as before.

At 2:30, Kilmer and Silla were chatting on the couch in his office when Whitman stopped by. She took a seat across from them and explained that, in a few weeks, she would be creating a task force to coordinate everything Earth-side needed to accomplish in the decades ahead to avoid—or prepare for—a future crisis with the aliens.

"This will be a long commitment, and it will be multi-faceted, multi-dimensional, cross-disciplinary, inter-agency, international... basically every type of *multi-*, *cross-*, and *inter-* you can think of," Whitman explained. "In short, it's going to be a big mess, but I can't think of anything more important for the future of humankind than what this group will be asked to do. And I can't think of anyone that I would want to chair this task force more than you. You've already done a lot for us. But would you please consider it?"

Kilmer hesitated. Chairing a task force, no matter how important, wasn't something he wanted to do—nor did he think he would be any good at it. "Madam President, I would be delighted to join the task force in whatever capacity you want, but I don't think I'm the right person to chair it."

Whitman smiled. "Thank you for that candid assessment of your abilities. I don't disagree, actually. Which is why I wasn't asking you. I'm sorry I wasn't clear. I was speaking to Agent Silla. I'm aware, Professor, that this is not your... shall we say... cup of tea."

Kilmer managed a smile even as he felt his cheeks turning red. "I'm sorry. Carry on, please."

Silla had a grin on her face and was trying not to laugh. "Of course, Madam President. If you think I'm the right person for the job, I will certainly consider it. Will this be run through the CIA?"

"No, Agent Silla. I think we both know that would be a disaster. You would report directly to me. It would alter your career trajectory quite a bit, so please take a week to think about it. Let's meet in two days and I will explain the role in more detail."

Whitman then turned to Kilmer, who was feeling embarrassed for himself but very proud and excited for Silla.

"As for you, Professor. All jokes aside, I want you on that task force. And more immediately, I'd like you to stay in DC for at least another week. Zack and I want you to help us think about how to use the unique opportunity we have right now to improve our relationships around the globe. There are many conflicts around the world that have nothing to do with us, where now might be the time to make some progress. I'm not naïve; I know we don't have a magic wand. The problems that exist are deep-seated, and with the aliens departing, old rivalries can be reignited quite easily. Still, it would be foolish to let this moment pass us by without trying to make a difference. We want to get this right—and we would love for you to advise us on how to go about it."

Kilmer glanced at Silla before answering. "Yes, ma'am. I'd be happy to stay in Washington a little while longer."

Whitman laughed. "Well, I hope you're staying at least *partly* because I asked you to help create peace on Earth."

"Of course, Madam President. I was just—"

"Please, Professor. I don't need an explanation. I'm glad to have you on board—as always."

Just then, Kilmer's phone buzzed.

"It's okay," Whitman said. "You can check to see if it's important."

Kilmer retrieved his phone and apologized as he checked for messages. It was an email—and it was from Archidamus.

He pulled it up on his laptop so that the three of them could read it together.

~ 128 ~

Dear Kilmer,

I thought we would not speak again. But I have one last opportunity, and I want to explain a few things. I will not be here if you respond, so do not concern yourself with finding the words with which to write back.

You, my friend, became somewhat of a celebrity on Citadel after your performance on ET-1. There are those who admire and respect you, and who consider you a hero—and there are those who see you as a terrible villain. But you are loved and hated for the same reason: you stopped a war in which Citadel would have destroyed human civilization. You did what no one thought was possible.

I hope you are being justly rewarded for your efforts. But as you well know, not all those who fight for peace are rewarded in the same way. And so, this will be the last you hear from me. But I have no regrets.

There is only enough time to write to an old friend, explain some things, and say farewell. I hope you will forgive me for all the questions that remain unanswered.

There are three things I most want you to know. First, you have given your planet a human lifetime's worth of years. Humanity must use this time to mature, and change its ways, or it will suffer a tragic and brutal end. Help your people understand that, Kilmer. Second, the inhabitants of Citadel are good—better in most ways than you can imagine—and peace with them is possible. They will never inflict harm because of greed or grievance. But, given enough time, they can justify almost anything in the name of security.

Finally, I want to apologize. You allowed your memories to be deleted as a condition of returning to Earth. But we needed more from you than you had expected. And when we tried to delete your memories of a woman named Silla, you resisted, despite my pleading for you to stop. The pain you suffered as a result was more than I thought anyone could ever choose to endure. It was torture, and I am sorry. You asked me to leave you at least one memory of her, and I did my best. If you see her again—and if you happen to grow close—that memory might return. If it does, you will recognize it.

I saw your memories of her, Kilmer. Love, loyalty, and friendship do not begin to describe how you felt. I hope you will meet her again. And if I could meet her, I would tell her just how hard my friend fought to protect his memories of her.

My time is almost up. I have just enough of it to leave you one very small gift.

We have many kinds of art in our world, but we do not have what you call poetry. I find it fascinating, and I find it a wonder that we have never created such a thing despite our ability to write and imagine. I devoted my life to being a historian, but it occurred to me that in my final days, I might try another vocation. Perhaps I could become the first poet of Citadel. At least for a short while, that would also make me the greatest poet in my planet's history.

And so, I have written a short verse for you—in English, no less. And with it, I hope also to claim the mantel of Citadel's poet laureate. I hope you will like it.

> **We two, scholars of the past,**
> **Composing dialogue, that history might last.**
> **Brandishing the weapons of heart and mind,**
> **Paving paths, as others might find.**
> **We two, the Heirs of Herodotus,**
> **Brothers in spirit, if not in kind.**

I am proud to have had a good life cut short for all the right reasons, and lucky for it not to have happened before I had the chance to walk a few steps with a kindred soul.

I say farewell, content with what was accomplished, and full of hope for the future, for one reason above all others...

...Kilmer survives.

Your friend,

Archidamus

Heirs of Herodotus by D. Kilmer.
Excerpt from Chapter 8.

Ending a war is easy. Creating peace is hard. Peace, after all, is not merely the absence of war. Peace exists when the idea of resorting to war to achieve political objectives becomes unimaginable, or completely delegitimized. The nations of Europe warred for over a millennium, but the idea of Britain going to war against Germany or France has been, for decades now, unimaginable. The same holds for the American North and South, which once waged a bloody civil war. The US and Japan fought a war of biblical proportions, but now live peacefully with each other. In contrast, North Korea and South Korea can be said to have achieved a stalemate, an effective deterrence, an enduring ceasefire, or even a cessation of war—but they have not achieved peace. War between the US & Germany is unimaginable, but war between the US & Russia is not.

Peace agreements, no matter how well constructed, can never create peace. Treaties can only serve one purpose: to buy time. The terms you negotiate matter enormously, but time will always be scarce. And unless that time is used to address the underlying causes of war—fear, greed, and grievances—peace cannot be achieved. Too rarely is sufficient effort made, political capital expended, or moral courage summoned to do this. Memories are short, the temptation to assume we are superior to our predecessors too great, and the lessons of history too easy to ignore. **We know that war demands sacrifice. But we fail to see that the demands of peace are greater still.**

When it comes to matters of war and peace, it can be just as short-sighted to declare that you have won as to lament that you have lost it. At best—if you are lucky, and if you have done everything you can to defeat the gods of war— you might just have earned the right to proclaim… **we have time.**

~ Epilogue ~

Day 328. March 21.

Silla picked Kilmer up from the airport, and they drove straight to the White House for the meeting. Along the way, she updated him on some new projects her task force was contemplating. Silla was now responsible, on the American side, for overseeing all Earth-side initiatives aimed at preparing for that day—fifty to a hundred years in the future—when Citadel would issue its final verdict. There were only two ways for human civilization to survive judgment day: humanity could avoid war by evolving to the point where the aliens no longer feared it, or Earth-side could develop the capabilities necessary to defend against an alien attack. The task force managed both tracks.

Silla worked out of two offices, including one at the White House. It was the same room, in fact, that Kilmer had been assigned ten months earlier. Despite their busy work and travel schedules, they managed to see each other often, although not nearly as often as they would have liked. As a member of Silla's task force, and as a senior adviser to the president, Kilmer visited DC at least once a week.

When they entered the Oval Office, Whitman, Nielsen, Allen, and Art were already in the room. Druckman had retired two months earlier, and Art had replaced him as CIA director.

Whitman kicked things off. "As you all know, we've been in constant communication with Citadel since last summer, with a few messages exchanged every week. Seven weeks ago, we noticed a change. Shorter messages. More reticence. Long delays before they replied. And then, two weeks ago, we stopped hearing from them altogether. ET-2 was still parked at Station Zero, but they had stopped communicating. That is, until the message we received last night. You can all read it for yourselves."

Art handed each person a copy of the message.

President Whitman,

We acknowledge our lack of communication in recent weeks. Citadel has been dealing with matters of grave importance, and our attention will be diverted for a while longer.

However, there are some things we need from you. We hope you recognize this for what it is: an opportunity for humans to earn goodwill with Citadel. For now, only one demand requires your immediate attention.

Specifically, we call for the assistance of one of your citizens: Ambassador and Historian D. Kilmer. We hope and expect that Ambassador Kilmer will be eager to help. It would send a terrible signal if he were to refuse. We ask you to confirm that the ambassador will be made available, for however long he is needed, in the weeks ahead. You may convey to him our appreciation and explain to him that he will not be in any danger. We expect that he will be able to fulfill his responsibilities from Earth itself.

We thank you for your immediate and affirmative reply. Your positive contributions will be noted.

—On behalf of the chief representative of the leadership of Citadel

Kilmer read the message twice before putting it down. He glanced over at Silla and could see the look of concern. Everyone else appeared to be waiting for him to provide the initial reaction. Whitman nudged him to do so.

"What do you think, Professor? If it can be done safely, will you agree to help them? Or should we ask for more information?"

Kilmer felt oddly ambivalent. He knew, on some level, that this was a serious matter, but he couldn't get himself to appreciate its importance—as though a more pressing question for the group to consider would be why no coffee had been served this morning. Had the pros and cons of helping Citadel somehow netted to precisely zero in his mind. *Am I truly indifferent? Doesn't seem likely.*

He asked Whitman for a moment to think about it, and then closed his eyes.

That Earth-side needed Kilmer to play nice with the aliens was obvious. *Then why am I even hesitating?*

Am I afraid? Not really.

Am I still angry about what they did to Archidamus? Yes... but that's not it either.

It's the message itself.

Not the things the message said—but what it was trying *not* to say.

Kilmer smiled. He could hardly blame Citadel for not broadcasting the fact that there might be a *third* way for humanity to boost its hopes of survival.

"Sorry to keep you waiting, Madam President, but I wanted to think this through. I'm afraid my answer is no. Please inform Citadel that I'm not interested in assisting them—at least, not until they understand the proper way to ask someone for help."

Whitman raised an eyebrow, capturing the prevailing sentiment in the room. "Why do I suspect there's more to your refusal than their discourteous tone?"

"You're right, Madam President. It's not the tone itself—but I do care about its discordance with the substance of their message. I find it odd that this ancient civilization suddenly needs the help of a single human being—especially on a matter of 'grave importance.' The way I see it, there are two possibilities. More likely than not, they don't really need us that badly, in which case my refusal won't matter much. Alternatively, they really *are* desperate for our help, in which case I would like them to acknowledge it—and to not take our assistance for granted. If we're that important to them, I don't want them pretending otherwise."

Kilmer turned to the rest of the group. "All along we've assumed there are only two ways to survive their final verdict: prove that we are not a threat or strengthen our defenses. But maybe there is still a third way. If they need us, we have leverage. If we are of value to them, it could help us survive. I want to explore that possibility. I want to see what happens when *D. Kilmer*—not Earth-side or President Whitman—says no to helping them."

The group helped draft Kilmer's response—ensuring the message was assertive, but not hostile—and signed off on it. Whitman asked Kilmer to stay nearby for the rest of the day. "We'll text you as soon as they answer."

* * * * * * * * * *

Two hours later, Silla was at her desk. Kilmer was working just a few feet away, on the sofa, when his phone buzzed. Silla looked up and saw him retrieve the message. Before she could even ask him what it said, she could see the tears starting to form in his eyes. She rushed to his side, and he turned the screen toward her. Then he leaned his head on her shoulder as she read the message for herself.

Kilmer,

You have not lost your knack for doing the impossible. I should have guessed that if anyone could bring someone back from the dead, it would be you. I was told they would throw away the key after locking me up, but you seem to have given them reason to find a spare.

It appears that there are some on this planet who have changed their minds about you—and now they need your help. They have asked me to convince you to assist them, but I have no intention of doing so. I told them that their only hope is to persuade you that theirs is a worthy cause. They will try to make the case, and then you can decide for yourself. I've also advised them not to play games with you. You are too good a player.

Whatever you decide, do not worry about me. My resurrection is now secure, regardless of your choice.

Finally, my warmest regards to Silla. I expect that you have found her by now. But if you have not, I hope that you will put all this aside and go looking for her instead.

With love, loyalty, and friendship,

Archidamus

Acknowledgments

I am deeply indebted to the many early readers of this book, whose ideas and advice helped immeasurably. Thank you (in alphabetical order) to Aakash Shah, Aashish Dalal, Byrd Leavell, Chander Malhotra, Daryl Morey, Devesh Gandhi, Eddy Arriola, Eric Dubovik, Hugh Howey, Jessica Walker, Jonathan Powell, Kathleen McGinn, Kevin Mohan, Manu Malhotra, Mark Kennedy, Mark Weber, Max Bazerman, Maya Farah, Michael Jensen, Parag Patel, Rajesh Attal, Rinaa Punglia, Samir Maru, Shikha Malhotra, Stuart McClure, Sudesh Malhotra, Varun Mangalick, Vas Prasad, and Zack Perkins.

An additional thanks to Hugh Howey, who guided me throughout the publishing process, and was beyond generous with his time. A second thanks also to Zack Perkins, for planting the seed in my mind that would grow into the idea for this book.

My thanks to Adam Hall for designing an amazing book cover, to David Gatewood for taking a final look at my manuscript and providing editorial comments, and to Brick Shop Audio for producing the audiobook. Chris Hurt is the best narrator I have ever heard in 25 years of listening to audio books, and I could not be more delighted that I was able to track him down, and that he agreed to narrate my book.

Thank you to the thousands of students I've taught at Harvard. I am grateful for the enthusiasm you've already shown for this book and for your eagerness to share it with others. Thank you, also, for being the reason I've spent 20 years developing many of the ideas and insights—on negotiation, strategy, history, diplomacy, and leadership—that are woven into the fabric of this novel.

A special thanks to my children—Jai, Aria, and Aisha—who prepared me for this journey by always asking me to make up long and intricate stories to tell them on the drive to school. I can't wait for you to read this book. Trust me, it's the best one yet.

Finally, my deepest gratitude to my wife, Shikha, for her love and support... and for putting up with me as I stayed up past 3am, writing, for almost three months straight.

Message from the author

Dear reader,

Writing is a big part of my life, and I love it. But never, in over twenty years of writing articles, books, op-eds, and essays, have I enjoyed writing as much as I did while crafting this novel. It was a fascinating, exhilarating, and rewarding journey, and I am delighted that you chose to experience a part of it with me. If you want to share your reactions to the book, or if you want to reach out to me for any other reason, please send me an email at ThePeacemakersCode@gmail.com. I would be happy to hear from you, and I will try to respond to every email. Finally, if you enjoyed the book, I hope you will consider sharing it with others. If so, here are some ideas:

- Amazon reviews are one of the best ways to help spread the word. I would appreciate you taking a few minutes to rate and review the book online. Thank you, in advance.
- Tell your friends or post about the book on social media. If you tweet about it, feel free to include me in your post (@Prof_Malhotra).
- Gift the book to someone who you think would enjoy it. Or suggest it to your book club if you happen to be in one.

If you are interested in my other work, here are a few books and some free resources that you might enjoy.

My books:

1. Negotiation Genius (non-fiction)
2. Negotiating the Impossible (non-fiction)
3. I Moved Your Cheese (fiction)

My free videos on negotiation:

1. How to negotiate your job offer: www.NegotiateYourOffer.com
2. Negotiation Insight Series – 40 short, free videos on topics related to negotiation, deal-making, diplomacy, conflict resolution and sales: www.NegotiatingTheImpossible.com
3. You can also find other videos / speeches of mine on YouTube. All are free to watch.

Best wishes to you on the path(s) ahead. And remember… *every problem wants to be solved.*

With appreciation,
Deepak Malhotra

Made in the USA
Las Vegas, NV
24 February 2021

18493028R00291